The Beautiful Beast

Stephen G. Kirk
Copyright © 2020

The Beautiful Beast

1

On a sun drenched October afternoon in Hansel's Creek, a blue-eyed bronzed youth of seventeen summers nearly skipped down the foot worn bleached concrete sidewalks of Main Street. His movements were quick and light; a sleek panther whose platinum blonde curls flowed over his ears and fell below the back of his collar. The adults he passed couldn't help but pay some notice to the boy. Women of a certain age allowed themselves discrete second glances, while men found themselves forced to recall their own glory days, when their own futures sparkled, the winds of change both warm and assuring.

Timothy Russell Williams strode down Main Street oblivious to what was taking place around him, his mind anticipating the promise of what tonight's party might entail. When Tim and his girlfriend Cindy Lowen weren't working at their part-time jobs, the summer found the teens spending their free hours engaged in attempts to solve the mysteries of life their ages naturally presented. Tonight he and Cindy had determined the most pressing of these might finally be answered. Tim knew it still wasn't a sure thing. Even at this youthful age, a man instinctively knew every woman was inclined to change her mind on a dime, especially on the subject of sex. His eyes absentmindedly traced the spider-webbed cracks in the sidewalk as he analyzed the situation for the umpteenth time.

Tim set aside his caution, he couldn't let doubt cloud his enthusiasm, after all, hadn't he already visited the men's room at the Fast-Gas service station? Hadn't he already slid eight quarters into the wall-mounted vending machine, which as promised, promptly spit out a multipack of three "specially lubricated and textured" Rough Rider prophylactics, each guaranteed to fulfill every woman's most sensual inner desires? Suddenly Tim worried if the rubbers could have somehow fallen out of his pocket. He quickly slid a hand into the front pocket of his blue jeans. Relief flooded his mind as his hand caressed the smooth plastic casings. He flushed with surprise as he felt a wave of sexual urgency welling up deep within him, at the same time marveling at the fact that merely possessing the accoutrements of his desire somehow increased his confidence.

A woman's cheerful voice greeted him, "Good afternoon Tim." Tim's head bobbed up in a flash. Christ! It was his mother's best friend, Clara McAdams. Tim's face immediately reddened and he felt the heat rise beneath his collar. As Tim sputtered out his stinted reply, in the back of his mind he found himself actually wondering if Mrs. McAdams might have guessed the items in his pocket and the thoughts on his mind. This insanity was further supported when Mrs. McAdams smiled knowingly while inquiring if he were on his way to see Cindy, who was putting in a few hours scooping ice cream at the Tasty Freeze down the block.

Tim thrust the ridiculous idea behind him, forcing himself to carry on a courteous if rather brief conversation with the middle-aged woman that closely studied him. He caught his reflection in the lenses of her oversized eyeglasses… surely that wasn't a guilty look on his face! Tim forced himself to smile as he answered her questions obligingly. "Yes, I'm on my way to see Cindy. Yes, our whole family enjoyed the summer. Yes, Dad is much better since his fall off the ladder last weekend, thanks for asking." He shuffled his feet looking first down at the sidewalk and then glancing at his watch; "Well, Cindy is probably wondering where I am…" he let the statement trail off.

Mrs. McAdams nodded and smiled, "I was young once too you know. Now off you go then, I don't want Cindy thinking I was the cause of your delay."

Tim waved and began to walk away then turned as Mrs. McAdams added, "Oh, and remember to say hi to your mother for me." Tim nodded once again managing a few halting steps before the woman spoke once more. "Oh yes, and tell her I'll send my George over to return her cake pan." Tim smiled and stood facing her… the boy waited expectantly. The woman grinned with amusement before releasing the lad with a quick wave and a cherry "toodle loo," turning on her heel and walking off in the opposite direction.

Tim pulled on the door handle leading into the Tasty Freeze ice cream parlor, a refreshingly cool puff of air swept across his face as he stepped inside. Behind the customer counter, a petit teenage girl had her back to him while digging out a scoop of raspberry ice cream then stuffing it into a waffle cone. A young boy, the shops only customer was waiting impatiently at the countertop and spoke up excitedly, "don't forget - a scoop of licorice

2

too!" The girl paused and turned slightly toward the boy, "are you for real, strawberry, and licorice?"

"Yup!" The boy, noticing Tim had come up beside him, cocked his head and shot him a grin. "And be sure to make it a big scoop please!"

"Yuck! Your stomach kid..." The girl finished pressing the second scoop of ice cream into the cone and turned toward the counter. Her lavender eyes lit up when she saw Tim's beaming smile. "Oh? Good afternoon sir", Cindy's voice impossibly coy. She handed the cone to the kid with one hand and took the boy's money with her other, never once breaking eye contact with her boyfriend. The pretty blonde batted her eyelashes then continued speaking in the same manner, "and what can I do for you today?"

The kid turned from the counter opened his mouth, stuck a finger down his throat and made a loud gagging noise before continuing toward the door.

Cindy feigned a nasty glare in the young boy's direction, stuck out her tongue then giggled at her own antics. Returning her attention to Tim and recognizing the meaning of his expression, her smile faded as their eyes suddenly locked for a long, smoky moment. Now it was Cindy's turn to redden, and breaking contact, dropped her eyes toward the countertop while carefully adjusting the position of the silver napkin holder only less than an inch from its previous location. "Well?" she said in a small voice.

Tim's voice was soft, low, and somewhat hesitant, "Are we still on for tonight?"

Cindy's eyes remained fixed on the napkin holder while her mind tried to work out all the implications underlying Tim's question. After several moments, she looked up and seeing his cautious yet hopeful expression replied. "I think so... yes."

Each studied the other's face, both seeking that unaskable promise, the unspoken contract negotiated between young men and young women of that uncertain age. Discovering what they each sought, Tim's expression brightened immeasurably as Cindy returned a sly, conspiratorial smile confirming the likelihood of the evening's anticipated event actually taking place.

The atmosphere in the Tasty Freeze suddenly became anything but cool, but knowing smiles quickly faded to light conversation as the door squeaked open. An old gent propped the door open for an elderly lady and the couple entered the store. Cindy shot the two a friendly smile, and then with a quick glance to Tim said, "See you at eight then?"

3

Tim winked as he replied; "I'll be bringing Ed's van." He watched as her eyes smiled and her mouth rounded making a silent "Oh..." Tim turned away from the counter, gave a quick hi and a wave to the old folks and made his way out the door. Outside Tim squinted and brought up a hand to shield his face while his eyes slowly adjusted to the bright afternoon sun. Just before the door closed he heard Cindy ask the couple, "So what will it be today?"

Tim smiled and spoke to himself under his breath, "Oh I think you know sweetie... hubba hubba!" he chuckled to himself picking up his pace while walking down the sidewalk. By the time he reached the first corner, he was nearly strutting.

It was almost seven thirty and the late autumn sky was already surrendering to the creep of twilight. Tim ran from the front door of his house clearing the veranda's steps in a single stride. His brother Eddie was leaning over the fender of his newest restoration project, a lemon yellow 1978 Z-28 Camero. Eddie would buy interesting vehicles on the cheap and fix them up for resale. The car's engine would occasionally rev up for a moment or two then drop back into a low throb as Eddie played with the idle arm. Tim approached the vehicle and stood near the front bumper without saying a word.

His brother's muffled voice carried above the drone of the engine. "So... heavy date tonight bro?" Eddie stood up and turning towards Tim dangled the van keys in front of his brother. "Wouldn't be a certain Cindy Lowen by any chance?"

"Maybe, Then again maybe not," Tim's face wore a broad smile. "...these days a good looking guy like me has to beat them off with a stick!"

"A likely enough story as I've ever heard." Ed smiled and tossed the keys to his brother. "Ok Romeo. Let's go over the "shaggin' wagon's rules one more time shall we?"

Tim's face took on a bored expression while he flatly replied, "Yeah I know; watch my speed, don't let anyone smoke in the van, no toking, I'm the only driver." He stopped and watched Ed's face.

Eddie frowned, "And?"

"No more than a couple of beers?" Tim asked hopefully.

Eddie voice made a buzzing nasal sound. "Wrong answer, try again little brother."

"No booze." Tim said resignedly.

"And..." Eddie paused expectantly for several seconds while his brother puzzled out which rule he may have neglected. With no reply forthcoming, Eddie smiled mischievously, "And ... you have to fill me in on all the juicy details tomorrow morning!"

"Screw you too!" Tim feigned mock anger then quickly smiled, "Thanks for the wheels Eddie.

"No sweat bro." Eddie walked to the Camero's door, reached through an open window and turned the key to the left; the engine died but not before sending several coughs and shudders through its frame. Eddie frowned at his brother and quipped, "This is gonna take a little more time than I figured." He walked a few feet toward an open red toolbox sitting atop a folding table in the driveway then closed its lid. "About taking time," Eddie looked thoughtful for a moment then added, "Tim, remember not to rush things. Cindy's a nice girl."

Watching the enthusiasm on Tim's face waver slightly, Eddie instantly made light of the situation and followed up "Just remember I don't want to have to hide you from her dad and brothers when they drop by tomorrow morning for a talk."

Tim's smile returned to his face. Throwing a two-fingered salute toward Eddie, Tim walked to the curb where the van awaited then drove off moments later.

The party was in full swing, taking place in the center of a wooded clearing a hundred yards or so across the old South Bridge just off Lakeside Drive. Sixty or more local high school kids milled about the large bonfire and more were arriving by the minute. The location had long been a favored party spot of the younger crowd spanning several generations and though well known to the local cops, a cruiser seldom patrolled that stretch of roadway. As a rule most of the kids were pretty good sorts and the rather remote location seldom drew any noise complaints from the few people living in the area. The closest home was the old Meyers place and it lay nearly a mile south. According to most people living in Hansel's Creek, old man Meyers pretty much kept to himself, seldom venturing out except to fill his prescriptions or to buy a book or magazine from Teller's Drugs on 2nd Street. Word had it that couple of months back, the old gent had finally checked into a nursing home in Claremont City leaving a lone relative and her manservant to rattle about in the sprawling mansion.

Cars and trucks formed a semi-circle along the outer rim of the clearing while kids sat on logs or folding chairs, talking and laughing near the fire while a few couples had stolen away from the main group seeking a quiet spot hidden from the view of the other partygoers.

Tim and Cindy had arrived at the party a couple of hours earlier, spending their time socializing with their friends and ensuring they made a proper showing. On the drive out the two agreed to leave the party about ten, ten thirty at the latest; but the last time Tim checked his watch it was already quarter to eleven and Cindy had embedded herself between several girlfriends - just as tight as a tick in a hound dog. Every once in a while, one of Cindy's girlfriends would look up furtively in his direction then return to their obviously intense conversation with Cindy. Only several minutes ago, finally able to catch her eye, Tim recognized Cindy had that "deer in a headlight" look and knew the chances of getting her alone in the van tonight lay somewhere between slim and none.

As Tim sidled up toward the trio, the conversation between Cindy and her girlfriends fell silent. One of the girls elbowed the other and nodded her head toward the fire. Tim watched the two leave then turned back to Cindy, who sat mutely upon a stump nursing a diet cola. The girl raised her head looked sheepishly up at Tim as she quietly whispered, "I'm sorry." The conversation between the two teens went as one might expect. At first Cindy was openly apologetic, while Tim tried his best to hide his disappointment. After another ten minutes, Cindy's apologies having fallen well short of saving the evening, the girl became frustrated and angry, though in truth more toward herself than Tim, who for his part was trying his best to behave as a gentleman should about the whole thing. Unfortunately this didn't help the situation, but only served to increase her annoyance until it produced the result she unconsciously hoped to provoke.

"Maybe it would be best if I just drove you home?" Tim muttered flatly.

Cindy spat out, "Well don't do me any favors, I'm leaving with Sheila and Tonya, I've already been offered a lift." Minutes earlier, some of the boys had thrown several large logs and dry branches on the fire which had considerably diminished from its previous size. Cindy's attention was drawn to the bonfire which had suddenly revived itself with a roar; its flames soared well above the fire pit.

"Really?" Tim paused, "Really..." He watched the girl at his side; ignoring him she continued to stare into the fire. "Fine, have it your way, I'll talk to you later." He turned about and headed toward a group of his friends that had separated themselves from the main group and were now fully engaged in drinking beers and passing around a joint. Teddy Marks, one of his better friends he had known since elementary school had watched the interaction taking place between Tim and Cindy. When Tim walked up, the boy stuck a hand into the cooler beside him and came out with a beer that he cracked and offered to his friend. Tim took a long swallow then scowled, watching Cindy join Tanya and Sheila enter a car then drive from the clearing.

About midnight, the party started to die. By that time many of the girls and couples had already left; turning the gathering into a stag party. As the girls became scarce, the jokes became lewd and later simply downright filthy and juvenile. Not that it mattered to Tim, he found himself engulfed within a black mood, the stupid jokes and the three beers in his belly weren't helping at all. As the time neared 1:00 A.M. the fire was finally allowed to fall to embers while a group of fellows were talking about heading off to Denny's for a gut bomb. Tim told Teddy that he might show up but not to count on him, he was probably just going to drive straight home.

A couple of the fellows began to walk to their cars or trucks when Teddy reminded them someone had to stay by the fire until it had pretty much gone out, then douse it with water from the nearby creek. A couple of the boys nodded and began heading back to the fire. One of the town's largest employers was the Limpet lumber mill, and all the town folk had an inherent grasp of the importance of maintaining the surrounding forests; it wouldn't sit well to have this fire get out of control and put their fathers out of work.

Tim spoke up, "You guys take off, and I'll look after the fire and make sure it's out."

Teddy leaned in close to his friend making sure he was out of earshot of the rest of the gang he said quietly. "Tim. You want me to stick around for a while? That's what friends are for, right?"

"Thanks man, but I just need to be alone right now. I gotta think things out." Tim stared into the fire. The remaining cars and trucks had started up, their headlights swung about the clearing as the vehicles turned to leave. The driver of the last truck in the clearing leaned on the horn while one of his passengers warned Marks to get a move on or walk. Teddy gave Tim a light punch on the shoulder then ran off to join the others.

Tim watched the truck's red tail lights as the vehicle drove from the clearing, its brake lights glaring briefly as the truck slowed before making the turn on the paved road heading back to town. Every so often the truck's lights flickered in and out of the tree line before it finally drove from sight.

Tim sat on one of two folding chairs he had brought to the party for him and Cindy. Teddy had thoughtfully left an unopened can of beer on the second chair. Tim cracked the can and took a sip then prodded the dying fire with a stick. For a time he gazed into the flames. Raising his head, he noticed the clearings shadows had grown and deepened since the others left. He could see his brother's van parked maybe twenty yards away from the fire pit. The dimming flames reflected and danced in the bumper's polished chrome.

A twig cracked loudly behind his chair. Dropping the can of beer, Tim leapt up and turned about in a flash, standing stiff and alert; his fists at the ready. A slender figure was walking toward the fire, as it approached Tim came to realized it belonged to a middle aged woman. The fire was still bright enough to illuminate her features, which he suddenly found particularly attractive. Tim thought she looked a little familiar but not from school; he reworked his assessment, she was only at most ten years older than he. He'd no doubt seen her about town somewhere; Hansel's Creek was pretty small after all.

A cheery feminine voice greeted him, "I'm sorry if I startled you, I didn't mean to sneak up."

Suddenly Tim realized he still held his fists up before him and somewhat sheepishly lowered them to his sides. "No, no. Not at all. I just figured it was one of my buddies, ah they're always playing pranks." Tim measured his reply; good going buddy; that shit sounded weak if not just plain stupid. Looking up into the woman's face, Tim reconsidered; well if it had, the woman clearly hadn't taken any notice.

"I was out with my boyfriend, we had a huge fight and I wound up walking. After a mile or so I knew I'd gotten lost. I'd pretty much figured I'd be stuck out here for the night until I saw your fire." She smiled warmly and as she did so it appeared to Tim that he had grossly overestimated her age, she couldn't be any more than twenty.

She drew closer. Tim couldn't help thinking to himself but "God didn't she looked great! What fucking idiot would kick her out on the side of the road? Tim realized he was gawking and should probably say something and say it quickly if he wasn't to look like a jerk. What came out of his mouth next pretty much nailed it. "Oh no, that happens to me all the time!" Inwardly Tim groaned.

The girl's voice became light and musical; her body swayed suggestively as she drew closer, her eyes dancing and reflecting the fire's red and yellow flames. "Really? I hope you're not lost right now." She giggled. "Otherwise I might never get home tonight."

8

Her voice betrayed a slight accent, one that he couldn't quite place. He spoke up and held out his right hand, "Hi, I'm Tim. Tim... Williams. He had croaked out his last name. His throat and mouth had suddenly gone dry."

"Irma, nice to meet you Tim." Rather than a traditional handshake, slowly and delicately the girl laid the four fingers of her left hand in his palm. To Tim it reminded him of a princess offering her hand to a prince, expecting it to be held and kissed. There was something extremely sensuous about the whole thing. "Do you live in Hansel's Creek?" she asked.

"Yeah, ah yes I do." Realizing his voice sounded harsh in his ears he swallowed hard and fought to retain what composure he had left. Silently Tim scolded himself - say something you fool, anything! As it turned out, he really didn't have to. The woman was quite a conversationalist and easily took the lead setting the young man quickly at ease. As he became less self conscious, he spoke more and more fluidly. As the minutes passed it seemed to him that no matter whatever came out of his mouth sounded absolutely charming and witty.

As Irma continued to speak, she drew ever closer to his side. Taking his hand she slowly raised it up to her breast. As she moved in, Tim became acutely aware of her scent, the warmth of her body, the promise of intimacy. "Tim. May I have a ride home with you?" Her voice dripped honey and by the time he answered, he was surprised to find they had left the fire, crossed the clearing and would shortly arrive at his van.

Tim opened the passenger door, an arm supporting her slim waist and waited for her to step into the van. She paused and stared into his eyes, "Tim, do we have to go home right away? I'd like to spend some time with you." As he lost the remainder of himself in her charms, he could feel himself becoming aroused, then hard as rock. He asked himself - was this really going to happen?

A moment later she had climbed into the rear seat of the van. Tim joined her and closed the van's side door and now sat close beside her. She slowly unbuttoned and removed her blouse and then slid off her bra. She watched his eyes glide hungrily about her curves. Irma softly caressed Tim's face in her hands then pulled him close, burying his face between her breasts.

Over the next quarter hour the van shook rhythmically, its tempo rising and falling, driven by the intensity of the love making. Suddenly a flash of light burst forth from the van's windows and pierced the dark meadow while a hoarse cry arose inside, all movement came to an abrupt stop. For several long minutes, an utter, eerie silence filled the deep night.

Almost noiselessly the side door of the van slid open bringing with it the pale yellow illumination of the van's single interior light. The woman stepped from the vehicle, finished redressing herself and straightening her clothing. The fire had long since turned from deep red embers to blackened coals, their residual heat now nearly spent. Within herself, she felt the long familiar sense of exhilaration that coursed through her being; the life energy pervading every cell within her body. She stretched her arms over her head and felt the light breeze flow across and cool her sweat drenched body. Dropping her arms to her sides, Irma continued looking upward, her eyes searching the night sky and locating constellations whose names were already ancient when she was first conceived. Those cold hard points of light drifted above the wooded clearing where she stood. Irma recognized a familiar double star in the handle of the Big Dipper; Mizar, over time she had witnessed its companion stars wheeling about one another, engaged in their eternal cosmic dance. So much had changed, the long river of her life had meandered through the centuries, its leisurely turns measured in decades, its violent rapids merely years.

Looking back to the van, she frowned slightly then slowly leaned into the vehicle's interior, placed a soft kiss on her index finger and then gently laid the finger upon Tim's forehead. The boy moaned slightly and then slumped lifelessly on the seat. She whispered softly, "Auf Wiedersehen my darling." and slid the door closed. She would instruct Norman to drop by before dawn and deal with the wizened corpse.

With practiced ease and confidence, the woman strolled into the depths of the night's shadow, each footfall well placed and assured. At one with her element, within moments she was gone, swallowed up and shrouded within the dark forest; homebound, and making her way towards Meyers Hall.

2

He emerged from slumber to find his limbs partially ensnared amid a twisted tumble of white linen. Lying on the bed, he tried somewhat unsuccessfully to recall the previous night's events then made several halfhearted attempts to free his body from the sheets that bound him. Finding he was unable to immediately escape their clutches, the boy's irritation flashed and then exploded in a flurry of kicks and contortions that sent the sheets and blankets sliding from the bed and onto the floor. His head throbbed with the exertion.

Now freed, Teun de Torres remained atop the bed, naked and laying still, his face turned upward, he allowed his eyes to play over the elaborate series of interwoven rings of the ceiling's unusual design. A delicate series of chimes sounded off to his left. An ornate and very expensive timepiece positioned atop the elegantly carved nightstand beside the massive king-size bed suggested it was nearly four in the afternoon, high time to rise and get mobile. He swung his long legs and sat on the edge of the bed for several seconds, the chimes started up a second time, just slightly louder this time; he extended a hand and waved it above the clock and the room again fell silent.

Teun looked around him and not for the first time reflected on his incredibly good fortune. His host was a handsome middle-aged man whom Teun had met, no make that targeted, nearly a week earlier while making the circuit cruising Club NYX, one of Amsterdam's hottest gay clubs. Although he possessed an excellent set of false ID claiming his was twenty years of age, he seldom had need to present it; most of the line men and club security recognized him by sight and better still knew him to be an excellent tipper. He'd strolled into the sprawling three-story club well after midnight knowing that the evening's alcohol and dancing would have had time to release its visitors from the inhibitions of their humdrum everyday life. Teun knew exactly what he was looking for and wasted no time exploring each floor, wading through knots of LGBTQ tourists, half-drunken businessmen looking to score, and regulars that hung out and socialized within Amsterdam's De Wallen center, the city's famous "red light" district.

On each of the club's levels, a different variety of music, neon, smoke and glaring ambience beckoned seasoned and nouveau clientele alike to dally and partake in a wide spectrum of offerings. Teun had quickly scanned the tables and sidebars on each floor looking for that person possessing a very particular profile. Unable to find a mark, he'd given up the search and set himself down on a stool in front of a long bar. The large mirrored wall behind the bar and its opposite number lying some thirty feet distant were slightly offset. The placement lent the impression of infinite dimension, accentuating the contrast struck between the calm of the subdued lamps atop the room's small oblong tables and side booths, and that of the spectral dazzle and noise bursting forth amid the throng of dancers tripping to light fantastic on the small dance floor.

Teun had chosen to sit at the bar showing his back to the room. He glanced down the length of the bar and caught the eye of the bar tender that gave a curt nod in his direction then began preparing Teun's usual poison. The boy took out a pack of smokes from his chest pocket, shook one out, then brought it to his mouth as the barman arrived and set down a drink in front of him. Looking up he saw the barman slowly shaking his head and point toward the glass doors leading to the outdoor balcony overlooking a narrow cobbled stone street and canal that ran through the city's medieval center. Teun smiled and shrugged returning the pack to his pocket while handing his plastic to the barman, "Sorry, I forgot." The barman nodded and walked over to the till where he stood speaking at length to one of the club's servers; given their animated conversation, Teun figured it would be a few minutes before the man returned with his card. The boy took a long sip of his drink and examined his image in the mirror before him. An unabashed hedonist, Teun was pleased with his reflection. At six foot one, his slim athletic frame cut a fine figure among those of his peers while his long tinted locks of ginger were worn slicked back atop his head, but shaved close above the ears. Teun's delicate features and full lips were further enhanced by the dark highlights within the smoky Gray of his eyes.

Catching the approach of an intriguing figure, Teun managed to tear his attentions away from himself and focus on the man walking toward the bar. Within the space of only seconds, he evaluated the man now taking the stool to the right of him. The man's taste in clothing, his jewelry and watch spoke of affluence, his grooming was impeccable from the stylish haircut down to his manicured fingernails. The aroma of the man's exceedingly expensive cologne wafted into Teun's nostrils and he allowed himself a sly smile in the mirror amazed to find his favorite prey sidling up beside him, how natural an opportunity.

Teun's self-confidence allowed him the luxury of allowing the middle-aged man to make the first move, which was rather awkward and no doubt had something to do with the heavy gold ring worn on upon the man's left ring finger. Within the next half hour, Teun found out everything he needed to know about his mark. Yes, the man was married - to a woman – who lived in Brussels along with the couple's two children. An investment banker for a leading European firm, Bruno Jung virtually oozed refinement. Happily flaunting his wealth and good fortune, his vaulted ego busily wrote cheques that Teun was only too happy to cash.

As the early Saturday morning sky began to lighten, Bruno and Teun were only now arriving by cab at the banker's luxurious hotel suite; held on a long-term lease, rooms accommodated Bruno while he worked in Amsterdam. The doorman moved quickly toward the curb opening the rear door of the cab, greeting the resident by name, fawning and generally falling over himself in an attempt to curry favor. Knowing the game, Teun took the opportunity to ask Bruno to introduce him to the doorman. When Bruno turned to walk up the steps to the building's revolving doorway, Teun paused and turned shaking the man's hand while palming him a €20.00 note. In doing so, Teun inferred his position as an equal while quietly adding he was sure they would see much more of each other in the future. The doorman examined the note held in his hand then beamed his gratitude... Teun knew he'd made an important contact that he could count on in the future.

The two men spent the rest of the weekend together, Teun making sure they were seen together as often as possible by the hotel's management and staff. It was Sunday afternoon when Teun felt he knew all that was needed to take his plan a step further. Bruno fell into a light sleep while the two shared a long embrace within the afterglow of urgent lovemaking. It was then that Teun allowed himself to perform the "gimmick" as he referred to it. His mind probed that of Bruno's, seeking out and finding what he sought. He still marveled as his ability to gain access to some one's deepest thoughts, bending them ever so slightly, ever so gently securing an emotional bond between them. Still, it would take time for this bond to solidify, but time was the other gift that Teun could now bestow upon himself.

Still in deep embrace, Teun felt that familiar thrill rise in his chest, and a gentle glow began to form in the space between the two men. If Teun were pressed to explain what was happening, the boy might say it felt as though he had taken in a deep breath after coming to the surface of a lake, his lungs having been starved of oxygen now refreshed him with life and sustenance. Unfortunately for Bruno, this was a one-way transaction. The man would soon awaken feeling as though he were enduring a severe hangover or a victim of the latest nasty flu bug making its rounds. Either way Bruno wouldn't be off to the office or even leaving the hotel room for the remainder of the week. But not to worry; Teun would be taking good care of his new friend.

Over the following days Bruno slowly climbed the steps of a difficult recovery, while on Teun's part, he continued to reinforce their emotional bond while at the same time stripping the man's life expectancy by nearly a decade. Teun insisted a doctor attend the hotel room to examine his new friend. At first Bruno's wanted no part of the visit but upon seeing his ravaged reflection in the bathroom mirror he acceded to the boy's wishes and a doctor was immediately sent for. Of course the doctor could conclude little except to suggest fluids and bed rest, but stated directly that should Bruno fail to bounce back he must be admitted to hospital in short order. It was nearly a week later when Bruno felt sufficiently strong enough to leave the hotel and return to his home and family in Brussels. However before leaving the hotel, the banker ensured management understood that Teun would remain as his guest and that every consideration be shown to the boy just as if it were he himself making the request.

It had been several days since Bruno's departure from the hotel. Teun continued sitting on the bed while rubbing his eyes. Shaking his head quickly from side to side try to clear his mind he instantly regretted the action. A flash of pain throbbed between his temples causing Teun's hands to rise to either side of his head. "What and how much had he been drinking the night before?" he asked himself. It was nearly an hour later following a hot shower and shave when he felt human enough to dress and leave the hotel room. Teun made his way across the spacious lobby, his heels clicking upon the polished granite tiles as he walked past marble busts, eighteenth century bronze statues and several massive pieces of abstract artwork mounted upon its walls, all lending the voluminous room an almost museum like quality. Situated only a matter of feet from the imposing lobby, he entered a rather ordinary looking cafeteria that featured decent coffee as well as an "all day" breakfast.

The boy chose a small table near the entrance. A young woman approached and offered a menu. Teun didn't acknowledge her, waving away the menu while ordering his usual and carefully watching the people moving about in the lobby. The waitress frowned and returned to the kitchen placing his order and returned with her guest's coffee. Teun noticed a man seated in the lobby and reading a newspaper, he looked somewhat familiar. The guy might be a cop, or at the very least someone who could take care of himself. The boy relaxed when the man dropped the paper on a

14

side table and rose to greet a woman who had just exited the public lavatory. He watched the two stroll through the lobby and leave the hotel arm in arm.

Given the way he made his way in life, it paid Teun to be constantly aware of his surroundings and those who might be showing a little too much interest in his direction. While what he did could hardly be proven, much less place him behind bars, his previous conquests eventually regained their senses and concluded by their much reduced bank balance or soaring credit card debt that he had in some inexplicable manner, defrauded them. On one occasion he had found himself arrested and brought in for questioning by police and although he managed to avoid charges, the mere fact of his name being mentioned in future investigations would no doubt bring unwelcome attention from the authorities.

It also was understood that each of his marks were themselves affluent to a man. In one particular case his victim occupied a significant position of power and influence within the government. Only a month before, this well known politician had arranged for several associates to drag Teun into a dingy alley in the old quarter and beat him rather badly. Their original instructions had been to kill him and they may well have done so, but for his ability to reach deep into their minds and tip the balance in his favor. Instead the men left him lying broken, battered and bruised. When he recovered sufficiently, Teun managed to stumble off to a place he knew where the homeless and disadvantaged gathered within a collection of cardboard boxes or huddled in makeshift tents. Crawling unseen into one such abode, he slid up close to the unfortunate within, incapacitating his victim's mind while siphoning off the life energy his body craved. Several hours later Teun emerged having staged a near miraculous recovery while leaving his victim near the point of death. Teun had always felt badly about that day and promised himself it would never happen again. As such, he always ensured he knew the background of the mark.

Having eaten a small breakfast, Teun nursed his second coffee deciding what to do with the remainder of the day. Before leaving the hotel room, he had already taken a phone call from a somewhat confused Bruno. From their conversation, Teun gathered he'd milked this gig sufficiently and it wasn't worth over staying his welcome. Teun knew exactly what to say and how to say it and by the time the conversation ended, Bruno was relieved to discover the relationship was at an end and their parting was mutually welcome and accepted. Teun even offered to repay Bruno for his hotel stay and whatever charges he had run up on the banker's credit card, but as he knew before making the offer, it was refused out of hand. This left the boy with the task of finding a new mark to exploit.

He returned to the hotel room, packed and said his amiable goodbyes and tipping a few of the staff before leaving. Good manners and a few Euros went a long way toward ensuring a warm welcome in the future. Teun flagged down a cab, tossed his bags into the back seat and climbed up front beside the driver. He hadn't given any notice of the two women who had been watching him on and off throughout the afternoon and early evening.

When Teun's cab rounded the next corner and drove from sight, the older of the two women raised her arm and a cabbie that had been waiting nearby immediately arrived and pulled over to the curb. The driver watched the older of the two open and hold the door for the younger woman who slid into the rear seat. The younger woman spoke the name and address of a third rate hotel several miles distant. The man made no attempt at conversation, he simply followed his superior's instructions, pulling out from the curb and driving toward the address.

Teun arrived at his destination, the St. Louis hotel, a bit of a fleabag, but one where the price of the rooms could be had at reasonable price and could be rented by the week. As with the staff in the upper end establishment, they greeted the young man with considerable warmth and cordiality. He carried his own bags to the elevator and up to the top floor where his room faced north ensuring the morning sun wouldn't intrude and disturb his sleep. Meanwhile, outside the hotel entrance, the two women sat drinking coffee across the street at an outdoor cafe. Shortly afterward a man joined them and they spoke at length, every so often one or more of them would glance in the direction of the hotel even though they hardly expected their quarry to surface much before midnight.

It was raining lightly when Teun left the hotel some three hours later. He turned the collar of his coat up as he walked along the dark narrow streets that would eventually lead to the de Wallen section of town. There the streets bustled with pedestrians, tourists and partygoers, all eager to sample Amsterdam's myriad of dance clubs and bars. He still had some distance to walk before he reached his hunting grounds. Here the cobblestone streets were illuminated for the most part by irregularly spaced street lamps whose pools of yellow light huddled near their bases refusing to venture too far beyond their source. A short distance behind him, Teun picked up the sound of stiletto heels atop the sidewalk, he glanced back to see two women stepping out from an apartment building and walk arm in arm talking and laughing. A short distance ahead a cab slowed then came to a stop along the curb. Teun watched as a short fat man stepped out, reached for his wallet and handed several bills to the driver. The cab sat at the curb before its overhead light signaled it was again available for hire. The fat man walked toward Teun then stopped, patted his chest and jacket pockets, evidently feeling for something he had misplaced. The man looked at Teun and asked if he could spare a cigarette, explaining he had forgotten them at the bar.

Teun didn't mind. He reached into his coat pulling out his pack and shaking out a cigarette that he held out to the man. The fat man took the cigarette placing it between his lips thanking Teun before sheepishly requesting a light. Teun nodded good-naturedly while taking a smoke for himself then flicking his lighter in the man's direction. The small flame sputtered and illuminated the man's face just as the two women he'd heard walking behind him now passed to either side; he felt a small sting in his upper arm then his head swam and his knees buckled. His last recollection was that of the fat man wearing an amused expression while the two women grabbed his arms and guided him to the waiting cab.

Teun awoke to find himself confined in a small room having a single barred window set in a thick rock wall and positioned nearly nine feet above the floor. The ten by twelve foot room contained a single bed, a nightstand and lamp, a small desk along the opposite wall upon which sat a small television, quick inspection showed it provided a familiar selection of popular European channels. A small shelf mounted above the desk held a selection of books and magazines, none of the titles held any interest for Teun whatsoever. There were two doors on the adjacent walls of the room, a large wooden door, locked and reinforced with iron bracing that Teun correctly assumed led to freedom, while the other opened into a small ensuite bathroom with a sink, toilet and a narrow plastic shower booth.

Although he found he wasn't overly hungry, the slow passage of hours and the boredom accompanying these had him wondering about meal times. Perhaps he could garner some information concerning his plight from whoever delivered the food to his cell. It was quite late when he fell asleep.

He awoke the next morning to find a tray of fruit, cheese and bread sitting atop the desk together with a large bottle of sparkling water. Normally a light sleeper, he wondered how he slept while the food was being delivered. He chalked it up to the needle he'd been stuck with in Amsterdam. That second day, he watched some television, slept on and off and even paged through several of the magazines. Patiently he watched and waited, someone would show up eventually but in the meantime he was determined not to cause a fuss, resisting a growing impulse to bang on the door and holler at the top of his lungs.

A day later he had yet to meet whoever visited his room in the night and once again replaced his food tray and water. In a last ditch effort to discover and speak with his jailer, Teun lay atop his bed with one eye open awaiting his nocturnal visitor, but try as he might; he inevitably fell asleep and as in other mornings would awaken to find a fresh tray and water waiting for him on the desk. He began considering if they, whoever they were, could be doping the food or water, which might explain his inability to remain awake.

He determined not to eat or drink the water provided him and instead drank water from the sink in his bathroom. Later that night he turned off the television set and positioned himself atop the thin mattress of his bed and began to page through a selection of magazines while keeping a close eye on the door. Hours later found Teun still seated upright on the bed, magazine in hand and reading the same paragraph as he had moments before. Noticing the dawn's rosy glow emanating from his window, he set down the publication and forlornly looked about the small room. His gaze froze in amazement when it reached the desk. Yesterday's food tray had included several apples, an orange and a banana along with the usual cheese and bread, but here now was a different tray complete with slices of fresh melon. How had they managed that?

Teun had reached the end of his patience. He arose from the bed and marched to the cell's entrance door hammering on the wood with his closed fist. The booming noise of the impact shattered the still calm that had surrounded him over the past week and took him quite by surprise, but far less so as did the door that now slowly swung open before him. He stood motionless for nearly a minute, his doorway opened to reveal a long hallway composed of the same stone used in the construction of his cell. The boy stepped forward, pushed the door open wide and craned his head out into the hall taking a long look about.

The walls of the hallway were nearly twelve feet high running some forty feet in either direction before meeting with adjacent passages that led to God knows where. Along the immediate hallway and spaced at regular intervals were other doors; Teun deduced they opened into other rooms like his. A series of bare electric lights starkly illuminated the hallway, spaced high along the opposite wall and strung and suspended from simple hooks drilled within the rock; the wiring obviously a modern alternative to the black cast iron torch sconces still mounted beside each doorway.

18

Teun called out timidly to whoever might be within hearing distance several times, but received no reply. He retreated into his room sat at the desk and ate some cheese and bread while contemplating his next actions. Taking several melon slices in his hands he walked from his cell into the hallway and turned to his left while munching on the fruit and saving the rind carrying it along with him. In front of his door he bit off a small piece of the melon's rind and dropped it to the floor. Making his way along the various hallways, he bit off and dropped other pieces to mark his progress and the return trip back to his cell. He held little hope that whoever had gone to the trouble to abduct and billet him would allow him to simply leave the building and go on his way. It took Teun less than ten minutes to survey his new surroundings. The hallways indeed opened into rooms about the same size as his, each having a bed and table minus a bathroom or toilet. Locating a common bathroom at one end of the hall, he stepped inside. No plumbing here, the primitive toilets before him were simply holes in a rock bench covered by wooden tops. He removed one such top half expecting his nostrils to be assailed by the odor of ripe effluent but there was no smell at all. Glancing inside the rock passageways he found them to be clear and unobstructed, he surmised the toilets hadn't been used for years, probably decades or perhaps even longer.

Continuing his exploration he came to the assumption that he was housed in a sizable keep or a castle of considerable age. Having grown up and been educated within a city that could trace its historical roots back to the 13th century, Teun had walked Amsterdam's ancient streets and byways and toured through its public buildings and museums along with his parents and schoolmates. This portion of the building he now explored gave every indication of similar age; where the hell am I?" he asked himself.

So far, each windowless corridor he walked through was exactly as the one before it. If it weren't for his trail of melon rinds Teun felt it likely he would have lost his way. He was pleasantly surprised when the latest hall he walked through, unexpectedly opened into a larger but still windowless room, measuring perhaps twenty by thirty feet in size. The drudgery of the earlier stone floors, walls, arched ceilings and bare electric bulbs disappeared now replaced by tastefully painted drywall, modern electrical light fixtures, and a richly carved mosaic area rug on which sat two comfortable looking plush chairs that faced one another. Beside each chair was a small end table, atop of which sat matching brass lamps whose taupe Shades cast a warm inviting light within the room. An ornate oblong coffee table separated the chairs and atop of this sat a set of matching crystal decanters each containing amber liquids of different hues, a silver ice

19

bucket, two whiskey glasses and two short stemmed aromatic tumblers. Teun studied the room closely. A tall, heavy looking wooden door stood front and center within the opposing wall. Along that wall and those on either side hung a wide assortment of original paintings, sketchings and pastels worked in various mediums and encased within expensive frames. While Teun would scarcely declare himself a "connoisseur of the arts," even he surmised the extraordinary degree of talent possessed by the artists whose works were displayed before him. He walked over to an interesting and oddly familiar painting and leaned in for closer inspection. The canvas appeared to have been painted some hundreds of years before, in the low light Teun was just able to make out the signature scrawled along the lower corner. The name's recognition caused him to take a breath; he took a step backing away from the work.

"Johannes Vermeer" a masculine voice broke the silence and Teun's head snapped to his left where his eyes fell upon the speaker who stood by the far door. "I see you recognize the Dutch master, as should every good Nederlander." Tall and thin, a man wearing a distinctive Glasgow brown tweed suite shut the heavy door then walked into the center of the room. As he did so he pointed to his left, "did you notice our Rembrandt... the Monet?" the gesturing to his right - "or perhaps the van Gough?"

The young men stood his ground watching the middle-aged man approach and then extend his hand in greeting. Teun's arms however remained at his side, his face remaining impassive he continued to evaluate the man who stood before him. While he couldn't quite place the man's accent, it was definitely western European as were the man's facial features. His large expressive brown eyes, dark eyebrows and thick wavy hair together with an olive complexion and pleasant oval face suggested an Italian or Moorish background but these by themselves were commonplace.

Looking down at his still unfilled palm the man smiled and brought his hands to his chest with a light clap. "Given the circumstances I can't say I blame you for being a little stand offish. I regret being unavailable since your arrival, my work carries me here and there - often at a moment's notice." The tall man turned his attention to the decanters atop the coffee table. "May I offer you a drink; whiskey, perhaps brandy?" He smiled pleasantly in Teun's direction. "Please allow me to explain why we brought you here." He held out a hand toward the liquors.

"Whiskey. Neat." Teun replied coolly then took a seat in the chair nearest to him. If his captors had wished him any immediate harm they would have done so well before now. Patience was now the key. That and keeping his personal details and abilities unto himself alone.

"My name is Blas Velez; you might say I'm the assistant administrator here." He handed Teun his whiskey then poured a short brandy into a snifter for himself.

"Where is here?" The tone of Teun's voice was terse and flat.

Seating himself in the chair opposite, Blas continued. "Well, here is Spain. The building in which we presently sit is an abbey of limited historical importance except to that of the owner, my mistress, Valeria Diaz, who I dare say places great personal store in its legacy. But for now let's start at the beginning. It was several years ago when you first came to our attention."

"Our attention?" The boy's tone was almost brusque.

"Yes. You find yourself a valued guest of the Orden Sempiterno." Seeing the boy was about to ask, Blas held up a hand and continued; "The Eternal Order is a loose affiliation of a very select group of people, people having talents and abilities that would defy the belief of the general public." Blas saw his words had gained the boys attention.

"Before I detail exactly who we are, let me first tell you how we came to be aware of you." Blas tilted his head, his eyes asked continuance.

"Go head, proceed." Teun took a sip of the liquor, and then held the glass up before his face. "Very nice... Bowmore? " he said more to himself than his host. The scotch was a select brand running about a thousand US dollars per bottle.

"No, Laphroaig. Slightly less money, but a brand I personally prefer." Blas Velez continued. "And personal preference is everything in this world, don't you think Mr. De Torres."

Teun's face remained stoic. "Go on." Only partially listening, he permitted his mind to reach out to the man seated before him. This man's conscious mind was steeled and disciplined but it mattered not, his primary targets lay within the realm of the unconscious.

Blas continued. "In brief, you were born a single child, into an average Nederland family, where you were raised until the age of fifteen in an average but well kept home in Noord. Your mother, Eva de Torres, was a seamstress while your father Sem de Torres, served as a chief petty officer in the RNLN, (Royal Netherlands Navy) until killed in an accident at sea. Up until that time your school grades were near the very top of your class, not that you worked hard to achieve them; these simply came naturally as you possess an eidetic memory. After your father's death, your mother remarried, may I say poorly, less than a year later. Your stepfather, one Daan Bakker, is a drunkard wholly unsuited to domestic life and if possible

21

even less suited as a father to a gay teen. Bakker was abusive toward you while your mother took every opportunity to fail to stand up to her husband on your behalf. You seriously contemplated suicide but decided instead to leave home following your sixteenth birthday. You have never returned, not once, not even to visit your mother who now sufferers from stage four cancer. You still hold her responsible for your unhappiness." Blas paused and took a sip of brandy while he carefully studied the young man's face seated in front of him.

Teun's fingers of thought made their first tentative contacts and quickly mapped the underlying emotional levels of Blas mind until he found what he sought. Now on familiar ground, the boy would apply subtle pressures that would render the man's mind susceptible to his most outrageous suggestions. This sort of thing was now second nature to Teun; he allowed himself a smirk as he pressed his attack forward.

Blas stated. "It was only after you left home and had to make your way in the world by any means whatsoever that you discovered your unusual talents. Your ability to manipulate others, bend their emotions to suit yourself, but more importantly, to feed and absorb their life force, increasing that of your own." Blas' face wore a knowing expression of amusement.

"Ugh..." The breath left Teun's lungs in an outward rush. His attack on Blas had been immediately repelled and broken; Teun's mind and body recoiled from a mental rebuke so powerful that it struck the boy as surely as would have a physical assault. For the first time in his life Teun had encountered a mind similar to his own, but one of incredible power and resolve.

"Ah... I sense you have met my Master." Blas' face became serious. "At this point I would caution you to mind your manners and keep your thoughts to yourself."

His eyes wide and his mouth agape Teun asked "How?"

"Silence! You only need listen to learn. Are you willing to do that?" Blas questioned. "Or perhaps you should prefer to return to your room to contemplate your situation further. Either way you will not leave this abbey until you understand who we are, who you are, and the turn your life has taken from this moment on."

Blas was pleased to see an expression of wonder and acceptance sweep the boy's face. Teun nodded softly. "Good. Then let us begin."

22

Reggie Denton awoke to the annoying buzz of the clock radio's alarm when it sprang to life precisely at 7:30 in the morning. The old man couldn't stand the sound, which was the precise reason he hadn't rid himself of the forty-year old timepiece thirty-nine years ago. It was also the reason that he placed the radio on his high boy dresser, the chest of drawers placed some ten feet distant from his bed, instead of his night table where a half empty bottle of water balanced precariously at the tables edge. Aside from his seemingly incessant nocturnal visits to his ensuite toilet, Reggie had always been, and still remained a heavy sleeper who had a difficult time waking any earlier than was his habit.

He flung the blankets off and swung his legs over the edge of the bed. Despite the abhorrent drone of the alarm, he waited several moments before standing to make sure he was balanced and stable. Failing to take this precaution had occasionally ended with his dropping back onto the bed or worse, having to heave his carcass from the bedroom floor. Reggie slowly rose to his feet, swayed slightly testing his balance before hobbling over the high boy and stabbing the alarms off button with a finger.

After a ten-minute stint in the bathroom, Reggie walked into his kitchen and started making his standard breakfast, toast and coffee. While he waited on each, he turned on the TV to catch the news and weather. One after another, a series of commercials, each announcing spectacular deals to be had – if one acted right this moment. "Fat chance Charlie" he glanced at his cat clock mounted on the wall opposite the fridge and stove, beneath the clock's face, a tail swung rhythmically, as it marked the passing seconds. "Oh fuck! Top of the hour..." he croaked, those assholes at the station in Claremont City always threw in at least another four or five ads knowing their audience was captive and prepared to suffer through whatever drivel they offered, just so the people could catch up on all the hard news and weather in the first five minutes. Miss that and you had to wait a full half hour before the cycle repeated.

His toast popped up almost exactly as his coffee was ready to pour; he had the timing down to a fine science. The commercials finally came to an end and a pair of newscasters, a distinguished looking gentleman and a rather attractive woman introduced themselves. Reggie had it figured that if it was an average news day; the woman Katy what's her face, would usually start off yakking about uninteresting local happenings, the passing of some foreign dignitary he'd never heard of or ever cared to, or the newest political scandal to be visited on the country. Today however, Jim something or other started off. This was never a good sign, although if he imitated Tom Brokaw, Peter Jennings or heaven forbid Walter Cronkite, you could count on a plane crash, an approaching hurricane or the President launching a cruise missile attack.

"Good morning. Just minutes ago, the Channel Seven News team was notified of the mysterious disappearance of yet another local youth. Police have confirmed that Shelly Ann Connelly, seven years of age, was abducted from her bedroom in the family home sometime last night. We take you now to the rural residence of Harvey and Maryann Connelly... Jennifer Brown is reporting from the scene. Jennifer?"

The news camera first centered upon a large farmhouse for several moments, then swung to a front lawn choked with parked police vehicles before zooming in on a close-up of the veranda. A uniformed police officer was standing outside the front door obviously monitoring the entry and exit of detectives and other uniforms from the home. The camera panned out to include Jennifer Brown, a pretty little brunette in a swanky pantsuit.

"Thank you Jim. Claremont City, Hansel Creek and State Police personnel are working together this hour in an attempt to locate Shelly Ann Connelly. A photo of the cute little girl flashed up in the left corner of Reggie's TV screen. The seven year old disappeared from her parent's rural home sometime between the hours of ten thirty last night and six this morning. Police have confirmed moments ago that in their opinion this is not a missing person's case where the child could simply have wandered away from her home. Shelly lives with her parents, two brothers and a sister; we are informed that the other children are safe and with their parents this hour. Jim, that's all that we have for you at this hour. We expect a police statement sometime later this morning. For the Channel Seven News Team, I'm Jennifer Brown reporting. Jim?"

The image of the two news anchors returned to the screen. "Thank you Jennifer. We'll be keeping our viewers posted on this important story as it unfolds." With the utterance of that last syllable Jimbo's look of intense continence disappeared completely and was replaced with a bright Howdy Doody demeanor as he looked over to his anchor. "So Katy, what's happening on our weather front this morning?"

Reggie laughed to himself as he noted that even Katy what's her face looked a little surprised given Jim's spontaneous level of gaiety. "What a knob..." Reggie quipped using the remote to kill the TV. As he buttered his toast, he thought about the number of kids and young people who had gone missing over the past two years and came up with six, although if they didn't find little Shelly, that would bring the count up to seven, and let's not forget, to date none of them had turned up - either dead or alive.

As he took the first bite of this toast, there was a loud knock at the front door. "Who the hell is that at this hour" he muttered, only then remembered it was those two Pilipino cleaning ladies he had hired the week previous, those same ladies were the reason for his setting his alarm clock. Ever since his Margery passed away several years ago, the level of housekeeping in his home had taken a decided turn for the worse as had his desire or motivation to do anything about it. Sixteen months later he admitted to himself that the place was a dump and it could stay that way for all he cared; but that was two weeks ago and two weeks ago he hadn't known his only son, Martin would be coming for an extended visit.

Reggie greeted the ladies cordially and showed them into his home, taking their light fall coats and hanging them in the front closet. Aside from a howdy do, there was no attempt at small talk on the part of the two women; according to his friend Dorothy who recommended the cleaners, these two were all business and would put in whatever effort was required to get the job done.

As per their last conversation, Reggie had ensured he had gathered or purchased all the preferred cleaning solutions, mops, dusters, vacuum bags etc. requested by the ladies. He led them to the hall closet where he kept the supplies and opened the door. The older (and sterner) of the two inspected the supplies then gave a nod of approval. The younger woman piped up and asked if Mr. Denton would be at home or doing errands while they worked. When Reggie stated he had plans for the morning and would probably be gone several hours, it appeared that the ladies attitudes brightened considerably. No doubt they had assumed the old fellow would be underfoot and in the way.

After finishing his breakfast and placing the dirtied dishes and cutlery in the dishwasher he donned his hat and waist length car coat, bid the ladies goodbye and made his way out the back door. As he walked to the rear garage he heard the high-pitched twitter of the ladies emanating from an open window. He couldn't understand a word they spoke in their native tongue, but as he heard the women laugh, Reggie casually wondered if he were the subject of their conversation.

Using his key, the old man opened the side door of the garage and paused a moment before entering. A familiar odor drifted up to his nostrils, a musty combination of stale motor oil, tire rubber and old concrete wafted through the doorway. For many people, including his late wife, the smell was almost offensive. For him however, it brought back memories of when he was a young man pumping gas and checking oil at the neighborhood Texaco station. That particular gas station had changed ownership several times until it was finally torn down all together almost a decade ago. A 7-11 store now sat on the site and if you needed to fuel up, you had to travel nearly five miles north to the Fast Gas station way out on Big Bend Road. Fast Gas had put the other two stations in town out of business in less than a year; how does the little guy compete with low cost, discount bulk pricing.

He hit the garage door opener, climbed into his Honda Fit and turned the key. The little engine immediately sparked to life and within seconds he was on his way. His thoughts drifted back to the old Buick he used to love to drive and did so for the better part of twenty years. Christ, now that was one hell of a car! That said, the little Honda was more dependable and easier on gas than the Buick was by a long shot; but he missed the big cars feel and sound.

Reggie swung past the One Stop Flower Shop on Main, stopping in and buying a small bouquet. Upon seeing the old man's Honda pull into one of the angled parking spots out front, Judy, the shop's owner, walked back and entered the small, humidity controlled cooler picking out a small assortment of blossoms she felt Mr. Denton might choose to purchase. Without fail, on the twelfth of each month, rain or shine, the old man would buy the flowers he would lay at the foot of his wife's stone on his regular visit.

Judy felt a quick stab of envy as she tried to picture her own husband even bothering to visit her grave on a yearly basis, to say nothing of bringing flowers each month. That emotion was fleeting, the beer-drinking slob that barely passed for her husband wouldn't make it past fifty at the rate he was going through the suds. Five minutes later Judy watched the old man re-enter his little car and drive off having purchased the flowers she had selected.

Reggie parked the car in a stall nearest to the entrance to the large secluded cemetery that bordered the western outskirts of Hansel's Creek or just "the Creek" as the locals referred to it. The oldest parts of the graveyard dated back to the early eighteen hundreds, a full fifty years before the railroad arrived, an event of historic proportions and one that brought commerce and the trappings of modern civilization to the quickly growing town.

Over the next decade, the town had become a primary railhead in the region, the end of the line, where goods were unloaded and stored and then transported by horse and wagon to a score of smaller towns and villages surrounding the Creek. The arrival of the railway also encouraged the Limpet's out of Boston to invest in a lumber mill built on the eastern edge of the town. For nearly half a century, the old growth forest surrounding Devils Head Hill had been known as the source of some of the best high quality timber available anywhere in the country. There were also several producing gold and coalmines in the area, the gold was always rather sparse even before the mines themselves became played out, but the region's coalmines were still in production. Although the recent demand for the product had nearly vanished as the angst of global warming took hold around the world.

Reggie stepped out of his car, grabbed the flowers and a wooden cane he stored in the car reserved for longer than usual walks. The senior could never be sure when the arthritis in his knees would act up. The sun was hidden by clouds and a light breeze had risen. The air chilled him somewhat, though it was early May, the month had proven cooler and rainier than was usual. He propped the cane up on a thigh and quickly buttoned his coat and fastened the cloth belt about his middle then left the car. Making his way across the asphalt parking lot, his cane clicked and clacked on the hard surface providing a rhythmic counterpoint to his steps.

The entrance to the cemetery was wide enough to allow a single vehicle passage, most often the hearse and occasionally a limo bearing the immediate family members. The other mourners were normally expected to park their cars and walk in to the gravesite, although exceptions were made for the planting of a particularly prominent individual. A black wrought iron fence about four feet in height ran along the entire eastern side of the graveyard although most of it lay hidden beneath the large manicured hedge that followed the fence line. The other three sides of the graveyard were bordered in thick spruce and fir. The growth was cut back each fall to prevent the verge from overrunning the cemetery.

Reggie made his way along one side of the ornate iron gate that guarded the main entrance. The black structure rose a good twelve feet or so above the pavement below. Atop the gateway was an arch bearing the name of the hallowed site, "God's Angel Cemetery." The main gates were almost always closed and locked, but smaller regular breaks in the fence allowed access to visitors at all hours of the day or night.

Reggie walked south along the narrow paved roadway leading to the newest gravesites. Margery's would be found among these. Had Reggie walked along the now seldom traveled north road he would have come across the fire blackened stone foundations of the old church, once a primary focal point within the community. At the point where these two pathways forked north and south, a visitor had a third option.

A red shale path ran due west leading to the oldest part of the cemetery. Here the inscriptions on the stones were faded, most just barely visible while many more of the old graves now only existed as shallow depressions in the grassy field. The old original wooden markers had rotted away, never to be replaced in stone by family members who may have moved from Hansel's Creek or perhaps who still remained, themselves here interred beside their loved ones.

At one time, a written record existed, listing the occupant of each grave and its location within the entire cemetery. The death records being dutifully kept current by the series of Pastors preaching the Good News from the pulpit of God's Angel Anglican Church. This ended during the unusually dry hot summer of 1948 when the church burned to the ground, the victim of a random lightning strike. The ensuing fire, driven by a strong easterly wind, threatened to engulf the entire town until the local fire fighters were aided by a torrential downpour an hour later. The original church's replacement was constructed on a site only two hundred yards south of the cemetery boundary. The western extension of Main Street to the west of 1st Avenue led directly into the parking lot, a year after construction was completed the street was appropriately renamed Church Street.

At the turn of the century, the "Creek" began its slow decline. The railway had expanded ever further into the northwest part of the state bringing an end to the town's principal value as a railhead. As the railway continued its progressive march across the state, new communities sprang up and flourished, the most prominent of these being Claremont City. The members of Hansel's Creek town council often spoke hopefully of the day when the Creek would become a bedroom community of Claremont City bringing with the designation new growth and commerce to the stagnant town. So far this outcome hardly seemed likely. Unlike the smaller agricultural centers situated near the city, Hansel's Creek sat amidst heavily forested land and the only major roadway leading to Claremont was the Big Bend Road, named so owing to the nearly twenty mile semi-circular path it followed as it skirted the high country surrounding Devil's Head Hill. Unless something changed, the future of the Creek was likely to remain bleak.

Reggie had arrived at Margery's grave. The old man surveyed the surroundings and was pleased that he and Margery had chosen the location of their plots together. The site was atop a gentle rise that overlooked a small lake in the distance through a clearing in the evergreen forests to the west. A discrete distance from the nearby graves, a huge weeping willow tree stood guard as it had for probably close to a century.

After much reflection, Reggie and Margery's had been sold on the Companion Wing Memorial. The twin headstones sat upon a granite base and between the headstones was a carved vase for flowers. Reggie hadn't wanted to spend as much as they did. The plots and the monument set them back nearly five grand, but they could pay in monthly installments. He considered the monument salesman to be a little too smooth for his liking although Margery seemed to take a shine to the fellow, and she had always been a better judge of character than he. When Margery passed and buried he was content with their decision.

He stepped up to the granite vase, deposited his bouquet in the vessel then stepped back to the foot of her grave. Reggie wasn't a religious man, but a short prayer of some sort seemed appropriate. He crossed himself, placed his hand together and quietly prayed. "Eternal rest grant unto Margery O Lord, and let Your Perpetual Light shine upon her. May she rest in peace, Amen."

He spent the next fifteen minutes or so catching Margery up on the latest news and happenings in the Creek but saved the best news for last. "By the way, you'll never guess in a million years; Marty is coming to stay at our house for about a month." His voice dropped low, "I guess him and Cheryl's divorce last year has left him a little low. Marty finishes off his criminology courses this week and the department agreed he could take his banked overtime hours along with that holiday time he never bothered to take. You know what a workaholic he can be. (Reggie didn't say it but mused that if his son had taken a little more time to spend with Cheryl, the divorce might never have come to pass) And yes, the house is clean and organized... I bet you're surprised."

He grew very quiet for several minutes, lost in the remembrances of their time together while feeling his grief well up and then gradually subside. "Well old girl, I guess I'll mosey along and check up on the cleaner's progress. Next time I come back I'll have Marty in tow... Ok then, all my love sweetheart." He turned and walked back along the pathway, a single tear rolled down his cheek.

Approaching the fork he happened to glance to his left, his eyes following the red shale path toward the old cemetery and was surprised to see what appeared to have been a new addition to that section of the graveyard. The normally unbroken grass had been recently upended; a stain of newly

29

exposed rich soil lay about an oblong mound rising from the surrounding sod while a tall stone monument of some sort had been recently put in place.

Always the curious sort, Reggie changed course and walked toward the new gravesite. The old red shale path, while clear of any vegetation, was bumpy and uneven, the result of ancient tree roots rising up along the earth's surface and occasionally breaking free of the soil. Half way there, the toe of his oxford had snagged a root causing him to lose his balance and very nearly fall. After that Reggie kept his head bent downward and his eyes upon the path.

Upon reaching his destination he stopped and looked about. As yet not dug, the grave was awaiting its occupant. Reggie stared up at the large monument situated at the head of the new grave. To say it was unusual would be an understatement. The dark, otherworldly gravestone was a statue depicting a shrouded figure breaking free of its own tombstone and emerging from the grave, one arm stretched toward heaven. A second slab erected directly behind the statue declared the grave to be that of Johannes Otto Meyers and beneath that in what he assumed to be German; Gehorsam - Ehre – Pflicht , translated as "Obedience - Honor – Duty".

Reggie looked for the dates of the man's birth and death but found nothing, gossip about town said old man Meyers was well over a hundred but Reggie always took such idle speculation with a grain of salt. However odd, Reggie reasoned that perhaps the reason stonecutter had yet to complete his task centered on the fact his customer was still breathing. He decided to ask around down at Misty's the next time he hankered a beer or two.

Reggie had never met Meyers though he had seen him on several occasions, the most recent being nearly six years before, during the opening of the Creek's library across the street from town hall, one of the main contributors; the old boy didn't mind spreading his money around. Everyone living in the Creek knew of Meyers and the overly large stone home that bore his name. The family had built the Hall between the years of 1947 – 49; about the same time the old church burnt to the ground. The Hall, most locals referred to it as a mansion, had been erected on a one-section parcel north of town. The five mile tree lined driveway leading to the Hall forked off Lakeside Drive and ran eastward just past the South Bridge. As far as Reggie knew, no one in the Creek had been out that way for quite some time. He wondered if anyone still lived there.

Reggie turned to leave and was startled by a raucous cacophony of caws and squawks. A flurry of dark wings beat against the gray sky. Looking up, Reggie saw a large flock of crows, up until a few moments before, the birds had perched in the towering spruce tree near the gravesite. Now the birds rose up as if one, wheeling overhead they flew swiftly westward disappearing into the depths of the forest. Reggie queried his mind, now what did people call a flock of crows? No matter.

Walking along the pathway leading toward the parking lot he paused watching a man who was leaning against the side of the equipment garage smoking a fat cigar. The graying fifty something year old man was dressed in a Gray striped set of dungarees. His odd matching cap provided Reggie the distinct impression he was looking at a railway engineer. He chuckled to himself and threw a quick wave toward the man then carried on. The caretaker waved back, crushed the cigar's remnants into the pavement with the sole of his boot before entering the building. As Reggie reached his car and laid a hand on the door handle he heard the sound of the cemeteries backhoe start up then fall to an idle.

"Murder!" Reggie spoke aloud the word that suddenly popped into his mind. "That's what they called a flock of crows... a murder." A minute or so later, the little Honda left the parking lot.

31

4

Teun De Torres appreciated the mellow yet pungent flavor of the Scotch whiskey he swirled about in his glass. While it might appear that the youth wasn't paying the least bit of attention to his host, nothing could be further from the truth. His mental contact with Blas's master, Valeria Diaz, had provided the boy a unique perspective.

"You Mr. De Torres, as a potential member of Orden Sempiterno, must be told where you fit within our organization, as well as the wider world in which we live. For you Mr. De Torres, this worm has definitely turned."

The tall, thin and elegantly dressed gentleman sitting across from him, smiled confidently and crossed one leg over the other, then leaned forward.

"As a race of super-humans, you Sempiterno are extraordinarily long lived. It is possible that some of your kind may live as long as a thousand years, although this is conjecture rather than fact. The oldest known Sempitor currently living is slightly over seven hundred and fifty years of age, but a rough average of live span most probably lies closer to three or four centuries. It is only within the last two hundred years that individual Sempitors began to recognize themselves for what they are, and that while rare; they were not unique. The Sempitors inevitably found them drawn together in common cause, namely commerce and trade. You see, when accumulating enormous wealth over a great many years, one must also take steps to preserve it.

You have felt the power of my Master, but you are very young, the world to you is still very much a source of mystery. Try to imagine the amazement of someone who has lived in seclusion from others of their kind for hundreds of years and meeting quite by chance another of their kind; feeling that aura of power emanating from another being like yourself. In many of your race, these mental powers grow more pronounced throughout their lives, while in others they are limited; the extent of any ones talent, Sempitor or human always lies within the individual. Some, as my Master, have the gift of true telepathy, she has the ability to "transmit or receive" thoughts often at considerable distance. Yet even the youngest of the Sempitor possess an innate ability to empathize. Empathy, something rather ironic if not laughable given your race employs these abilities to gain sway over other humans who will shortly afterward become their prey.

The way Sempitors recognize another has recently changed. The use of modern technology has improved preliminary identification of other possible Sempitors. This is especially true of youngsters, not unlike you, who are just beginning to discover radical differences between themselves, their family and their friends. As children, Sempitors are indistinguishable from other humans until they enter puberty, at which time they begin to exhibit certain "talents" shall we say.

The Sempiterno enjoy other talents that routinely include extraordinary physical strength, stamina, and or speed; this would go hand in hand with their amazing regenerative and healing powers. Some enjoy a degree of sight and hearing well beyond anything within the merely human experience. All seem to possess a much higher than average IQ, an eidetic memory – the ability to remember nearly everything they experience, and finally the development of a highly organized mind to track the memories and information they retain. The inability to properly file data would result in information overload and possibly a mental breakdown of sorts."

Blas paused and turned his face upward and slightly to the right, as if he were listening to someone. "You will have to excuse me Mr. De Torres; I must attend to my duties for a time." The man rose from his seat. "You of course are free to remain here or go back to your room as you prefer, although you will not be permitted to leave or explore the rest of the abbey."

"Locking me up are you?" Teun smirked.

"Not at all. From this point on we have no need of such crude methods of control. Suffice it to say, you will have to deal with my Master should you stray. Mr. De Torres, I sincerely hope we understand our situation."

Teun simply nodded, "I suppose we do." He watched Blas leave the room through the far door and walk further into the abbey.

A midsized community of three hundred and fifty thousand, Claremont City boasted a centralized downtown core, an active cultural and artistic community, well designed bus and light rail transit lines, numerous parks, and several upscale lake side developments. The newest addition to the skyline, the Meyers Theatre for the Performing Arts had enjoyed its ribbon cutting that very evening. Most definitely a gala event, the opulent festivities drew a number of big names within the arts and theater industry, prominent local and state politicians, and more than a smattering of the crème de la crème.

At the top of this list was Otto Meyers, the nonagenarian patriarch of the American branch of the prominent Swiss family of the same name. Born in 1921 with a European background, the aged gentleman had managed to make a rare public appearance along with that with his considerably

33

younger cousin, Irma Meyers. His assistant guided his wheel chair onto the stage, positioning it to one side of the podium where he took his place with the other tuxedoed dignitaries who patiently awaited their turn in that white-hot spotlight of public recognition. Beside Otto sat a darkly veiled, diminutive woman wearing an exquisite and very costly Balenciaga evening gown. The obsidian dress had a high collar that concealed her neck, long semitransparent sleeves, gathering at her waist before falling to her ankles. The style of Irma Meyers clothing worn at all public events was constant, nothing changed but the colors of the fabric.

The woman enjoyed an unusual modicum of privacy and respect from the paparazzi ever since a particularly persistent photographer snapped a photo while she walked by a hotel window having a slightly open curtain. Irma had been wearing a bra and panties at the time. At first glance, the prying lens had revealed a shapely middle-aged woman. The photographer must have thought he struck tabloid gold until he zoomed in closer to discover a pathetic figure whose skin was a horrific mass of hypertrophic scarring that began at the top of her partially denuded head, extended across her torso, upper arms, thighs and calves. Ignoring any pretence of propriety, the man had offered the photo to several tabloids of particular notoriety, only to find himself chastised and treated as a pariah by everyone in the industry. Since that occasion, Irma lived her life cocooned within anonymity and freed from idle speculation and unwanted attention, a situation she had gone to great lengths to attain, right down to the purchase of the movie set costume, and tipping off the luckless photographer as to her room number.

The speeches given by the Mayor and Governor stretched out nearly twenty-five minutes, Otto thought it could have been worse; the opening could have taken place in an election year. The next person to take center stage was the architect who thanked the theater's civic and state sponsors and most especially the Meyers family who had coughed up fully one quarter of the building's two hundred and fifty million dollar cost. Then Otto had surprised everyone by rising from his chair, shaking off the proffered hand of the Governor and climbing to the podium. Otto spoke eloquently for five minutes or so before allowing his personal assistant to help him shakily down from the podium and into his chair while everyone else in the auditorium rose from their own in applause.

The midnight blue Mercedes-Benz S550 rolled quietly into the parking lot pulling up to the main doors of the Shawnessy Home for Seniors. The facility was near the best of any of its type in the State, or western States for that matter, catering to those select few who could afford the five figure monthly tab. The car's chauffeur, Norman Stiles, doubling as Otto's personal assistant stepped out of the posh vehicle and walked to the trunk where he retrieved the wheelchair. Setting it down, the man pushed it toward the passenger side of the sedan. As the old gentleman stepped out and sat in the chair, two of the lodge attendants exited the entrance and quickly approached the car. The chauffeur raised a hand toward the man and woman who were only yards distant; they immediately stopped in their tracks. Irma Meyers stepped out of the back seat then took up a position in front of the wheelchair, bending low she engaged in a hushed conversation with Otto. It lasted but a minute. Irma entered the back seat of the Mercedes while the chauffeur motioned the attendants toward the elderly gentleman, upon arrival the two attendants commenced to fawn accordingly. A minute later the dark sedan left the curb and began the thirty-minute drive back to Meyers Hall.

Otto Meyers had come to live in the creek following the Second World War, Irma followed shortly afterward. Claiming to be Swiss born, his family had made millions in munitions industry supplying prewar Germany as well as England and France, but didn't recognize the danger when Hitler and the Nazis swept to power. Like similar industries in Germany they continued to do quite well until war was declared. After that they couldn't find buyers for the companies they owned and took it on the chin when the Axis countries were defeated. Still, the Meyers' family was fortunate to have maintained a significant amount of their assets outside the Reich. It was rumored by Jewish investigators that the Meyers had stolen millions of Reichsmarks from the Jews who were sent to the camps, secreting the funds out of the Third Reich and funneling them into accounts in Switzerland, England and the USA. Precious metals, gems and artwork stolen from synagogues and private houses were stashed in Safety Deposit boxes around the world, even the reforged gold fillings of concentration camp prisoners teeth added to the Meyers' holdings. Even so, the amounts stolen by the Meyers paled before the vast fortunes pilfered by no fewer than twelve or more prominent European families all of whom became multi-billionaires on the backs of those whose lives were destroyed within the holocaust.

Otto Meyers was a Nazis sympathizer and supporter both during and before the war, but always made sure he kept a foot in any number of camps. At the end of the conflict, his money bought anonymity and a hastened immigration to America. Over the years since coming to the US, he donated significant cash to both the Republican and Democratic parties and established a charitable foundation under the family name as well.

Originally wishing to keep a low profile, Otto chose Washington State to live. In 1947, the state's population was just a little over two million, the land was wide open, and few people ever asked any questions if enough money changed hands. For fifty-six years Otto used Meyers Hall as a quiet haven and retreat while he jetsetted about the world conducting his international business operations. As old age and declining health caught up with him, he spent ever more time within the Hall.

It was coming on four years now since Otto needed more help than Irma was willing to give. Full time servants, other than Norman Stiles, had never been employed; the Hall's cleaning and routine maintenance and yard care was conducted under the auspicious of a property management firm owned by the Meyers and based out of Claremont City. All activities took place under Norman's ever-watchful eyes and a video security system that in every way was the equal of that installed in the White House.

When it became clear that Otto needed full time dedicated care he was shuffled into the Shawnessy facility. Irma Meyers, ever shunning the public eye and utterly suspicious of anyone who may gain access to her personal comings and goings, immediately suspended the scheduled cleaning and routine maintenance service. Since that time, the conditions within the Hall and its surrounding grounds had taken a significant turn for the worse. As far as the residents of Hansel's Creek were concerned, interest in the Hall or that of the reclusive family living there had never been a high point of conversation. When Otto left the Hall and no longer showed his face in the Creek, people quickly forgot that anyone still lived at the "out of the way" mansion.

For Irma Meyers the seclusion and disinterest were both welcome and very much central to her purpose. Independently wealthy, the woman had no need of another soul in the world, except of course, her precious Norman. Over the past year she had found herself becoming ever more dependent upon the man although not for the simple essentials of daily life. Their relationship was exceedingly complex, and if not sexual, was intimate never the less. She and Norman were bound by ties of loyalty and trust that knew no bounds, exceeding even those between a mother and child. The couple had walked through life hand in hand, or perhaps more correctly mind within mind, since their first meeting in the early days following the end of the Second World War. Their bond was a cerebral joining, a meeting on an almost spiritual plane. When the two were within a limited physical range, a distance nearing a quarter mile, their minds operated almost as one. Each knew the other's thoughts and shared experience; lately this ability had become intermittent and strained.

Irma feared this was a portent of the future, as did Norman, and this particular future did not hold promise. So unlike her distant past when the centuries spread before her, she allowed her mind to replay her memories that for her were as a vivid as the present.

5

July 10, 1799 was a warm sunny day near Andel, Bavaria. Within a dingy, dirt floored shack an old woman sat on a milking stool placed at the end of a rough hewn wooden cot. Before her, a woman lay upon the cot's thin straw mattress, her legs splayed wide.

The old midwife said encouragingly, "I know it is hard my dear, but God only gives us those tasks that he knows we can handle." She didn't add that all too often those tasks were beyond even the most doughty and stalwart. A tear fell from the old woman's eye as her heart went out to the girl who cried out and writhed in the midst of her difficult labor.

The young mother's efforts to give birth to her second child were now extending into their third hour following the easy delivery of the first of her twin daughters. The midwife's right hand pressed and massaged the young woman's belly, her perceptive touch bypassing the baby's feet and legs and coming to rest above its torso. Using her other hand to support the small of her patient's back, she allowed her free hand to apply pressure in alternating directions, her movements guided by her years of experience in dealing with difficult and sometimes complex births.

The old woman wiped the sweat from her brow using the back of her hand then cast a furtive glance at a second middle-aged woman who stood nearby wringing her hands while wearing a guarded yet still hopeful expression. Hope faded as the midwife's lips thinned and her head shook softly from side to side.

"The child is twisted about, coming feet first." The midwife continued, "Gertrud... this sometimes happens, more often if a twin is involved."

"Can't you do anything?" the second woman asked "Anything at all for my Emma?"

The midwife remained silent as she continued her work trying to turn the child's position slightly, easing its way into the world. The birth was a breech; the little body was tightly trapped and twisted inside the mother's body. The healer's immediate concern was for the child's wellbeing since the odds of the umbilical cord becoming strangulated were increasingly likely. Should this occur, it would deny the child oxygen and result in a stillbirth. Her second concern, of no less consequence, was for the child's mother, who in her valiant struggles appeared to have ruptured something deep within her body and was now severely hemorrhaging. Moments later the midwife's hand confirmed her original fear that the child had died. A hand of minutes passed, the young mother mercifully lost consciousness.

The midwife knew this was likely from blood loss, but knowing the child was dead, she could afford to wrest the tiny corpse from the mother. Perhaps with the delivery, the cause of the bleeding might be somehow stemmed. This eventuality was not to be, and Emma Wainwright shortly thereafter passed from this world.

The midwife had laid the body of the deceased twin atop that of her mother, and then covered both bodies with the blood soaked sheet. If only she had been consulted earlier in the pregnancy, her experience would have led her to suspect that one of the twins was likely breeched. The old woman might have been able to reposition the child before labor began, as she had done on numerous previous occasions. She turned away from the small tragedy and studied Emma's mother.

Gertrud was holding the surviving twin daughter in a bright shaft of light streaming through the partially shuttered window and was carefully examining the child's little body. Through her tears, Gertrud counted ten fingers, ten toes and the perfectly normal features belonging to her new granddaughter.

Wrapping the child in a small receiving blanket, Gertrud and the midwife walked some fifty feet from the cottage where Emma's husband was pretending to busy himself upon an outdoor workbench. As the women approached, the man turned to face them. Seeing the small bundle in Gertrud's arms, Ernst Wainwright's face brightened as a smile of relief crossed his face. A moment later, his cheerful gaze shifted to the stark faces of each woman in turn. As the women spoke of his loss he silently nodded, his face now blank of all expression. He turned his back to the two women and looked toward heaven askingly. His eyes closed in silent prayer for several minutes.

Upon their reopening, his attention was drawn to the imposing hilltop that dominated the local landscape in all directions for several miles. Doing so, his eyes fell upon the blackened ruins of Landshut Castle. The keep's massive stones were still placed solidly one atop the other, but the interior had been completely gutted. On one side of the rectangular building, a lone, wide girthed tower soared high above its base below. Bathed in the warm yellow orange beams of the nearly setting sun, the upper ramparts cast a long deep finger of shadow that extended in a southeasterly direction.

Struggling with his grief, Ernst stared blankly at the panorama before him. As the minutes passed, he became aware of the tower's shadow, its edge slowly engulfing the bright sun lit earth before it. As the sun dropped ever lower toward the horizon, its shallow rays illuminated and accentuated the top half of the huge granite boulders dotting the rough landscape below the castle walls, while leaving the boulder's lower halves embedded in deep shadow. "Islands within a river," Ernst mumbled.

Not catching his words Gertrud called his name softly. "Ernst?" The man remained silent. The woman repeated his name a bit louder. "Ernst!"

As that finger of shadow finally kissed the ground beneath those standing in front of the cottage, the man was suddenly released from his stupor and turned to face the women and the child that waited in his mother-in-law's arms. Ernst leaned toward Gertrud, extending his hands. Gertrud carefully passed the baby to her father, laying it somewhat awkwardly in his arms. The midwife smiled and quickly moved in close, repositioning Ernst's arms properly supporting the child's neck and head. He cradled the child, slowly rocking her back and forth while staring at her face. Suddenly the baby's eyes opened slightly, Ernst was quite surprised to realize the child was actually looking at him. Her eyes closed once again as she gurgled contentedly.

"Ayla." His dry voice croaked softly, then firmed; "Her name shall be Ayla."

Ayla enjoyed a relatively happy childhood, although in that age childhood came to an early end. Especially true if you were motherless, the only sibling, and expected to perform the domestic duties usually asked of a wife. The adage, "it takes a village to raise a child" couldn't be truer than when that child lived in the early eighteen hundreds. From the age of five onward, the neighborhood women taught Ayla to sew, cook, and launder; and the many other everyday household tasks. A quick learner, hard worker and well liked by the village's children and adults, Ayla was also the apple of her father's eye. Whenever possible, Ernst doted on the young teen, taking her along on errands or small jobs. This began to change the day that her father met the woman who was to become her stepmother, Elsa Becker.

Elsa had moved into a small farmhouse on the outskirts of the village with her family. Physically, the twenty six year old woman was tall and slender with light blonde hair and a pleasant face. In many ways she resembled Ayla's mother. Perhaps this resemblance and her father's loneliness was what drove him to become so quickly enamored and remarried.

It should be stressed at this time that Elsa should not be seen as a cruel or evil sort, but as most women approaching a particular biological age, having children of their own became an overwhelmingly urgent affair. Obtaining a loving attentive father that provided for her new children was also highly desirable. Had Ayla been younger, Elsa's maternal instincts would have drawn her close, but Ayla was fourteen, and would reach a marriageable age in two years time; as such her presence within in the new family order was seen as an impediment to Elsa's goals.

Following Elsa's and Ernst's marriage, Elsa assumed the domestic duties of the family, leaving Ayla free to work outside the home. Families were poor in that region of Bavaria, and there were strong economic benefits to a family that had a daughter or son capable of working outside the home and bringing in money, but more likely food or traded goods. Elsa was always on the lookout for such opportunities, especially those that involved Ayla spending considerable time and distance away from the family home.

It was six months or so later when an ideal position made itself available. Ironically, it was Ernst who first became aware of the situation; it was also he that negotiated the arrangement with a cobbler in Longkamp, a village twenty-eight miles distant. The small shop owner had lost his wife to fever eighteen months earlier leaving his three children without anyone to care for them. The man seemed to be a decent sort, holding high regard in the community. He could also pay in coin, a rare prospect, the twenty copper Kreuzers (pennies) that Ayla could earn per month quickly persuaded Ernst to close the deal. It was agreed that Ernst would bring along his daughter on his next trip to the Longkamp.

The morning sun was barely over the horizon when Ernst carried two cloth bags out from the cottage, placing the larger of the two, containing Ayla's clothes in the rear of the wagon laying it beside his tools. The smaller bag containing their lunch for the road would sit upfront with him and Ayla. Ernst walked over to where the horse stood patiently waiting. Quickly re-checking the bridle and harness, Ernst returned to the wagon and climbed up. Taking up the reins he held them in his calloused hands while resting his forearms on his knees as he watched the cottage door. He thought to himself. "Why do women always take so long to get ready?"

Presently his daughter and wife appeared at the door. While Ernst knew Elsa didn't consider her stepdaughter as her child, his wife was not uncaring. She teared up while giving Ayla a hug and kissing her forehead. "Don't worry Ayla, everything will work out fine, God will see to it."

"Good bye" Ayla replied quietly. The girl turned away and walked to the wagon. Before climbing up beside her father she studied the little cottage, making a mental picture of her old home that she could take with her to her new life.

The wagon bucked and bumped its way along the rock-strewn pathway that led upward toward the ruined keep. Just over the hill's summit lay the road that led east toward Longkamp and beyond. As the path passed near the keep, the faint smell of charred wood still rose up from the ash and the mass of partially consumed timbers that had once been the castle's upper ramparts.

Upon joining the main road, the ride smoothed out considerably as did the girl's spirits, which rose with her natural anticipation of seeing country she had never seen before as well as what waited at her final destination. They stopped in the nearby village of Andel while Ernst picked up some iron hardware from the blacksmith. The brief delay gave Ayla the chance to say good-bye to all those she had known in her life.

Ayla was surprised and very happy to find so many of her friends and especially those women who had helped care for her as a child. There were many hugs, kisses and tears exchanged that last morning. Her well-wishers eventually dispersed to go about the days toils leaving Ayla to walk back to the wagon; she could see her father already sitting up in the wagon's forward bench. About to hurry her pace, she noticed her father conversing with another man, one whom she recognized and knew had a reputation for being long winded. Her attention drawn to the wagon, she hadn't noticed the approach of an ancient woman wearing a long gray dress and a thick black shawl draped about her head and shoulders.

"Ayla?" The old woman's voice was so weak and shallow that at first the teen didn't notice it over the general comings and goings on taking place in the street. The old woman's voice strained in effort, "Ayla. Ayla Wainwright?"

Hearing her name, Ayla turned toward the person before her and studied her face. "Yes?" The network of worry lines and the wrinkles of old age had inscribed their story upon the old woman's face. The hands she clasped together before her waist were thin and bony, and the mottled skin covering those bones was gossamer. Wisps of white and gray hair poked out from beneath the shawl but what caught Ayla's attention were her eyes. Although becoming lightly clouded over her long years of life, they and the expression worn upon her face continued to suggest her mind was as sharp as it ever was.

"My, my. I see you've become a young woman." The woman's eyes shone and glistened as she assessed the pretty girl standing before her.

"I'm sorry mother, do I know you?" Ayla searched her memory for the woman's face but came up blank.

"My name is Mattie. At one time I lived in Andel and every woman knew of me. I attended the birth of nearly half of the people in this town, including your father as well as yourself." The old woman searched for a spark of recognition on the part of the girl, finding none she continued; her words fell soft and resigned; "but that was a long time ago." She paused, "I was the midwife who cared for your mother when you were born."

Ayla knew the present midwife in the village and had spoken to her on many occasions but she didn't know how to respond to the woman before her. "Oh," was all she could manage.

"You resemble your mother; you have been blessed with her lovely Shade of blonde hair and a fair complexion." The old woman could see that she had captured the girl's interest. "Has no one told you that?"

"My grandmother and some of the village women say I look a little like her." Ayla stated nonchalantly. "Do you live in the village?"

"No, I just returned today. My husband passed last winter and now I'm to live out my final days with my grandson and his family." She smiled. "Do you know Erik Dansen? He and Mia have twin girls."

Ayla nodded, "yes, very well, I often come with my father when he visits the village for supplies. It was Mia who showed me how to sew when I was younger and I've know the twins since they were born. My father, Ernst often works with Erik Dansen."

The old woman looked thoughtful, "Ayla, did you know you had a twin sister?" As soon as the words were uttered, the woman felt regret. It wasn't proper in the day to speak of the family's dead unless a bond of familiarity had been well established. Yet given her age and health, she no long felt iron bound to that particular compliance.

Ayla's eyes widened. "Twin sister?"

"I'm sorry my dear, I should have said nothing." The old woman knew she had to continue. "Yes a twin. Your sister died at birth. You were born the eldest, but your sister was a breech... and your mother was so brave." Her voice was a whisper. "Forgive a nosey old woman, but I always ask the twins I have delivered or others I've met if they have ever shared an unusual bond?" The midwife had a considerable gift of perception and insight and over her long life it was one she had learned to channel and direct to some degree. Now she chose to do so.

The question hung in the air between them. Ayla's expression remained indecipherable. The old woman decided it would be best to explain her meaning further. "Some twins' say they know what the other is thinking without saying a word, or know what the other is doing even when separated by distance. Very often if one twin is in trouble, the other twin is aware of it." The midwife's mind softly probed that of the young woman as she read the girls' face which outwardly remained passive. Inwardly Ayla maintained a measured control. The midwife became aware of an incredible amount of information passing between herself and Ayla, but its flow was completely one-sided, toward Ayla. The old woman attempted to turn round the situation then suddenly, her thoughts were brusquely rebuffed; the midwife instinctively broke contact. The old woman considered; the girl's mind was powerful and well disciplined... far beyond her tender years, far beyond anything in her own experience.

"No!" Ayla nearly shouted. The girl was badly startled and upset by what she had just experienced. "No I have... haven't." The girl suddenly blanched, then held the sides of her head in her hands and fell to her knees on the rough ground. "Woman, what have you done?" The girl said nothing further but knelt motionless in the street for several minutes. The old midwife placed a hand on Ayla's shoulders hoping to console the young girl but she shrugged off the caress and nearly yelled, "Don't touch me!"

The old woman looked about somewhat nervously; a few people had stopped in the street and were watching them. Not wanting to continue the public spectacle, the midwife offered a quiet apology followed by a louder offer of help to the girl. "My, my dear, are you alright?" she queried while searching the faces of a growing number of people who had gathered about.

Ayla remained quiet for a few more seconds, and then rose to her feet. Her face was ashen and her eyes appeared haunted but quietly she spoke to the midwife. "Yes, I'm alright, I don't know what happened... thank you." This seemed to dispel the onlookers who returned to their business. Ayla turned her head toward the wagon. Her father had finally broken free from his recent conversation and now regarded her intently, waving her to him, impatiently awaiting her return. "I'm sorry mother, I have to go now." Ayla didn't allow her eyes to meet those of the old woman and somewhat unsteadily, walked away.

The old woman looked after Ayla questioningly. She had seldom felt so strong a response with anyone with whom she had previously made mental contact and that included Lisa, her own twin who had been endowed with a much more generous gift than she.

After Ayla had walked several paces she stopped and turned; "Thank you for everything you tried to do for us." Ayla trotted off toward the wagon.

Feeling the sincerity of Ayla's gratitude, the midwife smiled and slowly turned away. With their meeting she had the answers she had sought. Across the street she saw her daughter-in-law exit a small shop and stop to chat with the proprietor's wife who had paused in her sweeping and leaned atop a straw broom. Mia held a hand of each of her daughters as they stood impatiently waiting on either side of their mother.

"Do you know who that was?" Ernst asked of his daughter. He slapped the reins lightly on the back of the horse and the wagon started off down the street on its way out of town.

"Not at first, but I do now." The girl looked back and saw the old woman standing with Mia and her children, all of them looked toward their wagon. Ayla could tell her father wanted to talk about her meeting with the midwife and said tersely, "Father, do we have to speak of her, I really don't want to."

"Of course we don't." Ernst reached over, wrapping his arm over her shoulders and giving her a hug. "No, of course we don't."

Ayla was very quiet for the next hour or so. She mulled over her recent connection with the old midwife; the way that odd feeling had started in the small of her back, how it had slowly crept up the back of her neck and play over her temples. Ayla remembered a collage of random images appearing then disappearing rapidly within her mind. Her father standing proudly beside a young and very pregnant woman in front of their cottage, a newborn placed into her grandmother's waiting arms, a mother's feelings of joy, followed by others of sadness, loss, and finally despair. In that single moment, Ayla suddenly comprehended she had witnessed her own birth and mother's death within the memories of the old midwife.

Yet on a lower level, there were other images, strange images that begged answers to questions she had not yet formed. It would take Ayla considerable time to sort out what she had been provided, to make sense of the nonsense that now pervaded her mind. Ayla also wondered at her mind's newfound power to resist and then fended off the foreign contact. The girl thought the woman's response was not unlike the astonishment an animal might feel at that very moment when the jaws of a steel trap sprang shut upon its leg.

Ayla wondered about the old woman's interest regarding a connection between herself and her dead twin. Perhaps if she had known the midwife longer, Ayla might have confided in the woman. She may have told her that only recently; she somehow became aware of what other people were feeling, sometimes their most intimate emotions. Ayla suddenly regretted

45

she was leaving the village; she felt saddened knowing she and the old woman would never meet again.

Her father pulled on the reins directing the wagon from the roadway's pebbled surface and onto a green pasture stopping the wagon beneath the shading branches of a huge willow. "Let's have some lunch my girl. I'm famished." Ayla placed aside her thoughts of the old woman, instead considering her future in Longkamp, the cobbler and his family.

6

It was toward the end of shift when Detective Marty Denton and his partner Tony Lee walked into the precinct's Criminal Investigations Division (CID) office. As they entered, a united chorus of voices rang out - "Way to go College Boy!" The surprise on Marty's face was captured by half a dozen cell phones before he showed his back to the small crowd of well-wishers, playfully shielding his face. His partner grabbed his arms and shoulders and turned him about.

Marty Denton's boss, Lieutenant Jane Forbes walked up and held out her hand, but when Marty reached his own out to take it, Jane simply slapped it away and went in for a quick hug. "You won't get away that easily," she laughed, "It's not every day we have a chance to congratulate one of our own for such an achievement." Marty flushed slightly as a line of his friends and colleagues quickly formed up in front of him.

Denton had finally earned his Master's degree in criminology from the local university. It had been a long three-year, uphill climb since he continued his work within the CID handling a full caseload and maintaining an excellent clearance rate. Detective Denton was a natural when it came to police work; his hard work, intelligence and frankly uncanny intuition proved an unbeatable combination. Topping it all, on and off the job Marty was congenial and always ready with a smile and a helping hand. Judging by the number of people who turned out that afternoon, many people felt the same way.

Lieutenant Forbes extended her palms towards the people; "I also have another announcement folks." She turned to Marty. "I spoke with Director Fitch of the FBI this morning. It seems the Director was highly impressed with Detective Denton's performance while he worked on the joint task force with the BAU (Behavioral Analysis Unit) last summer. I'd like to read from the Director's letter, and I quote "Special Agent in Charge, Doug Huston: Detective Marty Denton has performed in an outstanding manner while attached to the JTF. Personally, I have seldom seen an individual as diligent, hardworking and capable as Detective Marty Denton. I would strongly recommend and furthermore, request this individual be offered a three year term as an active field agent under the auspicious of the BAU."

The lieutenant folded the letter. "I spoke to the chief about this, and he has agreed to the transfer, with the insistence that you be returned to our department after your tour. I'll have this letter placed into your file, if they can squeeze it in with that stack of other commendations." The entire room laughed together. "Congrats again Marty."

The back slapping and cajoling carried on for the better part of half an hour before the cake arrived. A local bakery had done a terrific job on the cake forming it to mimic a graduation cap. The cake was carried in by Ann Oaks, affectionately referred to by her friends as Anny Oakley. The perky little brunette worked in the IT unit downstairs and she and Marty had been dating on and off on a casual basis for six months or so. Marty had the distinct feeling she wanted more, but they both knew that couldn't happen right now.

After an hour or so, the party wound down. People left for home or started their shift leaving Marty and Ann alone for the first time that evening.

"So what am I to do without you for the next couple of years?" Ann asked with a smile on her face, but a serious question in her eyes.

"Oh, I'll be back for a little R&R every now and then, besides what's to stop you coming out for a weekend? The Creek is only four hours or so away." He smiled, "besides you still haven't met my Dad. I think you and he would hit it off." Marty knew they would, Ann bore a more than slight resemblance to his mother. When he first asked her out he had hesitated, wondering if it was healthy or just downright weird for a guy to date a girl that reminded him of his mom. What was that old song? "I want a girl, just like the girl, that married dear old Dad? In the end, Ann's personality was nothing like his mothers; sure Mom was friendly but quite reserved, while Ann was a ball of fire.

"Well, I'd better keep an eye on you. I don't want you to pick up any strays do I?" she smiled warmly. "Maybe I'll just drop in on you without warning." She turned slightly exposing her side to him and giving him a demure look, "Would that keep you on the straight and narrow?"

Marty wrapped his arms around Ann drew her close and whispered something in her ear. "Me too." Ann confirmed, her bottom lip trembling slightly. "I'm going to miss you Marty."

Marty gently grasped her shoulders and turned her slowly until he faced her. "The last six months has worn me pretty thin; I need a break before starting the new job, but not from you."

"I still have some vacation time..." she let her words hang.

"I'd love you to come. Summer's pretty and so is the town. Give me some time with Dad first. The last time we spoke I thought he sounded a little distant. I know he misses Mom, they were inseparable, especially after he retired." He looked thoughtful, "I can truthfully say they didn't spend a day apart for the last six years before she passed."

"Sounds wonderful," Ann wore a serious expression. "They were very lucky."

"Yes they were." He extended his elbow toward her. "What you say we grab some dinner. I feel like Chinese, how about you?"

Sliding her arm beneath his, she leaned in. "You and your Chinese food! Do I at least get an eggroll?"

He grinned and said suggestively, "Any kind of roll you might want!"

The couple spoke and laughed warmly as they left the CID office.

7

The door to the sitting room entered without warning. Teun, somewhat startled turned and faced the door.

Blas Velez entered the room and closed the door behind him. "Ah Mr. De Torres, thank you for your patience, once again I apologize for my temporary absence."

The men sat in the chairs as before. Blas began speaking.

"I should start out by saying members of the Order refer to themselves as a Sempitor or in plural, Sempitors. When referring to your race, the term is Sempiterno, as in the "Orden Sempiterno," derived from Spanish and translated as the "Eternal Order." Similarly a Sempitor translates to one who is eternal." Using two fingers Blas picked a piece of lint from his pants, moved his hands away from his side and rubbed his fingers together dropping the offending particle toward the floor. "Old buildings..." Blas shrugged. What is one to do?"

The thin man continued. "There are two basic differences within the Sempiterno, not physical or mental differences, but simply the manner in which they choose to feed." Blas had Teun's full attention. "The Order of White, represent those ninety five percent of Sempitors who I suppose could be termed parasitic for lack of a better term. These Sempitors choose to remain undetected at all costs. They siphon off perhaps a few months, or at most perhaps a year from their victims life expectancy before moving on to feed elsewhere. You yourself, at this stage in your life appear to exhibit many of the tendencies and preferences found within those belonging to the Order of White.

The second sort, the "Order of Gray," form the other five percent of Sempitors. These individuals are entirely predatory. They prefer to consume the entire life of a human in a great rush of ecstasy, often combining sexual appetite with wanton greed. From the point of view of the humans they prey upon, the Gray must only be viewed as being truly villainous in nature, but within the Order, no such judgments are handed down to the Grays from their White brethren. It could be looked upon as someone being unduly judgmental as to whether someone prefers their meat fully cooked or bloody. It is strictly a matter of personal preference although there are physical downsides to the latter.

Members of the Order of Gray tend to possess a shorter life expectancy when compared to that of the Order of White. By consuming the life energy of their victims within an extremely short period of time, their own bodies tend to age much faster, however this detriment is balanced to some degree with a significant increase in physical, though not mental power. It is also interesting that the White Order drift toward living in the better developed countries, probably due to their interests of economic stability while the Gray are more evenly split, with many choosing to remain in primitive areas where they may kill at will and employ any manner they may wish to do so.

While reasonably large, Meyers Hall could hardly be described as a mansion, at least in the general sense of the term, and most certainly not if your definition was based upon having conveniences such as electric power, modern indoor plumbing and central heating. The house was a throwback - commonplace in centuries past, but today only a peculiar anomaly, a stark departure from the norms of contemporary life. Its only two doorways, positioned at the center of the houses' front and rear walls, were narrow, yet oddly high in stature; while the windows were uniformly square and small in relation to the oversized non-descript Gray stone walls in which they sat. The glass within the window frames was of ancient manufacture and being rather opaque and of uneven thickness, tended to distort and dim an image passing through their panes.

In the years immediately following the Second World War, if you had an opportunity to converse with the contractors and masons hired to not build, but re-assemble the unusual two story stone house. You would hear of old, time worn stones, each individually numbered, shipped over from somewhere in Bavaria then carefully reassembled at the new site. Some might speak of a deeply excavated square pit and the manner in which locally quarried stone was used to construct the thick foundations supporting the many tons of rock stacked above. Others could describe the five upstairs rooms, not a single one a bathroom; but each having a small fireplace, each adding yet another black smoke stack to the forest of piping jutting out above the slate roof.

You might hear tales of a huge kitchen with old fashioned wood burning stoves, substantial butcher block countertops, and long preparation tables, or perhaps the formal dining room capable of seating up to forty people while not one, but two massive chandeliers dangled above its twenty foot high ceilings. Without doubt, the men would provide an in-depth description of the Great Room that boasted a massive dual opening fireplace in its center easily accommodating six foot logs within its girth, and most certainly, the unique serpentine design flowing through each room on the main floor; its pastel of colored slates carefully inlaid among

51

the Gray travertine floor. The twenty oaken steps rising up to the second floor are resplendent as is the ornately carved, highly polished banister.

All would speak of the seven men who died over the twenty eight months while engaged in its assembly. There were a series of unfortunate accidents, easily explainable and without mystery. A section of the foundation wall collapsing on several workers, a man's fall from a second story scaffold to the frozen ground some forty feet below, as well as a spat of similar, but non-fatal incidents, yet far more than one would expect among seasoned and experienced tradesmen. Not to mention the myriad of flu and cold like illnesses that seemed to inflict the workers, four of whom died that second winter, while sparing the good townsfolk of Hansel's Creek.

Those visiting Meyers house will travel a five mile winding laneway of hard packed gravel. On either side of the narrow path, flat Gray limestone rocks, stacked expertly, one atop the other to a height of a man's waste run the entire length leading up to the house. Beyond the south wall stood thick stands of spruce and fir, growing upon the elevated hillsides, the trees blocked most of the direct sunlight, creating a dark and brooding aspect; especially true during the long winter months when the pale sun rode low on the horizon. Past the north wall, a series of shallow fens and bogs dot the landscape creating an equally unappealing panorama, and appreciated only by myriads of mosquitoes, a few muskrat and the occasional wayward waterfowl. It is only as the land begins its steady ascent toward Devil's Head Hill, do the trees make their return.

A massive eight foot iron gate guards the laned entrance leading up to the homestead. About its perimeter a six foot high wrought iron fence encircles a four acre lot. Along the fence top; series of sharp arrowed spikes protrude above their spindles at regular six inch intervals. The laneway's hard pack gravel surface continues beneath the gate rushing outward on either side to form a wide circle perhaps two hundred feet in diameter. At its center stands the skeletal remnant of a long dead willow whose bark has long since been torn away and scattered by the elements; pale bleached limbs still point skyward in a most pleading ghostly fashion. Across the compound, sits a somewhat more modern two car garage, its two overhead doors hang slightly askew while the gray wooden siding, blistered and pealing, is urgently in need of repair.

At the rear of the house, a long neglected and overgrown garden engorged with sprawling brambles, thistles and other assorted weeds finds itself surrounded by now feral shrubs, bushes and the dwarfed misshapen trees that were never meant thrive in these more northerly climes.

In short, if one were to choose a word to sum up the appearance of the Meyers House; foreboding might spring to mind.

Earlier on that particular morning, long before dawn graced the clouds floating in the eastern sky with Shades of violet and rose; when night still held sway over the world, a pair of headlights appeared in the lane growing brighter as a van quietly cruised towards the iron gate of Meyers House. Upon reaching the entrance, the driver's door opened. A dark figure exited and approached the gate. One hand held an oversized key ring while the other reached out and grasped the heavy chain that bound the gate shut. Finding the padlock it was turned about within the harsh glare of the headlights until the location of the keyhole was revealed and the key inserted. A loud click sounded throughout the compound. A moment later the clanging and ringing of steel chain, grating noisily upon the bars of the wrought iron gate was quickly answered by the high pitched squeal of metal hinges protesting their infrequent movement.

Returning to the vehicle, the driver entered the van driving it forward several yards into the compound before returning on foot to close and lock the gate. Moments later, the vehicle crept slowly into the compound, the sound of its tires cracking upon gravel marked its passage until it came to a stop at the bottom of wide stone steps leading up to the front door landing.

Once again the driver exited the panel van walking back to its side door. The figure slid back the door; the inner compartment remained dark owing to the purposely missing light bulbs in the vans interior. The figure paused and turned about facing the front of the building expectantly.

In due course, the front door opened and a slightly built, hooded figure stepped slowly down the steps pausing at the van's opening. Slowly the figure leaned in then prodded something with its hands. It stood motionless for several long moments before it once again stood erect. The hooded figure turned toward the driver who still remained standing several feet beyond, waved a bony hand bidding the driver to approach before it made its way back up the stairs and disappeared into the dark recesses of the Hall.

The driver retrieved a small wrapped bundle, lifting it effortlessly from the van's interior then walking to the front entrance. While doing so, something small fell unnoticed and came to rest on the lowest step. Climbing the wide steps Norman Stiles dutifully followed his mistress into the house. The front door slowly shut. Norman carried his light burden as he crossed the cavernous rooms of the main floor. Then upon reaching the carved oaken door that led into the depths of the cold cellar he slowly began his descent.

The next hour passed slowly. Finally the stars near the eastern horizon began to blend with the emerging twilight. The front door opened and Norman Stiles walked down the steps toward the waiting vehicle. Reaching the bottom step he paused, bending to retrieve that which had been dropped earlier. Continuing to the still open van, it carelessly tossed in the Raggedy Ann doll. Quietly closing the door, he made a mental note to burn the child's toy along with the rest; after his mistress had fed.

8

Marty Denton loved night driving and before he knew it found himself entering Hansel's Creek much earlier than planned, the light traffic and his silver BMW Z4 ate up the road covering the three hundred fifty mile distance from Seattle in a little under four hours. He was more than happy with his new cars performance, and had bought the vehicle after test driving many other small convertible sports cars in his price range, which on an honest policeman's salary was rather limited. The deal was sealed when he discovered the Z4 was easily able to accommodate his six foot three frame. Marty checked the clock on the dash, just after 5:45 a.m. He'd already passed the Fast Gas station with its small restaurant a few miles back and decided not to stop for breakfast, but cruise the town and maybe stir up some old memories.

As expected at this hour, the small shops and businesses along Main Street had yet to open. Marty passed the Town Hall and Sheriff's office where an officer had just exited the door and was walking to one of the patrol cars parked out front. The officer gave him a good long look before figuring Marty didn't warrant any further attention, entered his vehicle and drove off in the opposite direction. He rolled past the new library; a large sign out front advertized the used book sale was set to take place this coming Saturday. A block over on Adams all the lights blazed in the town's only bakery and several doors further on Marty saw a fellow in a cook's apron propping open the door of Jim's Cafe, the neon light flickering in the window proclaimed the eatery was open for business.

Ten minutes later, Marty had seen pretty much all of Hansel's Creek, nothing ever seemed to change in the town and that was just fine with Marty. He pulled a left onto Collegiate Street making his way along the deserted roadway. Pools of pale yellow light gathered in ovals beneath the occasional street lamp in stark contrast with the otherwise jet black asphalt. Most of the houses lining either side of the street were still in darkness, only the odd light indicated any one stirred. Marty passed by Hansel Creek's high school, his alma mater. A brilliant mercury vapor yard light illuminated the 1950's era frontage of George Washington High into stark relief.

Seeing the building immediately brought a flood of memories, most pleasant, some less so. The majority centered about old girlfriends, chums and rivals and his victories on the boxing team. He'd liked school and had done reasonably well on his studies, but like many adults wished later on that they had applied themselves a little harder. Still, Marty figured, he could have done a lot worse. Like Jimmy Grissom who developed a penchant towards crack cocaine; Marty wasn't overly surprised to hear Jimmy had found himself in prison a couple of years after grad. Or Mike Blakely who'd died after wrapping his car around a bridge abutment after his grade twelve midterms. Then there was Tim somebody or other, the kid was at best only an acquaintance. He had been a year behind Marty; the guy just disappeared without a trace at one of the local party spots. God how long ago was that, he couldn't immediately put a number on it but it was well over a decade.

A block later brought him to the front of his childhood home. Noticing an interior light shining through the thin living room curtains, "Well how about that..." he said aloud, "the old man must be expecting me." He made a quick u-turn pulling up in front of the small bungalow. Everything was exactly as he remembered from his last visit a year or so back and even then the only thing that had changed since he was a kid was the size of the trees in the front yard. He left the car, grabbed his suitcase from the trunk and walked up along the wide flagstones leading to the front veranda. Passing a particularly large spruce, he remembered planting the Arbor Day tree with his mom after school and then a week later when he had unintentionally run over the tree with the lawn mower. No harm, no foul. He'd reached the door.

Marty tried the bell but didn't hear sound. He tried it once more deciding it was out of order, reached for the lion's head door knocker, rapping lightly several times in succession. In the silence of that early hour, those small taps sounded more like cannon fire booming out across the neighborhood. He looked quickly around, almost expecting electric lights to appear in the surrounding homes, of course none did. He heard light footsteps approach the doorway then stop.

"Yes, who is it?" an overly gruff voice asked. He smiled to himself; his dad was trying to sound tough.

"Seattle Police, open up. I've got a warrant for one Reggie Denton. Says here; you're wanted for murdering the steaks at the community barbeque last year." Reggie had been tasked with tending the barbeque while the cook hit the can. Typically his dad had gotten into an animated baseball discussion with a friend and forgot to keep an eye on the meat. No one ever missed a chance to rib him about it since.

The door swung open, his dad stood in his bathrobe with a big grin on his face. "I wondered if you'd be here early."

"Dad, close up your robe, or the real cops will show up when your neighbors report a flasher in the area." Marty chuckled.

"Oops" Reggie quickly closed his robe and tied the cloth belt in a bow while looking around tentatively. "Come on in Son."

Once inside Marty put down his case and the two men hugged. "I've been looking forward to your visit Martin." He motioned toward the kitchen with a hand, "got fresh coffee on if you'd like one?"

"Sounds good dad." Marty replied as he watched his father part the living room window's drapes and peak out at the street.

"Those your new wheels?" His dad looked back in his son's direction. "What is it?"

Marty nodded, "BMW convertible. Just picked it up last week... how about I take you for a spin later."

"Sounds good." Reggie's rubber soled slippers squeaked atop the kitchen's linoleum floor as he semi-shuffled toward the coffee pot.

Marty noticing the old man's slow uneven gait casually stated, "Arthritis bad today?"

"Bad every day now." Reggie reached up into the cupboard and took down two coffee mugs. "You still take cream and sugar?"

Marty surveyed the kitchen and noticing the old black and white portable TV sitting in the corner upon the fading arborite countertop he thought; some things just never change around here.

"Marty?" his dad had poured the coffee and stood waiting, the creamer held above Marty's cup.

"Sorry dad, just black these days" Marty patted his belly, "Was putting on a little weight, those eight sweetened cups of coffee a day will do that to you over time."

The two men sat at the kitchen table conversing for a good hour. The neighborhood comings and goings freely poured from the old gent. Marty noted, that as with many older people who lived on their own, they spent many hours alone, and usually not by choice. When an opportunity to chat with others presented itself, there was simply no stopping them when they had the chance to do so.

For Marty's part, he enjoyed hearing his father's voice and watching his familiar mannerisms. Sure they spoke on the phone every week or so, but it wasn't the same as in person. Reggie's casual matter of fact attitude towards life was borne out in the timbre and cadence of each word uttered. Marty realized it wasn't as if his father possessed the abilities of a great orator, but the emotional ease and family memories that voice invoked were often surprisingly powerful.

As an experienced police investigator, Marty recognized the value of voice identification in many of his cases; especially those instances where the victim had been physically or mentally traumatized.

While working on a case of sexual assault against a seventeen year old Latino girl, the offender had worn a balaclava to hide his face but voiced a tirade of verbal abuse that accompanied the physical attack. A standard sexual assault examination was performed at the hospital and DNA samples were obtained. A registered sex offender fitting the general description of her assailant was found to have recently moved into her neighborhood.

Marty and his partner Tony had the suspect picked up for questioning. As per standard operating procedure, the interrogation was video recorded. Although the man said precious little regarding the accusation, other to deny it and demand a lawyer, the detectives had their CSI people assemble a voice only line up. Later that day, a sample of the suspect's voice together with those of seven other non-involved males was played to the victim; and her interview was recorded on video. Even though the girl said she couldn't be positive in her choice, Marty recalled the victim's unconscious behavior had radically changed upon hearing that particular voice. There was no question in his mind, or that of the Judge approving the search warrant of the suspect's apartment that a reasonable identification had been provided. A black balaclava and leather jacket similar to that worn by the girl's attacker was found stashed out of sight in the corner of a top closet shelf. The hairs found within the balaclava provided the DNA match that ultimately convicted the perp.

It was nearly seven when fatigue finally caught up with Martin. "Well dad, I think I'm going to hit the hay for a while." He yawned and stretched his arms wide.

"You know the way to your room. By the way, how do you like my housekeeping?" Reggie asked while swinging an upturned palm across the room.

During the first minutes of his visit, Martin had in fact noticed that the place actually looked pretty good, everything in its place, carpets recently vacuumed, floors swept, counters tidy. "Don't tell me you did this yourself." Marty knew full well the old man to be somewhat neglectful in that area and had actually prepared himself to face a bit of a mess.

"No, I can't take the credit, got a good maid. Actually two of them, good looking too!" the old man added mischievously.

Marty smiled, gave his dad a quick hug and then went into the living room to retrieve his bags. His dad returned to his coffee and turned on the

TV. Once again Jim and Katy were presenting the morning's regional news. "... and Shelly Ann Connelly, seven years of age, the child having been abducted from the bedroom of her family's home is still missing. It's now been ten days since her disappearance." Marty had stuck his head in the kitchen before walking to his room and caught a bit of the report.

"Awful. Just bloody awful!" Reggie stated with considerable vehemence. "When they get that guy they ought to just take him out and shoo..."

"Please dad, quiet for a sec, I'd like to hear this." Marty interrupted. He'd heard his dad's opinions on law and order on numerous occasions, especially where they concerned children. Marty listened intently. In his experience, it wasn't unheard of that such abductions were somehow linked to others locally, regionally or even over a number of states. One of his more unusual talents was the ability to match up and intuit subtle connections that many other seasoned investigators would often miss.

The report ended and as the weather girl made her first appearance of the day wearing in short yellow sundress, Marty waved a hand at his dad who stood engrossed in front of the TV. "Love you pops."

Reggie turned and looked toward his son. "Huh? Oh, love you too Marty." Reggie paused then continued, "It's so nice to have our boy home again."

Marty smiled and walked down the short hall to his old bedroom. Entering, a plethora of childhood memories immediately flooded back. The man thought to himself, yes dad, it is nice to be home again. Then, for the first time in some months, Marty immediately fell asleep shortly after his head hit the pillow. He wouldn't rise until the early afternoon.

9

Teun De Torres sipped a cup of tea within a garden terrace. Having chosen a table purposefully distant from tour groups and other members of the public who sat about them, Blas encouraged Teun to speak freely.

"So how long have we, er my people been around?" Teun asked.

"How long indeed?" Blas replied. There have been some who have taken it upon themselves to investigate the origins of the Sempiterno." Blas paused thoughtfully as he stirred his cup. "As Europe entered the Age of Enlightenment, the Sempiterno became curious as well. Some of your number funded historians and archeologists to delve into the ancient texts, excavating the ruins and riddles of civilization; and yes, your kind appear to have a significant place in human history; stories for another time, once again I beg your indulgence.

As science became front and center in the late nineteenth and twentieth century's, so did the quest for your people's origins. Extensive experiments conducted on our behalf during the Second World War in Nazi Germany revealed the Sempiterno are the product of a genetic anomaly, one exceedingly rare, manifesting itself among identical rather than fraternal twins. Of course at first, no one was interested in twins; instead the Order was scouring the millions of captives in an effort to rescue others of your people... turns out the Order found what they were looking for, and much more.

No fewer than three adults and nine young people, all identified within the Nazi's camps by our agents who had clandestinely met the trains that brought torrents of people flooding into the camps from every point on the compass. Of special interest were the children stepping across the threshold of puberty. Able to sense their auras, these children and where possible their mother's and father's were separated from the masses. Every fact and nuance concerning their personal histories were recorded, examined and compared to those of the other families and slowly a pattern emerged.

In every instance, the child Sempitor had existed sharing its mother's womb with a twin, but survived as a single child; its other twin either dying while a fetus or for whatever the reason emerging into the world as a still born. As far as similar characteristics shared by the Sempitor's parents or those of other siblings; there were absolutely none. Attempts by the researchers to artificially reproduce this condition had utterly failed. Yes, the Sempiterno are capable of producing children, many have done so numerous times, yet there has never been a documented case where one or even both Sempiterno parents have succeeded in created a progeny like themselves.

Today, with the advancement in genetic manipulation and the mapping of the human genome, it is not only possible but probable that others of your kind will emerge from the test tube in some distant future. This is something the Order cannot condone or allow to happen. The mere rumor of your existence among humans is an anathema, and quite unthinkable. As such we spend considerable funds each year keeping track of and diverting specific branches of research away from such areas, instead heavily funding religious and special interest groups that discourage all forms of genetic manipulation. So far these efforts have met with considerable success.

Like all long lived beings, the accumulation of wealth and property, education and life experience are trappings to be enjoyed and employed to conceal their true natures. The Sempiterno are also exceptionally gifted in the art of blackmail. Imagine having access to wealthy, powerful people and using your powers of persuasion to entice them speak of subjects they wouldn't utter to their closest confidant.

Yet, even while possessing such an array of advantages, eventually Sempiterno have no choice but to feign death in some manner. Before the advent of mass communication and the ease of long distance travel they would simply sell out, take their gold and simply disappear using their fortunes to build new lives far from where they used to live."

"Teun, have you heard of the term, changeling?" Blas asked, and then took a sip of tea. Teun simply shook his head.

"The Sempitors often make use of "changelings." A suitable young person assumed the master's surname either as kin or an adoptee. Sent off to a distant locale, they were raised and schooled, laying down a traceable history. Meanwhile the masters would use disguises that allowed them to appear to age normally. Once the stage is set, the young person returns, the master has a nice funeral, while his or her changeling publically assume the reins of dynasty. The master may travel or live elsewhere for a time until his or her close personal friends and relatives have passed on. After that they are free to return, without use of disguise taking a lowly position in the household or firm while pulling the strings of their changeling or reassume the mantle of leadership within the dynasty.

The village of Longkamp was picturesque by any ones standards. Significantly larger than her tiny one street village of Andel; Longkamp was a thriving regional commercial hub. As Ayla and her father bumped along the narrow cart path and drew closer to the town, their path was joined with others to form ever larger and more regularly traveled roadways, at one point they actually met several wagons traveling in the opposite direction. Ayla was so proud of the way her father so confidently conversed with the other drivers. She asked her father how he knew so many of the people they met on the road. Ernst simply laughed before reminding his daughter of how often he traveled these and many other roads while conducting business; the business, which as his surname Wainwright would suggest, was repairing these same wagons.

By the time Ayla caught her first view of the town, the hard clay cart path on which they had first traveled had miraculously grown to become a broad well tended roadway. Nearly all of the people living in the region were completely unaware of the roads' history, assuming that one of the Bavarian kings had commissioned its construction several centuries or more before. In fact, various sections of road were of Roman origin. Termed corduroy roads, their foundations consisted of logs placed perpendicular to the road's direction, most often crossing in swampy or low lying areas prone to flooding. The log base would then be covered with gravel, sometimes quarried tens of miles from where it was needed. These particular logs had often been embedded in peat; an acidic anaerobic soil that discouraged the decomposition of the wood, sometimes extending the roads useful lifetime tens of decades. The town of Longkamp owed much of its commercial success to the eighteen hundred year old road connecting the community to similar centers lying to the north.

The old Roman road ran up from the lowlands along a gentle slope that brought their wagon within sight of the town that lay perhaps a half mile distant. Ayla identified a church steeple, several large buildings, houses and cottages. She found herself suddenly excited at the prospect of visiting the town, but as the wagon turned south at the next fork she sadly watched the town disappear behind a stand of mixed forest and brush. Noting his daughter's disappointment, Ernst apologized while pointing to a sun that was noticeably approaching the horizon. Sunset would arrive in several hours and they still had some miles travel ahead of them.

Terell Fischer's small farm lay several miles from his shop in Longkamp and consistent with farms in the area, boasted a modest cottage, small barn, chicken coop, and in Terell's case a vegetable garden, that with the notable exception of a small square, was overgrown with weeds. Terell was a cobbler, not a farmer, and prior to his wife's passing, it was she that tended the garden.

Besides, Terell's shop was in Longkamp, an hour distant by wagon, a half hour by horse and rider, double that if the weather was bad; commuting in the early 1800's was uncommon to say the least. Long hours spent at the shop would occasionally see Terell and his young apprentice Rolf Hamner staying in Longkamp and sleeping in the back of the shop. This said, without fail Terell would ride back to the farm every Saturday, with or without Rolf, and spend the rest of the day and all of the next with the family. Attending the local Catholic Church, the only church in Longkamp; was a big thing back in the day and as such formed the social bulwark of the town. Anyone making their living within the town was expected to be seen in attendance or risk being shunned unless an exceptional reason existed for their absence.

Terell was eager that Ernst have a good opinion of himself and the position he was offering Ayla. As such he spoke at length to his children instructing them; threatening them, to be well behaved when their guests arrived. His children were lucky in their appearance, the boys taking after their father, a reasonably handsome man, while his young daughter was spared his prominent nose and chin, instead possessing her mother's delicate features. Shortly after lunch the children had been dressed in their Sunday best and having been forbidden to play and soil their clothes reluctantly sat about impatiently the entire afternoon.

Angelika Fischer had passed from a sudden fever just weeks prior to her thirtieth birthday leaving her two boys, Tab and Degen aged eight and five years and a two year old daughter Cay in the care of their rather preoccupied father. Since Angelika's death, Terell had employed no fewer than three young girls to tend the home and care for his children over the previous eighteen months. Given the misbehavior of the children and Terell's lack of support for their caregiver, specifically in matters of obedience, each girl had chosen to leave his employ, each choosing to remain a shorter time than that of her predecessor. Eventually it had reached a point to where the children's reputation was known throughout the town and Terell could no longer find anyone willing to fill the position.

Whether his dotage toward his children was born of sympathy or simply a lack of will to reinforce practical behavioral norms, his children had become ill mannered brats who were used to getting their own way as often as it suited them. When Terell discovered Ernst's daughter was available he instantly made a very attractive offer to which her father immediately accepted on Ayla's behalf. It was only later that same day when the children were acting up worse than usual that Terell reflected that the considerable distance laying between the girl and her home could be a boon by ensuring her remaining in his employ despite any drawbacks.

Terell and his children greeted Ernst and Ayla with smiles and charm. As he had been previously instructed, his eldest boy Tab took Ayla's small bag of clothes and possessions into their home and set it atop a small bed in the corner of the kitchen, the make-shift bedroom was separated from the living area by a thin thread worn blanket suspended from the open rafters. These modest arrangements were all together suitable to Ernst and Ayla, who had expected nothing more elaborate. The location of her bed would allow Ayla to keep the wood stove's fire alive throughout cold nights and go about her early morning chores without waking the household prematurely.

The cordiality continued unabated throughout the evening with Terell and Ernst perhaps over indulging in a fine local German draft. The next morning Ayla began the first of her duties, making breakfast for the household, getting the younger children dressed for the day and seeing her father off. Ernst hitched his horse to the wagon, hugged his daughter and bid goodbye to Terell and his family. Terell took Ernst aside for a moment, and per their agreement pressed several coins into Ernst's palm and sincerely assured the man that he would do everything possible to make Ayla's stay a happy one. In truth, Terell meant what he said; he saw no purpose in mistreating people and had every hope in creating a peaceful home for him and his children.

After some final goodbyes Ayla watched the wagon slowly make its way down the road for a good ten minutes. Several times she saw her father turn and the two would wave toward one another. Finally as Ernst's wagon disappeared from view, she allowed a small tear to run down her cheek. Brushing it aside, she spoke under her breath; "well enough of that, I'm an adult now, with position and responsibility." Ayla smoothed her clothes and straightened her apron then walked back to the cottage where Terell stood on the doorstep smoking a pipe.

The cobbler provided Ayla his expectations as well as the rules of the house. All were very normal with but one exception; she was not to travel into the village unless he accompanied her. Terell explained that he must answer to her father for her safety, but secretly he didn't want the town gossip regarding his rather challenging progeny to prejudice her outlook; a prudent position. Unfortunately for all concerned, it wasn't long before Ayla became aware that the children were badly spoiled and that their father now undermined her authority at every turn. For his part Terell grew impatient with the girl's tiresome whining about his children's behavior and her insistence that he discipline his household; didn't she realize that was her job, after all didn't he have a business to run?

Ten months passed, Terell and Ayla now seldom spoke. Ayla felt herself a prisoner of her circumstance. Held within an untenable situation, for which there was no remedy, not even the ability to leave and return home. Her frustration turned to disappointment and disappointment turned to sorrow. Ayla realized she was coming to detest Terell and the two boys, Tab and Degen, whose version of events were taken above Ayla's as gospel in nearly all matters.

Late October and the weather was finally changing. The unusually long "Indian Summer" the townsfolk had enjoyed in the early fall was finally coming to an end. The fair sunny weather had allowed the harvest to be completed some several weeks earlier than usual. The farmers and villagers now went about the final tasks of winter preparation.

For Ayla these tasks were considerable. Terell Fischer was a demanding individual and one who wouldn't tolerate excuse for delay, and his two boys and the young girl weren't making matters easier. The children were spoiled and coddled by their over protective father, and as such they could do no wrong, and worse they knew it. Constantly catering to the children and their many whims meant that her work and small projects were taking much longer than usual to complete. This infuriated her employer and created tension within the home.

If it wasn't for Rolf's kindness and welcomed attentions her position would hardly be bearable. Her position, she often reflected that her position was little more than serfdom. She could appeal to her father to release her from his agreement with the cobbler, but that would entail somehow getting word to him. It had been early summer when she last saw him and now with winter on their doorstep; inclement and unpredictable weather and near impassable roads made it unlikely that she would see Ernst again before next spring. In the meantime she would have to make the best of a bad situation.

Over the past year and a half, Ayla began to blossom into womanhood. Now reaching her sixteenth birthday, she had recently noticed Terell studying her figure when he thought she wasn't looking. Not that this was unexpected, if somewhat unwanted. At thirty four years, Terell was still a relatively young man, good looking and marriage minded while Ayla had reached that age when girls were urged to consider taking a husband, marrying young had its benefits.

For those residing in the remote and backward mountainous villages of Bavaria, life could be hard and oft times short in comparison to those living in the larger and more progressive towns and cities. Modern historians point to a temporal schism, where relative technologies, industry and medical knowledge existed out of sync between rural and urban folk by as much as a century, so caused by a lamentable lack of communication and mobility between the country's citizens. Aside from a small degree of necessary commerce, people on either side had little reason to mix with their counterparts, and as such new ideas and methodologies tended to languish in the smaller or more remote backwaters.

It was early evening and the sun was quickly setting behind a dark cloudbank. Ayla had finished feeding the children and had sent the oldest boy Tab out to bring the night's firewood into the cottage while Degen and Cay played with the dog. The dog had been a favorite of his dead wife and since her passing Terell found he was becoming very fond of the animal. Ayla reflected on the day, it had gone smoothly, the kids behaved themselves and she was able to keep to her schedule.

Ayla wondered when Terell and Rolf would return, they were already late. If they didn't arrive soon she would have to remove the stew from the stove or it would burn on the bottom despite her near constant stirring. "Degen, come over and stir your father's dinner." Ayla had discovered that the children responded much more quickly to tasks assigned to them if she referred to the duties being required by their father. The six year old left his sister with the dog and obediently took the offered ladle from Ayla's hand. '

"I'll be back soon." Ayla left the cottage and walked into the yard and heard a report of small bangs and cracks off to her left. Looking over, she saw Tab was sitting on a stump lobbing small rocks toward a stick he had leaned against the open door of the woodshed as a target; a small pile of firewood sat on the ground beside him. The girl paused for a minute watching him silently. Sensing he was being watched, the boy looked about and seeing Ayla quickly dropped the rocks and began picking the wood from the ground.

The wind was chilly and it would be getting colder yet. The ground was still bare of snow but she could smell it in the air. The approaching cloud bank covered more than half the western sky now threatening to blot out the waxing gibbous moon; already a vanguard of thin cloud blurred its bright limbs. Ayla made her way to the outhouse, opened the door and sat upon the cold wooden seat. While seated, she imagined her life as being other than what it was threatening to become; a lifetime of hard labor and poor recompense. Her daydreaming was interrupted by a series of distressed, high pitched cries. It was Cay, the three year old girl.

While she hurriedly straightened herself, Ayla pushed open the outhouse door open with her foot to see what was happening in the yard. Cay and her brother Degen were running from the cottage pursuing the pup that was doing his level best to avoid his young owners. Privately Ayla detested the animal; animals did not belong in a home but outdoors. When Ayla had once asked Terell if the barn wasn't adequate for the dog, she received a sharp rebuke where Terell stated that perhaps the barn rather than the house might be more appropriate for her. Since then she kept mum on the subject.

Finally able to leave the outhouse, she ran toward the cottage and saw that all three children were engaged in what was likely a futile pursuit. The dog made several expertly performed dekes and dodges before rounding the corner of the barn and leaving the now breathless kids in the dust. Ayla cursed under her breath then in the next asked for the Lord's forgiveness. She called the children into the cottage and removed the pot of stew from the fire. Walking over to the doorway, Ayla opened the door a crack and peered out into the gloaming. There was no sign of the dog or Terell's wagon.

Ayla stepped from the door and stood on the wooden landing calling out the dog's name; "Axel, Axel!" Terell would be livid if Axel was lost for good, something Ayla thought rather unlikely, since the beast was little more than a soup hound and wouldn't stay lost for long. Still it wouldn't hurt to walk the perimeter of the yard and see if she could entice the miserable creature back to the house.

Ayla grabbed her shawl, cautioning the children to behave for the short time she would be gone while reminding them of their father's imminent return. She wrapped her garment tightly about her shoulders, picked up a length of rough hemp rope with which to leash the dog then left the cabin shutting the door tightly behind her.

Over the last several minutes the cool breeze had become a cold wind that tugged on her long dress and flagged the edges of her shawl. The moon was still visible, but only as a brightening glow fully enshrouded within the weather front. Ayla walked along the dirt path that wound behind the cottage, crossed over to the chicken coop, the pigsty, the woodshed and finally the barn. She called the dog's name over and over, but her calls were muted within the gusts of a strong and icy north wind. Embedded within the blusters were fine pellets of hard snow which stung her face, hands and lower legs. The storm was quickly evolving into a blizzard.

She had nearly decided to turn about and head back to the cottage when she noticed one of the barn's doors were slightly ajar. Ayla stepped inside and immediately welcomed the cessation of the icy bombardment. Looking about in the dim gloom she saw Axel happily chewing on a piece of cow dung. Apparently no longer interested in continuing the chase, he allowed Ayla to approach and place his leash around his neck. She and the dog were nearly back at the open barn door when the dog's hackles suddenly rose. He emitted a low warning growl. Whatever was out there, she sensed the danger as well. They had better get back to the cottage as soon as possible.

Ayla and the dog exited the barn and stood at the entrance. The dog's attentions were drawn to the west side of the barn; he issued several sharp barks in that direction and then whined nervously. Ayla couldn't see anything through the now blinding snow, but in her mind's eye she could see the outlines of animals in full stride, running towards her and the dog. "Run Axel, come!" she yelled in a shrill and panicked voice.

There was no need to convince the dog, it had already slipped its leash and was running well ahead of the girl. She tossed her head quickly from side to side looking back as she ran. She still couldn't see the wolves but could hear a muted chorus of canine voices approaching rapidly. Ayla was now only thirty yards or so now from the cottage, the dog had already arrived and stood barking excitedly at the door. As Ayla continued her flight, she saw the door open slightly; behind the crack she saw Tab wide eyed and watching the proceedings. The dog squeezed through the opening and ran into the cabin.

Ayla estimated the distance she had to cover against that the wolf pack had to make up to catch her before she gained the cabin's refuge. "I'm going to make it!" she said aloud while at the same moment tripping on a wayward chunk of fire wood Tab had dropped on his final trip. Ayla sprawled and tumbled atop the hard snowy ground knowing she had lost the race. "Close the door Tab!" she shouted, "Close the door now!" and was relieved to see the door close and the bolt thunk into place.

She somehow rose to her feet and backed toward the door now only several yards distant. The wolves had moved to within striking range. Ayla could see the dark shapes now only feet away, they paused for a moment knowing their quarry was already theirs. The pack leader would lead the attack and charge first. The animal was large and fearless in the face of a slightly build girl, she would offer the pack little contest.

Ayla stood erect and motionless, suddenly time seemed to stand still, but she wasn't paralyzed due to fear, instead she felt herself gathering some inner strength. When the lead wolf began his charge, Ayla felt an impossibly strong torrent of energy pulse and rise up deep within her being. The wolf, now in mid-leap, could sense something was wrong, but could do nothing to change what was about to happen. Moving with incredible speed, Ayla sidestepped the wolf as it flew through the air, as it passed, Ayla's hand lightly brushed atop the length of its coarse outer coat. When the animal landed atop the wooden landing and thudded heavily into the cottage wall, it was already a lifeless corpse.

Ayla extended her mind; filaments and tendrils of conscious thought writhed and flowed outward into the snowy darkness, radiating into the farmyard actively searching for the creatures that pursued her. Within seconds, the pack's individuals, abandoning any thought of the hunt, now fell among themselves; mane to muzzle, fang to fang, rending and tearing at each other until pain and self preservation finally forced them to flee. Tails tucked between legs and heads slung low, each disappeared into the blizzard, all running in separate directions.

Ayla maintained her stiff posture, her hands rose to her waist, palms upward while her head tilted slightly toward the sky. She felt oddly elated, vitality coursed through her veins, and for the first time in her short life she felt truly alive. In fact, she felt as though she might live forever.

The moment quickly passed and those strange feelings subsided. Ayla wondered if perhaps they had ever been there at all, but the body of the wolf said otherwise. In the distance she saw a wagon approaching. Terell rode on the wagon holding the reins and restraining the animal that wanted to bolt toward the barn in the yard. Walking ahead of the wagon, Rolf held a hurricane lantern up lighting the way forward.

Ayla saw Rolf wave to her as he and Terell guided the wagon toward the barn. Ayla returned the gesture then walked quickly to the landing where the wolf lay sprawled out across its rough wood surface. She grabbed a hind leg and tugged. The girl was amazed to discover how effortlessly she dragged the nearly two hundred pound carcass off the landing and behind the cabin before discarding it among the tall grasses that danced in the snowy wind.

Re-entering the cottage, she surveyed her cramped surroundings. The children were glued to the small window looking out into the yard and toward the barn. Lanterns glowed within the structure, outlining the shapes and casting dim shadows of the two half frozen men tending to the horse and wagon. Ayla felt those powerless, trapped feelings experienced earlier in the day evaporating with her newly found confidence. A voice rose from her subconscious and spoke, the voice cautioning her to keep today's discovery to herself.

10

It was a warm early evening about a week later, Reggie and Marty sat sipping beers in a pair of Cape Cod chairs his father had built back in the early sixties. While they spoke Marty's fingers played over the smooth arms of the chair, he wondered how many coats of yellow paint he'd discover if he scraped down into the wood. Dinner had been fabulous; he and his dad had barbequed a couple of two inch thick steaks they picked up from the Albertsons down on Main. Reggie had an in with the stores meat manager Mr. Bob Davies. Reggie had been involved with Little League Baseball in the Creek and had coached Mr. Davies when he was merely known as little Bobby Davies. That's the way it is, or Marty supposed, the way it was, not so long ago in small town USA, folks grew up knowing their neighbors parents, grandparents, uncles, aunts, you name it. No longer, the big cities beckoned and the country's youth answered. Sort of like that old song, "How Ya Gonna Keep 'em Down on the Farm (After They've Seen Paree)."

He and Reggie were discussing the prospects of the Mariners making it to the American league's division finals this year. They had pretty much agreed that the clubs outlook wasn't too rosy when they heard the back gate creak open then swing close with a clatter. The men heard the sound of footsteps falling upon the concrete side walk.

Reggie listened intently then smiled. "Evening Saul... Adrian," Reggie spoke up in a bright cheery voice. The couple rounded the corner moments later and entered the yard. Reggie would recognize the sounds of Adrian's flip flops and Sal's heavy oxford walkers any day of the week.

Saul's expression remained indifferent while he dismissively waved a hand toward Marty's dad as he followed a couple of paces behind his wife. The contrast between the Kaplan's couldn't be more overstated. Adrian was tall, thin and quick, with almost birdlike movements while Saul was short, heavy set and moved like a bull dozer. Now in their mid seventies the Jewish couple had recently returned to their faith. Such reconciliations were commonly seen among people of any religion, who reaching a certain age and perhaps not quite at the end of the road, could clearly read the "dead end" sign posted ahead.

"Reggie," Adrian verbally acknowledged the older man, but quickly walked straight over to where Marty was doing his best to rise from the low Cape Cod chair and greet his long time neighbors. "Marty! You look wonderful, a sight for sore eyes!"

Adrian and Marty hugged warmly. "You too Adrian. Still keeping the old boy in check I see." She nodded, smiled and gave him another squeeze.

The couple were a long time fixture in the neighborhood, and like his father and a few others still living on their street, the Kaplan's had been among the first to build in the then new development. That was back in the day when the Creek was still thriving and the mill was booming. Marty had a sudden recollection of Adrian bringing him a humbug hard candy as he played on the front lawn of their house. Adrian and his mother had been good friends, alternately hosting afternoon coffee several times a week.

Reggie got Saul a beer and Adrian a club soda with ice, remaining sober, the old woman hadn't drank alcohol for over thirty years. The foursome sat about the yard reminiscing about the old days, discussing their kids, they're careers, wives, husbands and in the case of Adrian and Saul, grandchildren. Adrian as usual pressed Marty about any romantic prospects in his future. Marty remained mute on the subject until Reggie rolled on his son mentioning Ann and the possibility of Marty's new love interest coming out for a visit in the next couple of weeks. Upon hearing this Adrian pressed for ever more details concerning Ann. Marty supposed that if his mother was still alive and the roles reversed, she would be doing exactly the same thing. Eventually Marty threw up his hands laughing while saying that Adrian would simply have to wait until the two women met.

An hour had nearly passed when Reggie apologized and then politely inquired how Saul's mother was faring. The woman had recently celebrated her ninety seventh birthday, but her health had been in decline over the past year then only last month she suffered a fall in the bath. She was in the hospital up in Claremont City. Saul and Adrian didn't expect her to return home, during their last visit she told them God would come for her soon, she'd had enough of this life.

Rachel Kaplan had the misfortune of being born into a Jewish family November 21, 1923 in Berlin, Germany. At the start of the First World War, her father and an uncle on her mother's side had volunteered for duty with the German army. The two managed to survive the trenches and fierce fighting only to later succumb to the Spanish Flu as it swept across the face of the globe in several waves during the two years that followed. Rachel, her mother and her older brothers were taken in by her mother's sister and her family who lived in Frankfurt.

Despite their allegiance to their country and her family's service during the First World War, with the Nazi's rise to power, also came their family's persecution. Forbidden and unable to worship in their synagogue which was eventually fire bombed by the "brown shirts," they were also restricted to their homes during the Christian's religious holidays. In 1939 they were moved to Krakow Poland and housed in the city's ghetto for several years. Life was hard and times were dangerous, especially for a pretty twenty sixteen year old girl. In the ghetto, one didn't have to worry about just the Nazi's or their collaborators, when people were starving and destitute in those overcrowded, deplorable neighborhoods; law was a fragile thing at best. People tended to move in small groups but seldom alone, that would invite trouble.

In late 1942, Rachel and her extended family were moved out of the Krakow ghetto and into the neighboring Plaszow forced labor camp. It was out of the frying pan and into the fire. Children too young and seniors to weak to work were simply transferred to the nearby Auschwitz death camp for extermination. For Rachel's family this was not an immediate concern since Rachel was the Kaplan's youngest at eighteen years old while her mother, sister and sister's husband were still under fifty and in relatively good condition. Their fortunes would change when the family arrived in the Auschwitz camp in January 1944.

The neighbors laughed and joked for another half hour before the impromptu gathering broke up for the night leaving Marty and Reggie nursing the final beers of the night. It was getting dark and the small solar yard lights were beginning to shine in the darker corners of the yard. "Well, I guess that's it..." said Reggie, "mother always told me it was time to come in when the street lights came on."

Before going inside, Marty returned the heavy wooden Cape Cod chairs back to their usual positions on the patio while Reggie checked and locked up the garage. Five minutes later, his father sat in front of the living room television nodding off to sleep. Marty was in the kitchen, seated at his laptop conversing with Ann on Skype. After twenty minutes, the young couple said their goodbyes. Marty shook his father's shoulder awakening his dad then both trundled off to bed.

11

Ayla hadn't seen her father for quite some time; summer had turned to fall and fall to winter. Ernst would seldom venture out on the long trip to Longkamp, certainly not with a heavy wagon that could become bogged down in snow until spring. No, winter wasn't the time for travel; winter was the time to busy himself along with his partners, a village carpenter and a leather worker preparing for the spring. Through the cold months, the three would work constructing wagons, various parts and a backlog of hitch repairs then Ernst would deliver the equipment made during the previous winter to his customers during the warmer seasons.

For his part, the cobbler would send Ayla's wages to Ernst via his apprentice Rolf, who made deliveries of Terell's wares from village to village by way of horseback. As was the custom of the age, Rolf was housed in a small hut at the rear of his employer's family home and would take meals with the cobbler and his family. On Sundays the entire family together with Ayla and Rolf attended Mass, as did the vast majority of Longkamp's citizens. At that time, Catholicism was the prominent religious belief in Bavaria. The church formed the social fabric of the community and failure to attend on a regular basis was nearly unthinkable. Rolf and Ayla looked forward to Sundays as this would be the only free time for the apprentice who consistently worked twelve hour days throughout the week, and Ayla, while still expected to make meals, would have a few free hours for herself.

As the long winter passed, Ayla and Rolf found themselves spending more time together. Rolf was only several years older than Ayla, and she came to have a crush on the hard working young man. She looked forward to Sundays when they could spend the afternoon and evenings together. These affections, previously lost on Terell, came to the forefront when speaking to the wife of a prominent town elder following Easter Mass. She remarked that Rolf and Ayla made a fine match then blathered on for some time about announcing the banns of marriage in the next several weeks, and the possibility of an early summer wedding.

Over the next week, Terell found himself in a quandary. Things had improved on the home front and while he and Ayla could not be considered best of friends, the children had come to accept her and with that acceptance had come to mind her in most things. Losing her to marriage and having to start again from scratch with a new girl, if he could find one willing, was not in his best interest.

To thwart any possible engagement, the very next Sunday Terell announced Rolf's graduation from his apprenticeship to the entire congregation. Now while the lad was certainly capable of performing the work without further supervision, Terell's release of his apprentice was much earlier than was normally the case. It was customary at the time for the graduated apprentice continue to work for his master for an additional term and in this way repay his benefactor for being taught his trade.

Terell's explanation for Rolf's early release was to allow the young man to open a shop in another town, a town a considerable distance from Longkamp. Terell had purchased the storefront from the family of a recently deceased's cobbler and had done so at a bargain. For Rolf's part, he was ecstatic to learn that he could work in his own store and repay Terell over time, something that wasn't often done for anyone who was not immediate family.

When Rolf told Ayla of his opportunity he was surprised by her reaction. Not only was she not happy for him, her tears told him she was crushed by the news. Her attitude changed immediately when the young man proposed to her on the spot saying that once he had gotten the business established they could marry. After Rolf left for his new shop, nearly fifty miles distant, Ayla couldn't help to feel abandoned and for several weeks was rather sullen.

Her mood was dispelled during one of her father's infrequent visits. Ernst arrived carrying a letter for her from Rolf. The reason for this unusually lengthy journey was owed in large part to Bavaria's part in the ongoing Napoleonic Wars that were taking place throughout Europe. While too old to be a soldier, he and others in the area were temporarily pressed into hauling supplies for the army. Now Ernst's wagon arrived in Longkamp, laden with three badly wounded men and a small troop of bedraggled soldiers slogging along behind it. Unknown to them all, something else had stowed away and travelled with the group.

Her father stayed with Terell's family for several days as his horse required a badly needed rest. During that time, Ayla was once again her cheerful self. She read and reread Rolf's letter until it was very nearly in tatters. The letter stated that the little business was doing well and he was making a modest profit, even after taking into account his repayment to Terell.

The evening before Ernst left Terell's home, the two men sat together on the porch drinking ale, and Ernst brought Terell up on all the news from elsewhere. Bavaria had fought alongside France from 1805 until 1813; and their King regarded himself as a partner to the French, rather than a subservient auxiliary. Recently the political landscape had undergone a radical change and Bavaria had to switch alliances and was now pitted against France. Several months ago the Bavarians had fought their first battle attempting to block the French withdrawal at Hanau where their forces were swept aside. The now battered army retreated to lick its wounds and prepare for the next campaign while numerous wounded and nonprofessional soldiers decided to leave the field permanently and return to their distant rural homes. These were the men who now passed through Longkamp.

Ernst awoke the next morning with a splitting headache that he simply put down to having drunk too much ale the night before. Ayla brought the lunch she had packed for her father's journey and gave him a long bear hug. Ernst in turn assured her that Rolf spoke often of how much he missed her. Terell and the children bid her father goodbye while Ayla road up upon the wagon beside her father for a mile or so before taking leave. Ernst told her it would be several months before he returned; she in turn told her father she wanted to remember him and took a good long look. She stood in the roadway and walked back toward Terell's cottage. The young woman would never see her father again. Had she, Ayla would no longer resemble the loving, trusting person seated upon the buck board this fine summer morning.

It was nearly a week later, one of the injured soldiers Ernest had returned to Longkamp came down with a high fever. The soldier was the youngest son of a farmer who worked a modest plot of bottom land along the small river on the outskirts of the town with his family. The young man's back and torso were covered with multiple shallow shrapnel wounds he received from a cannon ball's nearby airburst. The most pressing concern was infection, but the wounds soon scabbed over and the lad remained relatively healthy even venturing out of doors to take in some fresh air and sunshine.

It was the following afternoon when the farmer walked into town with his eldest son looking for Doctor Fuchs. Dieter Fuchs was a relatively young man who had unintentionally become a resident several years back when he became snowed in and stranded by a blizzard of near monumental size. The family, who owned one of the town's three inns, had put him up for several weeks. It was there that Dieter had met their very attractive daughter. It was a case of love at first sight. They were married within a fortnight and he opened his practice a week after that.

Dieter had been an ardent admirer of the famous traveling surgeon Johann Andreas Eisenbarth, a popular figure living in the previous century, Eisenbarth and his large entourage traveled extensively throughout Germany. Eisenbarth's fellow travelers, occasionally numbering in excess of one hundred people, were a mishmash of entertainers, musicians and pantomimes. The good doctor's principal trade was that of an oculist and what was known at the time as a "barber-surgeon" who specialized in the treatment of cataracts and the practice of calculus surgery – the later being the rather painful removal of kidney stones and the like without the benefit of anesthetics. While the man had no formal medical credentials, he was in fact highly skilled and held in high esteem by members of German Royalty. Like Eisenbarth, Dieter had a romantic notion where he saw himself traveling the roads healing the sick in remote villages and hamlets, that all changed when he met his young wife.

It took some time to locate Dieter, who was assisting another farmer on the opposite side of the town delivering several lambs experiencing a difficult birth. Fully half of Dieter's fees were gained as a result of treating livestock. Dieter often pondered if someone could actually make a living by treating only animals, joking with his wife that they, unlike his human patients, complained much less when being treated.

It was nearly sundown when Dieter arrived at the farm house carrying his small leather satchel that accompanied the doctor wherever he traveled. The long slender shadows of the trees growing along the laneway to the farm produced an unusual striped pattern upon the road's surface. The doctor and the farmers approached the door of the home, and light from burning lanterns filled each window. The farmer's wife met them at the door, her face full with concern. Their son had gotten much worse in the hours that her husband had been gone in search of the doctor.

Dieter Fuchs entered the house and his free hand was immediately grasped by the farmer's wife who praised God for his arrival while she pulled him towards a small room where a young man lay upon a bed. As he entered the room, the familiar smell of sickness struck his nostrils and Dieter knew that whatever malady the boy had contracted, it was likely serious. The doctor set his satchel upon a small table beside the bedside and asked that a lantern be brought closer so that he could make a proper examination of his patient. The appearance of the man lying before him caused Dieter to groan audibly. He had seen this disease many times before, in many stages within its victims. Fuchs knew that in its present stage the disease was extremely contagious and that most of the farmer's family members were no doubt exposed and would fall ill. There was also a thirty percent chance that any who did would not recover.

The boy had become feverish only several days before his mother noticed an odd rash had appeared consisting of small red spots on the victim's mouth and tongue. When the rash began to reveal itself on his face and spread to his chest she became alarmed and had sent her husband to find the doctor.

Fuchs knew the rash would evolve into small sores spreading to all parts of the body within a day or so. At this stage the victim often began to feel better, but the improvement was only temporary. Within several more days the sores began to fill with a thick opaque liquid. At this stage the body temperature often rose alarmingly. Over the next ten days or so, the rash grows to become a beadwork of hardened pustules or pox that gives the illusion that small peas are lying just below the victim's skin. This condition lent the disease its famous and dreaded name; Smallpox.

Dieter did not touch the patient, he had no need to do so, nor did he stay in the room any longer than it took him to diagnose the cause of the boy's condition. Instead grabbing his satchel he briskly walked from the bedroom and out of the house entirely. Stopping when he reached the front porch, Dieter set his case down on the rough wood fumbling about in his long coat searching for his pipe and tobacco. While he did so, Dieter said nothing, choosing instead to fill his pipe and light it quickly; hopefully thinking there might be some truth in what he had heard about the smoke having purification qualities. Taking several deep draughts of the smoke into his mouth and lungs, he held it there for many seconds time before expelling it in a rush; the smoke gusted out into the cool evening air. The farmer's family had followed him out and were now crowded about him, the women folk wringing their hands wearing worried expressions, while the farmer and his sons were curious and not somewhat angry given his sudden unexplained departure from their home. Their anger immediately turned to fear when the doctor utter two words; Small Pox.

Over the next two months those living in Longkamp experienced firsthand what a community underwent during a serious epidemic. Fear and apprehension embraced the town. This was a dangerous time for other nearby communities since Small Pox has a relatively long gestation period where the victims may exhibit no outward signs of infection for a week to ten days time. Travelling to another village where the illness had not yet taken hold, the contagious refugees would unknowingly place themselves in a position to pass along the virus to others when they fell ill.

Doctor Fuchs, like many physicians of his day believed the Miasmic theory that stated these plagues and serious diseases were caused by exposure to noxious vapors produced by rotting organic matter. These vapors labeled "night air" owed its name due since people would wake in the morning to find themselves or their family member's ill, when they appeared in perfect health only the evening before. These "miasma" were thought to linger about outdoors, waiting to infect new victims and so it came as no surprise that when the good doctor spoke at the town meeting, he urged the citizens to shutter themselves indoors, and refrain from going out into the open night air. This theory would persist for decades given that the unintentional isolation of potential victims from those already contagious, would deny exposure to the malady and help contain the epidemic.

When the disease struck down the first individuals among family and friends, what had previously been a vague threat now turned to heated panic. Newly infected having no family or close associations with the community would often flee, but seldom make it to other villages before dying; one of the benefits of slow means of travel and distance. Often epidemics would "burn" themselves out since the virus or bacteria ran out of potential victims in the region. The fortunate majority would be cared for as best as could be expected, the caregivers going about their tasks without regard for their own safety.

Given the degree of care required, the number of patients, as well as the speed of the epidemic; initial panic finally gave way to odious drudgery. Inevitably the sick were moved to a central location, not to isolate them from the general population so much as to allow the caregivers to take shifts caring for multiple patients rather than one or two individuals.

As the illness continued to spread and run its course; swift burial or disposal of the dead became paramount. While the average person living at the time didn't understand the mechanics of viral and bacterial infections; everyone certainly understood the concept that having a lot of rotting corpses lying about was something to be avoided. The smell of decomposing human bodies probably lent support, if not initially giving rise to miasmic theory. Since the epidemic occurred in the summer month's burial was not generally a problem since the ground was soft and graves easily dug; during epidemics occurring during winter months the bodies would often be cremated. But there would be no mass graves for Longkamp; the deceased were well known or had kin living in the town who would insist upon proper interment. Where epidemics occurred in much larger centers, mass graves were often the last resort when the ability of the community to individually dispose of the huge number of dead were overwhelmed, many victims would go to their deaths forgotten and unnamed.

Coming into contact with most of the townsfolk while working in his shop, it was not surprising that Terell was the first of his family to fall ill, but he wouldn't be the last. Although he like many other shop owners promptly shuttered their shops when hearing of the outbreak, it was already a week or more since they had been exposed and the virus was already working within their bodies.

Next Sunday Ayla woke as usual and began her day seeing to the many household chores. After lighting the wood stove she walked to the shallow well Terell had dug at the rear of the cottage. It was a beautiful morning and promised to be a lovely day. She smiled thinking how the children would enjoy a little fresh air and sunshine after spending several dreary rainy days in the house or playing in the barn. Ayla drew up the cool water using a small pail attached to a length of hemp rope. She was dumping the well water into a larger pail that would in turn fill a large clay firkin that sat on the floor in a corner of the kitchen when she heard Degen cry out in the house. Ayla didn't think much of the wail since the young boy and Tab, his older sibling was constantly fighting.

She frowned and thought if the children woke their father there would be cause for wailing. Since closing his shop, the fear of the illness had become of a secondary concern to the loss of his income. Terell had busied himself working at the farm; there were always repairs and upkeep that never seemed to get done given the long hours he spent in his shop, especially since Rolf had left. Over the last several days, Terell had become ill tempered and short with the children, something he had never been in the past. Ayla considered with some satisfaction that in staying home perhaps their father was finally seeing what she had to deal with on a daily basis. These thoughts vanished when she heard Tab and Degen calling her name urgently; their younger sister crying in the background.

Releasing the pail from her grip, it fell to earth, the contents splashing her long dress and shoes as she ran toward the house. Her first concern was that perhaps the stove had caused another fire in the series of pipe sections where the smoke from the stove could be directed to flow across the ceiling of the cottage before running out a wall and above the roof. In winter this design allowed the stove's hot exhaust to run through the overhead pipes heating the home. The difficulty here lay in the creosote buildup in the pipes which occasionally caught fire. More than once that past winter she had extinguished the stove's fire using heavy gloves to remove sections of the smoldering piping, hauling them out into the farm yard where she shook out the smoking ash and soot. She dismissed the thought, in the warmer months those pipes were sealed off by a flue; the smoke directed straight up and out of the home's chimney.

The children's cries of alarm became louder and more pronounced. Ayla burst through the doors to see the two brothers standing at the open doorway to their father's bedroom. Looking past the boys, she could see Terell unmoving and sprawled out on the floor near the bed. She shooed the children into the kitchen and quieted the now screaming Cay. Once the young child settled down, Ayla instructed the boys to sit beside their sister on the floor and hold her hands while she looked in on their father.

Knowing full well the likelihood that Terell may have fallen ill, Ayla approached the prone figure with some trepidation as to what she would find. Terell had gone to bed earlier than usual the night before complaining of pains in his lower back and a nagging headache. Both he and Ayla had simply dismissed his discomfort as his having over stressed himself while repairing the stalls in the barn by himself. Now looking at the man lying at her feet she felt a cold chill run up her spine.

Terell's head and bedclothes were bathed in sweat and his face and what she could see of his chest were covered in a dull scarlet rash. While Ayla had never heard, much less seen a case of Small Pox before it appeared in Longkamp, the description of the illness Terell had related to her certainly seemed to fit with what she saw here. She paused for several minutes considering her next actions. This was obviously a case of fever despite the underlying cause; she would treat the illness in the same manner she had been instructed as a younger girl.

Before assisting Terell, she went into the children's bedroom and gathering up blankets, pillows and clothes handed these to the older boys while she scooped up the toddler and instructed the boys to follow her into the barn. Quickly Ayla laid the clothes and bedding on the back of the buckboard wagon then sat the kids down in front of her on a small bench. She explained in the simplest of terms that their father had come down with a fever and that for the next few days they would all be sleeping in the barn. It was important that they not enter the house under any circumstances without her permission. She assigned Tab the duty of gathering clean hay in an empty stall and gave Degen the task of taking his sister outside and playing together.

In another minute or so, the kids seemed to accept the situation, especially the boys who relished the idea of sleeping in the barn on piles of hay. Once the children were busy Ayla walked back into the house and saw to Terell. Terell wasn't a large man, but at her present age, Ayla was small for her size and it took some doing to lift the man's dead weight onto the bed. She'd get his upper half onto the mattress and then grab hold of his legs only to find Terell would once again slump to the floor. It took nearly five full minutes before the man lay on the bed.

Over the next two days, Terell would pass in and out of consciousness and Ayla would try and cool his body using a rag to wipe his heated skin. Ayla had almost convinced herself the fever could be some other than Small Pox, but the unmistakable pebbling appearing beneath his skin and now covering the entire surface of his body proved otherwise. As the disease ran through its stages there were many times when Ayla wondered if Terell would survive, one time in particular, hours after the sores had burst and oozed a thick Gray liquid. Terell's temperature had shot up dramatically since Ayla could feel the heat arise while suspending a palm several inches above his skin. Terell stopped breathing on several occasions, the longest pause approaching several minutes. Fearing the man had passed, she reached down grasping the sheet bunched at the foot of the bed and began pulling it across his body, and just before his face was covered he suddenly gasped for air. She retreated in shock then continued the tiresome well worn routine of bathing his face and chest with water for several minutes then leaving to see to the children.

It was several days later when Ayla felt Terell had passed the worst of the disease and would recover when Degen and Cay became ill less than forty eight hours later. Several days later Cay lost her fight to the disease, passing away sometime in the night's long hours. Degen put up a better fight, although in the end he too would finally succumb. Throughout the nightmare only she and Tab seemed untouched by the malady and she thanked God for their deliverance.

Several days after Ayla had buried the younger children atop a gentle hill next to their mother's grave, a friend of Terell's ventured from town to check on the family. Terell grieving and a much weakened state, was still able to greet his friend Hans while propped upright in a kitchen chair. Hans, like Terell, had himself lost his only child and wife and no longer having any responsibility to provide care to his family set out to see what good he could do in the community. Terell and Ayla agreed that Tab could see to his father's needs while she would accompany Hans to town and assist helping the afflicted townsfolk. Terell and Tab would make do with the vegetables and other staples stored in the root cellar. Tab had surprised Ayla showing that the young boy had mastered a few basic cooking methods over the last difficult weeks while Ayla busied herself caring for the stricken members of the household.

For Ayla, the trip to town passed quickly while Hans spoke of the news and happenings within the town. When Ayla asked about Hans' family, he changed subjects quickly, the wounds being too fresh for him to speak of. From what Hans did tell Ayla, it appeared that Terell's family was one of the first to be infected and the town was now in the full grip of the epidemic. The sick, numbering over a hundred were being treated within several of the town's homes, in the case of a particularly large house, it had been available given the recent passing of its elderly owners, while two smaller homes nearby had been generously offered as refuges for the sick.

When Hans and Ayla neared the outskirts of town Ayla became aware of a foreboding silence that had replaced the typical bright tumult of town life. Their wagon rolled past the church and Ayla saw individuals coming and going from the entrance, she couldn't make out who the parishioners might be as their faces were draped in scarves and veils. The one person she did recognize was the parish priest who stood near the entrance, appearing worn and haggard. Holding a thin chain in his left hand the padre gently swung a silver thurible or incense burner by his side, for a moment Ayla caught its familiar and comforting scent within her nostrils before the fickle breeze shifted bearing the small wisps of smoke elsewhere.

After passing the frontage of the church the cemetery came into view. Its normally unbroken lawn had sprouted fresh and numerous mounds of earth and clay, small wooden crosses set at the head of the grave sites would have to pass for carved stones or monuments until supply caught up with the demand. Four men toiled in the day's heat, their shovels and picks rising and falling rhythmically among the cries and wails of several mourners who were unwilling to leave the graves of their loved ones.

Along Main Street, the store fronts were shuttered and knots of people with hidden faces moved about the wooden walkways and paths in silence. Rather than riding upon the wagon, she bid Hans to carry on, she would walk and stretch her legs. Ayla motioned to Hans to stop when his wagon reached Terell's shop. Ayla walked up to the front door; a padlock still secured the door, the same was true when she checked the shops rear door. At least Terell would receive some good news when she returned - if she returned that is.

Over the next several weeks Ayla worked tirelessly while tending to the Longkamp's sick and dying while Hans took on the responsibility of visiting the outlying farms, as he had done with Terell's home. Hans would often return carrying one or sometimes two victims in his wagon, and of course the bodies of those who didn't survive; their loved ones either unable to bury their dead on their farms or wishing to have them interred in sacred ground.

The townsfolk marveled at Ayla's ability to carry on working almost without rest for several days at a time. The girl herself began to wonder why she hadn't slept, or hadn't desired sleep. At first she assumed it was the underlying crisis that kept her going; certainly there were other caretakers who were making their rounds, moving tirelessly from cot to cot seemingly caught up in a dreamlike state like zombies. But that in no way described her condition.

Rather than feeling haggard and careworn, Ayla felt energized and almost euphoric, strange since she hadn't eaten much over the last several days. When her odd behavior was noticed by several older women working beside her, Ayla became concerned that it might be a symptom of the disease, but failing to fall ill she put aside this concern. This suddenly changed one morning when relieving herself, Ayla discovered bright scarlet blood staining her underclothing and inner thigh. She was alarmed to find herself bleeding! It took only moments for the girl to trace the discoloration to its source and once found she immediately calmed; she was experiencing her first period.

For Ayla, and like a smaller percentage of other young girls, menstruation had come much later that was commonplace. She was seventeen, and before the current crisis arrived, she had grown increasingly concerned that there was something wrong with her. Was the arrival of womanhood providing her with her seemingly perpetual supply of energy or was it something else entirely?

That very morning Doctor Fuchs approached Ayla asking if she could administer to those victims who would more likely than not die from the disease. These patients had been transferred into one of the smaller homes, now designated a death house, where they would receive care, but no longer any treatment from the doctor or some of the older women who had some homespun medical expertise. The number of people volunteering as caregivers had dramatically dwindled of late since recognizing that close proximity to the infected increased the chances of the caregiver falling ill despite the scarves, veils and incense being deployed to counteract the miasma.

Ayla had acquiesced to Fuchs request and immediately set about caring for the unfortunates in the final stages of their fight with the disease.

During the long and lonely hours of the death watch, Ayla had plenty of time to think. As with any young woman in love, Ayla's thoughts centered about Rolf and their future life together, when would they marry, soon? What sort of house would they live in? How many and what sort of children might they have?

As the days and nights dragged on, Ayla believed that she had an unusual gift that led her to comfort those patients who were about to pass. The girl would sit beside their cot on a little three legged stool and hold their hands. After a short while, despite her best efforts to stay awake, Ayla found herself drifting off to sleep. Upon awakening she would find the person had passed on. The first time it happened Ayla thought it mildly interesting that following her short bedside nap, she felt amazingly refreshed and invigorated. As these sessions occurred with increasing frequency, Ayla came to feel elated, powerful, just as she had on the "night of the wolf," a name she coined whenever she recalled that strange evening.

Dr. Fuchs and another nurse discussed an interesting observation each had made separately concerning Ayla's assignment in the death house - while most of the patients transferred to Ayla's care were not expected to survive their ordeal, there were always one or two who would get better. This ceased to be the case once Ayla took over. There was a one hundred percent mortality rate of those under her care. Concerned by this sudden turn in mortality, Dr. Fuchs and the nurse would steal into the death house from time to time, carefully watching Ayla without her knowledge of their presence. Rather than failing to perform her duties adequately, it appeared to the doctor and the nurse that the girl was doing more than was humanly possible to care for the needs of her patients, especially those who although deathly ill, were possibly on the cusp of survival.

Aside from her infrequent naps, Ayla scarcely required any real sleep. To be sure, she often rested upon her cot that sat in the far corner of the room and failing to fall asleep would stare up at the beamed ceiling for several hours before rising and tending to the needs of her patients, but true sleep eluded her. During these quiet times, Ayla thought she could feel a part of her mind busily at work within her, a powerful turbulent force, forever in motion. Occasionally that part of her would break free and rise to the surface of her consciousness. During these moments of unusual clarity, she believed it was almost as if another version of her were struggling to reach up and out, claiming her life for its own. At first this thought was rather frightening, but over a space of a few days Ayla came to first accept, and look forward to its arrival. Ayla came to believe that rather claiming her life;

the force was transforming her being in some magical and wonderful manner.

With the emergence of this new found reality, Ayla discovered that if she concentrated she could find herself picturing her childhood home in detail, almost as if she were actually there. She could recall, or perhaps more descriptively, replay events that occurred in life with incredible clarity. The next night, Ayla attended the bedside of a young woman who she knew without doubt, would die within an hour or less. Once again, she held the woman's hand then within moments, felt herself slip into a light dreamlike state. It was as if she could view herself sitting by the patient, as if standing outside herself. As she watched, she saw a slender wispy thread of light arise from the woman's torso. Ayla, a devout Catholic, jumped to the immediate conclusion that it must be the woman's soul. The spirit, emerging from her disease ravaged body would no doubt continue to rise toward heaven and salvation. A warm feeling of confirmed belief flooded her heart; she recalled feeling the same way after receiving her first communion and later during her confirmation.

As Ayla continued to watch the scene unfold before her, she became aware that the light feathery glow no longer rose higher, but now turned and drifted in the direction of where her body was seated. This was puzzling and somewhat troubling. Closer and still closer the thread wound its way, approaching her sleeping form until the tip softly touched her own chest. Ayla immediately awoke from her trance. She saw the young woman lying before her on the cot suddenly convulse, her spine rising upward and away from the sweat ridden bedding at a frightening angle. Ayla saw the thread of light brighten in union with the woman's contortions and become a streaming torrent of energy she felt surge into her very being before radiating outward in a rush toward her extremities. Overcome by emotion and sensation, Ayla closed her eyes while feeling every cell in her body become saturated with a power that flowed through; flowed over her. It was to end as suddenly as it began. Ayla's eyes opened to see the thread of light fade then vanish while the woman's body slumped limply into the mattress; her life force now utterly spent.

The physical euphoria Ayla continued to experience became secondary to her concern for the young woman whose lifeless body now lay before her. Difficult questions arose and begged for answers far faster than Ayla could contemplate. Had she taken human life? Perhaps they were simply parting gifts from people who had accepted their fate and passing along whatever they had left and no longer needed, but if so, why had she not heard of this before. Surely other people must have experienced this miracle; or curse... she physically shuddered at the thought.

As she and so many others had, on so many other occasions when perplexed by the unexplained twists and turns of life, she now looked to her religion to explain the unexplainable. If so, she should not have bothered, Christianity, and in particular Catholicism, has no room in its halls for nonconformists, to say nothing of one who might somehow benefit from another's death; with the notable exception of our Lord and Savior, Jesus Christ. No... Catechism placed her situation squarely in the realm of the supernatural, and any supernatural event or semi deity that wasn't blessed and accepted within the Bible was deemed to be evil in nature.

Those indoctrinated into Christianity saw themselves as guilty in some manner before they were born, Original Sin was the term and no one escaped its grasp. The concept of guilt was an effective and overriding motivator within the Church and the institution held itself out as the only source of salvation. There were no accepted alternatives. As such Ayla's mind followed such reasoning; the rationalization having ruts that were cut both deep and well worn.

Ayla followed this path and arrived at the only possible conclusion. The glowing threads she witnessed arising from the bodies she touched were obviously souls, what else could they be? Then rather than going up to heaven, the souls instead entered her body and since she felt strengthened when this occurred hadn't she consumed a soul? Wasn't this in the same vein as taking the Body and Blood of the Savior into her heart every Sunday? But if she personally benefited from another's loss, how then could this be seen as anything other than evil. How could she herself... be anything other than evil? And then there was the "night of the wolf," were these not all logical proofs and conclusions.

Ayla promised God and herself that she would never again partake in this unholy practice. Perhaps the devil himself had devised this abomination as a means of temptation? She would go to her priest and confess what took place; yes that is what she must do. Even as this thought took root in her mind, common sense cautioned against it. If Ayla followed this plan at best the priest might think her mad or worse a witch, a being enthralled by a demon or perhaps even the devil itself. The seven hundred year history of the Inquisition was still fresh in the minds of the faithful, and if somewhat diminished, its final victim would be executed in 1826, a decade of so from the present. No, Ayla thought, she had better handle this problem on her own.

Ayla retreated to her cot. Lying atop the blanket, she closed her eyes and clasped her hands tightly together in prayer asking Jesus for absolution and that He spare her from this accursed affliction. After some time she found she felt much better and did her best to put the disquieting events and thoughts behind her. To do so, she focused on her past; the happy times spent with her father traveling about the countryside in their wagon and the exciting future she would enjoy with Rolf. Ayla fell into a deep unbroken sleep that carried her through the long quiet night. This night there would be no need to rise every few hours to treat and comfort the sick and dying.

The next morning Ayla woke with a start when Dr. Fuchs gently nudged her shoulder. Groggily, she swung her legs over the side of the cot and slowly sat upright. The doctor set himself on the bed beside her and shook his head solemnly watching two men pick up and carry out the last of the bodies from the room. Ayla's remaining three patients had died sometime in the night. Doctor Fuchs considered asking Ayla if she had heard anything to indicate their passing but immediately reconsidered, after all, he had borne witness to the dedication the girl displayed toward those in her care. Instead Fuchs simply took her hand in his and gave it a tender squeeze.

Another week passed before the number of patients arriving in Ayla's ward began to fall. The medical crisis was in its last days. The virus had burned itself out, finding fewer and fewer potential victims to infect; those who somehow avoided exposure and of course those who had died. Then there were the others, the majority of sick who survived the illness and who were now immune, and still others like herself who seemingly enjoyed a natural immunity to the disease.

With the number of patients rapidly declining, Dr. Fuchs finally declared the epidemic to be at an end. Surprisingly, with fewer patients to attend, Ayla also noted a similar decline in her own energy levels. The young woman returned to sleeping longer hours and eating regularly. The odd rumors of Ayla's unbridled and unexplainable vigor disappeared as quickly as did the disease. Ayla's concerns regarding the matter remained, but in the last several days she had nearly convinced herself that it was simply a result of over work and little sleep.

Over the course of six weeks, the epidemic had savaged multiple towns and villages throughout the land and the authorities had prudently sought out and obtained lists of the dead. The reasons for doing so were both a humanitarian and a proprietary necessity. While it was only morally proper to pass along these grim notifications to distant relatives; matters of business, taxation and the transfer of property ownership demanded quick action. These lengthy listings were posted in town halls but more sensibly distributed directly to the churches in the region. The majority of the rural population being illiterate; the priests and vicars read the names out to their congregations or if known, would notify the victim's family personally. In parishes were the dead had been born and raised, records of their passing were dutifully added to church registers.

The following Sunday was the day when Ayla's world took an unexpected and unwelcome turn. Ayla, Tab and Terell sat on the long hardwood pew listening to the Father read from of a long list of names provided to him by a government courier the day before. Every so often a gasp or cry could be heard within the congregation as a loved one's name was read aloud. Ayla felt her heart stop the moment the name Ernst Wainwright of Andel was announced. Hearing her father's name Ayla gasped, and gripping her bible in both hands pressed the book to her chest. The rest of the names droned on for several more minutes. Many of the victim's names were unknown to her, but even some she had known well in her old village upon reaching Ayla's ears remained unacknowledged, her heart and mind deafened in grief. It was only when the minister reached the name: Rolf Hamner of Longkamp that the words punched into her stomach like an iron fist.

Ayla, along with many others remained in the church for some time after the Mass had ended. Some like Ayla were seated with their heads bent low trying to make sense of the world, while others knelt in prayer within the pews; several members humbling and prostrating themselves on the marble floor before the alter. These newly unexpected losses were a hammer blow to the townsfolk, many who had already suffered heavy personal loss while the epidemic raged in Longkamp.

Terell and Tab had offered their condolences and had stayed along with Ayla saying prayers for Ayla's father, Rolf, and an uncle of Terell's who lived in a town some distance from Longkamp. Wishing to stay in the church and not yet ready to leave, Terell and Tab took their leave, Terell placing a hand on her shoulder saying they would stay near the wagon and would be waiting when she finished prayer.

Ayla tried to pray, but couldn't form a mental connection with her God, it was if the Almighty had turned his face from her. Instead Ayla now considered her rapidly dwindling options of a woman utterly left alone without means or family in what was definitely a man's world. The fall out resulting from the recent events would not be lost on Terell. Ayla was now totally dependent upon Terell for food and lodging. Her inheritance was nonexistent, her father's farm, house and property passing directly to her stepmother.

Ayla had developed into an attractive young woman, and Terell was still a relatively young and virile man without a wife to help him tend a home, raise a son and perhaps in the future, additional children. When it became clear to Terell that Rolf and Ayla were to be betrothed, he abandoned the idea. Instead, he turned his attentions to a young widow just weeks prior to the start of the epidemic. Terell decided to approach Amelia Schneider, a rotund twenty something woman who had lost her husband in the recent conflict with France. Amelia had proven receptive, but had been lost to Small Pox, her only child, a son, was shipped off to live with distant relatives. The epidemic had changed all that went before it.

With Rolf and Ayla's father now out of the way, Terell considered if Ayla might now be persuaded to take up a domestic role in his household. After waiting an acceptable period of time Terell began cautious and rather awkward advances toward Ayla, but the girl could not put aside their past animosities and rejected Terell's romantic gestures out of hand. Instead, much to Terell's vexation, Ayla instead proposed she continue in his employ retaining the same conditions and rate of pay of the current agreement.

Terell reluctantly agreed to the situation, he required help at the farm while he attended to his shop; following the epidemic, employees of any sort were hard to come by. In another year or so, his son would be of suitable size and age to become an apprentice which would eliminate the need for someone to watch his boy, but this didn't change the fact that he required someone immediately to help run the small farm and once again, help of any sort was hard to come by right now. Terell considered selling the farm and moving into town but the population had been slashed by ten percent or more and land values had crashed. Many of the farms about Longkamp and other towns and villages were abandoned and could be had for next to nothing save registration fees. After approaching the problem from every possible angle, Terell accepted that the current agreement with Ayla would have to stand.

The situation although at first awkward became less so in the passing months, but Ayla's growing physical beauty had become a constant and overriding distraction for Terell whenever he was home. Being a man, he found it nearly impossible to restrain his desire when he was around Ayla. As for her, Ayla held no illusions concerning the circumstances women of the day often found themselves. Lately she was finding it more difficult tactfully rejecting his attentions.

One evening Terell showed up at the farmhouse after drinking in the ale house with a friend. It was unusual for Terell to drink, much less become drunk, but he arrived on the doorstep with an empty flagon of ale and an appetite for something more. Terell and his friend discussed his predicament at length over the evening. Eventually their conversation turned to Ayla. His friend stated in no uncertain terms what he would do in Terell's shoes, sometimes a woman didn't know what she really wanted and required some persuasion. At first Terell dismissed the suggestion out of hand, this behavior was repugnant and socially unacceptable in the eyes of the townsfolk not to mention his standing in the Church, but as they continued to drink the boundaries of social morality became blurred in the looming perspective of sexual imperative.

The idea took root within his mind and he allowed himself to visualize Ayla's firm young body, her gentle curves, her pretty face, and the way she smelled. By the time he arrived home he had decided to bring his fantasy to fruition, he would have the girl tonight. After all, she slept beneath his roof, ate at his table, enjoyed his protection from the outside world; surely she was obligated to him; surely it was his right as a man.

Tab would be asleep in the house by the time he arrived home, but Terell had no intention of forcibly taking Ayla while in the home; he wanted no unwelcome surprises or interruptions. Terell would ask for her help in the barn. He would claim the horse had come up lame and that he needed her to hold and pacify the animal while he examined the hoof. Once they were alone, he would press his advances, gently though persistent; he still had hope that she had needs as urgent and equal to his own. Who knew with women, perhaps she would surprise him and acquiesce to a common desire? If not, she would bend to his will; her acceptance of their changed situation would come later.

When Terell half stumbled through the door, the look in his eye told Ayla he was not himself, and within felt an ambiguous warning, but upon seeing the empty leather flagon and smelling the ale on his breath she stifled caution and put the uneasy feeling down to his inebriated condition. Ayla had prepared for bed, donning her night gown, she drew toward the kitchen table preparing to snuff the candle when she had glanced out the window and had seen Terell walking on foot, leading his horse when he entered the dark farmyard. As she continued to watch, she saw Terell had lit a lantern within the barn, and had left it burning while he approached the house, he obviously intended to return to the barn for some reason so when he requested Ayla lend a hand with the horse, she fell completely at ease.

Terell left the house and walked out toward the barn, swinging an arm casually motioning for her to follow, all was going to plan, he felt himself stir and grow hard. It had been so long since he had lain with a woman. For her part, Ayla grabbed her shawl threw it overtop her night gown and obediently followed the man walking into the night and out to the barn.

When they were both inside the small barn, Terell bid Ayla to take the horse's lead while he backtracked and walked to the barn door. After staring back at the house for some seconds and assuring himself that Tab was asleep he shut the door tight while Ayla busied herself petting and gently reassuring the animal.

Terell sat down upon a nearby bench asking that Ayla sit beside him, he had a matter to discuss and it shouldn't be in front of Tab. Her vague unease returned but still she wasn't frightened, Terell could have pressed his advantage over her on many occasions, yet hadn't. She sat down beside him and placed her hands upon her lap looking up at his face, and into his eyes. Ayla grew worried about what she saw reflected in both.

Terell took his hand and caressed her cheek, "I know you know how I really feel about you." His hand slid down and covered her small hands on her lap. His eyes were glazed and held the gleam of excitement.

Ayla pulled her hands away and tried to stand but a pair of strong arms grasped her shoulders then drew her close. Rather than struggling, Ayla simply and firmly said, "No Terell! No!" Looking into Terell's face, she saw hesitation, for a moment she believed he would release her with an apology. The thought flashed in her mind; things had not moved past a point that couldn't be undone, she could remain in his employ. This was not the case, she misread his intentions completely. Rather than contemplating an apology, Terell was simply working out how he would proceed.

When Ayla turned toward the door and leave, Terell grabbed her from behind by the waist, lifted and carried her over to a small pile of clean hay where he set her down. When she struggled to regain her feet he lay down beside her and restraining her arms above her head, he began kissing her cheeks, his lips searching for her mouth.

For Ayla's part, she was doing everything she could think of to discourage the assault but feared that putting up too strenuous a struggle might place her in serious physical danger. She was a small woman, less than half the weight of Terell and the man could badly hurt her without intending to do so. When struggling failed to discourage the man, Ayla cried aloud, her tears flowed down her cheeks. Tasting the salty tears and feeling the warm flush in the girl's face further intensified Terell's desire and his physical need for release overwhelmed any sense of guilt he felt in the moment.

Ayla felt a rough hand reach beneath the folds of her nightgown. The realization of what she had feared could happen caused her to resume her struggle more vigorously, but no matter what she did, she could not break the iron grip that held her hands firmly above her neck, nor budge the man's weight that bore down upon her. Unable to mount a further defense, Ayla retreated within herself. Doing so, she perceived time slowing, Terell's hand paused and then froze as it reached her womanhood; the passage of time came to a stop, much as it had on the "night of the wolf."

Deep within her being, Ayla was now apart from her physical self. Ayla could feel herself searching for something... but what? It was something possessed by the man that laid atop her... something very familiar... something... very desired. A brilliant flash of comprehension illuminated the landscape of Ayla's consciousness, knowledge flooded forth, encompassing her completely and starkly revealing a part of her she had first denied then buried deep within herself. That night at the farm when she destroyed the wolves, and more recently only a month earlier when she witnessed herself draw forth and absorb the life force of a dying young woman in the death house.

Now fully aware of who and what she was, Ayla allowed that part of herself, to probe and access the man atop her body. She watched her alter ego locate a bright knot of entwined strands of light deep within Terell's chest, gleaming far brighter than had the sickly glow emanating from the diseased woman. She unwound the dazzling knot, pulling free and redirecting its slender pulsing threads and thicker tendrils downward, taking them into her own body while remaining motionless beneath the man. Ayla sensed that the visions she saw within her mind's eye were merely her futile attempt to describe the indescribable, a vague translation of what she could not comprehend.

Suddenly, the beat and flow of time restored itself and Ayla once again felt Terell's hand pressing upon her mound, his fingers probing her crevices, seeking entry; but something was quite different than before. Now rather than fighting his advances, she sought to aid him and parted her legs wide to allow him greater access. On Terell's part, he hadn't expected her consent and was most certainly surprised when the young woman took an ever increasingly active part in what had become lovemaking.

Ayla's sexual awakening coincided with what she could only sense as an intense hunger for life; the life of the man she had taken physically and spiritually within her body. The couple writhed and twisted atop the bed of hay, their previously separate existence now welded in a glorious union. Moments to seconds, seconds to minutes, then time itself lengthened impossibly for each of them and seemed to approach eternity. Abruptly, the brilliant warmth faded and she felt Terell disappear within the folds of a velvet blackness that folded in upon itself then disappeared entirely.

The connection utterly broken, Ayla gasped for breath and found herself sitting upright and straddling Terell's lifeless body lying on the bed of hay strewn upon the barn floor's wooden planks. Terell's face appeared sunken and pale, his hands wrinkled, his previously strong arms withered; a lifetime of vitality entirely spewed forth in a matter of moments, a vitality she had taken for her own. Now flushed with a pleasure the like of which she had never dreamt, Ayla bathed in the energy that pulsed and surged through her entire being. Surprisingly the passage of time itself appeared to her to have grown less meaningful; her mind raced and danced with ideas, thoughts and plans for the future. Throughout the remnants of that night of rebirth, Ayla explored her heightened sense of self awareness. A new standing and purpose had yawned open before her, one which would replace what she had previously accepted as her lot in life; her modest, acquiescing and yes, thoroughly pathetic life. No longer, as of this moment now she would set no one above herself, she would be her own master... and perhaps the master of others.

At dawn Ayla woke Tab. The boy's young mind still developing, at this stage was extremely malleable was easily mesmerized. Ayla was surprised how easily she manipulated his memory, to accept her version of the night's events; how the two of them had awakened to find the home on fire, how they tried to save his father but were driven back by the heat and flame. Yes, the boy was obedient to her will, and he would be of some use to her in the future, whether as a willing accomplice, or as a meal. To Ayla it mattered not, just as with any predator Ayla could no longer afford sympathy for the weak... for her prey.

That dawn, an attractive woman and a young boy rolled away in the horse drawn wagon following the rutted rock strewn pathway that would eventually lead to Longkamp and points many leagues and years beyond, a path that would see Ayla abandon a burning farmhouse and her own past far behind.

12

In the abbey, Teun De Torres awoke within his bedroom. He and Blas had talked until the wee hours of the morning, but here he was, fully awake and showering only several hours later. His need for sleep was drastically reduced although he recalled with a small touch of regret the luxurious feeling of remaining within a warm bed while drifting in and out of sleep only rising in the early afternoon. Teun exited the shower and dried himself before dressing and partaking in a continental breakfast laid out on his table by one of the servants in the employ of the Order.

Today when he entered the sitting room, Blas was already present and dressed in a brilliant white suit rather than his subdued Gray uniform. Noticing Teun's surprise, he explained. "A wedding. Today I'm accompanying my Master to the wedding of a prominent member's daughter." Blas paused. "Because of this, I apologize before hand; this will be a limited session."

"You may have sensed upon our first meeting that I myself was not a Sempitor; but rather am a Servicio or servant. I do not emit an aura as does my Master; I am but a reflection of her power. I and my Master enjoy a unique and intimate mental if not in fact spiritual relationship. While so connected, we share every memory, thought and emotion. I will not enjoy her life expectancy, her physical or mental powers; in every way, I am completely human.

You might inquire if just anyone could become a Servicio. I assure you this is not the case. As I have previously explained, as the birth of a Sempitor seems to rely upon its own twin perishing within the womb or very soon after birth, so too is it a requirement of a potential Servicio. No one knows why this is, although some speak of the unusual bond that exists between those who grow from a single seed and share a womb during the first months of life. You may scoff at the notion, but there are many documented cases where two identical twins, separated at birth, raised in distant locals, by adoptive parents having distinctly different lineage and custom grow to adulthood. If by chance they meet much later in life, they often discover they have similar hobbies, careers, perhaps pick wives that look as they themselves could be sisters, or even provide the same names to their children.

Far less well documented, but I assure you to be absolute fact, is the unusual ability to communicate using thought alone or at the very least share a state of consistent empathy, one twin knowing when the other is happy, sad, fearful, injured and so on. Perhaps it is here that we can look for an explanation as to the intimate connection between Sempitor and Servicio. Each having lost such a twin early in life, the surviving twin remains an open connection awaiting its counterpart. Once that connection between the master and its servant comes to be, it is permanent and unique. Think of this as if a radio transmission were locked upon a unique channel, one totally secure and scrambled. In any case, twins, such as me, may be identified by a Sempitor who is not yet bound to another Servicio and if desired, a connection can be made, with or without the permission of the potential Servicio. If the connection between the Master and Servicio is later broken through the death of the servant, the Master can re-establish a new connection with another who is suitable.

While we both live, our bond is lifelong and unassailable, with one notable exception; should my Master enter her final years, among other things I will later explain, this connection will become at first intermittent, then broken entirely. At this point the Servicio's obligation to its master remains steadfast and he or she will try their best to convince the Sempitor to take their own lives, or allow their Servicio to assist them in doing so. But... should their ministrations fall on deaf ears, their obligation then turns toward the Orden Sempiterno. Contact will be made by way of our Servicio brethren. Operating under the Order's instruction, its agents will be sent to dispatch the aging member in any way possible while doing so with the utmost discretion. Above all else, our overriding purpose is to avoid exposure of our existence to the humans. A Servicio is not required to take an active part in their master's demise, as neither I, nor any other Servicio could possibly bring us to kill one so dear. Once the master is no more, we are willing to take our own life; our lives no longer hold meaning. Even if we could somehow face such a singular existence, the Order will seldom accept the risk we would pose to its secrecy. Its agents would dispatch us.

While closely joined with their masters and able to share thoughts, feelings and memories on a uniquely personal level, the Order encourages indirect dialogue between those of the servant caste knowing loyalty is never a question, the Servicio's only concern is that of the welfare of their masters. This same degree of loyalty has prevented ego driven Sempitors to attempt to wield the Servicio as a weapon against others in the Order. To date, this uninterrupted and impartial flow of information has pre-empted conflicts that might lead to open warfare if one Sempitor or as a group thought they could hide their intentions let alone their actions from the Order's other members.

The long Gray panel van sped along the highway heading west from Claremont City. If the all too familiar route had proven long and tiresome for the driver, Norman Stiles could only imagine how the journey must be for the three illegal migrants he had stashed in the back of the stuffy windowless van. The van's occupants had adequate water and sandwiches for the trip north and knew enough to keep their mouths shut whenever the van came to a stop. The situation also demanded that rest stops be kept to a minimum over the twenty six hour trip. At roughly six hour intervals Norman would routinely stop the vehicle and stretch his legs while keeping a wary eye out for anything or anyone unusual before banging lightly on the side of the van. A moment later he'd slide open the side door, grab the full piss bottles from the floor, pour them out, toss them in, close the door and drive on.

Norman only stopped to pay cash for gas or to swap out the van's rear license plate each time he crossed into a different state. Any cop checking the plate registrations would find himself looking at a similar Gray panel van belonging to Jed's Paints and Textures. Unless the officer carefully checked the Vehicle Identification Number bearing a close sequence, he would conclude the vehicle was properly registered, if the difference was noticed, it could be easily be explained as a simple record keeping error. There was no point taking a chance that his vehicle might fall victim as a random profile target. Norman had even gone to the trouble of having magnetic signs advertizing his vehicle as belonging to his bogus house painting company, the ladders atop the roof rack lending a distinct air of credibility to the ruse. So far, none of the cops he'd seen paid the least interest, why should they?

Unassuming and mild mannered Norman Stiles presented the antithesis of a character that the authorities might consider a person of interest. In his early fifties, average height and weight, short cropped Graying hair and moustache, black rimmed glasses, and wearing a Steelers ball cap, a pair of paint stained overalls and cheap runners, Norman's attire dovetailed nicely with the van's phony motif. Stiles went by many names, each possessing authentic Federal and State photo identification. His employer had even purchased or rented properties in each state associated with his various aliases. Operating on a cash only basis, Norman would utilize any of the properties as the need arose, eliminating any paper trail. Anyone performing anything other than an in-depth check on Mr. Stiles or whatever handle he proffered at the time, could only assume he was who he said he was; a small time painter from the town of Bum Fuck, Idunknow.

The sun had set half an hour before and the overcast sky was quickly darkening, but he was nearly home. Norman left the main highway onto the Big Bend Road heading towards Hansel Creek. The van drove over the North Bridge, kept to the right of Devil's Fork then turned east before reaching the town limits. The smooth asphalt turned to hard pack gravel and Norman heard muted voices in Spanish interspaced with the low rumble and occasional ping of small stones against the van's fenders. He chuckled to himself, "the natives were growing restless," and their long ordeal would be over soon enough. The young trio had made it all the way from El Salvador to Washington State; all they wanted was a chance for a better life, a chance to make a decent living. Norman smiled grimly while recalling a favorite line from the movie The Outlaw Josie Wales. A bounty hunter intent on brining the outlaw to justice says to Josie, "a man's gotta make a livin'" to which Clint Eastwood replied, "dyin' ain't much of a livin' boy."

Half a mile or so further, Norman approached the heavy steel gate guarding the compound's entrance. Norman slowed the van to a gentle stop, stepped out, and walking a few steps unlocked and fumbled with a thick chain and padlock. Pushing the gate open, he drove the vehicle a short ways into the compound stopped once again, closed and locked the gate securely before continuing to the main doors of the Hall.

He stopped the vehicle and placed it in park, stepped out then reached back into the van; beneath the dashboard he found a hidden toggle switch. Flicking it to the on position, Norman heard the quiet but unmistakable hiss of a small canister filling the rear of the van with an odorless, but potent fentanyl based gas that would incapacitate the men and render them unconscious. He shut the door and let the gas complete its work. Checking his watch he counted off several minutes before banging heavily upon the side of the van. As expected, hearing nothing Norman slid open the side door waiting several more minutes to allow the gas to disperse before checking on the men inside. They were sleeping like babies and would remain that way for at least an hour or more. More than enough time for him to cart them off to the dank cells that awaited them in the Hall's cellars.

Norman completed the prisoner's transfer, ensuring the captives had food and water waiting for them when they awoke. As usual he turned the radio to an easy listening station, before climbing the series of long steep steps leading up from the basement. Reaching the top of the stairs, he turned off the main lights leaving the cellar bathed in the dim light provided by several dim bulbs dangling on thin black electrical wires several feet below the main floor's joists. Neither he nor his master would return for some hours. It was always a better choice to allow the prisoners to adapt to their new surroundings in their own time. This would no doubt include a number of hours filled with yells, curses, threats and finally pleas for freedom or at least explanation, but none of that sort of unpleasantness would be heard within the upper rooms of the Hall, thick walls and soundproofed ceilings would see to that.

While Norman transferred the unconscious men from the van and into the cells, he considered for the umpteenth time what his life might be like if his Master had been a White Sempitor rather than a Gray. He had known a fair number of Servicio although briefly. The Servicio or assistants to the long lived Sempiterno were indoctrinated to their roles at an early age, when their minds were still open and easily influenced. His own service began in France, just after his thirteenth birthday, only five months after the end of World War Two. He had met the Gray Master quite by accident. Norman had gotten turned around and lost while following a trail meandering through a forest near his home. He came across the Sempitor as it consumed a young man. Norman thought the young fellow to be about thirty, handsome, and in his prime; an unfortunate circumstance given his Master's preferences.

An innocent, Norman had never before witnessed physical love making, although he and his friends had speculated on the matter at some length. Still, what he witnessed that day was hardly love making in any ordinary sense of the word. He could still recall his initial amazement, watching the couple as they entwined and writhed on the green grass, completely immersed in the throes of passion. From what Norman could see, there was no question that the fellow was enjoying himself immensely, that changed when Norman noticed an unusual blush of light appearing to form between the two. As his Master sat astride the still smiling young man who moaned in pleasure, he noticed the Gray's smile take on an impossibly hungry countenance. Its eyes burned and smoldered with an unearthly desire and that odd radiance between the two brightened appreciably. Up until that very moment, Norman had thought his eyes merely tricked by the dappling afternoon sunlight sifting through the forest canopy. Norman stared open mouthed as the ambiguous glow resolved itself into a brilliant stream of pure light. To Norman it appeared the stream began in the young fellow's chest then flowed and pulsed into that of the Gray. Over the space of perhaps a minute, he watched as the young man seemed to strangely whither and fade, while at the same time his Master's features seemed to surge in vitality.

The young man's body fell to the grass, his Master brushing aside the corpse as easily as brushing a crumb of bread from a shirt. Although the Gray never looked in his direction Norman had the distinct impression it knew he was present. Wanting to beat a hasty retreat, he started to turn about when two strong hands fell upon each shoulder holding him fast. The boy cranked about his head looking past his shoulder to see who held him and saw a middle-aged man looking down on him.

Held securely within the man's grip, Norman had little choice but to watch his future Master turn to face him for the first time. That wanton expression, those piercing eyes he beheld only moments before no longer held any trace of what transpired just moments before. Instead the Sempitor's eyes appeared thoughtful, benevolent, and even... kind. The Gray spoke to him and as it did so, the words and the rise and fall of their intonation calmed his racing heart and quelled the sick terror arising within him. Those calming words playing in his ears; on a deeper level, Norman's mind felt the first subliminal brush of the other's thoughts upon his own.

During those first years, he often found himself trying to analyze, examine, and describe in terms of words or phrases, the nature of their cerebral relationship, but failed at every turn. The attempts at explanation continued to elude him even when speaking of the experience with other Servicio having undergone a similar indoctrination with their Sempitors. The best description that he had yet heard came from a young woman who described her intimate conversations as a form of mental imagery immersed within a constantly changing series of emotion, similar to the manner in which music and dance intertwine; a ballet and chorus of thought and existence.

The one thing agreed upon among all the Servicio, was that the connection between themselves and their masters were both confidential and exclusive, truly a meeting of minds between two singularly suited individuals. The Sempitors possessed the ability to initiate the transmission of ideas between themselves and their servant in a manner that was somehow attuned only to their individual minds, an exceedingly exceptional occurrence. One Servicio could not connect to a Sempitor who was not his or her own, even if they had not been already bound to their master; it was highly unlikely that they could connect to any other. It was as if their minds were radios, each tuned to an impossibly narrow channel that once joined could never become separated. Sempitor's were also bound by a contract of exclusivity, and were bound to their Servicio just as tightly as the other was to them. The relationship was both deep and fulfilling, of one mind; while the Sempitor was the senior personality, thoughts and emotions passed freely between the two without need of filter. The bond would continue until one or the other failed to exist, truly an "until death do you part" qualifier.

The Gray Master spoke quietly while they stood within the small glade; Norman felt himself grow calm and relaxed. As his apprehensions evaporated the strong hands gripping his shoulders gently slid away. Stepping out from behind him, the man patted his head then approached the body of the other that lay motionless upon the trampled grass. Norman watched as the man gently and respectfully began to administer to the corpse. Suddenly pausing his undertaking, the man slowly looked up toward Norman and the Gray Master standing at his side. "Thank you Otto," said the master. "I will see you back at the house when you've completed your task." Otto smiled and nodded slowly, the expression on his face reflecting an appreciation of this most unique moment, an appreciation soon to be shared between Norman and his new master.

Norman and the Gray walked along a trail leading away from the small clearing while Otto continued his chore disposing of the emaciated corpse. They walked together in the summer sun, the warmth of the afternoon sunlight only exceeded by his growing love and devotion for his new Master as Norman began a new chapter in his life. The boy would later see the man he had met in the forest glade on that day months later and thousands of miles distant, in America.

Norman closed the thick cellar door pausing for a moment and wondered how long these three new additions would fill the masters' ever growing appetite. Over the last several years Norman witnessed the Master's behavior and peculiar feeding habits changing with increasing and rather disturbing rapidity. The last five months in particular had proven extraordinarily difficult for Norman personally. He and his Sempitor had slowly drifted apart, their minds didn't meld and flow in the same easy manner as they had before; sometimes his Master intentionally blocked communication for days at a time except to demand Norman resupply the Hall with new victims.

In the years following their initial joining, the Master would only feast two or three times per year. Norman would take care to ensure none of the Master's victims had local ties that might complicate their lives. Instead the two would travel and explore the post war world while the master sampled a diverse and sometimes exotic menu. When their union was new and fresh, Norman thought the Sempitor's feeding habits were universal, Gray or White, but this was not the case. Feeding habits were a matter of choice rather than need. The Gray preferred to take the lives of those they consumed in a single violent rush and flurry of sexual and occasionally sadistic excitement while the White consumed only what they needed to survive and would feed from a group of humans simultaneously, often the young.

The victims on whom the White fed were fortunate indeed since the Sempitor would only consume a minute portion of their life force, consuming only months from the victim's life expectancy at a single feeding. If the victim was young, no one, most certainly not the victims would ever become aware of what had been stolen. The White Sempitors often placed themselves in positions where they had access to a large number of hosts; the term hosts being particularly suited since the White Sempitors lived lives of a parasitic rather than that of a predatory nature. The White often donned the guise of charitable benefactors; running orphanages, asylums for the mentally ill and challenged, or as doctors working in areas where they had access to the very sick or dying. While feeding, the Whites were careful never to draw undue attention. By "sipping" or slowly siphoning off their victim's energy, the intense glow and light show Norman consistently observed while his Master fed remained all but invisible. The Whites hid in plain sight while the Grays lived solitary and secretive lives.

Norman learned from his Master and the other Servicio he had occasion to meet; that White or Gray, all Sempiterno would eventually approach old age and in doing so would "turn"; becoming what was termed a Black or Shade. In past centuries, "turning" became an exceedingly dangerous time for the affected Sempitor as well as his Servicio since the chance of discovery increased exponentially as did the Sempitor's requirement for an ever growing supply of victims. Old age demanded the creatures consume ever increasing amounts of life energy, the previously adequate quantity now failing to provide sufficient nourishment to sustain their life.

As this troubling situation progressed, hunger became extreme, causing irrational behavior. Like an old tiger missing its canines and forced to change its manner of hunting, eventually becoming a man eater; the Shades were unable to control the manner or quantity of their feeding. At some point, towards the end, they experienced increasing periods of dementia, eventually becoming insane. Now unable to control their hunger, the Shades violently drained their victims. Worse still, Shades fed upon whoever was at hand, without regard to secrecy, leaving a trail of corpses in their wake, a trail that eventually led back to them. This eventuality faced all Sempitor, and some recognizing the situation choose to end their lives by their own hand, or with the assistance of their Servicio.

Norman had suspected for some time that his Master was in the process of turning. As the number of killings mounted, Norman had to range ever further from the Creek to ensure he found victims who would not be missed. Six months before he felt that he had stumbled upon the perfect solution, by posing as a trafficker of illegal immigrants. For a time this seemed to work, but more recently his Master had begun leaving the Hall at night and wandering out alone. Simply watching the local news he mentally tallied the number of missing person stories reported to the town's constabulary. As would be expected nearly all would eventually turn up safe and sound. Teen runaways would show up in Seattle or another large city, husbands or wives taking sabbaticals from a troubled marriage would re-appear holding divorce papers, boozers chasing lost weekends would finally run out of cash or plastic and sober up, and on and on. But the reports cited a few others that would never resurface, and Norman prayed they never would. He knew every facet of his Master's taste and habit, and a few of the missing dovetailed perfectly within that category. Norman would do his utmost to manage the situation; as his was an existence of willful obedience, unbridled loyalty and yes he supposed... love. Together, he and his Sempitor would face their uncertain future together.

13

It was early evening and Adrian and Saul Kaplan were preparing to leave the house and visit some good friends of theirs in the nearby town of Knots' Ridge. "Mom, are you sure you don't feel like coming with us tonight? You haven't been out of the house in nearly a week; a little fresh air would do you good."

"No dear, you know my favorite program is on in a few minutes." Rachel tried to keep the exasperation from her voice as she explained to her son her reason for remaining home for the third time that evening. "Beside, my arthritis is acting up again..." She paused. "I think there must be a weather change on the way." That last remark always worked to redirect the conversation, her son was an addict when it came to watching the Weather Network on TV. If Saul were forty years younger Rachel figured he'd be one of those storm chaser nuts going after tornados and such.

Adrian's voice reached out to her from the master bedroom. "Mom, have you taken your Aleve?"

Rachel lied. "Yes dear, I just took one. It will take time to work." Rachel grabbed her cane from behind her bedroom door and made a point of limping into the kitchen where she found Saul in the refrigerator grabbing several beers for himself and a couple of club sodas for Adrian. "What type of friends are these you're seeing tonight? They can't even offer you a few drinks?"

Saul answered his mother. "You know I like my own brand, that stuff Arthur drinks gives me gas."

Adrian entered the kitchen joining her husband and mother-in-law. "Now Rachel, do you need anything at all before we go?"

"No I'll be fine." Rachel replied as the three walked into the living room. Rachel sat down in her favorite chair directly facing the television, making herself comfortable. Saul and Adrian moved toward the front door.

Just before the couple left, Adrian turned away from the front door her husband held open. "Ok, now remember if you need anything you call us. The number is on the kitchen table."

"Fine, fine. Now off you go and enjoy your evening." Rachel threw a wave toward the couple and reached for the television's remote control that lay on the side table next to the chair.

Adrian walked onto the front stoop, Saul followed, "OK, bye mom. We won't be too late." He closed the door. Rachel watched the couple stroll down the sidewalk and enter their car parked at the curb. A moment later they were gone.

Rachel left her cane where she'd propped it against the wall and lifted herself from her chair, "Finally!" Rachel thought to herself. The old woman comfortably walked into the small dining room approaching a fine hardwood side table upon which sat a small crystal decanter of Sherry surrounded by six tiny crystal sipping glasses of similar design. She took a quick glance at the clock, seven-twenty eight. Pouring a small glass she took a sip and topped up the glass before walking back into the living room where the familiar theme of Jeopardy announced the start of her program.

Rachel's program had ended with the sun's setting a half hour before. Now the cool lavender of early summer twilight descended upon the homes and businesses of Hansel's Creek. This was quite unlike the approach of dusk taking place at Meyers Hall some five miles distant. The deep forest and brush surrounding the Hall abetted the growth of gloom and shadow that crawled and deepened atop the Hall's weed choked garden, unkempt lawn and along its dark Gray stone foundations. A single light burned in a window on the main floor then went out leaving the building in complete darkness.

Presently the front door swung open then closed behind the dark outline of a man who walked out across the dark stoned gravel of the compound and entered the dilapidated garage through a side door. Moments later the overhead door swung upward and a dark four door sedan emerged from the garage, the vehicle pulling up and stopping in front of the Hall. Leaving the vehicle running, Norman Stiles stepped from the vehicle walked to the passenger side of the car where he opened and held the door. A petite figure of a woman stepped from the Hall, crossed down the steps and entered the expensive vehicle. Norman gently swung the car door shut, enjoying the familiar solid thunk as it closed. He glanced for a moment observing the dim reflection of his somber lined face within the deeply tinted glass. Walking back to the driver's door he wondered how many times he had seen that face smile back at him through the years; far too seldom he decided, but no matter, c'est la vie; that's life. He guided the heavy vehicle down the laneway and turned left onto the Big Bend Road which would take him and his master into Hansel's Creek.

At the Kaplan home, Rachel was finishing her second glass of Sherry when a loud knock sounded against the front door. A knock, not the doorbell; Rachel thought that rather unusual but never the less rose to answer the door. Arriving at the front door as was her habit, she leaned forward to peer through the peephole before remembering her son and

105

daughter in law hadn't bothered installing one. "Why bother" she thought as she opened the door, nothing ever happened on the sleepy streets of the Creek. The door swung wide but failed to reveal anyone on the stoop or down along the walkway. Across the road a street light flashed briefly several times before achieving a stable glow and brightening. "Hello" Rachel called; her voice sounded frail, even to her ears. She frowned as she closed the door and returned to her seat. Kids... she decided, kids. Well now that the street lights had come on most of the youngsters would be heading back home or risk facing the wrath of their parents should they arrive much later.

It was nearly a minute later when she heard two more door knocks in rapid succession. This time Rachel hesitated before rising from her chair. It may well be kids she thought, but what if it weren't? A chill ran through her sending a light shiver up her spine. Instead of proceeding directly to the door, she detoured toward the living room window. Pulling down on the drape string, the curtains slid apart to reveal a partial view of the front yard and sidewalk. On the opposite side of the street a couple walked a dog and passed beneath the street light then paused while the dog lifted its leg on the pole. Rachel craned her neck to see who might be at the door but the angle of her viewpoint denied her eyes access to the front steps. She glanced back at the couple and then to the wall clock checking the time; almost nine. She chided herself for her caution; it was hardly the middle of the night. Now - exactly who was at the door?

Once again the door swung wide, but this time she had taken a moment to flick on the porch light before doing so. Just as before, no one stood upon the stoop. Catching sight of the porch light and the old woman who stood silhouetted within the door frame, the couple walking their dog gave a brief wave before continuing on their way. Emboldened by the presence of neighbors and the nearby light, Rachel stepped down the stairs and walked half way across the front yard. "You kids will be getting home if you know what's good for you!" No answer, no movement among the trees and shrubs that lined the sides of the yard.

Muttering under her breath Rachel turned, climbed the front steps and re-entered the house. She closed and locked the door but left the porch light burning. She'd be sure to ask Saul to inquire with the neighbors and have words about their children's antics this evening. Rachel walked toward the easy chair, picked up the TV remote and turned off the set. It was time for bed. She reached for her cane, clicked off the brass table lamp then turned to leave the room. The old woman froze in her tracks.

"My God!" The old woman croaked raising her cane against a figure standing nearby. "Who are you?! What do you want here?!"

A disdainful leering voice spoke aloud in German. "Hallo Rachel, hast du mich vermisst? " That voice, dreadful and somehow terribly familiar echoed within her ears settling atop her heart like a leaden weight. The feeble light from the distant street lamp splashed and pooled upon the portion of the living room carpet before the open curtain. Rachel's eyes struggled to adapt to the room's dim lighting. Within that subdued ambiance, Rachel strove to identify the face that remained hidden within the deep shadow only several steps distant. Shifting her stance slightly to one side, the old woman's efforts were rewarded, no... perhaps punished. Like herself, the figure standing before her appeared aged and withered. Had it not been for the startling piercing eyes staring back into her own she might have added frail to the description, but those soul less eyes belied great age, malice and power.

"Miss... missed... you?" Rachel's voice quaked with question. She stood transfixed as the figure stepped out of shadow, suddenly casting away its mantle of time. The facade of decades fell away to reveal a vivid and unwanted reminisce from a past she had gratefully discarded years before. Forced to acknowledge its existence threatened to tear apart whatever thin veneer of sanity remained to her. Rachel blanched and felt bile rise in her throat. A moment later she managed to choke out a sentence. "No! No! You are dead... dead and rotting in hell with the other monsters from the camps!" Rachel's voice grew shrill and full of hysteria.

The creatures eyes brightened with hatred and brimming with what Rachel could have only have described as lust. A bitter, contemptuous snarl rasped out; "No not dead Rachel, just simply too busy to visit old friends." It swept towards the elderly lady before it.

As the dark shadow enveloped Rachel's shocked face, the old woman's expression now tinged with horror. She felt her heart quiver within her chest as would the struggles of a small bird held within a raptor's steely talons. Her heart thudded heavily one last time in her chest then suddenly stilled as she surrendered whatever number of days she still retained in her twilight of her existence, days that fled her body and consumed by the raging hunger of the creature that grasped her close.

14

It had been a cold night, even for late November and was likely to remain an equally cold morning. One of a pair of SS privates on guard duty at the door of the camp's hospital checked his watch for the fourth time in as many minutes. Their night shift concluded fifteen minutes ago and they waited impatiently on their relief. Even though the young soldiers had permission to warm themselves one at a time, standing guard within the hospital's lobby for a maximum of ten minutes per hour, it was barely enough time to begin to warm their feet. The soles of their boots were worn to nearly paper while their socks were threadbare and worn through in the heels and toes. There had been a time when SS soldiers were the pride of the Fatherland and being Hitler's favorite corps, its members could count on receiving the best equipment, training and conditions. That all changed as the tide of war turned in favor of the allies.

Sharing a cigarette the two guards stamped their feet on the frozen concrete landing in front of the hospital doors and took turns cursing their tardy replacements before their attention was drawn to an approaching figure striding toward their position. This particular figure could be expected to visit the building at any time of the day or night. Many of the camps' soldiers offhandedly joked that he never slept. The soldiers posting the longest duty within the Auschwitz-Birkenau complex had long since ceased musing of the senior officer's erratic comings and goings.

The men snapped to attention and saluted smartly in the direction of the SS officer approaching the hospital entrance. The officer paused in front of the still closed set of double doors and shot a warning glance toward the young soldier on his right. The guard proffered an apology, "Verzeihung bitte Sir" while he immediately grasped the door handle, pulled open, then held the door while at attention.

Hauptsturmführer (Captain) Josef Mengele nodded curtly in the young man's direction and passed into the hospital without a word. The officer pulled off his great coat and hung it along with his forge cap on one of the wooden clothes hooks in the hospital lobby. Beneath the coat, instead of a regulation uniform, the man wore a knee length white lab coat, a pair of thick, gray wool trousers and a pair of comfortable oxfords ensuring he passed the long hours on his feet with at least some measure of comfort. Mengele stretched out the arms and straightened his lab coat which had become twisted beneath the heavy winter coat then strode down the hallway with purpose.

He had duties to perform, important tasks at hand, of a type that must be completed swiftly before external factors could intervene and force the termination or at least delay his life's work. His high level contacts within Berlin told him the camp would be overrun by the Soviet armies no earlier than December, but certainly not later than mid February.

The war was a lost cause and had been for nearly a full year, but like nearly all lost military causes, the country's soldiers and civilians would find themselves caught up in nationalist fervor, urged to fight on to the bitter end despite the absence of all hope of victory. Very soon "sacrifice" for the sake of the state would replace that of "duty." This was the endgame; when ridiculous pronouncement would drown out any semblance of rational decision. Mengele knew that the time had come to activate his long conceived plan in the hopes that he and his work might escape the inevitable destruction that would coincide with the fall of the Third Reich.

He had already forwarded much of the important results of his research to associates in Brazil where arrangements had and were still being made for his arrival and the continuation of his work. Arriving at his office Mengele opened the door, didn't bother turning on the harsh overly bright overhead lights but walked over in the darkness to his desk, slid into the seat and leaned forward. His fingers reached out toward the small desk lamp and finding the small chain, he gave a light pull that turned on the lamp. A small oval of yellow light spread out across the even grain of polished mahogany. Leaning back in his chair, he opened his top desk drawer and pulled out a pack of French cigarettes, pulled one out and lit it using a heavy crystal lighter. He inhaled the smoke, taking it deep into his lungs, returning the lighter to the desk and placing it beside a matching ash tray. The lighter and ash tray were gifts from his chief sponsor; Heinrich Himmler. Himmler held the lofty position of Reichsführer of the Schutzstaffel, and was a leading member of Germany's Nazi Party. As one of the most powerful men in the country, Hitler had appointed Himmler as the main architect of what would eventually be known as the Holocaust.

Mengele looked at the wall clock mounted a few feet from where he sat. In the diffuse light he read the time to be nearly seven thirty. The nurses and orderlies would be preparing for the next shift and as usual he would be present to receive their reports. He grabbed his pen and clipboard then walked out of the office. As he made his way down the wide aisle leading to the ward containing his most precious patients, he flipped through the notes he made the night before, refreshing and focusing on his goals for the morning. He was greeted by a nurse who stood in front of a counter at her station. A large pot of very black coffee sat on a warming tray. "Sir?" the nurse held out a mug and pointed to the pot.

"Nein fraulein" He shook his head from side to side and frowned heavily. "But perhaps if you were to brew a fresh pot?"

"Yes, Herr Doctor, at once." The woman picked up the pot and left to drain its tar like contents and obtain fresh water.

Mengele walked into the ward and surveyed the scene. There were nearly thirty beds in the ward, but only eight held patients of interest, these cases held the most promise. The other beds in the room would fill or empty with terrifying regularity; those specimens either quickly dying or having fulfilled and more correctly outliving their purpose, were disposed of. They would take their place among the multitude of other unfortunates, to be gassed, and then cremated at an increasingly frenzied rate as Himmler continued to strive in his efforts towards Hitler's "Final Solution."

The captain accompanied by the head nurse and a uniformed orderly made their rounds methodically moving from bed to bed. The nurse spoke only when spoken to, the orderly spoke not at all while obediently following the direction of his superior, adjusting or repositioning the little patients so as to provide the Doctor or nurse clear access to the intentional wounds, operative incisions, and other points of clinical interest. After accessing each set of young twins, Mengele would smile and make an encouraging comment as to their recovery, even if it was highly unlikely to be forthcoming. Having been born an identical twin himself he could relate to the children's plight if only on the most basic of levels.

Frankly, Captain Mengele had long ago concluded that further tests and experimentation yet to be conducted on the little ones were useless and a waste of his precious time. Still he had to keep up the charade and provide forward looking statements to Himmler et al to ensure his true work proceeded as planned. Finishing his rounds in the children's ward he caught the aroma of fresh brewed coffee, and walked over to the nursing station.

15

Midmorning. From their high vantage atop the Stone Pines growing nearby or hidden within leafy thickets, small songbirds gaily twittered and chirped while a scurry of red squirrels tussled and chased one another beneath the verdant spring foliage. The warmth of the season had also enticed small groups of visitors to explore the grounds of the medieval Spanish monastery. Several of the tour groups meandered about the grounds and partial ruins of one of Catalonia's less famous yet well visited historical sites.

An impeccably dressed, very tall, very thin man carried a large leather satchel cradled in his right arm. Walking through the familiar halls, chapels and recesses of the monastery he paused as his corridor opened into an ornate presbytery. There, an attractive young woman with dark hair and deep brown eyes captivated a dozen or so camera toting tourists while occasionally gesturing here or there with a hand. Her pleasant voice and lilting Spanish accent held the tourist's interest and his own as she continued to describe the significance of this most sacred site within the church.

The man had heard all of this before; residing within its walls for most of his lifetime, he could have led the tour of the monastery himself. The old building possessed a long and interesting history that intertwined among some of the most famous figures in history.

The tour group began to move down the nave which would lead them back to the front door of the church where they had originally entered. The woman spoke of that history as they slowly walked on. Her voice carried and echoed within the thick stone walls and floor..."up until 1492, this church, its walls and grounds housed the Carmelites. The Carmelites were a Roman Catholic order established by St. Berthold of Calabria, and its members had spoken vows of poverty." The woman's voice continued to speak but diminished as the tour proceeded a little further.

Blas finished the abbey's secret history in his mind. Unfortunately for the monks, while Columbus sailed westward toward the Bahamas; Pope Rodrigo Borgia inexplicably ordered the monastery to be passed onto the Orden Sempiterno or Eternal Order, an obscure group under the direction of Abbott Cruz Diaz. Those poor Carmelite monks were immediately displaced and while some were taken in by other abbeys, many others simply wandered homeless and destitute.

The woman's voice increased in volume as the group began walking back toward Blas. "Corrupt, worldly, and ambitious, it was rumored that Pope Borgia had been unduly influenced by Cruz Diaz. Hardly a man of God, Cruz was simply a wealthy Baron who only very recently had supposedly taken his vows of poverty and penance. According to the gossip at the time, Borgia had handed the monastery over to Diaz in return for a generous donation of lands and monies. Some historians thought that Diaz was attracted to the site for reasons completely removed from that of piety. There was talk among the local peasants of odd happenings and rituals, even a wild rumor of Diaz living a life of unnatural length. All of this was of course untrue; the peasants of the day were very suspicious of anything or anyone new."

One of the men in the tour group spoke up remarking. "This place reminds me more of a castle than a church." The young woman continued.

"You're quite right for thinking this. In fact, this particular monastery, like many others of its day, once functioned as a military stronghold before its conversion toward more peaceful pursuits. The religious group continued to occupy the monastery until civil war broke out in the early twentieth century. Under direct attack by forces on either side of the conflict; the group was forced to abandon the site… they have never resurfaced. The monastery sat empty until the end of World War Two when the bombed out church and outbuildings were purchased and partially restored by a wealthy industrialist... who as it turns out... is none other than a distant relative of Cruz Diaz. The family retains a small portion of the monastery as a private residence, but has generously allowed the Catalonian government to administer the building and grounds as a historical site." The small group made their way down the length of the cool nave and then out the main doors into the warm spring sunlight.

The ancient building commands a position atop a prominent hill separated a considerable distance from the nearest village. Its towering walls, towers, and ramparts long provided security and privacy for the Order Sempiterno sequestered within and even now continued to fulfill that promise, offering sanctuary to those few special souls still choosing to dwell within its stone walls.

Walking along the pale gray stone floor, the gentleman's black oxfords, each polished to mirror like perfection, clicked and echoed as he made his way down one of many ancient narrow hallways within the monastery. Coming to a large wooden door, his left hand slid back an iron bolt giving a resounding thunk as it slid into place. Placing his shoulder to the heavy door he shifted his weight forward. The tall door swung slowly open upon well oiled hinges to reveal an elegant rectangular room of significant size, the doorway occupied the precise center of a twenty foot wide stone wall while some thirty feet opposite several hefty logs blazed within a massive fireplace. Exquisite works of art from more than a dozen well respected painters graced the walls on either side of the room, while small statues and busts of stone or bronze sat upon long hardwood tables positioned along the rooms perimeter.

Two enormous ornate crystal chandeliers dangled down from the nearly thirty foot high ceilings, the soft glow of their recently modernized electric fixtures provided a peaceful ambience to the room. Below the chandeliers, several long French provincial tufted sofas sat opposite the other, their gracefully carved arms and backs matching and complimenting those of the stylish end tables on either side. In front of the fireplace two huge leather armchairs sat positioned at forty five degree angles, enabling their occupants to comfortably view both the fire and each the other. In one of these chairs sat a middle aged woman, it was her that the thin man approached with an air of deference.

The woman sat motionless in the leather chair. Her flawless ivory skin and aristocratic features flushed warmly in the close proximately of the fireplace. Her dress was not what you would expect from an ageless beauty whose degree of wealth would embarrass many of the world's leading magnates and business tycoons. The calf length royal blue dress she wore was at once elegant yet understated, as were her beige stockings and the light brown slippers each sporting a tiny white bow to the outer side. All of these articles served only to accentuate the exquisite rings on her fingers and most especially, the intricate gold medallion that graced her slender neck.

Blas Velez walked up standing patiently off to one side of his Mistress, whose eyes remained lightly closed in deep contemplation and deliberation. Even so distracted, she had been aware of his coming long before he first entered the long hallway leading to this room. She was in fact aware of the approximate location of the tour groups and all of the abbey's twenty three staff members at any particular moment. The woman's physical senses, while honed to a nearly supernatural plane, could be viewed as almost pedestrian in comparison to this significant clairvoyant ability. It was rumored by some within the Order that her gift of intuition, perception and prediction was unequalled. Events presently occurring near or even at considerable distance from the abbey were often clearly discerned, recognized and suitably acted upon. Her abilities concerning matters of business were legendary; though carefully hidden and guarded, known only to those moving within the most private of circles.

A long moment passed. The woman's eyes opened, her steady unfathomable gaze already trained on his face. Her eyes darted to the satchel he held. "You have the details we require." Her words were a statement rather than a question.

"Yes Madame. The Servicio has confirmed his earlier suspicions that his Mistress, a Gray member of the Sempiterno, has entered the twilight of existence. We have identified the member and pin pointed her location." The thin man's face wore a puzzled expression.

"Yes Blas, I will answer your question." Her gaze left the satchel and returned to his face. Without pause she continued, "This particular member while relatively young in years lived, has engaged in a life of depravity, wonton gluttony and excess. It debased and abused its powers over these last centuries, and now time has prematurely decided to deal with this... succubus." The intonation of that last word was laced with loathing.

Blas nodded respectfully, "We of course will take the appropriate measures."

"Truly there can be no alternative." While those born into the Sempiterno entered without personal choice, the membership cannot permit such a discovery. This had become an ever increasing likelihood - a linear result given the 21st Century's embracement of universal surveillance and the open exchange of information.

"The Servicio may yet convince his Mistress to accept suicide, but given this Sempitor is a Gray, I think this very unlikely." The woman shook her head from side to side. Her memory flashed back to a rainy morning sixty years before to a day when her love told her that he had made the decision to end his life of his own accord. How sorrowfully they embraced upon the cold bleak rampart, that morning he flung himself from the forty foot high inner wall of the monastery, a thin wire noose about his neck. How he dropped thirty of the forty foot height before the wire lead upon reaching its length, tightened abruptly. The force of the drop allowing the wire to slice through flesh, muscle and bone with equal ease, his head separating from his body and both plunging those final feet to the wet grass below. How she mourned her one true love, Cruz Diaz, of the White.

Her mind sprang back to the present. "You will instruct our most trusted associate. Inform him he may employ an assistant of his choosing within America and quietly..." she emphasized and repeated the last word, "quietly convince our errant member to either depart this life with what dignity

114

remains to her, or do what must be done in a most expedient manner. Our agent will also graciously thank and assist our loyal Servicio on his way towards eternal peace."

"Madame." Blas bowed his head ever so slightly and prepared to leave.

"Oh yes, and Blas." The woman paused for several long seconds, "Blas, ensure our friend is fully apprised of this particular individual's considerable talents. While in this stage, our member is exceedingly dangerous and unpredictable, extreme caution must be exercised while engaged in this mission."

Blas nodded and left the room. He would make the necessary arrangements this very night.

Valeria Diaz, Director of the Orden Sempiterno; the Eternal Order, now closed her eyes. Her razor sharp mind considered each possible action and weighed the likely result, much as she had done so over the past five hundred years. Diaz had long known of this particular member's unusually sadistic and sexual proclivities, but those were of little concern to the Order, so long as those activities did not shine an unwanted spotlight in their direction.

16

Two nights later 3:15 a.m. Marty awoke to the sound of a door opening and then closing. Always a light sleeper, Marty walked from his bedroom into the hallway and checking his dad's bedroom, found Reggie's bed empty. He walked down the hall into the dark and empty kitchen and then into the living room. The room was still dark but through the drapes he could see a parked vehicle's headlights in the street and flashing red and white emergency overhead lights; an ambulance.

Marty walked to the front door, opened it and stood on the front steps. The night was warm and the sky was clear, a waning gibbous moon hung low near the southern horizon. Marty scanned the front yard for any sign of his dad or the neighbors, seeing no one he popped back to his bedroom and donned his slippers before leaving out the front door and over to Saul and Adrian's home.

The front door was ajar and all the lights on the main floor of the house were burning. Marty knocked on the front door causing it to swing open. The scene was familiar territory to the experienced detective. Family and friends stood about the room's periphery their expressions a blend of concern and anguish, meanwhile a pair of EMTs, a man and a woman gently lifted a patient onto the ambulance gurney in the middle of the brightly lit room. Marty did a quick inventory of the people in the room feeling relieved to see Saul and Adrian standing nearby. An elderly woman laid motionless and unresponsive on the gurney, an ambulance attendant pulled a sheet across her face. Marty quietly made his way over to his dad and stood beside him. Feeling absolutely powerless, Marty looked on trying to think if there was anything he could do for the family.

A minute later, the female EMT approached Saul and Adrian. The attendant quickly spoke with the couple explaining where they intended to deliver Saul's mother. Saul told the woman that according to Jewish custom, the body could not be left unattended and since there was no question as to why she died, he expected her interment could take place within the day. The ambulance attendant made a quick phone call and spoke with Rachel's doctor. Given her recent decline in health, the physician had expected her demise and gave permission to leave the body with the family. Before leaving the home, the attendants lifted Rachel's body atop a portable cot in the living room. Reggie and Marty remained with the couple after the ambulance departed.

Saul and his wife took the news in stride, given her advanced years and full life. A half hour later, Marty and his dad left the couple to make contact with their children and relatives. Reggie promised to call the Kaplan's neighbors and friends later in the morning notifying them of the remembrance gathering at the Kaplan's home. It would take place the day following the funeral, but today, the synagogue and graveside service would be attended by family members only.

Friends, neighbors, out of town guests and family crowded the Kaplan's living room, kitchen and backyard patio. The dining room and kitchen tables were overflowing with appetizers, cakes and deserts of all kinds; most of the food had been brought over by the neighbors and local friends. Judy the owner of the Creek's One Stop Flower Shop had brought over several exquisite flower bouquets that graced a long sofa table and bracketed a large photograph of Rachel taken a decade or so earlier on the occasion when several of her black and white paintings were hung in the Metropolitan Museum of Art.

While Marty's dad mixed with the older guests and neighbors, Marty found an unexpected opportunity to catch up with two of Saul and Adrian's kids who Marty had grown up with and attended school. He and Jacob Kaplan had played Little League and at one time had been best friends up until the last semester of high school when a pretty red head had come between them.

"What was her name?" Marty asked with a smile.

"Marion Barton..." Jacob replied.

"Well, it's been a little over twenty years; my memory isn't what it once was." Marty winked and took a sip of his beer. The two men chuckled over the affair, laughing loudly they recalled the young woman spurning both their advances, choosing instead to attend the prom with a player of the school's football team. That jovial outburst earned the pair rebuking looks from several older women sitting across the room.

"I was talking with your dad earlier. Sounds like you're quite the ace when it comes to solving serial murders." Jacob wore a thoughtful expression. "You know he's very proud of you Marty."

"Yes, I know." Marty replied. "I just hope I can live up to his expectations."

"Oh sure, as if anyone in Hansel Creek has ever held high expectations of you!" Jacob smiled broadly. "Seriously, it must be a tough job, not just catching the bad guys, but dealing with what I'm sure are some pretty gruesome scenes, not to mention dealing with the grief of the victim's families."

"When it comes to the crime scenes, we might attend a few of them, but even at those we do attend, the CSI (crime scene investigator) crews do all the real work. They're amazing people but unlike the TV series, the tests and conclusions often take several months to come in, pretty complicated work and there are a lot of other people working in the background no one ever sees. Did you know there are over five hundred specialists and scientists working in the FBI crime lab alone?" Marty paused and politely waved off a desert plate offered by a smiling and very pretty young woman. "Maybe later, thanks anyway though." The young woman turned and walked toward another small group.

Marty intently followed the woman's progress across the room and was somewhat embarrassed when she suddenly turned and discovered he was watching her. The girl's smile only brightened and her voice twittered happily as she engaged the others with her offering.

Jacob grinned, "Mary Ellen Hastings; my sister's best friend. Hey, by the way, I thought you were already taken?"

"Did I ask her name?" said Marty somewhat defensively. "...you know I can still look, besides, Ann and I are just dating."

"Hmm I hear your "date" is coming to meet your dad and visit for several weeks." Jacob took a sip of smooth twelve-year old whiskey from a crystal hi-ball glass. His comment was greeted by a shrug of Marty's shoulders.

"Dad doesn't leave much to guessing when it comes to keeping folks up to date on my personal affairs." Marty's smile returned.

"Don't worry about Mary Ellen. I'll be happy to take her off your hands, after all I'm still single and fancy free." Jacob drained the dram of whiskey from the ice cubes in his glass. "Time for another refreshment, besides, I guess I should really check if mom needs me to do anything." Jacob nodded toward his friend, "catch you later?"

Marty watched Jacob cross the room and enter the kitchen where Adrian was fussing with a serving plate of fresh hors d'oeuvres. Mother and son spoke for several moments. Marty watched as Adrian patted his shoulder obviously dismissing his offer of assistance where upon Jacob approached the kitchen counter's temporary bar refilling his glass. His attention was distracted by his dad's hand on his elbow; "Marty? There is someone I'd like you meet."

The gathering lasted several more hours before one by one the guests began leaving for their homes. Reggie left the affair somewhat earlier than he intended, evidently one of the hors d'oeuvres disagreed with him and put him out of action. Jacob, his sister Sarah and her friend Mary Ellen had left for a walk around the old neighborhood several minutes ago. As the three of them passed by, Jacob stepped back, momentarily leaning in close to Marty then winked and whispering "now all I have to do is ditch Sarah and I'll be home free!"

That left only Marty and a few final hangers on. Adrian asked if Marty would see the last of their guests out while she busied herself in the kitchen. Several of the neighborhood women offered to help Adrian straighten up but being particular, she insisted doing that sort of thing all on her own. Truth was she very much enjoyed it and today she felt she needed the distraction.

Marty was looking at the selection of Rachel's paintings and sketches that were set up on make-shift easels in the living and dining rooms. The young detective reflected on the fact that while Rachel Kaplan's works obviously pointed to an incredible talent, her subject material was extraordinarily narrow in scope and frankly; rather cheerless. The display consisted of charcoal sketches and black and white painted renderings of the years she and her family had spent imprisoned within the Nazi camps.

Marty spend several minutes examining two, ten by fifteen inch oil paintings. The first painting depicted a female SS guard sitting on the side of a prisoner's bed with her head and face low and bent close to a young woman who lay on the bed. The guard wasn't touching the woman, but judging by the frightened open mouthed expression on the woman's face and the way her hands were held rigidly at her side tightly gripping the bed sheets, the guard wasn't there out of concern for the prisoner's wellbeing. Marty could see the woman's eyes were wide, staring up at the hidden face of the guard. Looking more closely, he wasn't positive but he thought there was also a trace of a white cloudy mist floating in the air between their bodies.

In the painting next to the first, the guard was standing with her back turned to the woman prisoner. The guards' face appeared bright and refreshed; what Marty's mother would have termed a healthy glow. For a moment, Marty thought the guard appeared quite attractive... Marty quickly admonished himself; the guard and others like her had proven themselves monsters in their treatment of the prisoners in their charge. Chiding himself, he consciously directed his eyes back to the image of the prisoner still lying on the bed. Marty was shocked to see the woman's features had changed appreciably from the first rendering. While the woman in Rachel's first work appeared emaciated, probably from lack of food and overwork, she certainly appeared to be in much better shape than that depicted in the second painting. No longer did she retain any semblance of youth, but rather, looked emptied, gaunt, maybe used up would be the best term. Marty wondered as to the significance of the paintings, if any.

"Did you know my Mother donated all the money she received from the sale of her paintings to groups like B'nai Brith and Amnesty International?" A little startled, Marty hadn't heard Saul's approach. "Uh, no. I hadn't." Marty's attention was again focused on the two painting before him.

Saul noticed Marty's interest. "Unusual aren't they? There are other sketches and water colors showing this very same guard." There are still two large chests full of mom's stuff downstairs, rough drafts of these and other paintings, sketch books, and even a couple of diaries that are so detailed that I assume Mother must have written her thoughts down shortly after the Soviet Army liberated the camp."

Marty closely looked at the female guard then muttered, "She ain't pretty; she just looks that way." Marty quietly chuckled as he recalled the line from an old song then immediately regretted saying it aloud.

"Sorry Marty, what was that?" asked Saul turning his face toward Marty's.

"Nothing Saul, just my bad attempt at humor, nothing more." Marty continued to examine the paintings and found it difficult to turn away.

"Most of them are very disturbing..." Saul continued, "A few I came across I wouldn't dare bring into a room of decent people; they are thoroughly offensive." He shook his head, "I suppose there are few people that could imagine what it was like to live under those conditions. Mom actually gave evidence at war crimes trials just after the war."

"Saul, I wonder if I could read your mom's journals... that is, if you don't mind, I'd like to approach Rachel's notes from a professional view point. In my work I run across criminals... sociopaths, psychopaths and the like, I believe that many of these people have similar characteristics. It could benefit my work; maybe even help catch more of these animals. Serial killers are notoriously difficult to identify and even harder to convict."

"Marty, I can't believe my mother would object." Saul added, "Why don't you come over next week? We'll be a little more organized by then."

"Sure, that would be fine." Marty put a hand on Saul's shoulder. "In the meantime, if you and Adrian need any help from either me or dad, please let us know."

17

Sitting at the kitchen table, Reggie rubbed his eyes then turned to the sports pages of the Claremont City Post's Late Edition. With the wire rimmed reading glasses perched upon his nose, the old man worked his arms moving them in and out, trying to bring the newspaper's fine print into proper focus. It wasn't working. Reggie slapped the paper down onto the table, took off his readers and studied the lenses intently as if the prescription might somehow have changed since the last time he wore them. Marty had seen the time honored ritual several times and watched his father with some amusement.

"Dad. What you say we give Dr. Stephenson a call tomorrow and make you an eye appointment?" Marty cleared away the remainder of the dishes placing them in the sink to disappear among the wash suds.

"Maybe I should, these things don't work worth a damn." Reggie grinned. "You know I haven't seen that old quack for some time." The good doctor became the "old quack" ever since Stephenson moved ten miles north to the town of Knots Ridge and started pitching for the local softball team. Reggie wouldn't have normally minded, but Stephenson was the best pitcher in the regional league.

Marty continued to sponge and dry the supper dishes and cutlery while half listening to his father going on at some length about the leagues teams, players, coaches and statistics. When Marty had placed the last glass in the cupboard he politely interrupted his father who was pretty much talked out on the subject anyway.

Knowing his father's answer before he spoke Marty asked, "Feel like going to Misty's for a beer tonight?" Marty felt the need to get out of the house; the last several days had been rainy and dismal.

A half hour later the couple left the sidewalk, the younger man pushing open the pub's frosted glass door onto which the name "Misty's" had been etched . It had been years since Marty had walked through that very door, and many more since he and several young friends had leaned on or carried each other out the same door after concluding a raucous night of carousing. Entering the small dimly lit establishment brought a flood of memories to the detective, the place hadn't changed a lick; it even smelled the same.

There was a smattering of regular clientele, men for the most part as well as a few women with escorts. Reggie knew them all, conducted a gruff roll call while waving an arm in their general directions as he did so. Marty picked out an empty table near the center of the room. The small circular table, like the others in the room, was fitted with a tight terry cloth cover that would help soak up any spills.

"Still no TV's I see." Marty remarked to his dad. Reggie nodded absentmindedly and cast a wave to the middle aged woman minding the bar. "Not exactly what I'd call a sports pub." Marty exhorted mildly, he'd hoped to catch part of the Mariner's game.

Reggie replied, "Nay, Mitch still refuses to make any changes; says people should talk to each other rather than quietly stare or shout at a screen... otherwise why bother going to a pub, just stay at home." Marty thought on it for a second and had to admit the guy had a point.

They ordered a couple of beer that were delivered shortly afterward along with a complimentary bowl of salted peanuts. Marty took a long quaff from his mug. Replacing the now half empty glass on the table he wiped away a small trickle of brew from his chin with the back of his hand. His thirst surprised him.

The two men spoke on a number of subjects, though it was mostly Marty's dad who provided a running commentary of those seated at the tables about them. Every once in a while Marty would catch a wayward glance in their direction; no doubt he and his dad were the subjects of other conversations as well. Presently Reggie ran low of gossip and excused himself to use the facilities.

Alone now, Marty took the opportunity to survey the tavern. On the wall opposite the entrance stood a long, dark stained wooden bar, a well worn brass foot rail running its length. Behind the elbow polished bar top, mounted upon the mahogany panel wall were several thin glass shelves and behind those, a row of smoke mirrored tile reflecting bottles of seldom requested liquors, many of them unusually shaped or colored glass, all of them for display only; the bar brands being stored handily beneath the bar's countertop. To the left were three beer spigots, each bearing the name of a popular beverage. Mounted upon the pub's left wall, a neon sign reading "Drink Coca Cola" glowed cheerily, the fire engine red trademark surrounded by a selection of beer and whiskey signs, a number of the signs were clearly antiques. Upon the right wall, near the far corner a dart board bristling with a collection of colorful missiles beckoned while to its side stood a black wrought iron cue stand presenting the players a bridge or as the fellows referred to it, a "ladies aide". There were cue sticks of various lengths, weights, warps, and nonexistent tips, all guaranteed to make a good shot next to impossible. The ancient three by seven foot, coin operated pool table sporting oversized pockets, a thin beverage stained felt and tired cushions occupied a position just a tad too close to the back wall requiring that a player use an undersized cue, none of which were present. Above the table, a brass table light with a green Shade was swagged overhead of the table doing what it could to illuminate an entire section of the barroom.

Marty felt a hand on his shoulder and jumped a bit. Reggie returned to the table with another gent in tow. "Marty, I'd like you to meet our sheriff, Norm Billings." He turned to the large heavy set man standing next to him. "Norm; my boy Marty." The two men shook hands.

Norm was about to carry on and walk back to his own table then paused waving to a very attractive young woman about Marty's age. She sat watching the men or perhaps more to the point; Marty. The sheriff asked, "Say... is it ok if I join you fellows for a few minutes?" Marty nodded and waved to an empty chair though his gaze was still held by the woman seated at the sheriff's table. Norm pulled up a chair and noticing the subject of Marty's attention offered, "My daughter Julie, she's up to visit Maggie and I from Seattle." Norm swung his considerable bulk forward, moving closer to the table. "Speaking of which, your dad here tells me you're a detective with Seattle P.D."

Marty didn't answer. Norm continued, "Says you work homicide?" Still receiving no response Norm waved his hand before Marty's face. The young man immediately blushed and offered a hasty apology to which the older man just smiled and quipped, "Don't worry son, it happens all the time. She's the spitting image of her mother when she was her age. "

Marty collected himself, "I'm sorry Norm, you were saying?"

"You work homicide?" Norm repeated.

"Yes, for the last two years, but I've recently been reassigned to an FBI taskforce investigating serial killers operating in the northwestern region." Marty tried not to appear overly self-important. "I'll just be a small cog in a much bigger machine, but it will be quite a learning experience. I feel pretty lucky."

Norm's face turned serious then remarked, "It's been my experience that coppers make their own luck. Never sell yourself short. In this business you have to look sharp, act sharp and be sharp. Missing something obvious can cost people their lives." The sheriff face was expressionless then he continued. "Look Marty, let me get to the point. I know your visiting your dad and I don't want to intrude, but I'm facing a tough situation here. There are people missing, too many people for my liking and of the kind that shouldn't be going missing and simply never turn up." Marty's face showed Norm that he had the sheriff's full attention. "I was wondering if you could spare an hour or so and go over our files; maybe a fresh set of eyes could pick out something we might have missed. I've got good people, but aside from me, none of them have any experience in this sort of thing. It would mean a lot Marty."

Marty looked thoughtful and then grew determined. "I can't promise anything but I'd be happy to do whatever I can." He paused before continuing, "I could drop by tomorrow... say mid-morning?"

The sheriff nodded and stood up from the table. "Fine, that'd be just fine. Thanks Marty. Be sure to get Reggie back home before he has too many beers and I have to lock him up again." Reggie just grinned and waved the man off.

Marty and his father watched the sheriff walk toward his table where his daughter was already on her feet, a small purse in hand evidently prepared for their departure. The sheriff removed his wallet and threw a couple of bills on the table. Julie tried to be nonchalant, panning the bar before casting a quick but purposeful glance towards Marty's table. Happily seeing she still held the young man's attention, Julie gave Marty a smile and a quick wave then followed her dad from the bar.

"I'm glad you're going to help Marty. Norm worked in Chicago for years, from what I hear he was well thought of. He's good people and we're lucky to have him as sheriff." Reggie finished his glass and set it down on the table. "Well, I'm a little tired son, mind if we go?"

"Sure Dad." Marty glanced up at the Budweiser clock, there was still an hour or so left in the ball game. "Yeah, let's head out pop." On the way home, Marty had already begun making a mental list of what he wanted to check on during tomorrows visit to the sheriff's office.

The next morning dawned clear and sunny. After his morning run followed by a light breakfast, Marty put on his Shades and fired up the beamer. Marty drove the Z4 the long way about town, first stopping at the Fast Gas to fuel up and check the oil before continuing on to the Sheriff's office.

The office was smaller than he remembered, being attached to the county court house it could be easily overlooked by a casual visitor driving through town. Marty parked his car in the parking lot beside the court house and walked toward the building. He passed the series of large frosted windows providing natural light to the lower floors, their heavy iron bars mounted atop the Gray cinder block walls gave a strong hint as to the location of the sheriff department's holding cells.

It was turning into a gorgeous day and Marty promised himself to take the BMW for an afternoon spin by way of Lakeside drive. The scenic secondary highway wound its way between Lawrence Lake and the Ingalls Forestry Reserve. For a moment he thought he might take the side road leading up to the viewpoint atop Devil's Head Hill, but reconsidered remembering the road's rough graveled surface and his car's low clearance.

Entering the front entrance he stood for a moment, taking in his surroundings and removing his sunglasses sliding them into his shirt's breast pocket. A long flight of marble steps to his right led to the second floor and a wide mezzanine stretched out before the county's two court rooms. A single, large elevator was situated against the far wall while to his left a set of double glass doors led into the sheriff's office, the right door was propped open with a stop.

Marty walked into the front of the office approaching a long blue counter that stretched out on either side of the entrance. Several sets of imitation ivory pen holders together with cheap plastic black pens chained to the bases graced the worn arborite top. At the far end of the counter a small wooden gate controlled entry to the office recesses. At present, the front office was unmanned although the steaming mug of coffee and the partially eaten Danish sitting beside the desk's computer screen and keyboard promised someone would appear shortly. Moments later, a uniformed deputy appeared from the doorway of a small office along the back wall.

"Yes Sir, good morning." A young deputy gave Marty a quick wave as he strode up to the counter. "How can we be of service?"

A quick glance at the deputy's shield provided Marty with the officer's name. "Morning Henry, I'm Marty Denton, here to see Sheriff Billings."

"Right..." The officer took a quick glance toward the large office clock that hung on the wall to his right. "The boss told me you'd be coming in this morning after ten; looks like you're here a bit early. He's discussing an upcoming case with the A.D.A. (the officer referred to the Assistant District Attorney), but he should be back soon."

"Ok Henry, is there a place around here I can score a coffee?" Marty asked.

"Well you could nip on over to Dead Man's Doughnuts cross the street or take a chance with our pot in the coffee room." Henry noted the detective's puzzled expression. "Ah bad joke... Tim Horton's, cross the street." Henry referred to the famous Canadian hockey player who was killed in a car crash after beginning what would later become one of the leading coffee shop franchises in North America.

125

Marty replied, "Thanks anyway, I'll take my chances here." The telephone at the officer's desk rang loudly, the young officer gestured toward the small gate at the other end of the counter.

"Go on, I'll buzz you in. The coffee room is back there down to the right, can't miss it." The deputy arrived at his desk and picked up the telephone receiver, "Hansel Creek Sheriff's Office, Deputy Templar speaking." The deputy continued to watch Marty's progress toward the gate. Henry reached over to the side of his desk and held down a green button. The gate latch buzzed and released, Marty walked into the office.

Pouring himself a cup of java he took a sniff. Still pretty fresh, he wouldn't have to lace it with sugar and creamer. A familiar voice drew his attention away from the coffee counter.

"Detective Denton?" The young deputy stood in the small room's doorway.

"Just call me Marty." He paused, "Sheriff back yet?"

"Matter of fact that was him on the phone, he'll be tied up a while longer than he expected. Sheriff Billings asked me to show you to our report room. You can look over the files he had me pull this morning."

"Great, thanks." Detective Denton followed the officer several doors further down a long hallway. Noticing a lack of personnel in the office Marty remarked. "By the way, where is everyone?"

"Well, our secretary is out with the flu," the officer tilted his head, "that's why I'm answering phones this morning. Half the day shift is in court and the other half is out on the street taking B&E calls. Some drunken asshole decided to bust in the door of a strip mall, once inside he just kicked his way through the drywall separating each store, didn't steal anything, but petty cash. By the time he got to the last place I guess he passed out, the store owner found him sound asleep on the floor. One of our guys is processing him downstairs as we speak but either way, we got stuck with a ton of paperwork."

"Been there, done that." Marty replied. "In uniform I worked in an industrial area, every Monday morning our day crews would be guaranteed to get at least two or three shop break-ins. By lunch time your hand would cramp up." They'd reached the report room.

Upon a three by eight foot table sat along one wall, a selection of manila files, a pad of standard lined paper, several pens and a yellow highlighter were carefully laid out upon its surface. The deputy walked to the left side of the table and pointed down at the paperwork. "These here are the thirty-three missing person cases assorted in chronological order, left to right. The oldest we have is just over twenty years, the most recent about a couple of weeks ago. None of these people have ever been seen again."

Noticing a nearby photocopy machine Marty asked, "You think the Sheriff would mind if I make some copies for the file summary?"

The deputy just shook his head, "No problem. You need anything at all, just ask; hear?"

"Will do Henry, thanks." Marty pulled up a chair and flipped open the first folder. The face of a handsome blonde haired youth grinned up at him from a 5x7 photograph attached to the body of paperwork below. Marty read the now slightly yellowed label: Timothy Russell Williams – October 25, 2012.

It was just after twelve noon when Sheriff Billings stuck his head in the report room. Marty was shuffling a selection of photocopies together accompanied by several pages of handwritten notes.

Billings walked into the room and stood at Marty's shoulder. "Damn sorry I'm so late Marty." The Sheriff shook his head wearing an air of frustration. "Got ambushed at the A.D.A.'s office, the presiding judge unexpectedly kicked up the court date by a couple of weeks... the boys upstairs had a bit of a melt down... no matter."

"No apology necessary Sheriff. I work alone when I go over case files; I like to let the officer's reports and witness statements speak to me in their own language. By the way, you were quite right last night."

"How so?" Billings looked at him quizzically.

"You have some good people working for you. I've seldom seen such detailed reports except from seasoned investigators. I especially appreciated the typed witness statements, not having to decipher the usual chicken scratching makes my job a lot easier." Marty wore a sincere expression.

"Thanks Marty, but I can't take much credit; I've only been Sheriff here the past five years." Norm Billing's proud countenance grew expectant and hopeful. "Any luck?"

"Buy me lunch and I'll let you know." Marty jested.

"You're on." Norm smiled, what do you feel like eating? Marty picked up the papers and the men left the room while Marty considered the question. They were half way out of the office when Marty gave his one word reply, "Chinese?"

Half an hour later, the waiter cleared away the dishes and after refilling the coffee mugs left the two men to talk in private.

Marty handed the manila envelope to Norm. "Have a quick look at my notes and I'll fill you in on some ideas I've come up with." He watched the Sheriff as he opened the folder, removed the content's photocopies and loose leaf papers, carefully reading Marty's observations.

After five minutes or so Norm looked up. "I was afraid you'd come to some of the same conclusions I arrived at earlier."

Marty nodded. "Yes, given the striking similarity of the victims, especially over the first fifteen years, as well as the steadily decreasing periods of time between disappearances, I'd say we are unquestionably dealing with a serial killer."

"What about the lack of bodies?" Norm asked.

"People can always be expected to go missing from time to time and never be heard of again. These are usually your accidental deaths where people head off into the woods without telling anyone, maybe fall into a tight crevice or are swept away in a river... that sort of thing. But given enough time, most of these bodies will eventually resurface somewhere. You probably remember investigating mysterious disappearances that turn out to be suicides after the bodies are discovered; often the person didn't leave a note hoping the insurance would pay out, or maybe they did leave a note, but relatives got rid of it for the same reason." Marty saw Billings nodding.

"We also see teens running away from home, wives leaving abusive situations, and in rare cases men or women running from criminal situations; all of these share a commonality – they don't want to be found and often go to great lengths to ensure they are never discovered." Marty paused.

"I think I've eliminated seven cases that might possibly fall into one of these groups I've mentioned. There is no reason to waste time and resources chasing down red herrings. This leaves twenty-six possible victims of foul play, whose bodies have never been discovered. Our killer has been active for at least a couple of decades, perhaps more. Given the longevity of his crimes I think we can assume we're dealing with a very selective and very careful individual... or individuals. We could be dealing with a team of killers, this has happened many times before, in many places. If they're able, people will naturally gravitate toward others like themselves; the internet has made this increasingly likely. Take the "incels" for example, men who remain involuntarily celibate."

"Incels? You mean those losers that can't get a date to save their souls then decide to murder folks?" Billings derided.

"I never like referring to anyone as a loser, but yeah most of these guys are definitely deranged and in need of some serious help. The incels or even the "me too" movements are clear examples of how things can spin out of control when like minds team up... for good or evil. Collective extremism makes society less safe and our jobs that much more difficult."

Billings spoke up, "So you saying if the original guy took on an accomplice it could explain the variation in the choice of the victims over the last five years or so."

"Quite possibly, or as the killer ages he or she becomes physically less able to prey on a certain type or their tastes simply change along with whatever sick fantasies turn them on." Marty looked at the Sheriff. "This could be especially true seeing that some of our most recent cases involve young teens. I'd also like to look further into the case of that abducted child that went missing from her parent's home a short while ago, what was her name? "

"The little Connelly girl? Shelly." The Sheriff ventured. "Just outside our jurisdiction, but we do whatever we can to help the investigation if asked. The State investigators are handling the case."

Marty produced a small map of the region bearing a smattering of circled numbers 1 through 26. "Yes, I've plotted the disappearances on a map. You can see her home sits only a couple of miles distance from the event epicenter."

"Marty, this isn't common knowledge, but one of the canine guys came across some partial foot prints near the edge of the property while conducting a perimeter check. The dog didn't react at all but the trail led into and out of the property from the south, then disappeared in heavy bush; it can get pretty thick out that way. At first some thought they may have belonged to the missing child, but the State Police Crime Scene investigator enhanced the photos and given his measurements concluded they belonged to a man." The Sheriff sighed and then continued.

"Let's face it though; those tracks could belong to a reporter or newscaster, they swarmed the place before we figured it could be an abduction, by then any hope of securing the perimeter had come and gone. Even so, it could be that whoever it was came in on foot, made the snatch then took the girl through the woods to a waiting vehicle somewhere else. I can't see someone driving up to the farm house and parking in the yard, it would be pretty brazen."

"Yes. Unlikely. Have they considered it might be one or even both of the parents?" Marty asked.

"The State Police are working that angle, especially since the kid had a yappy little dog that usually slept in her room, though they can't say for sure the dog was there that night." The Sheriff added, "Both passed polygraph tests and underwent multiple interviews, looks like a dead end, at least for now."

"Hmm." Marty looked thoughtful while Billings continued to study the map.

Norm commented, "Looks to me that for a while the events were moving closer to the Creek, and then two years ago they stopped completely, before starting up again eighteen months later."

Marty suggested, "Police aren't the only ones who use maps and police investigation techniques to avoid detection. Could be for a while he, or they hunted elsewhere, just in case someone was getting too close to figuring out what was going on. I hate to ask, but when did your department start wondering if these missing person's cases were something more? "

"I see your point, could it be a cop? Could be, but I doubt its one of ours, we pulled these cases after the Connelly girl went missing and the state boys asked us to review our files. Christ I don't know why we didn't think to put the pieces together before that. That's why we're trying to get a handle on the situation ourselves, and why I asked your opinion. Aside from saving a little face, we'd all like to get this guy ourselves. These are our people he's been preying on."

18

Teun De Torres and Blas Velez walked the hallways of the abbey. Over the past week, Teun had gained limited freedom within the abbey's walls and may in time earn the right to leave its grounds. In the meantime, the boy's continued education was paramount.

Blas leaned against a warm sun dappled rock wall and took a deep breath of the fresh blossom scented air surrounding the well tended garden.

"Yes, causes of premature death are often suicides. Mostly due to boredom in old age, or guilt and depression in youth; the term "youth in this case" should be taken to refer to the first hundred years or so of life. Obviously accidental death rates must be very low, given your incredible powers of regeneration and healing. Still, this is balanced to some degree by the much increased likelihood of a mental illness occurring at one time or another in your overly long lives. Studies indicate that as many as 1 in 5 humans may suffer episodes of some mental illness at one point or another within their lives. Now extend that lifetime by a factor of five or ten and draw your own conclusions."

"You might identify with another young person who finds themselves disassociated from societal norms and just possibly responsible for the deaths of people close to them. Such people might contemplate suicide, or as they drift toward the psychopathic and sociopathic realms, begin associating with criminal misfits? Later at some point, they might conclude that in many ways they are superior to those humans that surround them. In the end it is inevitable that Sempitors consider themselves totally divorced from the rest of the human race. Isn't that mental distancing a necessity? A prerequisite to survival? Ask yourself how many predators can afford to feel sorry for their prey? Can a lion empathize when taking down a wildebeest or do you consider the welfare of the chicken when you go out for wings?

As a Sempitor, you may wonder what happens as you reach the end of your life. Here is the hard, fast and irrevocable rule. Every Sempitor whether White or Gray, if they manage to survive the centuries, will eventually reach old age, and at that time, they face a final decision. Do they commit suicide or seek an assisted death? In doing so, they would pass from this world with some degree of dignity or dare I say nobility? Or do they refuse to accept the inevitable and try to outrun their destiny in a cowardly race with death?

Should you choose the latter, rest assured you will not "go gently into that good night," oh no, those Sempitors instead choose to "burn and rage at the close of the day." The transformation will begin within your mind, a creeping dementia, towards the end you will be robbed of all reason and thought, all your will and intent shall be bent towards a single end; that of feeding.

Within the space of a single year at best, you will find yourself aging with incredible rapidity. As I have referred in the past, you will become what we term, a Shade. Growing ever more ravenous you will be driven to consume the life force of humanity in ever greater numbers and quantity and yet, this will never satiate your hunger or act to sustain your body. Within humans, the nearest condition approaching this process is that of a cachexia, where despite eating, extreme weight loss and muscle wasting may be brought on by cancers, HIV, or multiple sclerosis to name just several causes.

In the final stages you will experience a drastic change in appearance; your face and skull become misshapen as you lose fat and muscle tone. Your skin will grow pale, thin and scaly; pulling and distorting your facial features. Many will sport a terrible grimace in which your gums recede from your teeth, giving the false appearance of long fangs. The skin will cling and hug your frame and you will appear and in fact become a walking skeleton.

Yet... despite this lurching rush toward physical ruin, the life force you consume from your victims will continue to fuel and augment the carnage you will sow among your human victims.

At this stage, your body is now sieve-like, the life force falling away almost as quickly as it is consumed. Appearing wraithlike, these deathly white, living corpses finally desire an end to their plight. Experiencing a wish for death's release they will often seek the companionship of the dead, going about sleeping in cemeteries, mausoleums and such. Somewhere deep within their subconscious, they somehow realize their actions will attract unwanted attention. These dying creatures hide themselves away where they won't be found, often only venturing out after dark. In the end, like animals sensing the approach of imminent death, they crawl away to hide and die; alone.

Does this sound even vaguely familiar to you? It should if you've ever heard the name of Dracula. You might be interested to know that the origin of that particular tale is tied to your own kind... but I speak prematurely, there are more central themes to discuss. Such as, how did your kind come to exist?

"Woo-hoo!" Ike Tate gunned the engine and cranked the wheel sharply to the left sending the Black vintage 1955 Chevy pickup yawing to the right, the rear tires spinning in the loose gravel and sending up a rooster tail of dust and rocks. The truck skid and swept about the turn in a graceful arc, Ike might be liquored but he could still drive better than a lot of folks could sober. He loved to run the length of the winding forestry road bordering Devils Head Hill, especially on a belly full of beer with a whiskey chaser. He glanced at the small clock mounted in the center of the dash, just after 9:15, hell if he kept up this pace he'd set a new best. "Gonna make it happen buddy!"

That buddy, Eddie Swan, who would normally be fully engaged and egging on the driver, found himself rather subdued on this particular evening. Guts rumbling, seeing double and his head swimming, all the while hearing his father's time honored adage repeat over and over in his head like a skipping record, "Beer before liquor, never been sicker, liquor before beer, you're in the clear." What a load of shit, pretty much like everything else his old man ever told him before he was sent off to prison to complete a fifteen year stretch for slashing a guys throat open with a broken liquor bottle during a barroom brawl. Truth was, too much booze or beer on an empty stomach was always a disaster... he should have known better. Now they were only half way around Ike's favorite route and he figured the odds were fifty-fifty that he'd puke his guts out by the time they hit the next corner.

Eddie shouldn't have worried. He'd closed his eyes and was busily holding back a wet burp he feared might turn into something more substantial when it happened.

Half way through the familiar turn Ike suddenly yanked the steering wheel in the opposite direction yelling "Christ, what the fuck!" The truck's center of gravity first shifted violently to the left and then to the right as Ike fought to keep control of the vehicle. As the truck veered toward the ditch, Eddie heard Ike shout something that sounded like, "grab your ass buddy, we're going in." Then the lights went out.

Eddie awoke some time later lying face down on a mossy embankment within the Ingalls Forest Reserve. The dried blood caked on his face and eyes gave him an indication he'd been out a while. He wiped them open with the back of his hand. Eddie winced, if he thought his head hurt before the crash, it was nothing like the pain he experienced whenever he shifted his head. Even so he forced himself to look about and take stock of the situation. Somehow in the process he'd been thrown clear of the wreck, landing on a bed of spongy moss some twenty feet higher than Ike's pickup that lay in the rock strewn ditch. The Chevy sat on its roof some thirty feet distant, even from this vantage and the meager light provided by the moon's first quarter; he could see Ike was going to have one hell of a time restoring the truck, not to mention the cost and time trying to find original parts anywhere in the state. But meanwhile, just where was Ike?

"Ike. Ike. Man, you out there?" There was no reply. Eddie leaned forward. Reaching for a nearby sapling, he gripped the trunk to steady himself as he rose to his feet. He stood erect swaying on his feet for several minutes and balancing himself precariously on the bank's tilted surface. He took a tentative step forward then immediately regretted the attempt. Still half drunk and dizzy Eddie lost his footing and fell back, his tailbone striking the rock hard root of a tree. The impact sent waves of pain shooting up the length of his spine and reverberating within his injured head; he very nearly passed out. He sat motionless for several minutes before he chanced moving again and carefully shuffled his butt off the tree root and onto the mercifully damp soft moss. For a time Eddie considered staying where he was for the night and climbing down to the road in the morning light, but there was Ike to consider, what if he was badly hurt, maybe bleeding out in the overturned truck. No, sitting tight wasn't an option; he steeled himself as he began his slow descent down the steep embankment.

"Grab your ass man, we're going in." Ike yelled as if a banshee. He fought the steering wheel and the laws of physics that dictated the inevitable and incontrovertible finale of the night's festivities. In taking the turn in the road with speed, Ike had guided the Chevy into a controlled yaw that saw all four wheels spinning and sliding in the pea gravel. When the headlights revealed the danger ahead, he found himself faced with a series of split second decisions, none of which had a chance of preventing a bad outcome.

Rather than hit whatever was crossing the road, Ike yanked the wheel and braked hard at the same time. From the moment the trucks wheels locked in a full skid, what little control Ike had over the vehicle disappeared completely. For Ike, time had slowed to a crawl, the event playing out as if in slow motion. The trucks right wheels were the first to leave the road's sharp shoulder and drop downward toward the awaiting ditch. When the left tires followed suite, Ike felt the truck enter freefall and begin a roll that wouldn't slow or stop until the vehicles forward momentum had been entirely spent. At some point as the vehicle rolled and spun about, while Ike was jostled and wrenched about in the cab, his eyes fell on his passenger;

for a brief second the passenger door flashed open then closed, and Eddie was gone.

Ike was pretty sure he hadn't passed out, but after Eddie disappeared he couldn't seem to recall anything else until after the truck came to a stop; resting upside down on its roof. He hung upside down in the cab suspended by his seatbelt looking out where the front windshield had been. One unbroken headlight remained, dutifully illuminating the rock strewn landscape before him. Ike heard the engine run on for several more seconds before it began to cough, chug and finally shut down. Fumbling with his seat belt for a minute or so, it finally clicked loudly releasing his body. He dropped in a graceless tumble striking the roof below him abruptly, the impact painfully wrenching his neck and shoulder. Seeking an exit, Ike tried opening both of the trucks doors, but they remained tightly jammed even when he sent several good kicks their way. Ike cursed himself for his stupidity as he simply crawled out of the missing front windshield's opening. Now outside the truck, he remained on his hands and knees for several long seconds before standing shakily.

Ike stood looking out at the boulder strewn nightscape. Where was Eddie? He yelled out several times and listened, but there was no answer to his calls. He'd have to look for his friend, then he became suddenly afraid of what he might find waiting for him in the dark. He was surprised how the crash had seemed to sober him up, "chalk that one up to adrenalin" he muttered "or shock." Christ maybe all he needed was a smoke; that might set him to right. Ike felt for the cigarettes he always kept in his left breast pocket half expecting it to have been thrown out during the rollover, but sure enough it was still there, along with the pack of matches he had thoughtfully stuffed in with the pack. He lit up and inhaled deeply savoring the flavor of the tobacco and the immediate effects of the nicotine rushing into his system. As he exhaled, he suddenly gagged and coughed up a huge hunk of phlegm. Spitting it onto the earth he admitted to himself that like it or not he'd have to quit sooner than later, hell only last year his favorite uncle had passed away from lung cancer.

Half way through his smoke, Ike figured he'd better start looking for his pal. His eyes searched the swath of ditch within the yellow glow of the headlight but found nothing. He started to circle the truck. Stepping carefully as he walked atop the rocky uneven ground, Ike called out Eddie's name. He took his time, moving slowly while he watched and listened for any sign of his friend. Reaching the rear of the truck, Ike was grateful to find the tail lights still working and although relatively dim, in the pitch black along a deserted stretch of gravel road they appeared as bright as search lights. Ike surprised himself realizing for the first time since the accident he was giving thought as to what he had seen crossing the road ahead of them. At first glance he took it for an animal of some sort; maybe a deer or coyote, but now as he tried to mentally visualize the figure; he came away thinking he was pretty sure it must have been a person, but who in their right mind would be out here walking about in the dark. Bathed in the reassuring glow of the tail lights, he took another puff of his smoke then dropped it on the ground and crushed it out with his heel. Like everyone in the Creek, growing up in the lumber town, it was second nature never to give fire a chance to start.

As he continued to walk about the far side of the truck the vehicles lights suddenly dimmed, flickered and died. "Fuck!" He exclaimed, as if things weren't bad enough already. He set about using his hands to guide him sliding them along the smooth side of the truck, every once in a while stopping to light up a match, checking to see if Eddie lay near the truck.

Ike made it back to the front of the truck and propped himself up on the bumper; he checked his watch - almost ten. The night sky was slowly clearing and the clouds present earlier in the evening were slipping away. Another half hour would reveal the moon and stars in their full glory. He'd give it another fifteen and have another smoke. Hopefully someone would drive by... highly unlikely he thought, but you never know. If no one showed up, he'd have to hike out, following the forestry road until it met Big Bend, after that it wouldn't be much further to the Fast Gas station.

Ike opened the match book, then as an afterthought used using his fingers to count off how many he had left in the pack. He was grateful to discover more than half a dozen still remained. Striking a match he brought it towards the cigarette held in his lips. Through the glare of the match, Ike saw a dark outline of someone standing a short distance away. "Eddie? Eddie, is that you man?"

-Silence -

Quickly lowering the match from his face, Ike held the sputtering flame before him peering into the depths of the night. With impossible speed the figure swept close, who, or whatever Ike met in the darkness, was certainly not his friend.

After nearly falling several times, Eddie reached the bottom of the ditch. The moon, though hardly bright, sailed high in the sky above him providing him with a modicum of light by which to navigate. He made his way to the truck and peered into the cab, it was empty. He walked about the vehicle, calling for Ike, exactly matching his friend's movements only an hour or so earlier. Failing locate his friend, Eddie figured he might as well start walking the four or so remaining miles that led to the gas station, or maybe he'd meet someone driving out along the Big Bend. Although Eddie couldn't have known at the time, he'd only have to walk a much shorter distance before his nocturnal journey, and his life - ended.

19

It had been a pleasant drive out from Seattle, the weather cooperated and the miles flew by while she listened to her tunes. Marty had told her Hansel's Creek was pleasant, but that was an understatement. The tree lined streets, green lawns and parks recalled what had been the best of small town America, a throwback to earlier decades, where the future and globalization had yet to intrude.

Ann's Gray Honda Fit rolled up and stopped in front of a small bungalow she suspected was the house number on Collegiate Street that Marty had provided, at least that was the location her GPS indicated. Unsure, she exited the little vehicle walking half way up the sidewalk until she saw the house number peeking out from behind an overgrown shrub. "Must be the place..." she said to herself. She turned to retrieve her bags from the Honda then heard a man's voice call out behind her.

"Can I help you miss?"

Ann turned about. An elderly man stood on a patio stone walkway at the side of the house. The gent must have walked out from the backyard; from the description Marty had provided during their last phone call, she assumed the fellow must be Marty's father.

"Mr. Denton?" Ann flashed a warm smile and gave a little wave then approached the house.

"Reggie, please, you must be Ann. Marty said you'd be coming up sometime this afternoon." Rather slowly, the man walked toward her. Meeting the girl half way up the walk he extended a hand and a smile. Ann was taken aback by Marty's uncanny resemblance to his father and found herself giving Reggie a quick hug rather than taking his hand, then backed away quickly wearing a slightly sheepish expression.

"Well, nice to meet you Anny. You've certainly made an old man's day." He chuckled. "I don't get many hugs from pretty girls too often these days." Ann pegged Reggie's age to be in around seventy or so. His thinning Gray hair was parted at the side while a pair of oversized round eyeglass frames gave Reggie a somewhat owlish appearance. Although slightly hunched, Mr. Denton was on the tall, slim side and in his younger days she thought he had likely been quite athletic.

The sound of the front screen door loudly slapping its wooden frame drew their attention. Marty was already walking toward them.

"Any trouble finding the place?" His face beamed toward the pretty little brunette.

"Nope." She drank in the man's appearance. They hadn't seen one another for nearly three weeks. They hugged for several long seconds then slowly separated, still holding hands while their gaze locked and steadied. She found herself loving the way his eyes held hers. "Maybe there was more to this than either of them realized."

Obviously preoccupied with the girl, Marty had found himself thinking along the same lines. A moment later they remembered Reggie's presence and turned in his direction. "Oh sorry Dad..."

"Ann... this is my dad Reggie Denton; Dad this is Ann Oaks." The old man wore a wide smile while Ann sported a slight blush.

"Already had the pleasure; we were just getting acquainted when you walked up." The old man gestured towards the side of the house. "Got the chairs set up in the backyard, some ice cold lemonade in the fridge that I made only this morning, all by myself." He set off toward the side of the house without waiting for a response. "I'll leave you two to say your hellos and get settled."

Marty and Ann shared another quick hug, grabbing her bags from the car, depositing them in the spare room before Marty presented her with the "five cent" tour.

Holding a beer in one hand and a bowl of potato chips in the other, Marty hip checked the back door open, walked onto to the Shaded patio and joined Reggie at the table. He found the man holding a smoke between his fingers. "Really Dad? Really?" Marty's face wore an exasperated expression. "I thought you gave that shit up?"

"I'm seventy-six years old and I'll do as I please thank you very much. Besides one every once in a while never hurts." Reggie wagged a finger in his son's direction. "Everything in moderation. Moderation... that's the key... makes all the difference." As if to make a point Reggie took another puff. "Where's our guest?"

"She's just freshening up; she'll be out in a minute or two." Marty took another look at the smoke in his father's hand, shook his head then looking upward considered the few fleecy cumulous clouds sailing high in an otherwise clear afternoon sky.

"Seems like a lovely girl Marty." Reggie said matter of factly. After another moment he leaned forward, his voice grew conspiratorial as he whispered, "See anything happening in the future son?"

Marty was about to say something but was interrupted as Ann walked through the back door wearing a white and blue sundress, she grinned happily to discover Marty noticing her tanned and shapely legs. A glass jug sat in the center of the table, "I'd love to try a glass of your lemonade Reggie." The old man smiled and poured out a tall glass.

Like the gentle afternoon breeze, the easy banter and chitchat swirled and drifted about the table. Losing track of the time, an hour or so later, the small group realized that supper time was fast approaching. That was Marty's cue to fire up the barbeque and cook up the juicy steaks that he and his dad had purchased from the Albertson's only that morning.

After dinner, Ann helped her hosts clear away the dishes. She and Reggie took on the task of washing and drying while Marty scraped and cleaned the barbeque. The domestic duties now completed the group returned to the patio to enjoy the remainder of the evening.

As it goes, join people who work together and eventually the conversations inevitably turn to the job. This is especially true of cops and support workers; as a rule they are a close bunch, everyone seems to have a finger on the pulse and departmental gossip. According to Ann, Marty's old partner, Tony Lee, had been assigned a detective trainee from the field. At first he wasn't happy about having to show a newbie the ropes, but as it turned out the guy had been in uniform for nine years and was a far cry from needing a baby sitter. The new team had in fact made a number of good collars; turns out the guy even brought a few decent informants of his own to the table.

There was also the talk of a serial killer resurfacing in the Seattle area. Several bodies had recently been discovered; as with others some months before, the victims appeared to have been killed in the same fashion then dumped in clean packs. This led to Reggie's mentioning Sheriff Billings request that Marty lend a hand looking over some files. Marty cautioned his dad about discussing anything he'd hear at the table with friends in town then went to describe the area's missing persons and what he thought they might be facing.

"All those years... so many poor people." Ann looked thoughtfully at the two men while shaking her head gently.

Marty looked toward his dad. "I told Norm..." then looked toward Ann, "Ah, Norm Billings, the Creek's Sheriff." The girl nodded, and then he continued. "I told him that I'd be starting with the FBI taskforce in another week or so. I'll recommend the team take a look at the situation."

Ann asked, "What office will you be working out off?"

"Not too sure just yet. The team I'll be joining is in the field, we sort of go where we're needed, work out of the closest office." Marty took a sip of the beer he was nursing.

Reggie spoke up with a start, "Hey, look at the time! The Mariners game's already started, probably half way through the second inning." As he rose from his seat he waved at Ann and Marty. "You kids stay and yak."

"Not on your life! I love baseball and they're my hometown team. Let's go!" Ann was the first one through the back door.

Reggie held back a second longer grabbed Marty's arm then leaned in close, "Son, you sure there's nothing major happening between you two? This one sure seems to be a keeper to me." His father released Marty's arm before hightailing it into the house right behind Ann.

Marty remained on the patio watching the two making their way through the kitchen and down the short hallway that led into the living room and the television. Giving his head a slow scratch, he found him asking himself the same question.

20

A light sleeper these days, Norman Stiles awoke at twelve thirty A.M. to his room's flashing lights and the soft, but insistent chime of the house alarm that if ignored soon promised to become a loud annoying siren. He slid his feet out from the bed sheets swinging them to the floor. Sitting on the bed watching the monitor screen on his night table told him all he needed to know. Someone was trying the Hall's front door, and Norman knew exactly who that someone was. He pressed the alarm code silencing the chimes and returning the lighting to normal.

For several minutes he studied the antics of the person standing in the doorway. The security system's night vision cameras clearly showed the shadowy hooded figure busily stabbing random codes into the access panel beside the door. He wondered how many combinations the Master would enter before the Sempitor got it right unlocking the front door. Tonight it appeared a new record would be set. Norman planned to wait several moments longer, but quickly allowed entry when his Master began to push and hammer on the door with a gloved fist. The Master's incredible strength would quickly demolish a simple wooden slab door, but would have little effect on the reinforced steel, even so the heavy impact caused the door to shudder in its frame, while the noise reverberated and echoed throughout the entire structure.

The electric bank vault type locks moved within the sides, top and bottom of the door, the heavy door swung open on silent hinges. Norman watched his Master body fall into the Hall's foyer, landing atop the Gray travertine floor on hands and knees, its black hooded cloak swathed and blurred the figures outline. The outside camera no longer providing an image automatically switched to an inner camera mounted high on the foyer wall. From this position, the camera zoomed in and out, focusing and refocusing on the figure below, the security camera seeking facial features, if found that face would be quickly identified by the system's powerful facial recognition software.

When Norman first installed the system, his Sempitor had coughed up a cool half million dollars to the Orden Sempiterno and a further one hundred thousand per year to gain and retain access to their pirated image data base registry. The amount paid would be excessive and of limited value if the images scanned were gathered merely from the house and ground's cameras alone, but the Order also could hack and access any number of online connected cameras in any given area around the globe in real time. Something even the NSA or CIA could only dream about.

Norman could hear the Sempitor speaking to itself in a garish archaic version of the beloved language he learned as a child. The soft reasoned voice he had grown to know and love decades before was nowhere to be found, misplaced among the manic growled ramblings that spewed forth from the monitor's speakers. Norman steeled and mentally prepared himself to leave his room and attend his Master. He must and would do everything in his power to bring about a return to reason within the Sempitor's mind, just as he had done many times over the past year.

In these instances it now fell to Norman, rather than the Master, to initiate the "joining"; or melding of minds. In doing so, Norman would steady and guide the Master back the long road toward reason and the reality of the present.

Only two weeks earlier, Norman wrestled and fought over twelve hours before he succeeded in rescuing the Master's consciousness from the black yawning abyss into which it had floundered. That most recent episode had been brought on after the Master had fallen upon the three young immigrants Norman had procured and placed in the basement's cells.

Norman hadn't been present that particular afternoon spending nearly three hours in Claremont City performing various errands. Upon his return he found his Master incapacitated and raving. From the state of his Gray Master's clothing, Norman guessed at what he would later discover in the cellars. Norman quickly initiated the "joining" and his exertions continued until nearly five the next morning at which time his master finally recovered. Afterward, he saw to the Sempitor's needs; first removing and stowing the soiled clothing caked with dried blood, moist tissue and gore, then drawing a hot bath for his exhausted friend, remaining at the bedside until his Master rested peacefully.

Nothing in the past had prepared Norman for what he discovered when he entered the cellars to carry out the basement's clean up. Norman had most certainly glimpsed some of what had transpired in the cells during the previous afternoon while joined with the Master; he had not expected the enormity and extremes of violence and mayhem attested to in the scene before him. Tears fell on Norman's cheeks as he went about sanitizing the cell floors, walls and bars. The blazing 980 ° C heat of the crematorium's flames soon made quick work of his master's ruined clothing and the victim's bodies. Norman's outpouring of emotion and dismay did not result from the gory spectacle set before him. The Servicio was well acquainted with the scope of his duties and as such the servant had long ago shed any sympathy for those his Master consumed, irregardless in the manner of their consumption.

Rather, the deep sorrow and desolation that troubled Norman so lay embedded within the knowledge that his beloved Master had now entered the twilight of its life. The Sempitor had begun its transformation from that of an esteemed Gray Master to that of a blacked outcast. Sooner or later, it was impossible to tell, his Master would adopt the tortured and demeaning existence of a Shade. Norman shook his head thinking of the eventuality... not if this Servicio had anything to say about it. He would do everything in his power to persuade the Sempitor to end its life by way of suicide, a decidedly noble means to an end given the alternative.

If Norman's efforts were successful, he would contact the Order and make arrangements to transfer his master's wealth and property to their control. As dictated by tradition, once Norman's duties were completed, he would be permitted to follow his friend and confidant into oblivion; his days ended by his own hand. Such was life for the Servicio of a Gray Master, a mere human who had no doubt witnessed and taken part in atrocities beyond the scope of reconciliation within the human experience. It was different for those serving the Order's White Sempitors; if those Servicio actually witnessed a single death meted out at the hands of their Masters, no doubt it would appear gentle, if not benign - perhaps even as an act of kindness? As such, those fortunate servants would continue in service to the Order, albeit in a less substantial and indirect manner. They would interact and maintain good standing within the human family. As Norman now reflected - those fortunate few would retain their souls.

Tonight, following his Master's unanticipated early morning arrival at the Hall, Norman performed the "joining" and was pleased when the Master responded more quickly than he had expected might be the case. During the meld and later when speaking with his Master, Norman learned a good portion of what had taken place earlier that evening but not all the details as clearly as he would have liked. The Servicio was dismayed, his Master's one time eidetic memory was failing more often now, there were frequent gaps and lapses, Norman thought it not dissimilar to a form of dementia. After caring for his Sempitor's immediate needs, Norman excused himself and made his way across the compound toward the garage. The van's engine purred as it emerged beneath the wide overhead door and within minutes the vehicle had cleared the perimeter gate and now idled at a stop sign positioned on the West end of the Hall's long laneway and its intersection with Big Bend Road.

Norman checked his watch… nearly three A.M. He figured he had a couple of hours at most before the odds favored a motorist coming upon the site of Ike Tate's rollover. Little likelihood of that happening, he turned the van to the right and headed North towards the Devil's Fork intersection. Instead of continuing along Big Bend Road that would take him past the Fast Gas station and onto the Claremont City turn off; Norman took another right onto Lakeside Drive. Five miles later the van passed atop South Bridge, its non-descript Gray metal girders and arches spanned the headwaters of Hansel's Creek before it swept southeast toward the town that bore its name. As Norman crossed the bridge he glanced to the north catching the last glimmer of the setting moon upon the gentle waves of Lawrence Lake lying only a hundred yards or so north of the bridge.

Norman turned onto the Forestry Trunk Road only another mile or so further. He hadn't seen another vehicle since he left the Hall, a good sign. He was nearing the half way point in the Forestry Road when the van's high beams glinted off what Norman correctly assumed was a bumper. He arrived at the accident scene moments later. The head lights revealed the extent of the truck's damage as a result of the rollover… a write off if he ever saw one, not to worry; its owner wasn't in a position to care one way or the other. Norman stopped the van, leaving it parked and its engine running while he used a powerful flashlight to scour the surrounding area for the body he knew was waiting to be found. Several minutes later, he returned to the van and drove it forward another hundred feet or so then stopped, sliding open the side door.

Before continuing, Norman paused, swiveling left, and then right he searched the length of gravel roadway for any sign of approaching lights or engine sounds. All clear, he removed a brand new six by eight foot blue tarp from its cellophane wrapper then carried the tarp over to the body's location. He let his flashlight play over the corpse, the face held that commonly seen expression of open eyed terror forever frozen and preserved in the final moments of life. Pleasantly surprised and grateful, this time it appeared his master had drained her victim's life force without inflicting any of the extreme traumas he had had to recently deal with in the residence's cellar.

Before continuing Norman bent low, taking time to examine the corpse and surrounding ground closely. There wasn't a drop of blood to be found anywhere. Excellent, this shouldn't take too long at all. Too bad the body couldn't simply be left at the scene. Unfortunately the victim's withered, emaciated and frankly unexplainable physical condition, not to mention Mr.

145

Tate's dreadful death mask, would leave far too many obvious questions unanswered.

Norman spread out the tarp, pulled what was left of Ike Tate onto its surface then wrapped it tightly about the body securing it with several bungee cords. He picked up the load and placed it carefully in the back of the van's hidden compartment, the same place he stowed the immigrants earlier, then slid the side door shut. Walking to the other side of the vehicle he stood beside the driver's door and took another quick look about before he got inside. At one point in his "joining," he had the momentary impression that there were two victims, not just one, but he had allowed himself to conduct an adequate search of the area assuring himself Tate was the only one on the menu earlier tonight. Still, he'd keep an eye on the ditches further down the road just in case.

Norman put the van in gear and continued onward down the Forestry Trunk Road making the lonely loop that would take him onto Lakeview Drive, Big Bend Road, then past the Fast Gas station and back home to the Hall. It was one of those odd quirks of fate that a mile further on, several deer crossed the road directly in front of the van. Their passing distracted his attention away from the crumpled, rather bloody remains of Eddie Swan lying upon the road's shoulder allowing the body to linger there for all the world to see when the sun rose later that morning.

21

The black wall phone rang six times in a row. Standing in the bathroom and thinking she heard something, Ann turned off her hair dryer for a moment, listening. The kitchen phone continued to ring. Ann laid the dryer on the bathroom counter and walked to the kitchen remarking, "Doesn't anyone around here answer the phone?" Her comment went unanswered, through the kitchen window she saw Marty and Reggie standing out in the back lane looking under the hood of Reggie's car. The engine ran noisily and black smoke spewed out the exhaust pipe.

"Good morning. Denton residence." Ann said.

"Good morning to you ma'am. Deputy Templar calling, may I speak to Marty Denton please?"

"Sure, he's just outside, I'll call him." Ann walked outside the back door, called out and waved to the two men who looked her way. "Marty, telephone, it's a Deputy Temple?"

Marty yelled back over top the car engine, "Templar?"

Unable to make out what Marty had said. "What?" Ann asked holding her palms up and shrugging.

"Templar, Deputy Temp..." Giving up, Marty just waved and yelled out, "BE RIGHT THERE."

A minute later Marty picked up the phone, "Henry? Marty Denton..."

"Hi Marty, sorry to bother you on a Sunday, but the Sheriff asked me to give you a call. We got a stiff out on mile 7 of the Forestry Trunk Road, Sheriff Billings thinks it might be related to those missing person cases you two are looking into. The boss tried your cell but ..."

"Yeah, working on my old man's car; left it in the house. How long has Norm been out there?" Marty asked.

"Not long, besides he's still waiting on the county coroner; she's up at Knots Ridge. Some guy committed sideways (suicide) in a barn. Just a sec Marty..." Henry's voice suddenly became distant as he'd covered the receiver briefly with a hand; "Yes Sir, I'll be right with you, give me a second." The deputy's voice returned, "Sorry Marty, got a citizen at the counter and I'm by myself. Will you be going out that way?"

"Yes, I'll leave in a couple." Marty replied.

"Know where you're heading?" Henry asked.

"Oh yeah... back in high school us kids used to party out that way" Marty stated.

"Ok, I'll let the Sheriff know, talk later Marty, bye for now." The call ended before Marty could say his goodbyes.

Marty's twenty minute drive to the scene was pleasantly familiar, old memories flooded back as he rounded each bend of Lakeside Road. Little had changed since he and his high school chums had partied out this way. Turning onto the trunk road, he slowed somewhat. The gravel spit and spun up into the wheel wells and pinged off the undercarriage of Ann's Rogue. Knowing his Z24 was ill suited to the short trip; she had traded him vehicles. He checked his rear view mirror; Mile Marker 6 had disappeared after he took the final turn onto the straightway ahead of him. There was a vehicle in the roadway.

Marty slowed the SUV and crept up beside a tow truck. The operator stood at the winch controls near the rear of the truck, his full attention given to a length of cable that snaked off into the ditch in the direction of a Chevy truck that had since been turned onto its side. Marty watched the cable rise level with the tow truck's winch as it slowly tightened, then snapped taught when the slack was removed. The rear tires of the tow truck slid in the gravel slightly for a second before digging in. In response, the half ton twisted slightly, beginning to rise and tilt upward in the direction of the tow truck. A moment later, gravity replaced the pull of the winch and the half ton crashed down on its wheels.

The operator, suddenly noticing Marty's vehicle beside his own turned toward him, "Morning mister, rollover... happened last night. Say what can I do ya for?"

"Hi. Looking for the sheriff, told he was out this way?" Marty said.

The operator nodded and flicked his thumb down the road. "Just around the next bend." The man began walking into the ditch toward the Chevy.

Marty said his thanks then drove down the road. A minute later Marty pulled up behind the Sheriffs Suburban. A patrol car was parked ahead of the Sheriff's vehicle. Norm Billings stood beside the driver's side door, his head and one shoulder propped up in the open window while he spoke on the radio. Exiting Ann's vehicle, Marty noticed a deputy, poking around the tree line some fifty yards distant.

Norm Billings slid the radio mike back into the holder on the dash and met Marty at the back of the Suburban. "Thanks for coming Marty. Wait... you're not thinking about putting in for overtime I hope." Billings laughed.

"Hell no, just having the opportunity of spending a Sunday morning with you is worth my time and more." Marty chuckled. "What have we got?"

The sheriff waved Marty toward the front of his deputy's police car and began to walk over toward the vehicle while Marty followed. Ahead, a yellow tarp was draped across a section of the road's narrow shoulder; Marty noticed a running shoe peeking out one end.

The sheriff bent over the tarp and held up an end exposing the corpse beneath. "Eddie Swan. A local fellow, friendly enough, but still sowing his wild oats."

Marty bent low. Marty immediately looked into the face of the deceased and at first glance was taken aback by its unusually gruesome expression. The corpse of Eddie Swan stared blankly into the blue sky, the pupils of his eyes, opaque in death peered out from their sunken sockets while the shriveled facial skin clung to his facial bones, the medium brown hair he wore in life now appeared nearly black when taken in contrast next to his pale skin. Still, it wasn't anything Marty hadn't seen before; he began to stand then stopped abruptly bending low once more. "What the hell..." he mumbled beneath his breath. He'd only just noticed there was something very odd in the way the body's head sat upon its torso. It took him a moment to figure out what it was.

The sheriff's voice spoke behind him. "That's right; neck broke - head turned right 'round." The chest, waist and legs of Eddie's corpse lay against the cold gravel, but his face on the other hand...

"Fell off, maybe thrown from a vehicle?" Marty immediately made the connection with the wreck down the road, but remembered the skid marks leading to the ditch meant the vehicle was traveling towards this point when it crashed. He also instantly discounted the possibility that Eddie may have walked to this point and then collapsed; no the injuries he sustained were immediately fatal and unless the body had been deliberately moved, this man had fallen where he had died.

"Kind of spooky ain't it." The sheriff continued, "Unless this is a re-run of that Exorcist movie, I think we have to search for some answers."

Marty stood up. "Well it's a might strange that no one found the body earlier, I mean, it is right out in the open." Marty waved his hand towards the roadway. "Judging from the condition of the corpse, off hand I'd say our friend's been dead for a couple of days or so. Still, out here you'd think the critters would have gotten to him by now; he still looks to be pretty much intact – 'cept for the broken neck."

"Yup, I'd agree with your assessment if it weren't for the fact that he and Ike Tate", the sheriff gestured in the direction of the wrecked Chevy. "Ike's being the owner of that black '55 Chevy back there in the ditch. My deputy saw both Ike Tate and Eddie Swan having a couple of drinks and playing pool in Misty's only last night."

"The hell you say..." Marty scratched his chin then examined the corpse one more time. His opinion on the time of death remained unswayed. Something else was at work here. Something he didn't understand... not just yet.

"I was just speaking with the coroner when you pulled up. She'll be out here in about an hour or so, Karen's at a call up in Knots Ridge." The sheriff commented. "Oh yeah, I've got the State CSU (Crime Scene Unit) coming out on this one as well. They'll photograph and go over the accident scene up the road and our friend here."

Marty frowned and stated. "Norm, you're aware the tow truck driver is already loading the pick up?"

"Son of a bitch, that tears it! I told him not to touch anything until I gave him the ok." Billings roared loud enough so that the deputy looked up in the distance to see what had set off his boss. "Jimmy, do me a favor and drive back to the wreck and tell Melvin to stop whatever he's up to. If I go back there I'll kill him for sure." The deputy waved back and started for his car.

"Marty, makes no sense having you hang around here all day. I've shown you what I thought you should see. The rest can wait 'til tomorrow's autopsy if you'd like to tag along?" Denton took the sheriff's outstretched hand gave it a firm shake, "wouldn't miss it for the world!" before say goodbye. Tomorrow should be interesting.

22

Marty Denton pulled his BMW Z4 off the boulevard and into the Claremont City General Hospital parking lot. It was still pretty early in the morning and aside from the employee parking; most of the stalls were still vacant. He drove his small car to the front of the building noticing a Hansel Creek Sheriff's vehicle parked in a stall posted "Police Only"; the man behind the wheel wore a Stetson. Marty pulled his silver sports car into a nearby stall and stepped out just as did Sheriff Norm Billings.

Seeing Marty in the parking lot, the Sheriff waited for him to join him on the front steps where they shook hands and entered the hospital together. They made their way past emergency and then admitting before catching an elevator to the basement where the medical examiner's office and morgue were located. As soon as they left the elevator, Marty felt the air grow cooler and the air conditioning fans grow louder, although he was sure it was his imagination, the clinically sterile atmosphere bore a distinctly sour underlying odor. It was the same in every morgue, Marty figured it was nearly impossible to completely filter and erase any trace of decomposition.

When the two men stepped into the reception area the odor quickly faded and the air warmed to a reasonable temperature. Uncomfortable plastic chairs dotted the room's perimeter while a young woman sat behind a small desk near the back typing on a computer. When the men approached she stopped what she was doing and smiled pleasantly. "Yes gentlemen. How can I help you?"

"Morning miss, we have a meeting with Karen Dodd." The Sheriff glanced at one of two doors leading from the reception area. The clear glass door on the left led to Karen Dodd's office while the frosted glass door to the right led to a viewing room where the next of kin could identify their loved ones bodies. That particular room brought too many sad memories back to the Sheriff.

The woman checked the day timer on the desk and drew a line through the time block reserved for the scheduled meeting. "Please have a seat; I'll let Coroner Dodd know you have arrived." The men turned toward the chairs before a woman's voice greeted them.

"That's ok Sharon." A forty something blonde smiled broadly while she motioned toward her receptionist then extended a hand out to the sheriff. "Hi Norm, how's tricks?"

151

"Can't complain, unlike your customers I'm still on the right side of the turf." Billings chuckled while he shook hands with the county's chief coroner.

"Who's your friend?" Karen shot Marty an inquisitive smile as she turned and pushed open and held the clear glass door behind her.

"Hmm? Oh sorry, Karen Dodd this is Detective Marty Denton out of Seattle. He's been helping us out going over some open cases." The Sheriff and Denton thanked Karen as they walked through the door and down the hall toward her office. She opened the door and entered a small waiting room ahead of the men. Arising from a comfortable plush chair a tall black gentleman grinned toward Marty.

"Marty, I believe you and Elijah know one another?" Karen smiled and stood off to one side.

"Elijah thanks so much for coming down on such short notice." Marty shook the big man's hand. "Elijah Cole, this is Sheriff Norm Billings."

"Deputy Director Cole, it's a pleasure to meet you sir, Marty's told me a lot about you." Another round of handshakes.

"A pleasure Sheriff. Marty tells me you have a strange one on your hands. I can't promise to be of much help but I do have access to a lot of people who can." The Deputy Director turned to Marty. "I should let you know I've spoken to your Lieutenant, Jane Forbes, she tells me that as far as Seattle is concerned, you are now our problem and on our dime. Welcome to the FBI son."

"Thank you very much, I'll do my best." Denton nodded toward the man.

"I'm sure you will." Cole smiled warmly at Marty then turned toward the coroner. "Well, I guess that leaves us in your hands now Doctor."

"This way gentlemen." Karen Dodd led the way down a long hallway, through a large metal door leading into a cool, brightly lit medical theatre where the autopsy of Eddie Swan would begin in a few minutes. At present the body was hidden from view, being covered by a long white plastic sheet.

The coroner slipped on a long lab coat, placed a mask and medical splash guard on her face then walked to the table and removed the sheet. The three men looked on as she stood above a cross vented stainless steel gurney and drain supported by a single heavy square pedestal. Several sinks were positioned near the autopsy table's head, as well as a set of scales. A smaller table set off to her right displayed a carefully placed set of scalpels, rib spreaders and bone saws.

Karen reached above her head grabbing hold of a black microphone with an adjustable spiral cord, flicking the on switch then pulling it down toward her head. She began to recite a well practiced, ordered litany describing each autopsy she conducted beginning with the date, time, and persons in attendance then moved onto the identity of the deceased.

"The subject is twenty eight years of age, 5'10" in height... weight approximately 170 lbs, hazel eyes, medium brown hair. The facial muscles are fully engaged, a pronounced risus sardonicus is present." This abnormal sustained spasm of facial muscles after death lends a horrific grinning appearance to the corpse known as the "rictus grin." "Prior to beginning this general autopsy, the body's head faced 180 degrees about and completely backward. I and assistant Ken Williams completed a post mortem examination and exploration of the cervical vertebrae before returning the head to its natural position... refer to the notes made this date at 07:30 hours. Upon inspection at that time, the Atlas and cervical vertebrae of the spine all showed evidence of extraordinary crush and dislocation... please refer to photos 1 through 8 taken by Ken Williams at that time. It is quite possible that the risus sardonicus or facial grin came as a result of the severe factures observed within the subject's neck and trachea; note this is occasionally seen following a hanging death.

From a visual perspective, "post mortem lividity indicates the body lay on its back for some time after death. Unusually there is no rigor at present whatsoever, nor was any witnessed by me when I attended the scene some fourteen hours after death; the time of death derived from body and ambient temperature. It also appears that the body is in the intermediate stages of decomposition, however this is not supported by my estimated time of death or the facts of the police case which state the victim was alive only the evening before.

The skin is Gray and ... withered in appearance, this unusual condition is observed over the entire surface of the body. Note the eyes are heavily glazed and sunken..." Karen took a measure "to a depth of approximately 3mm within the sockets, possibly a result of unusual structural deterioration of underlying tissues or perhaps a result of moisture loss, again both conditions unusual and unexpected given the recent time of death." The coroner moved onto the rest of the body.

"Back, arms, legs, and upper thorax all show typical contusions, shallow cuts and scrapes remaining consistent with an ejection from a motor vehicle and subsequent contact with road and or ground surfaces." She began working her way into the chest cavity, removing and weighing the principal organs before cutting the scalp near the back of the neck then pulling the entire flap of hair forward - turning it inside out and draping it over the face to fully expose the skull. "The skull has not suffered any visible fracture... but there are four points of discoloration, er... four visible contusions are present on each side of the skull and two more located near the forward cranium indicating a very considerable exertion of pressure has been applied, there are no indications of what might have caused these." The coroner went on to saw open the skull, removing the brain and placing it on the scale. "Brain weight is... 1410 grams... and normal in appearance."

Karen Dodd continued for another five minutes or so before delivering her belief that the direct cause of Eddie Swan's death was that of a broken neck and subsequent asphyxiation. "This is a very strange case. Considering the evidence I'd say it almost appears as if someone had gripped the top of this man's head in both hands and tried to twist off his head." She frowned. "Look, I'll take tissue samples of the organs, muscle and skin and get them off to the lab later this morning. We should have the results back by the end of the week. I am interested to see what they make of the body's desiccated appearance."

Doctor Karen Dodd turned toward the men standing several feet away and studied their faces. "Any comments, seen anything close to this?" she asked with raised eyebrows, "I know I haven't."

Billings and Denton each shrugged and casually stated the circumstances were certainly very strange but when Karen looked to Deputy Director Cole she saw hesitation on his face, almost as if he had something of interest to add to the conversation, but then just as quickly the expression vanished. Instead the big man just quickly shook his head explaining that no matter how often he attended these things, he never felt comfortable. Karen considered it a likely explanation, many seasoned health professionals admitted to feeling the same way. Treating the sick was one thing, dealing with the dead, especially those meeting a violent end was quite another.

The trio of men said their thanks and goodbyes then saw themselves out. The sheriff went back to his office, while Denton invited Cole over to his dad's house for beers. Elijah thanked Marty for the invite but declined saying he had another meeting in Claremont City. Elijah watched Marty leave the parking lot then took out his cell phone and quickly dialed up someone he knew would be interested in what he had just learned.

None of the three bothered going out to lunch that day.

23

The day was Gray and overcast and the forecast called for a steady rain later that afternoon causing Ann and Marty to postpone their planned hike up to the summit of Devils Head Hill. Instead the young couple stood on the neighbor's front step waiting for Saul or Adrian Kaplan to answer the door. Marty reached for the doorbell for a third time before Ann gently smacked the back of his hand. "I hear footsteps - they're coming. Why are you so impatient?" Ann chided.

"No their not, when I phoned over Adrian was vacuuming downstairs and Saul's as deaf as a post." The moment Marty's last word came from his mouth the door swung open.

"Deaf as a post..." Saul stood in the open doorway. "Not by half, least not as long as my hearing aids still work." Seeing Marty's embarrassment the senior grinned broadly. "And Marty, who is this beautiful creature." Adrian was rushing up toward the front door waving.

Marty made the introductions, "Saul, Adrian Kaplan, this is Ann Oaks from Seattle, she's visiting with Reggie and me for a couple of weeks." Ann smiled sweetly and extended her hand to the couple, but Adrian simply brushed past her husband leaving Ann's hand dangling at the end of her arm while the slight woman embraced the girl in a tight hug.

"Oh my!" Taken aback by the warmth of Adrian's greeting, Ann reddened slightly, "It's so nice to meet you and Saul, Marty's spoken of you so often." Adrian released her grip before grabbing Marty and kissing his cheek.

Meanwhile Saul just tilted his head to one side and shrugged. "Don't worry Ann; Adrian's the hugger in our family. Marty, Ann please come in." The senior, very much still a broad-chested man backed away into the living room to allow the couple to enter.

Adrian had laid out some of her best china atop the dining room table along with a plateful of her wonderful chocolate raisin babka. "Coffee or Tea?" she asked expectedly.

Saul broke in. "Or maybe something stronger Marty?" the old man said hopefully.

Marty stole a glance toward Adrian knowing the woman watched her husband's health like a hawk and didn't approve of his fondness for alcohol. Adrian herself was a recovering alcoholic, and Marty knew that no one suffering from the disease ever suggested they were an ex-alcoholic;

155

they never lost sight that a relapse was never more than a sip away. Adrian checked the wall clock; it was nearly twelve in the morning. "Well, I suppose, it's almost afternoon, but just one Saul."

"Yes, yes, just one dearest." Saul winked at Marty and grinned like a schoolboy. Adrian turned to Ann.

"Coffee is fine thank you." Ann took a seat. "You have a lovely home." then paused and continued, "Mr. Kaplan, I was so sorry to hear of your mother's passing."

"Yes." Saul Kaplan smiled thinly. "Thank you Ann, my mother Rachel had a full life although I can say I wish it had been happier. As a young woman she and her family spent time in the death camps." His face grew reflective then brightened once more. "Well. Marty come on downstairs; let's leave the women to gossip while we see what trouble we can get ourselves into."

"Remember, only one husband." Adrian called after the two men as they disappeared into the kitchen then walked down the steps to the basement's rec room. "So tell me Ann. How did you and Marty meet?"

Downstairs the men caught up on the major league baseball standings over several beers while upstairs Adrian softly grilled Ann as to the future of her and Marty's relationship, a subject Ann was only too happy to discuss. Ann had yet to meet anyone who knew Marty as well as Adrian, especially one willing to fill her in on his family's history going back to when he was just a child. Half an hour later Ann felt she had known Adrian for a lifetime; and both women knew they had found a good friend.

Saul was standing in front of the open bar fridge and looked back at the other man. "Another one Marty?" Marty shook his head and held up his half full bottle. The old gent reached in and pulled out another and was just about to crack his third beer when he heard the sound of small feet atop the stairs leading to the basement. Saul quickly returned the beer to the rack and shut the door quickly while Marty just smiled to himself, nothing ever changed.

Saul and Adrian showed Marty and Ann to a spare room that Saul's son Jacob had turned into an office slash studio for his Grandmother's work, it was a shame she used it for such a short time. Either way, a number of her favorite works hung on the longer walls, while a fair sized desk with a tower computer and monitor filled an entire corner. The curious pair of oil paintings Marty had seen upstairs a week or so earlier following Rachel's death hung together upon one of the shorter walls. A large four drawer file cabinet sat beside the desk. Along another wall, a highly polished rosewood

156

bureau with a lift top sat on the carpeted floor; the open lid revealed what were dozens of outlines, unframed paintings and charcoal sketches.

Saul spoke up. "There's a lot to go through. I'm pretty sure it will keep you busy." He looked at Ann who was busy surveying the office.

"There certainly is… your mother was a busy woman." Ann replied. "I did some research. Your mother was highly thought of in many circles." She saw Saul nod.

Marty broke in. "Saul, I appreciate you letting Ann and I dig through your mother's diaries and notes. I know how much they mean to you and I can assure you they're in good hands."

"I'm sure that is the case." Saul considered the young woman who had made her way over to one of the walls and was now studying a charcoal sketch she found of particular interest.

Before asking if Ann could assist him in his review of Rachel Kaplan's notes concerning the years she and her family spent in the camps, he filled Saul in on her background. Before Ann joined the Seattle Police Department she had studied and trained as an IT professional but prior to that she had considered entering into a career as a museum curator. Having obtained her Bachelor of Arts degree, she attended the Ontario College of Art and Design in Canada working towards a Master's in Curatorial Practice. A very clever individual, she was about to begin her final term when she simply decided the field wasn't for her and switched horses midstream toward a career in IT. She hadn't regretted her decision.

Ann looked over her shoulder to where Marty and Saul stood watching her. "Saul, would you mind if I have access to what I assume is your mother's computer?"

"It's actually Jacob's, but he doesn't use it, he's never here. He said he whipped it, ah… wiped it; and set it up for my mother. Strange how an old woman could use such things when her son is completely at odds with these things…" Saul pondered. "No please… you have permission to everything in this room."

Adrian added. "Ann, consider yourself part of the family, please come over anytime." She turned to Marty with a sly look, leaned in and whispered. "Lovely girl Marty… how could you possibly do better? Don't let her slip through your hands."

Marty just smiled while Saul rolled his eyes. Back at the desk, Ann had already seated herself and her fingers flew atop the keys. Looking at the list of entries and titles she remarked silently; "Rachel, you certainly have been busy…"

Ann had grown oblivious, already lost in her work. Marty and the old couple looked at each other, smiled then left the room.

"Marty... how about one for the road?" Saul suggested.

24

Inside the 7-11 store, a tall well built, forty something black man stood in shorts and a T-shirt at the magazine rack thumbing through the newest edition of Today's Golfer. The weather outside was as hot as a fire cracker and the summer heat wave was predicted to last through the end of the week. Not unexpectedly, the air conditioned store did some of its best business during these spells, not too many passersby could resist stopping in, cooling off and grabbing a cold drink or two.

A rainbow haired twenty something rocker with bad skin threw a comment out to his customer as he swept past, "Hey pal, you gonna buy that thing or read it here?" The white clerk smirked and rudely brushed past the man on his way to the cashier island where a long line of customers waited impatiently in front of a lone female clerk doing her best to serve the latest swell of customers. Cole didn't deign to answer but simply raised his head and watched the clerk break through the line of customers without offering any apology before returning to the article entitled "the perfect putt." Continuing to read, he concluded the author of the article certainly knew his stuff." Throughout high school and college, Elijah Cole had made a name while on the amateur circuit, but when faced with the difficult decision of turning pro or concentrating exclusively on his studies chose the latter. As things went, FBI Deputy Director Elijah Cole was glad he made the right decision.

Several minutes passed by far more quickly than Elijah had figured and he quickly glanced out the store front's window. His wife Tina sat in the front of the Lincoln Navigator wearing a pout and pointing to her wrist watch mouthing "let's go already." Ok it was official, he was in Dutch. Elijah and the wife were supposed to have been at the Jensen's pool party over half an hour ago. He and Tina were wrapping up a two week vacation in Mississippi, visiting family and friends. Tomorrow evening they'd board a plane that would take them back to Seattle Washington where Cole would begin the fourth year of his five year mandate.

Quickly making his way toward the cash out, he reached down into his shorts and dug out his wallet. Arriving at the cashier he was grateful the long line of waiting customers had dissipated. Only one person ahead of him, a young boy carried a slurpee almost as big as he was, set the oversized cup on the counter in front of the rude young clerk who spoke to Cole minutes ago. The young boy dug into the front pockets of his jeans then one by one his little fists emerged holding a selection of pennies, nickels and dimes that he spilled across the countertop in front of a now frowning pizza faced clerk.

The clerk began scathingly "Whoa kid, if you think I'm going to count all this shit you got another thing com..." He never had a chance to finish his sentence.

A skinny Latino man came up from behind Cole, shoving the young boy to the floor with one arm and flashing a 32 cal handgun in the clerks face before quickly turning the weapon in Elijah's direction looking him dead in the eye, "Don't even think about trying anything negro!" The robber turned spun the gun back on the clerk. "And you make with the cash right fucking now!"

Elijah watched the clerk's face blanch while his mouth opened and closed without making a sound. Cole predicted the clerk was gonna lose his lunch any second now but surprised Elijah by managing to mutter out; "ok... ok..." Unfortunately for the clerk, the robber decided he wasn't moving fast enough and jumping the counter pistol whipped the man across the nose. The clerk face exploded in a gout of blood as he tumbled to the floor. Behind the counter, the gunman rifled through the register grabbing the larger bills in his fist and leaving the Washington's in the till before vaulting over the counter once again waving the gun in Cole's direction. "No tricks or someone gets hurt."

Cole raised his hands to his shoulders, "You got no problems from me brother..." He glanced down at the young boy who lay on the floor in tears.

Elijah saw the last thing he wanted to see walking toward the store's entrance. A uniformed police officer pushed through the glass door, the gunman's back was to the officer and although he couldn't see the gun, he did notice Cole's arms held in the air. Something was up; the officer's hand fell to the butt of his gun while his fingers flipped open the snap that held the weapon securely in its holster.

As the sound of the door chime rang out announcing someone had entered the store, the gunman spun about to confront the new comer. Even before the gunman started to turn toward the policeman, Elijah knew there was almost no chance the officer could outdraw the robber. Without a moment's thought, Cole acted decisively, his FBI training automatically coming into play as did his championship years as captain of his school's wresting team.

Cole launched himself forward, rotating his body to the left as his right hand flashed downward in front of the robber, striking the man's gun hand downward toward the floor. A moment later the gunman's finger tightened on the trigger firing off a single round that ricocheted off the floor tile that redirected the bullet toward unopened bundle of newspapers lying only a foot or so from where the police officer stood. Absorbing the bullet's momentum, the round spent itself buried in the classified pages of the Natchez Democrat.

Cole's right hand had succeeded in knocking the weapon from the gunman's grip; it hit the floor and spun away from the man. Meanwhile Cole had shifted his weight toward his rear foot bringing his right elbow in a powerful upward arc catching the culprit just below the jaw line. Elijah heard the gratifying crack of a jaw bone breaking and knew the man was out for the count even before his body hit the floor.

It was only now that the officer's hand yanked the 9mm automatic from his holster aiming it at Cole. Elijah threw his hands upward above his head, speaking quickly and identifying himself as an FBI agent. The police officer didn't lower his weapon but kept it leveled at Cole while his eyes roved about the store. It was only when the officer's partner entered the store behind him that he regained some degree of composure and began conversing with Elijah. That was the moment that the rude clerk finally came to and jumped up behind the counter. Now for the second time in as many minutes the clerk found himself staring down the barrel of a loaded gun, just as Cole had predicted earlier he commenced spewing his guts out across the counter.

Several weeks later, Elijah Cole found himself behind the Deputy Directors desk of the Special Crimes Task Force, a section formed under the auspices of the FBI's Criminal Profiling Program. Unlike the Behavioral Analysis Unit or the Criminal Profiling Unit whose mandate included method analysis, offender profiling and identification of serial killers and their targets, Coles task force' mandate was that of apprehension and enforcement or as some within the group referred to it, search and destroy; a term severely frowned upon by the FBI's upper echelon. Even so, the unquestionable success of the unit gave Elijah and his men considerably more autonomy than was generally extended to other units. This unusual degree of independence could be traced back to the unit's direct funding by States in which the task force operated and the assignment of City and State law enforcement investigators that served to augment the units manpower.

At the moment, Deputy Director Cole and his chief investigators were preparing for a meeting that would outline his Task Force's next assignment. Members of the FBI's Behavioral Analysis and Criminal

Profiling Units along with the representatives of various State and City law enforcement agencies would identify pressing situations suggesting that a serial murderer or murderers could be active within the states of Washington, Oregon, Idaho, or western Montana. As with any such conglomeration of interested parties, politics always reared its ugly head and Cole was quite aware that if he were not extraordinarily careful, the most promising cases could be swept aside while catering to less productive but more politically viable investigations. This morning Elijah didn't give it much thought, he was still preoccupied with the intense discussion he and his wife Tina endured following the altercation in the 7-11. Besides, this was hardly his first rodeo, and he had a talent for steering things in their proper direction while expertly managing to keep agendas and egos in check.

The meeting ran from 9:00 am and ended just before 11:30. As usual, Cole and his team of analysts were able to satisfy everyone as to their target selection; especially since it appeared that multiple citizens from each member state had turned up dead or had mysteriously vanished over a period of only three years, and more importantly – the rate of frequency had more than tripled over the last eighteen months.

The term serial killer encompasses a selection of murderers who commit multiple killings over various periods of time for a wide variety of different reasons. Often these include "thrill kills" where the murderer enjoys the rush of adrenaline given by excitement of the kill or the risk of being discovered and caught. Other murders are motivated by profit, black widows that do away with husbands for the insurance money or even contract killers.

Yet by far, the most common motivation within such killers was the hedonistic self indulgent tendency to seek sadosexual gratification or absolute control over their victim. In these cases the killer inflicts pain, torture and sometimes mutilation in an attempt to fill some bizarre inner need. The murderer will often wait a considerable period of time before committing another killing. In the mean time, they relive past murders and fantasize of future killings and the methods they will employ while doing so. Many of these psychopaths will take personal articles from their victims. Fixating on these trophies as a means to escalate the degree of pleasure derived from the remembered destruction of their victims and their unquenchable thirst for the blood of ever more innocents. Eventually when fantasy and dark dreams no longer satisfy these inner demons, they are once again driven to act and kill again. In many of the cases the period between murders shrinks over time, a result of the ever diminishing ability of the killer's fantasies to satisfy the growing urges.

As the number of murders increase and the body count piles up, investigators are able piece together and gain insight into the psyche of the killer identifying consistent patterns or profiles of the person. Since the majority of these killers are mono-faceted, or obsessed with recreating specific and narrow patterns of behavior, a profile of the killer becomes ever more detailed often pointing toward individuals having a certain background, employment, psychological or medical history. Matching physical evidence and clues to possible suspects known to possess such profiles often gives the investigators the edge required to identify and bring these people to justice.

While it was true that Elijah Cole used these standardized methods to close such cases undertaken by his task force, there was one method commonly employed by the police to identify common criminals and yet almost never available to those investigating serial killers: a confidential informant.

Yes, most certainly citizens would phone in tips or report unusual circumstances they thought might prove useful to the police, but "dropping a dime," and providing a name and specific details of the person responsible for mass murder was nearly unheard of. Having such an informant provide that degree of information on multiple killers, operating independently within disparate geographic areas simply didn't happen, and yet Elijah spoke regularly with just such a confidential source whose information was always unerring in its accuracy.

The Deputy Director had spoken to this particular informant only the day before, it was he who supplied the background of one such killer operating in Washington State, that killer who the task force would now focus its investigation. Unfortunately, the nature of the relationship between Cole and his source demanded that two caveats be observed. The first proviso bound Cole from openly disclosing the name or specifics of the target to his men and women while allowing him to steer and move the investigation forward in subtle ways that would ultimately reveal the killer and provide irrevocable evidence as to their guilt. The second stipulation demanded that the suspect would never be taken alive under any circumstance and on rare occasion might necessitate the need to ensure the killer's body was never found.

Following Cole's conversation with the source, Elijah sat for several minutes considering what he had been told and how to best act on the information while maintaining the covenant between he and his source. A complex issue, Elijah needed a break from the office. Sometimes he found it helped to walk. Cole often found the exercise helped put things in perspective and provide him new avenues of thought. It was nearly lunchtime and Cole skipped eating at the local cafeteria in favor of a stroll through nearby Olympic Sculpture Park.

It was a beautiful day; the sun had finally broken through the persistent morning fog that for some reason ad refused to dissipate until only a half hour before. The pathway he followed meandered through the nine acre park passing by large and small artistic sculptures, some remarkable, others less so. Walking along the waterfront, the hustle of the city, its people and vehicle traffic faded into the background and Elijah became immersed within in the sounds of the nearby water and the unmistakable briny aroma wafting off Elliot Bay; each timeless reminders of the ocean's omnipresence. By the time he was halfway through his walk he had decided on how to best move on the information provided to him earlier that morning.

Cole allowed his mind to relax as he sat upon a wooden bench overlooking a concrete train corridor whose series of locomotive tracks ran north and south along the coast. His eyes followed the boardwalk as it continued across a small pedestrian bridge that straddled the tracks then continued alongside the beach. Cole watched small knots of office workers walk or jog along the path while the sunlight glinted off the small waves in the bay. It was following one such day that he had first met the person that would later become a trusted friend and powerful ally in his fight against the monsters that roamed the country at will preying mercilessly upon an unsuspecting public.

Before being promoted Elijah Cole had been a member of the Behavioral Analysis Unit for several years and was often called into the field to assess a crime scene from the perspective of a criminal profiler. He arrived in Tallahassee on a chilly October morning to meet with the primary investigator and a member Tallahassee's crime scenes unit. The facts suggested a most unusual case, even as serial murders went.

The first of eight bodies had begun showing up three months earlier, the hapless victims discovered by chance as folks stumbled across shallow hastily buried graves where, in at least several instances, a leg or an arm protruded from the disturbed soil. Most of the cadavers were in various stages of advanced decomposition, something quite expected given the hot summer weather and the autumnal heat wave that finally broke in late September. The local coroner had made a determination of death owing to trauma; extreme trauma indicated by the display of dislocated joints, broken bones and twisted necks.

But it was the latest victims that drew the most attention, all three disappearing only days before their ruined bodies were discovered within the grounds of Tallahassee's historic Old City Cemetery. Here the recent dead lay unburied, their bodies strewn carelessly upon the lawn only mere feet from a most elaborate monument marking the grave of one Elizabeth Budd-Graham.

Elijah attended the scene where the bodies had been callously discarded. In order of discovery they were those of a teenage girl, a fifty two year old woman, and a latest, a thirty three year old man. Detective Ruth Laramie, the primary investigator and Sid Morgan a crime scene investigator turned to greet Cole as he approached the raised rock barrier that enclosed and defined the large gravesite. Noting the aged caretaker who had insisted upon showing the Deputy Director the way to the grave, Laramie and Morgan had exchanged knowing glances; the old timer had no doubt enjoyed regaling Cole with the strange legend associated with the grave's occupant. Separately, each of the men wondered how to broach the nagging suspicion that the legend may yet hold sway in their investigation.

Minutes before meeting the two detectives, Elijah Cole wash trying to make sense of the faded cemetery site map when the kindly black caretaker, one Benjamin Aloysius Jackson had appeared and taken Elijah under his wing. He approached the big man with a friendly hello and stood beside the younger man taking a moment to light up a smoke before asking who Elijah was there to visit. Upon hearing the name of the deceased, old Ben began reciting his position, length of service and unique qualifications as chief historian of Tallahassee's Old City Cemetery, who by the way had been employed as such since November 22, 1963. Old Ben went on to say that he remembered the exact day of his hiring given that was the day that nice young president JFK had been assassinated in Dallas by that no good Russki S.O.B. Having gotten introductions out of the way, old Ben took the Deputy Director by the arm leading him towards the center of the cemetery.

"Yes siree bob, ol' Bessie gets lots of visits from lots of folk. You know she was a witch don't you? O'course you do. You're a policeman ain't yah." The old man paused a moment to draw another puff on his cigarette. "Sad thing ya know. Poor woman was only twenty three year old when she went to meet her maker, bad heart ya know. Left her man and chillens, way back in 1889."

Elijah looked down the worn path. Some sixty yards distant he saw a man in a light sport jacket and a woman in a pant suit conversing near a large monument he assumed was their destination. The old man went on to tell

Cole that the burial was unholy, the headstone faced west, dead opposite the direction of a properly seated Christian stone that always faced east, toward the rising sun and eternal glory.

Ben continued, "Folks have it, the grave digger his' elf said the woman was buried face down in the coffin, feet west, head east. Yup." Elijah listened as the man continued to speak while they walked along. Ben stated it wasn't long after Bessie was buried, that rumors surfaced that she had been a "white witch", a practitioner of magic, but not evil; least not as how the story went.

Ben added. "Yup, Bessie would concoct spells for to help folks out. Help women cure the seven year itch that steered a husband ta stray, scart away bad dreams, cure da fevers, an even the Yella Fever itself!" Elijah knew Yellow Fever to be a particularly nasty scourge of the day. Apparently, Bessie had cast a love spell, enticing her well to do husband, a man some years the girl's senior to take her as his wife. It was said her ghost was sometimes seen admiring her grave, which was the finest of any in the old cemetery.

Reaching the other officers, Cole shook hands with the old man thanking him again as he left the grave site. The three men made their introductions. Morgan, the scene investigator spoke first, "Well, here's what we know for what it's worth. The victims all lived in Tallahassee, though in neighborhoods lying some distance from the other. We think they were all killed elsewhere before being dumped here. We couldn't find any tell tale signs of violence in or near the cemetery."

It is common knowledge among police investigators that people locked in a life and death struggle tended to leave a lot of clues and evidence lying about.

Morgan continued, "As mentioned in the coroner's report, these injuries are more or less similar to those of the previous five victims; dislocated joints, broken bones and what have you."

Cole spoke up; "Yes, I noticed those reports state a number of victims suffered the breakage of a femur. From what I understand the thighbone is far and away the strongest bone in the human body. I do find it interesting that although they suffered significant trauma, almost all of it was internal. None of the bone breaks resulted in compound fractures; essentially the skin remained intact aside from shallow cuts and scrapes. Is that right?"

Ruth Laramie spoke up. "Yes, very odd, at first I suggested they may have died as a result of significant falls. Maybe the killer threw them off a building or something like that but our coroner nixed that. That sort of injury would require falling from a significant height, a fall like that would result in massive contusions along whatever side of the body absorbed the greatest impact, basically a bloody splat for want of a better term. That didn't happen here. It appears that the torn joints, broken limbs and crushed torsos were damaged separately, by incredibly strong forces applied from differing directions. It would be similar to you or me killing a chicken with our bare hands, but stopping just short of ripping it to bits."

Morgan watched the puzzled expression on Coles face. "Yeah, that's pretty much where it leaves us too. Can't make head or tails of it, but there is something else, gets even weirder." Cole glanced at Morgan then back to the female detective who began to speak.

"As you know, the first bodies found were partially buried, by the time they were found they were in advanced stages of decomposition. The coroner figures they were killed and buried in the summer or early fall, as such he couldn't tell us much more than how and when they likely died. Since nearly all of them were reported missing soon after by friends or relatives, we have a pretty good idea of when they were taken anyway." Ruth stopped and looked toward Morgan before continuing. "Now here's the rub. The last three victims dumped at this grave site were reported missing less than twelve hours earlier before being found, and yes they each bore the same massive injuries as the others; we're almost positive we're dealing with the same killer. But... the condition of these bodies suggests cellular interference possibly disruption on a massive scale. "

"Sort of desiccated like, Morgan offered." Ruth looked at him and shook her head.

"No, not desiccated, not dried out. Yeah, I have to admit I thought the victims looked sort of withered like; as if their skin had been dried out, but I left a meeting with the coroner just before I drove here. The lab results came back from the first two bodies that were found here, we're still waiting on the results of the last victim." Ruth brought out a small notebook and read from it. "According to the examiner's interpretation of the results, he says it appears as though the cells simply - surrendered their consistency and structure - while retaining normal levels of moisture." Ruth looked at the faces of the men standing beside her. "Now what exactly does that mean...? I had to ask too."

The detective continued to read, "It appear as though the majority of the body's cells had suddenly and inexplicably - aged and atrophied. He'd seen similar results when applying a chemical fixture to skin, muscle and organ samples while preserving them in case they might be required for evidence later on. He uses a combination of formaldehyde and some other preservers, but all the samples they tested turned up a lack of any foreign chemicals or substances. Absolutely nothing out of the ordinary was found."

Cole commented, "I'd hardly expect our victims to have been drowned in formaldehyde at any rate. Can the medical examiner give us any hint if the older bodies showed similar evidence?"

"The late stages of decomposition would make that quite impossible." Morgan stated.

"So where does this leave us?" Ruth asked.

Cole shrugged, "Good question." Ruth's and Elijah's attention was drawn by Morgan who wore a strange expression while motioning a thumbed fist in the direction of the graves monument standing behind him.

"Yeah right Sid." Ruth frowned and gave a little chuckle, but her laugh failed to dispel the chill she suddenly felt run up her spine.

"I assume you've checked any video feeds near the cemetery. It would be nice to have some idea of who is dumping the bodies." Elijah stated.

"I've got officers checking out traffic camera feeds and security video from the businesses in the surrounding area." Ruth continued. "As of today they haven't come up with anything but I wouldn't give up hope just yet."

Morgan spoke up. "Little of interest from the crime scene, no recognizable footprints, not surprising on its own, there's nothing but grass around the monument. We went over the entire area with a fine toothed comb but found nothing that couldn't be traced back to the victims. They may as well have been dumped out of a helicopter as carried here. We couldn't find any indication they were dragged here, and believe me... we looked. We had officers walk the entire cemetery and the pathways that lead here... nothing."

"No drag marks. That leaves us to assume they must have been carried?" Elijah added.

Ruth piped up, "That would be quite a feat for anyone, given that our male victim weighed in over two hundred and forty five pounds. Dead weight too."

Cole spoke. "Any tire tracks? Perhaps they were brought here in something like a wheelbarrow?"

Morgan spoke up. "Sorry, nothing like that." He glanced at his notebook. "There was something else I wanted to impart." Cole and Ruth looked his way. "I hesitate to say this, but the bodies may have, again may have - been

168

crudely "arranged or staged." Their bodies were found with their heads generally pointing to the west, and their feet to the east. Opposite to that of a Christian burial, as I'm sure old Ben informed you while on your way over here."

"I think we're going to have to wait and see if the video can shed more light on the situation." The small group began to walk from the grave site. Cole asked, "I haven't had a chance to check into a motel, can you make any recommendations."

Morgan laughed, "Well there's the Marquis, it's clean and has a great view of the cemetery from the top floor."

Ruth ignored Morgan. "Don't listen to Sid, the Marquis's a dump. We usually put visitors up in the Hilton Double Tree just off West Park Avenue. It's close to downtown and near some decent restaurants."

Cole surprised both of the detectives saying, "Actually I think I'll try the Marquis, I'm a bit of a night owl; I'd interested to see what goes on here at night for myself."

"Don't say you weren't warned." Ruth laughed handing Elijah her card and a small map of the city. Reaching the Palm Court parking lot, the officers shook hands and Cole watched them drive away from the cemetery.

Looking to his left Elijah saw the Marquis Hotel's main entrance sitting only a hundred yards or so from his car, "well... I guess I'm home." He took out a small suitcase and a folding garment bag containing his suits and began walking toward the old three story hotel enjoying the heat of the early afternoon sun.

Elijah Cole wasn't one to simply accept everything he was told. He'd been involved in enough cases to know a little poking about on your own often offered a better perspective of the situation as a whole, even if it didn't provide any ground breaking leads or evidence. He walked up to the front desk. Fully aware of his customer's presence, the middle-aged clerk continued to sit nearby, eating a sandwich and reading his paper until Cole stabbed the small bell sitting on the counter top several times. The man frowned and put down his paper. "Lunch time don't you know. Now sir, what can I do for you?"

Cole walked into the west facing room rather gratified to see a rather large window looking out across the grounds of the nearby cemetery. If the detective had gone out specifically seeking a prime observing location he'd be hard pressed to find one any better. He hung up his suit, sport jacket and pants in the small closet and opened his suitcase on the small luggage rack at the foot of the bed. Reaching inside he took out a pair of big 10x70mm binoculars from their case and attached them to a small tripod he positioned in front of the window. He took several minutes scanning the grounds. Aside from old Ben the caretaker, the place was deserted. There wouldn't be too many visitors; the cemetery was full, the last plot being sold in 1902. Cole figured it was a safe bet that its residents no longer had any close family still living to visit.

After a quick conversation with his wife Tina and giving her the number of the hotel, he hid the binoculars and tripod flat beneath the bed's mattress. The place looked ok, the hotel lay in a decent neighborhood, but you could never tell. He grabbed a quick bite at the hotel's cafeteria, not too bad at all, and then left the hotel driving to police headquarters intending to meet with Ruth's superiors before checking up on the progress being made on the video feeds. Even though the FBI's presence had been requested by the local force, there were often some who were put off by what they considered jurisdictional trespass. Making a proper introduction and commenting on what he considered to be a thorough and well run investigation, would place most, if not all these predispositions to rest. As it was, Elijah found there was no basis for his concern, Lieutenant Jameson, the officer in charge of the Homicide unit was himself a seasoned investigator who welcomed and understood the importance of gaining any edge when it came to complex investigations.

Ruth Laramie greeted Elijah and Jameson as they entered the homicide office. "I think we might have at least a partial explanation as to how our victims came to arrive at their final destination. Have a look at this feed taken off a traffic camera only two blocks distant from the cemetery."

The two men approached the counter where she stood. A thirty two inch monitor sat beside a laptop computer. Ruth took up the mouse and dragged the cursor overtop a thumbnail image showing a street intersection. The caption below the video clip stated the location, date and time; 3:30 am. She clicked the play button and the scene two days earlier played out before them.

The men stood spell bound watching two figures walking hand in hand while jaywalking across the empty street in a direction that would take them directly to the Old City Cemetery. Ruth clicked the image to full screen and zoomed in. "The man on the right, closest to the camera is our latest victim, one Allan James Johnson, thirty three, six foot with a build like an ox. The small man walking next to him with his face turned away from the camera is at least a person of interest if not our prime suspect."

"Do we have a facial shot of the suspect?" Jameson asked.

Ruth shook her head, "Unfortunately not, it appears the other man is constantly talking to Johnson as they walk along."

"They're arm in arm." Cole commented. "Any chance we're looking at a gay liaison?"

Ruth spoke up, "The thought crossed my mind as well, but it's not too likely. The officers checking on Johnson's movements that night say he was drinking at a local cowboy bar, a pretty rough one at that. Johnson was married and according to his friends had a reputation as a lady's man. The guys he was with that night said he walked home alone just after the bar closed at 2:00 am. Johnson didn't drive, he arrived and left on foot, his house is only a few blocks from the bar."

"How far is the bar from this camera?" Cole asked.

"Hmm. Looks like a good five miles or more. That would fit into the time frame, might take a while to walk that far." Ruth suggested.

Jameson commented. "Look at the way Johnson walks, certainly doesn't appear that he's drunk or drugged."

"I agree, but the other man appears to almost be leading him?" Cole remarked.

"Can't comment on that but remember I said "person of interest" rather than suspect? Watch what happens next after these two cross the street." Ruth pointed to the top left of the screen while the victim and the other man walked off and left the image frame. Nearly three minutes passed until the hooded figure of a man dressed in dark colors appeared moving furtively behind the trees and bushes bordering the roadway. Every once in a while he would stop and inspect the ground or move in small circles before looking up in the direction taken by Johnson and the other man. The detectives watched as the figure crouched down before stepping into the intersection choosing instead to remain in the shadows while a solitary car approached. Once the vehicle had passed from sight, the figure rapidly crossed the street obviously following the other men. Ruth fiddled with the zoom control but it was evident by those viewing, that this man knew exactly where the camera was positioned and was careful to avoid showing his face.

Jameson spoke up, "We've seen our victim, suspect and person of interest, but exactly who is who?"

It was nearly four in the afternoon. There was nothing else to be done at headquarters and Jameson invited Cole and Ruth for a social drink in the bar next store. Ruth excused herself; she had a husband and kids waiting. Since the bodies started turning up she hadn't spent a lot of time at home.

The two men went for a drink, shared some war stories then parted ways. Stopping at a liquor store, Elijah picked up a mickey of bourbon on the way back to the hotel.

He reached the Marquis a little after seven, Elijah grabbed a burger and fries then slipped up to his room and gave his wife a quick call. The setting sun shone in through the west facing window, the trees and light posts cast long shadows across the grass and pavement below. A young couple walked arm in arm along the paved walking path bisecting the cemetery. It was a lovely evening, Elijah watched the two sit at a park bench where they snuggled for several minutes before leaving and continuing their stroll. The sun dropped below the horizon leaving the city in twilight.

Elijah retrieved his binoculars and tripod from beneath the mattress. Positioning the instrument at the window he slid a hardwood chair up behind the tripod. All was ready. Closing the curtains on either side of the binoculars he poured himself three fingers of bourbon and watched the local news for half an hour. Looking at the time, Elijah removed a wind up alarm clock from his case, checked the tension of the spring and set the alarm at 12:00 midnight. He turned off the room's light then lay atop of bed spread intending to catch some shut eye.

Cole awoke just a minute or so before his alarm sounded. Deactivating the alarm, he once again found himself continually amazed with the often unerring accuracy of his inner clock. The room was in semidarkness; the feeble ambient light of the surrounding neighborhoods providing the room's only illumination entering through the narrow opening in front of his binoculars - all fine and dandy. He poured a second light drink sitting his glass on the wide window sill then parked himself on the chair and peered through the binoculars into the night.

The 10x70mm binoculars provided a wide bright field with plenty of eye relief. Back at home he used the instruments to scan the Milky Way on clear summer nights, now he turned them toward the cemetery grounds. He watched on and off for the next several hours, sometimes using the binoculars but more often his natural eyesight. As a reward for his time and effort he saw nothing but a cat passing by the old grave markers. Elijah was about ready to pack it in for the night until he caught something move out of the corner of his eye, and that something was creeping about, hidden for the most part as it moved among the bushes and the deep shadows cast by the street lamps bordering each side of the cemetery.

Cole brought the binoculars into play and focused them in the area where he had detected the movement. An ancient decrepit mausoleum came into view, from this angle; Cole noticed the gleam of the street lamps as they struck the tomb's stone roof. He also noticed something else, in a corner of its stone roof was a large black hole. A section of the roof had evidently caved into the tomb's interior. Elijah recalled the little building when he walked to meet Ruth and Sid earlier in the day. He'd noticed the entrance to the mausoleum was sealed shut with stone and mortar, no doubt to prevent unwanted entry by people or animals. As Elijah continued to watch, he saw a shadow emerge from the hole in the roof and climb down where it skittered across the grass and out of sight entering some brush nearby. Could it be a person, or perhaps only the cat he saw earlier? In the dim light and without reference to place what he saw to scale, it was anyone's guess. Cole wasn't about to call in the troops to investigate the sighting of an alley cat. Still, he wasn't tired... he'd take a stroll and see what he could see.

He checked his 9mm semi-automatic and returned it to his shoulder holster, making sure there was one round up the snout. Satisfied he took the small but powerful flashlight he kept on his belt turning it on and off to ensure the batteries were good, then donned a dark blue windbreaker before leaving the room and locking the door behind him. Down the stairwell and stepping out into the hotel lobby he saw the night clerk, a young woman he spoke with earlier in the evening. She was speaking on the phone standing behind the registration desk. Recognizing Cole she gave him a friendly wave before returning to her conversation.

Elijah left the lobby and walked across the Palm Court parking lot pausing several moments at the door of his car. He scanned the other side of the street for any sign of movement within the cemetery. Had he seen anyone watching him he would have entered the vehicle and driven away, removing any indication of his own interest. He'd then park on a nearby side street before approaching the grounds from a different angle. Cole paused for several long moments then satisfied he was not being watched, left the parking lot, crossed the street and entered the cemetery.

Instead of immediately walking in the direction of the mausoleum, he held back at the edge of the grounds allowing him to blend in among the shadows. Crouching down, he studied the grounds in detail. From this low vantage, he eliminated a good number of the lower tree branches while expanding his view along the brighter patches of lawn that sprawled across much of the park's grounds. If anything crossed the grass, he would readily distinguish a moving object from its surroundings.

He waited several minutes before standing up, slowly walking into the park and taking advantage of the trees and shrubbery to mask his approach. As a young teen, he'd been taught to hunt by his father, an experienced hunter. His dad had two truths when moving in the bush. The first was that movement kills, the second being that the only animal that walks in a straight and steady line through the forest is man. Elijah reverted to his training, taking only two or three quiet steps before pausing, sometimes for nearly a full minute, keeping his head stationary he would only allow his eyes to move side to side slowly scanning ahead of him while his ears were keenly pricked to detect any sound. Continuing to move in this manner it took him nearly twenty minutes to reach the mausoleum; he hadn't seen a thing and was glad that he hadn't asked the local police to assist him checking out the cemetery grounds. Cole quietly made his way about the perimeter of the small building and then stopped. Stalking game while making small, slow and careful movements while doing so was draining, as any hunter would tell you, it took much less effort to walk normally. He glanced down at his watch, nearly one thirty, time to go to bed. He arched his back and stretched his arms skyward, that was when he saw a dark shadow drop from the mausoleum room onto the ground some ten yards distant.

Landing with the agility of a cat, it swept toward him, he reached into his coat in an effort pull his weapon but the figure sprang at him covering the last nine feet for so in a single bound. He tensed and readied himself for an impact that never came. Out of the corner of his eye, he saw a second figure he had somehow missed. Hidden close by, the second figure rose up to meet and intercept the dark shape lunging at him. For a brief moment, Elijah caught the unmistakable gleam of steel sweeping along the surface of a long blade as it arced upward and buried itself within the dark folds of clothing worn by his attacker. A loud almost unworldly cry broke free in the night and chilled him to the bone. Elijah stood frozen in place watching the two figures tumble across the grass only a scant few feet from his side.

Several seconds later, Cole's attacker lay motionless on the ground, a pool of glistening shadow gathered at its side; blood. Now recovered, Elijah reached into his jacket for his gun. The second figure was on him in a second, the blade of a long Bowie knife held at Elijah's throat. A smooth calming voice spoke softly. "Mr. Cole, I wouldn't do that if I were you." Cole pulled an empty hand from his jacket while the person beside him reached in and removed the gun from his holster. "A wise move Elijah. Now be a good boy and wait here for another moment, I just have to do one more thing."

Elijah watched the man approach the prone figure in the grass and pull back the cloak that up until now hid its face, or what might pass for a face. Even in the dim light Elijah could see the features were oddly misshapen, the eyes larger by a considerable degree than that of any person he had ever encountered, they seemed to shine outward. Cole saw the person's hands, well, perhaps more accurately, the claws of whatever lay there. Two sets of long dagger like talons protruded from beneath the folds of the loose clothing covering its body. His eyes glanced back toward the gleaming orbs within the pale skinned face. Rather than a reflection, Elijah saw that eerily cold, silvery light might actually originate within the eyes themselves. That ended a moment later when the odd glow was extinguished as the long knife flashed downwards biting deep within the creature's neck and severing the head from its body. The person wielding the knife wiped the blade clean on the dew soaked stems of grass then stood erect. Placing the knife in a sheath at his side, the man approached Cole and they stared at one another for several long seconds before Cole broke the silence.

"Who are you... what have you done." Elijah asked in a quiet voice.

"First off, I'm the person who saved you from what would otherwise be a certain and most gruesome death. That's why you're standing here talking with me instead of becoming a snack for our dead friend over there. Secondly my name is Lyle Fox and we have much to discuss. I hope you're the reasonable sort, once I explain myself you'll be given the opportunity to work with me... or not. Keep in mind I'd much rather dispose of one body tonight rather than two."

The long and fascinating conversation, in which Elijah Cole and Lyle Fox had engaged on that night some seven years before, had irrevocably changed his worldview, the course of his life and his career within the FBI.

25

"Marty! Don't be such a poop!" Ann Oaks feigned anger with her man, giggling and pushing his shoulder with her hand very nearly spilling his morning coffee. "It'll be fun, you'll see."

Reggie chimed in. "Marty, why don't you go son. Always best to keep a lady happy you know. I let your mother drag me to Spring into Spring Flower Show down at the rec center every Mother's Day, even though my hay fever would raise hell the next week."

Marty put on a grimace then smiled. "Well, it looks like I'm outnumbered." He looked at his dad, "you up for coming?"

"Me... no I don't go in for that type of thing, besides your mother would never have approved." Reggie shook his head. Margery had been raised a devout catholic, the only ghost she believed in was the Holy Spirit, and the only contacts from beyond the grave came from the Virgin Mary or another Saintly figure properly sanctioned by the church.

Resignedly, Marty looked at Ann. "So where and what time is this thing?"

"The Otto Meyers' Library, at eleven this morning." She grinned at him. "I have a brochure right here." She waved it in front of his face. "She's not a crackpot you know; she has a PHD in Astrophysics from Cornell and has written several books."

"Boo... did she help write that John Carpenter movie plot, "Ghosts of Mars?" Marty smirked.

She checked the brochure. "It says here she's written several well received books regarding Quantum Mechanics and String Theory."

Marty looked up, just a bit surprised as Ann continued, "And... the Ghosts of Mars..." She giggled once more as Marty and Reggie smiled and laughed.

It was a lovely Saturday morning. Marty left his sports car parked on the street in front of their house, he and Ann chose to walk the four block distance to the library. Ten minutes later they arrived. The couple had never been in the new library, it was only built four or five years ago, when Marty was already living in Seattle.

The building was certainly different than the older structures it shared the block with. The building faced south, three large arched front windows rose up a full two stories, and each window had motorized vertical blinds that extended the entire height of the windows, adjusting automatically with the amount of sunlight falling on the building. Comfortable chairs and couches were positioned near the windows on each floor as were the selection of books sitting upon shelves to take full advantage of the natural light while the conference rooms and management offices were set toward the rear.

As the couple walked through the front doors, a small purple sign supported on a single chrome pedestal announced that Christine Webb's lecture and book signing would take place in the library's "Red Room" located on the main floor. Entering the small forum, both Marty and Ann were surprised at the number of people already seated, looking about, they finally located and occupied a pair of empty seats.

A rather attractive forty something woman wearing a white blouse and a form fitting red mid-length skirt made her way up to the front of the room. Just to the left of the polished hardwood podium a second woman fussed about a table on which sat several piles of books, no doubt readied for the book signing.

The woman in the red skirt looked up to the black wall clock and checked her own wristwatch. Half the audience followed her gaze then checked their own watches. Marty smiled to himself finding he too was doing exactly the same thing. Sort of like yawning when you just saw someone else doing it; things like this were catchy.

"Ok, I guess we can start." The woman in the red skirt nodded to the lady who had been fussing with the table. The second woman walked to the back of the room closing the double doors. "Thanks Joanna," Said the woman at the front of the room and stepping up to the podium.

"As you probably guessed, my name is Christine Webb, author of "A Speculative Science." I'd like to thank and welcome you all." She adjusted the microphone. "I'm just going to dive right in and explain the basic tenants you'll find in my newest book. If you have questions, please wait towards the end of the lecture, I might cover your question in due course. Following this discussion, I'd like to provide a reading; as most of you know, I'm a recognized member in good standing within several American and European Associations of psychics and mediums." A few of the people in the front row clapped enthusiastically.

Marty leaned into Ann and whispered in her ear; "I see she brought her fan club with her..." Ann responded with a "shush" and gave him a light elbow in the ribs.

"Many scientists, including myself believe in the theory of multiversity." Dr. Webb stated, and then continued. "Wikipedia defines the multiverse as a hypothetical group of multiple universes. Together, these universes comprise everything that exists: the entirety of space, time, matter, energy, information, and the physical laws and constants that describe them."

Christine Webb smiled; "Well... that's pretty heady stuff. You have probably read books, watched TV series or science fiction movies where the story line involves alternate or parallel universes co-existing with our own observable universe though on different dimensions or planes. In these stories it's not uncommon for one or more characters to have the ability to move or shift between these universes in some manner; it certainly makes for an interesting plot.

As an astrophysicist and one who understands a good deal of the quantum and relativistic theory pertaining to both the very small, and the very fast, I can tell you I think we may have run ourselves up against a brick wall. The wall in this case represents the impossibility of studying and experimenting on impossibly small objects and infinitesimal amounts of energy without our experiment or perhaps even just our mere observation being enough to affect the outcome of the experiment in some way. No matter how carefully we proceed, we always seem to reach an uncertain outcome, something scientists like me work very hard to avoid.

It is my personal belief that we have to look beyond science and mathematics to find proof of other dimensions of existence. We need only look inside ourselves or contemplate our shared human experience and ask ourselves "how" rather than "why" we exist. The answer as to "why we are here" can only forever remain uncertain, so we are left only with the certainty that - we are. As for the "how" let's consider some universally held beliefs commonly found among nearly all peoples; an instinctive belief of another life existing after this one, life after death.

Now before any of you recite the old argument that this is a fabrication of organized religions on behalf of whatever agenda they might be pushing, consider this. Paleolithic or Stone Age burials taking place as early as three hundred thousand years ago were found to contain "grave goods" entombed with the dead. The Neanderthals; an extinct and separate species of man and the Cro-Magnon, our earliest European ancestors, both placed objects such as weapons, food, and tools presumably useful to the deceased in the afterlife. Before you pooh pooh this idea, think about this: these individuals, so few in number and walking a fine line of survival in a savage world, dispossessed themselves of the very items that might well spell the difference between their own life and death, not to mention that of their children. Obviously they placed tremendous store in this belief; just as many of us do still to this day.

I personally hold that humans recognize this particular belief as an "ambiguous certainty," an oxymoron to be sure, but one with incredible staying power. Reincarnation and other forms of cyclic existence where people relive their lives over and over again, or the more judgmental eternal after lives of a heaven or a hell, are all peripheral evidence of the multiverse.

The same is true of supernatural experiences; clairvoyance, prediction, seeing ghosts and the like. For example, take common déjà vu, the French meaning "already seen"; almost everyone has experienced that odd feeling where they find themselves in a situation they immediately recognize as familiar, but are unable to recall exactly when that situation actually took place.

Now I'm going to lay some groundwork to support my ideas, so please bear with me a minute or two.

It is important that we accept that every individual person is unique in both the physical and mental sense, this has been proven by our mapping of the human genome; those bits of DNA code responsible for creating each of us. Even identical twins, those derived from a single fertilized egg, are still found to display slight differences within their genetic makeup, however small. The probability of two people being exactly the same approaches that of zero. Yet even so, urban legend has it that such twins share an innate ability to empathize or even communicate at some basic level. Now if that is true among twins, just imagine what two absolutely identical people might be able to accomplish. Keep this thought.

Let's proceed under the assumption there are an infinite number of universes that co-exist with that of our own. From everything science has witnessed on earth... and beyond; fundamental similarity rather than radical differentiation appears to be the rule rather than the exception. Only several decades ago it was held that planets were an exceedingly rare phenomena among the stars in the sky. Today modern astronomy tells us solar systems are in fact overwhelmingly common, in fact planets believed able to sustain life are now discovered on a frequent basis. So why should we expect anything different of alternate universes?

If there are an infinite number of universes co-existing with ours, some of which are highly similar if not identical in nearly every important aspect, should we not expect identical versions of ourselves living on identical worlds? Imagine, near infinite numbers of people exactly like you; same looks and thoughts, same world, same friends, same relatives – same everything. What if it was only a matter of sequential time being "out of sync"? Some versions of our nearly exact universe existing in what we think

179

of as our distant or recent past, still others within recent or even very distant futures. Now, remember what I said about the possible communicative ability of two identical individuals?

Isn't it possible that communication of some sort, between you and another version of yourself in the past or future is not only possible, but almost certain? Even if this communication consisted of nothing more than a vague feeling that you are not alone, the feeling that if you were to die at this moment, some part of you would continue to exist and would do so ever more. If we consider common déjà vu in similar terms; you experience an extraordinarily familiar situation because an alternate self, perhaps only moments earlier, had lived it and transferred this memory to you, its future counterpart, allowing you to "relive" the same experience.

What of a near death experience? As people die, their normal senses withdraw from the world, it is quite possible that during these desperate times other unused senses may be stimulated and reach out, crossing boundaries of communication previously closed to them. Do they make contact with a version of themselves living in a past universe? Visiting now deceased loved ones and friends who continue to exist on the "other side" before recovering and being yanked back into this world? Could this sort of communication or transmission also explain visions of the newly deceased appearing to close friends and relatives within mere moments of their death?

Most of us have or will experience an event in our life that defies common sense, or our everyday acceptance as to how the world works. I've coined these occasions as "God Moments." I like to think of these as times when nearly identical universes overlap, approaching so closely that our identical selves are able to breach thinning boundaries, reach out touching the minds and sharing thoughts of our "alter egos." This flow of movement of information goes both ways. Now please remember that these God Moments do not occur for everybody in the same instance. You must think of time as a river in which you are afloat, every once in a while you drift past one of your alternate selves perhaps brushing shoulders and sharing something special between you; a God Moment. This could also go a long ways to explaining the appearance of specters and ghosts, premonitions of another's death or injury, some unusual event, or even a mass prediction as what might happen in the distant future.

For most people these special moments are exceedingly rare, for others, mediums like me, they are rather common, sometimes too much so. I actually work to insulate myself. I sometimes imagine myself as caught within a particular eddy in that river and unable to escape. I'm nearly always in contact with other versions of myself. As a medium, isn't it true then that those other versions of me must also have this ability. How many other universes, with all their possible futures and pasts are me and my alternates able to sense and communicate? It's mind boggling.

Before someone asks the obvious, such as why I can't obtain the winning numbers to next week's lottery. I think this can be explained as an inability to significantly interfere with the timeline we currently experience. Think of it as trying to swim upstream against a vast and irresistible current, in my book I term this force "temporal momentum," otherwise simply put, "fate." Events must unfold in ways very similar to those in the other timelines we inhabit at a specific time, at least if those particular universes are to remain in sync with our own. For example, say my alternate wins the lottery, unfortunately I exist in a universe where I didn't win, and as such I won't be able to afford that world cruise I've always dreamed of."

Dr. Webb saw an insistent hand raised near the back row. "Yes?"

A woman stood up and addressed a question. "Sorry to interrupt but what about future knowledge of our own deaths?" She continued hesitantly, "Say if a past version told us of our accidental death in say a car accident? Could we avoid that?"

"Well documented premonitions forewarning those individuals who will actually suffer some serious trauma is rare, probably because a person receiving such a warning might subconsciously take precautions to avoid the tragic outcome or might simply assume that the danger posed to themselves was a natural extension of the risk they assumed when performing a dangerous activity.

As far as people knowing that a disaster was imminent, and then taking steps to avoid it prior to the event occurring thus saving their lives? An extremely rare event, if it ever occurs at all. Also rare, yet documented are events where a person experiences a premonition, but unable to escape the path of danger; goes on to actually experience the event, but upon surviving may speak of it.

Premonitions warning a person of his or her impending sudden or accidental death are a challenge to understand. Obviously if a person did experience a premonition of their death, that person might be reasonably expected to take steps in order to avoid the event, but if for some reason they did not and died anyway, they would have had to share their premonition with another person, who would then inform the rest of us. No, I think this falls into the category of our lottery predicament. Say a previous version of us had suddenly and unexpectedly died, doing so they would be immediately removed from the time continuum supporting that future, their unique universe could no longer connect with our own, your individual timeline having become too dissimilar. That said, perhaps we can at least partially sense the passing of an alternate self, when this happens do we get that cold shiver, that foreboding sensation that "someone just walked over your grave".

The type of premonitions so often related, such as having sudden knowledge that a loved one has passed away or perhaps another who had been involved in a serious incident of some sort both point to a telepathic event. Again this would depend upon an extrasensory connection formed between two or more properly attuned individuals, certainly existing in this universe but also likewise connected within an alternate past universe, but the event would only reveal itself during a significantly traumatic episode. Anything less would probably go completely unnoticed. It is logical to assume that such well attuned individuals may always be connected, but have learned from early childhood to shield their minds or simply ignore the day to day whisperings sent back from their counterparts. Yet such people would perhaps be unable to block out a shouted transmission taking place during a serious life changing event.

I've tried to explain my theory as to how we communicate with ourselves on the other side. So how does this work from the point of view of a medium? One who acts as a go between for those in her immediate presence and their friends and loved ones "other side," especially those having the ability to connect to those who have actually died? One thing I can say is that when I connect to people who still exist or live within another dimension, in the past or future, I find the communication of ideas to be quite clear and organized.

Quite different than when I connect with someone who has passed on. I and other mediums, often have to interpret what the dead are trying to say to us. In such cases, mediums sometimes see what could be termed snapshots or partial images; other times perhaps disorganized words, but more often simply intense feelings; relief, peacefulness, fright, anger, envy and the like. It is only the name of the deceased and those people most important in their lives that most often come through. That and of course the details of the life ending event itself.

Given these vague peculiarities in the manner of contact, I can only float the idea that we mediums are somehow picking up "psychic echoes" from past worlds, in a universe where the person's death only took place recently. More than this I can't comment.

I do apologize for my brevity; but we must move forward. I would only add that a copy of my newest book is available for purchase following today's reading. I'll be happy to sign the book, or any of my books you might have with you. I'll need several minutes to prepare for today's reading; in the meantime there is coffee or juice, at the back table."

The group adjourned for the next ten minutes forming little knots of three or four people discussing points of interest. Dr. Webb had vanished into the back room after her lecture and had yet to reappear. Slowly the people filed back to their seats, the last of them skittering back when Dr. Webb entered the room.

Instead of going to the podium, the doctor grabbed a stool and placed it several feet from the front row of the audience. Now seated, the woman sat quietly, eyes closed, with her hands in her lap. Nearly a minute passed before Dr. Webb began to speak.

Her eyes opened and stared blankly into the audience. "Is there someone here named Saul who recently suffered a loss?"

Marty watched the woman's face closely, if she was feeling any emotion, her expression didn't show it. Suddenly her eyes shifted quickly to the left and came to rest on someone in the third row. "Is there someone here named Alex who recently lost... a mother?" She repeated.

This time, a dark curly haired man about thirty years of age, looked toward her, their eyes locked. "I'm Alex, my mother Julian Harper passed away several weeks ago."

Dr. Webb continued; "She is showing me her chest and stomach." She paused then continued, "I sense a lot of pain just before she passed on... cancer?"

"Yes, she battled the disease for almost three years, but it finally won." The man dabbed at his wet face with a handkerchief.

"Know that I sense a calm feeling of relief from your mom, Minny's at peace now." The woman tilted her head and paused again.

"Minny was dad's nickname for mom." The waterworks started anew.

"Your father went before your mom... she's showing me water... a boating accident?" Marty saw the man nod slowly. Webb continued. "Know too that both of them are together again. I get a strong sense of happiness... they were close in life?"

"Inseparable, they had a home based business, they were together twenty-four seven." The man smiled.

"I'm glad I was able to read for you today Alex." Dr. Webb ended his reading.

"Thanks so much Dr. Webb. I'll let my sisters know what you said." Alex replied and fell silent. A long minute passed.

Suddenly Christine spoke up once again. "Alex. Tell your sister Tina, that you're mother's missing broach had fallen behind the dresser in the spare room."

A look of wonder crossed the man's face. "Yes, ah yes, I certainly will. Thank you."

The medium closed her eyes once again and sat quietly on her stool. After another minute or so had passed, Christine's eyes opened once more and this time fell to her right, skipping along the front row and stopping when it reached a young woman.

"Blue eyes... blonde hair...Tim..." Christine said slowly. The woman's blonde hair bounced about her shoulders as she vigorously nodded her head.

"I see an image of you and him together..." Christine said slowly. "... A boyfriend?"

Wide eyed, the girl blurted out, "Yes, yes. Tim Williams, he went missing thirteen years ago this Friday. Is he still alive somewhere?"

This got Marty's immediate attention; he had read the old missing person's report concerning Tim Williams only days before and recalled the name and circumstances.

Christine Webb closed her eyes for a moment then shook her head sadly. "No, he has passed on." She continued. "I sense deep sadness and anger towards his killer. I'm also sensing great confusion - a person yet not a person - something very old... malignant, a burning hunger... feeding a burning hunger." Her eyes opened wide.

"Someone else who has passed on is also with us, a woman... both young and yet old... her memories are strong." Christine's eyes searched the audience and for a brief moment alighted on Marty, then fell upon Ann. "You! You have seen them...these young women... a prison cell, so long ago, such a bad place..." Tears coursed down the medium's cheeks. "This night a uniform moves among the women... an enemy. An ancient hunger that still lives." Christine gasped then nearly screamed; "a woman who is yet not a woman, a beast - the hyena of Auschwitz is among us!"

Marty felt Ann's hands grasp his own and squeeze hard. His own heart thumped and rose in his chest and he couldn't take his eyes off the medium, she was now a woman possessed. Suddenly her gaze shifted and her eyes locked with Marty's.

Her voice became a dusty croak. "Policeman... you search for the beast but do not yet know her. Allies of power soon arrive. Together you will save many though others die before the end. Beware the lover of the beast, the Todesengel. He will seek to avenge her destruction with your own."

Dr. Christine Webb's eyes shut, her chin dropped to her chest. A moment later she swooned and fell to the floor in a heap. It took several seconds before the people seated before her reacted and rushed to help her. Her assistant ran forward and addressed the group. "Can someone phone an ambulance?"

Dr. Webb stirred, "No, I don't require an ambulance. Please just help me to a chair."

Ten minutes later or so, her assistant had finally persuaded the last of the Doctor's audience to leave the room, but upon Christine's insistence, her assistant allowed Marty, Ann and Cindy to remain. Introductions were made all around.

Now fully recovered and seated in a comfortable chair sipping a glass of water, Christine spoke to the three people who had remained with her. "Well, that was certainly interesting. This has never happened to me before, although I've spoken to others who have experienced such things. I recall some of what I said but not all of it apparently. Could you please fill me in?"

Ann and Cindy patched together the conversation they recalled while Marty stood by quietly.

Christine listened carefully then spoke. "Yes, I clearly remember speaking to you Cindy; I started to drift when your friend began bombarding me with images and strong emotions. I suppose I must have become overloaded, maybe that's the best description of what I felt."

The medium paused, "As I said earlier, others have experienced this sort of trans-like state, and these aren't typical readings per say. I was no longer in control. I simply became a conduit for whatever came through. Although I can't recall everything, I do remember this."

Christine began. "It was night, late at night. I saw Tim in a wooded clearing, he was alone and sitting close to a small fire. A beautiful woman approached and spoke to him. I'm sorry Cindy, I saw Tim and the woman close together, having sex, but then suddenly it became an attack. Tim was powerless; all he perceived was an intense hunger. Just before he passed, he sensed she was somehow feeding upon him." She shook her body slightly as if experiencing a chill. "Ugh. I've read people who have passed on before, as I said in my lecture, these readings are usually quite vague... this experience on the other hand was extremely vivid." Christine looked at Marty questioningly.

"I'm familiar with the investigation, I read the Sheriff's report just a couple of days ago." All eyes were on Marty as he spoke. "It seems Tim Williams had been at a party spot out near the South Bridge. When I was in high school, all us kids used to go there. The party broke up and Tim volunteered to stay and douse the fire. He was supposed to meet his buds later on but never showed up."

"A van, he and the woman, or whatever she was, they were in a van..." Christine blurted. "I don't recall anything else."

"Yes, his brother's van. It was never found." Marty confirmed.

Ann looked at Christine, "Do you remember what you told me?" she asked.

"Yes but this is very strange, even to me but I'll try to explain as best I can. There were two women communing with me, no - not two women - the same woman but at a time when she was quite young, then later, when she was very old. The young woman showed me a guard, a female guard wearing a uniform and carrying a short whip. I can still see the guard's face; pretty yet cruel and pitiless. The young woman and other prisoners are Jewish ... are, no were, in a camp, a concentration camp. The young woman watched the guard walk up beside a girl lying on a cot and crouch beside the girl. There's a bright light of some sort, the guard stands up. Now the girl on the cot looks old and withered, and she's quite dead."

"My God!" Ann exclaimed. "I've seen that before." Christine, Marty and Cindy stared at Ann. "Marty, the paintings... the odd paintings I saw in the Kaplan's basement, do you remember?"

Marty nodded. "Yes, I do, but I saw them upstairs at the old lady's wake." Marty saw Christine glance his way, he explained. "Rachel Kaplan's wake, she died just a week or so ago."

Christine placed her hands on her cheeks, "The old lady, the one who spoke through me, must have been Rachel."

Ann asked, "Do you remember what you said to Marty, just before you fainted?"

Christine looked up at the young woman. "Why no, not even vaguely, not at all."

Ann continued, "A search? Allies that would help find the beast?"

Cindy broke in, "Yes, you said allies of power, and then gave Marty a warning, something about the lover of the beast, Todesengel."

"No I'm terribly sorry. I recall nothing of this." Suddenly Christine's face became unreadable, her eyes glazed and her hand began to shake, spilling water from her glass. Several moments later she appeared to recover her senses. The medium reached toward with her free hand and grasped the hand of the detective. "Marty, I know the person who killed Tim, it was the same guard Rachel saw in the camps, the same face the old Rachel saw just before she died... this thing whatever it is, is prowling about Hansel's Creek!

26

Returning from the library, Ann and Marty arrived back at Reggie's home a little after two that same afternoon having taken the long way home window shopping on Main Street, grabbing a small lunch at Jan's Diner, and sitting on a bench near Parkside Pond. Ann found herself quite shaken from the experience with Christine Webb, Marty could hardly blame her. Before this morning, he'd never believed any of these sorts of things nor had Ann who had approached the reading as a lark, just something interesting to do on a Saturday morning.

Marty considered something he once heard; "keeping a closed mind is to risk that some unforeseen eventuality will rip that mind's doors from its hinges." This morning certainly seemed to qualify that remark. Normality finally seemed to gain the upper hand as the couple walked across along the park's red shale path that wound itself among the trees that lined the pond. By the time they reached home Marty sensed that Ann wanted to talk.

The couple had the house to themselves; Reggie had gone to watch an afternoon baseball game in Knots Ridge. Normally, the young couple would have taken advantage of their time alone, but neither of them was in the mood. Instead there were things to discuss, important issues that couldn't wait or be denied. Marty made him and Ann a strong gin and tonic. While carrying the drinks out to the picnic table in the backyard Ann brushed past him saying she had to get something from her room. She came out minutes later with her Ipad and a handful of notes scribbled on various sized pieces of scrap paper. Ann sat at the table beside Marty buying time while shuffling through the papers for nearly a minute. Finally, she was ready to say what was on her mind.

"I can hardly believe what I heard this morning. That Dr. Webb how did that woman..." a long pause, she shook her head and continued. "Sorry, doesn't matter, what matters is that Rachel Kaplan believed that this Nazi guard, Irma Grese, was something other than merely human. Up until now I thought the poor woman had just suffered a mental lapse while living in the camps; who could possibly blame her. Men, women and children, all starved, beaten, worked close to death - surviving only to wind up in a gas chamber." A tear rolled down Ann's cheek.

"It's ok." Marty offered his hand but Ann pushed it away.

"No, it is not ok." Ann grew angry. "I believe what Rachel diarized was the truth, as crazy as it sounds to us. Rachel says the guard was a monster of some sort, not just in the inhuman way she and the other Nazi's treated the prisoners, but this particular guard somehow fed off the prisoners." Now, you have to remember that most details in her diary were not written down at the time, prisoners weren't allowed many possessions much less pen and paper; still Rachel was able to somehow scratch out and hide some papers containing key dates and words to help her document the ordeal should she survive.

Ann placed her notes on the table and picked up her tablet. "I have most of her diary on my tablet, but some of them I figured were only crazed ramblings." She opened the screen, activated the tablet's Word program and opened the file she had labeled Auschwitz. "I transferred these entries from Rachel's computer. There is quite a lot of information here. The lady had an impressive memory."

"Here is a quote - this November morning is dark and cold. One of us has died during the night. The Kapos took her body moments ago."

"Kapos?" Marty asked.

Ann explained. "The Kapos were Jewish collaborators living within the camps. They acted as policemen and did the Nazi's bidding getting special treatment in return. Most of them were recruited from criminal gangs and they were particularly brutal towards other prisoners. If they didn't perform up to the Nazi's standards they would be returned to prisoner status and would have to answer to other Kapos in turn. This head female guard in Auschwitz, Irma Grese, had a half dozen or so of the worst of them accompanying her as she made her rounds about the camp."

Ann returned to the tablet. "Emma, one of the girls in our barracks is suffering from dysentery and confined to bed. Shortly I'll be leaving for work, I don't expect to find her here when I return." She goes on to write, "No one has seen any supply trucks for nearly a week. We hear shelling in the distance every day now. Some have overheard the Kapos saying the German's are losing and the war will soon be over, but none of us expect to survive and leave the camp. The Kapos say the Germans will make sure no one does." Bear with me a second Marty, there's another entry I wanted to... here it is.

Ann continued to read. "The hyena was on the prowl this morning, but Grese didn't have her Kapos with her. She came into our barracks, she looked ill. I hoped the bitch had dysentery, but maybe the guards didn't have much food either." Ann took a deep breath. "I was sitting on a chamber pot and crouched down in a corner when I saw her come in. Emma and I were alone in the barracks; I'm sure Grese didn't know I was watching, she didn't even look around but immediately walked straight to the sick girl's bed. I saw Emma awake while the guard stood over top of her, I remember the terrified look on her face; truly awful. Then something very strange happened. Grese bent low and took Emma in her arms squeezing her tightly to her own breast. I wondered what Grese really had in mind. Irma Grese was a jealous, inhuman monster who delighted in torturing and disfiguring women who still retained any semblance of beauty. A moment later I saw a light glowing between the two women. It grew brighter by the second before blazing like a photographer's flash bulb, it nearly blinded me. At the same time I heard Emma wheeze and gasp then fall silent. Grese rose up from the cot and turned to leave. I couldn't take my eyes off the guard's face, Grese's eyes were now clear and bright, her cheeks had color; she looked just like one of those Hollywood pinup girls. After she left, I crept out of my corner and walked to the cot to check on the girl. I couldn't believe what I saw. Emma, who I took to be about sixteen, looked as if she had aged many years in the space of only a few seconds. I shook her shoulder, her eyelids fluttered for a moment then closed... she was dead. What sort of creature is Irma Grese?"

"This inspired those paintings we saw." Marty said quietly.

Marty watched Ann's fingers fly among the letters of the screen's virtual keyboard, she pulled up the "find" feature and typed various key words - nothing found – appeared on the screen. She entered a number of other words and searched, but nothing came up. "Any suggestions?"

"I don't know, maybe try - flash?" he offered.

"Flash? Oh yeah, like that'll work." Ann said rather sarcastically but punched it in anyway. To her surprise there were several entries on the screen. She opened the first on the list and began to read aloud. "One of the Kapos has been buying one of the women's sexual attentions with bread; the Kapo is her husband."

"Her husband?" Marty asked.

"Yes, the women would sometimes prostitute themselves for scraps. When you're starving, relationships and taboos go out the window." Ann explained then continued to read. "The girl told us the Kapo told her that the hyena and Mengele have a thing going on. He watched them together from a window within a hospital ward where Mengele works with the twins. The two of them were kissing and touching each other near one of the beds where a young boy lay sleeping. The Kapo described a bright flash running from the patient's chest towards each of the Nazis; he said it looked like an electrical arc." Becoming fearful, the woman's husband didn't stick around, but left the building to have a smoke. After a while, he and another Kapo were called in and directed to remove a body. It was the twin he saw earlier. He described the boy's face as looking like that of an old man."

Ann opened and scanned the other entries, nothing really here that relates. "Let's try Mengele. I'll bet he's Josef Mengele, the crackpot doctor who experimented on twins." She entered the name. A couple of hits appeared.

"Hmm, confirmed... Grese and Mengele were romantically involved. Seems that both of them were disliked by the other guards in the camp or maybe mistrusted is a better word, aside from that there's little else. I thought there would be more but then I haven't gone through everything at the Kaplan's, besides Rachel was noted more for her artwork than anything else."

"What has the internet to say about these two?" Marty asked.

"Let's find out." Ann replied. The two of them spent the next half hour reading the long list of crimes and accusations arising from Mengele's and Grese's actions while in the camp. There were also numerous photographs of both. Comparing the photos of Grese to the photos Ann had taken of Rachel's paintings, there could be no question, Grese was the person shown in the artwork. "Irma Grese didn't leave the camp after the liberation. She was arrested, tried and hanged shortly afterward. Mengele apparently escaped to South America before the Russians and western Allies crushed the Reich between their armies. According to this next article, Mengele took on a new identity and disappeared, but later it came out he had suffered a stroke while swimming and had drowned."

Ann went on. "And listen to this. Captain Josef Mengele was a physician working in several Nazi camps. He was known as the White Angel of Death since he would wear his white smock while watching new prisoners arrive at the rail yards. He would separate mothers and children, selecting some who were taken to the hospital and others who he had sent directly to the gas chambers..." Ann gasped, "Look at this photo." A man in a German uniform was shown, the caption below read: Mengele, known as the Angel of Death or in German - Todesengel.

"Todesengel! Wasn't that the word Christine had used when she warned me of danger?" Marty asked.

"The lover of the beast... Todesengel." Ann confirmed. "What do you think?"

"What on earth am I supposed to think?" Marty replied. "Are we to assume the dead are walking about Hansel's Creek?"

27

At a hardwood table within Meyers Hall's spacious kitchen, a thoroughly dejected man stared at a lap top computer screen while nursing his fourth gin and tonic. The sun had just set below the forest's tree line and twilight shrouded the Hall in gloom. The stark glare of the computer screen illuminated the tabletop. Norman rose and walked several feet toward a nearby wall, flipping a switch, a small fluorescent light suspended by silver chains above the porcelain sink came to life and provided the room a little more light, it would do.

His first request had been received and he was told help would be soon in coming and to wait for instructions; but that was nearly two weeks ago. Given the deteriorating situation of late, he had sent a second message; although the request had been acknowledged, no one had shown up nor had he heard a thing. God you'd think someone could just pick up a telephone, but he knew better. Within the United States of America, the NSA routinely intercepted all manner of phone calls and unscrambled, unencrypted communications, as did the Russian Federation, as did the Chinese and on and on.

Over the past year, what had been a trusted symbiotic union between Norman and his Sempitor had instead deteriorated into suspicious sporadic conversation. His mistress, fully knowing what lay in store as it entered the final stages of life, continued to brush aside Norman's benevolent suggestion of suicide or assisted death. As a Servicio, Norman was mentally unprepared and physically incapable of dealing with a creature of such power on his own.

Three full days had passed since Norman Stiles' last urgent appeal, now he was growing desperate. Given what he'd witnessed so far, he wondered if he should have acted much sooner. During their last intermittent joining, Norman had availed himself of the Sempitor's memories regarding the transformation of others of her kind entering the final stages of life. Although the process was difficult both for the Sempitor and their servant, the outcome was at least hopeful that there could be a peaceful acquiescent resolution.

Unfortunately for Norman, his mistress's vivid memories were, but only limited conversations with others of her kind; direct observation and experience was sorely lacking. While these beings lived for centuries, their lives up until several hundred years ago were extremely isolated, the odds of any of them directly witnessing such a turning, were about the same as someone seeing a supernova light up the daytime skies. From her recollections, it also appeared to Norman that such subjects were considered impolite conversation within their own circles.

Norman's contacts among his Servicio brethren had provided him a better insight as to what to expect, but again none of it was direct experience, after all, any Servicio who's Master had required termination by the Order's agents found they themselves also dispatched in short order. Consequently the best information had been passed down to the Servicio through those same agents; unfortunately by the time the agents became involved the transformation had already taking place, whatever happened in the months or weeks prior to their involvement was of little concern. Worse yet, all of the available background centered about those of the White Order, of the Gray there existed naught but speculation, and what there was of that was chilling.

The change in the Master's appearance had been as rapid as it was alarming. The pleasant visage his beloved had shown to the world was now a gut wrenching repulsion. The chronic wasting, her deathly pallor, the thin skin stretched tightly about her limbs and trunk seemed nearly reptilian while the strange shifts and deformation taking place almost daily within her facial structure very nearly prevented Norman from any recognition of the beloved person who he believed was still present, though trapped within that insatiable horror.

Lately his mistress had embraced a nocturnal lifestyle. He had done his best to satiate her ravenous appetites, providing victims who would not be missed in their disappearance; the homeless, transients, and illegal migrants; but now she had taken to leaving the Hall during the hours of darkness to prowl the nearby woods and parks.

Several nights before, his mistress had disappeared causing Norman to worriedly search the forests to the north of the Hall, but his efforts had come up empty. Hours later he discovered an abandoned sedan, its engine still running out near the old South Bridge. From the evidence, his mistress had chanced upon a young couple parked in the secluded area, and there she had ambushed them. He dealt with the vehicle but could find no trace of the couple or their bodies. Upon his return to the Hall, Norman discovered the girl's mangled corpse lying in the Hall's overgrown garden, and later that of the boy who been taken into the lower cellar and slowly consumed.

The problems were piling up at an frightening rate, only a week before that Norman had to retrieve a corpse she had left discarded near a truck wreck out on the Forestry Trunk Road; it was only later he learned that her second victim had been found a mile further up the road. The police were now involved, Norman figured if they were lucky they were still one step ahead of the authorities. Norman thanked God Meyers Hall was bordered on the south by nearly impenetrable brush and forest, separating itself some miles distant from the town, but eventually even this formidable barrier would prove insufficient to discourage his mistress from seeking better hunting within the town of Hansel's Creek.

For the past hour, Stiles had been surfing the internet, scanning news sites for anything associated to suspicious disappearances or heaven forbid, additional murders in the area of Claremont City and more specifically Hansel's Creek. So far, only the body of one Eddie Swan had the authorities convinced foul play had taken place. The vehicle of the young couple his master had consumed only days before hadn't yet surfaced, nor was it likely to, given Norman's choice of a particularly deep and rarely visited inlet along the shores of Lawrence Lake. He continued to peruse the news articles before systematically moving into the social pages of Facebook, Twitter, and Instagram.

Meanwhile within the Hall's cavernous cellar, a dark shape moved within one of the holding cells that previously housed the luckless souls awaiting his mistress's convenience. An irrepressible, gnawing hunger stirred within the Shade causing her to wake from a series of endless nightmares. What remained of the aging Sempitor, who had gone by so many names over the last several centuries; Ayla Wainwright, Ida Frank, Irma Grese, and most lately the persona of Irma Myers, now rose from the bloody soiled mattress where she had lain for the last forty eight hours. Her sensitive ears probed her surroundings for the slightest sound while her eyes, a pair of grotesquely enlarged silver orbs crisscrossed and pierced the darkness within the basement, but it was her nose that whispered a promise of relief, a brief respite from the hollow, aching pit consuming her.

The dark form arose and approached the bars of the cell doors. Reaching out, Irma pushed gently on one of the steel cross bars - the unlocked door opened with a soft creak. Whoever deposited her within the cell hadn't bothered to lock her in. In a remote corner of her mind her consciousness sparked to life and questioned as to who might have done so? For the briefest of moments, that part of her insisted that she knew, but what should have been a familiar name or face completely escaped her, these memories were jumbled, discordant or missing entirely. As quickly as that part of her semiconscious mind had surfaced, it was swept down and drowned within the dark waters of a base, animalistic hunger.

In the smothering blackness of the basement, Irma moved silently, her night adapted eyes just barely allowing her to pick out and allow her to avoid obstructions in her path. As iron filings to a magnet, the scent of nearby prey drove her on and then upward. The Shade ascended the steep cellar stairway in a rush, the soles of its clawed feet scarcely resting any step but for the briefest of moments. Reaching the heavy oaken door leading onto the main floor its talon- like hand fell to the handle, the cool immovable steel rebuffed her effort; it was locked. Once again the Shade listened intently, and in doing so was surprised to find it could reach out and wander among the many rooms of the Hall as easily as if it physically walked through each. The dark beast, the Shade of Norman's beloved mistress had located what it so desperately sought and required. The Shade slowly placed both of its hands upon the steel handle and bringing its incredible strength to bear, felt the locking mechanism resist and then succumb to its powerful grip. The metal gave way. A series of metallic clicks and groans echoed through the cellar.

It paused listening for any indication its prey may have detected the door's breach. Although hearing nothing, it waited patiently. Presently, it sensed movement.

In the kitchen, something had drawn Norman's attention away from the laptop; a noise perhaps, had it come from the cellar? His blood ran cold. There was another sound, one at once more familiar. He walked to the kitchen window that overlooked the ruined garden and peered out hearing a faint tapping. Looking down he could make out the naked boughs of a straggly unkempt shrub. Set too closely to the building, its branches now rapped against the window's wooden shutters. Looking further out into the yard, Norman could see the dark branches of a tree near the edge of the yard swaying rhythmically in a newly arisen breeze. Unlocking the window's latch, he slid the pane open and felt a gust of fresh air sweep into the room, the air currents pushed gently against the fluorescent light fixture causing it to slowly swing back and forth. Satisfied and at ease Stiles returned to the task at hand and reseated himself at the table.

After several long minutes, the Shade pushed lightly on the door; it swung open on silent well oiled hinges. Entering onto the main floor, making sure the long claws on its toes didn't make contact with the stone, it padded softly into a hallway that led to the kitchen. Instinctively the beast sensed Norman's location, its keen nose failed to detect the unmistakable stink of panic its presence normally inspired from its impending victims. Reaching the kitchen entrance, it saw Norman sitting at the table, his attention focused on the computer screen, his back towards the thing that now decided to take full advantage of the opportunity before it. It moved forward with incredible speed.

Norman heard something approach behind him; the rapid staccato of hard claws upon the stone floor spoke to his worst fears. He spun about in his chair coming face to face with the monstrous apparition that his mistress now presented to the world. Strong hands gripped his shoulders lifting him from his chair as easily as a leaf caught within a dust devil; he gasped then shrieked in pain as the creatures taloned claws bit deep into muscle and scraped across bone. The kitchen's previously weak ambient light, flashed and steadily brightened as the Shade drew out the man's life energy in a luminous stream directed towards its own misshapen bony chest. Norman was only vaguely aware of the life that fled his body, hidden within his anguished cries, gasps and screams echoing back and forth across the room's stone floor and rock walls. Suddenly Norman saw himself through the eyes of the Shade who was fully engaged within his appalling agony of breaking bones and rending of muscle and ligament. Totally immersed in the ecstatic rapture of his own demise, Norman's mind joined with that of the creature that gleefully tore him apart in bloody ruin. Then for just the briefest moment before his death, Norman thought he detected his beloved's presence, followed by an intense unfathomable sorrow.

28

The night sky was a sack cloth curtain, moon and starless, the forecast called for a major storm front moving into the area by tomorrow morning. An immaculate cherry red 2000 Ford F150 rolled along two of the four lanes of Big Bend Road. The truck slowed before stopping on the road's shoulder just past a sign stating "Important Intersection Ahead." The driver glanced down at the map app on his phone, the usually accurate map now failed to indicate any turnoff in the road for the next ten clicks. He threw the phone on the seat next to him and reached into the glove compartment where he still kept regional maps of Western Canada and the North Western US States. Seconds later he discovered what he needed to know, put the truck in gear and drove down the road. A minute later he drove past a small sign - "Devil's Fork" - the sun bleached print was barely visible as was an arrow pointing eastward, a narrow unmarked two lane blacktop ran off into the distance. "Important Intersection my ass..." the man muttered.

He stayed the course, and carried on southward. A minute later he caught sight of a large service station and cafe on his right. A brightly lit, oversized green and white sign cheerily proclaimed he'd arrived at Hansel's Creek Fast Gas" while a small sign on the roof of the combined convenience store and cafe, simply said "Mary's Famous Pies." He checked his watch, nearly ten thirty; he'd made pretty good time. The driver pulled the truck onto the lot, drove past the pumps and parked in his choice of vacant stalls in front of the cafe. Inside the restaurant, a number of people seated at the tables turned their heads to glimpse the new arrival.

Turning off the ignition, the man stepped down from the cab, closed the door, hit the lock on the fob and walked toward the single glass door leading inside. Obviously a quiet night, a bored young clerk at the counter looked up hopefully from his magazine when the door chimes sounded then seeing the aboriginal man that entered simply frowned and returned to reading.

Lyle Fox was used to such greetings, small towns in America might enjoy the reputation for being visitor friendly, but that was only valid when the visitors were white. He didn't look twice in the clerk's direction but continued through the aisles of the small store and into the adjoining cafeteria. Standing in the entrance way, Fox surveyed the customers seated at the small rectangular tables. A matronly looking waitress clad in a blue and white floral print dress and a sparkling white apron had just finished refilling a customer's coffee mug and turned in his direction.

The old gal gave Lyle her best smile and walked his way. "Hi darling, you can sit anywhere you like. Can I get you a coffee?"

Lyle smiled back, thinking the friendly woman had just earned herself a fat tip. He glanced beyond her and recognized the man whose coffee mug she had just refilled. "Coffee's fine - black, no sugar." Lyle gestured past the woman. "I'll be sitting right there Ma'am, beside that good looking fella over there."

The waitress followed his eyes to where a middle aged black man sat digging into a slice of peach pie. "Ok hon. Menus on the table. I'll be with you in five or so to take your order."

Lyle walked up to the table, pulled out a chair opposite to Elijah Cole and sat down. "Elijah. Been a while hasn't it?" His face was expressionless for the briefest of moments before he allowed a trace of a smile to appear on his face.

The black man nodded, finishing a mouthful of pie and washing it down with a sip of coffee. "It has indeed. Thanks for coming down." Elijah looked into the face of the man sitting across the table. The relationship between the two men was cordial, but no more than that. The nature of their business demanded an arm's length association, the dangers involved required an unemotional, logical approach, and cooler heads would go a long way to winning the day if things went south.

"I got a message from Blas just after I spoke with you. You are aware this is sanctioned by the Order?" Lyle stared at the man.

"Yes, I received the same information about an hour ago." Elijah added. "I wonder why we hadn't gotten wind of this before. I only arrived at this conclusion several days ago when I witnessed an autopsy that had all of the usual signs of a Shade killing."

"Actually this isn't all that unusual; remember here that we're dealing with a member of the Gray Order." Lyle stopped speaking as he noticed the waitress arrive at the table and pour out a cup of coffee.

"Decided on anything yet dear?" the waitress asked.

"Grilled cheese... and a piece of the peach pie my friend is chowing down. Must be good!" Lyle flashed a small smile in her direction. The woman left and he continued.

"This sort turns a lot faster than the White." Lyle grew serious. "You know you have to admire her Servicio. He followed the guidelines, did everything he could to prevent this. I think in the end, the turn took her even faster than she thought it would have. Still, most Grays never do the right thing, just not in their nature."

"Hmm, doesn't help all the folk she's murdered since she got here, how many decades ago was that?" Elijah scowled.

"About six, give or take a few years. If it's any consolation, before she started to turn, she did nearly all of her hunting abroad. The Gray aren't stupid you know. When they get the urge they usually visit those "shit hole" countries your president is always going on about. They take what they need, have their jolly's and then come home."

"And how do you know this, someone ask her?" Elijah queried.

"Her Servicio gave reports back to the Order whenever they traveled. Some countries were on the menu, others weren't." Fox replied.

"So the Order sanctions these murder sprees?" Cole nearly spat. Although he and Fox had worked together coming up nearly six years, Elijah still couldn't get his head around the ease which the Sempiterno dispatched human life, nor those of the White order who parasitized humanity, stealing months or years of life expectancy from men women or children, anyone vulnerable to whom they had access.

Fox knew where Coles thoughts and emotions were leading; he could read Elijah like a book. "Yet you don't have any problem accepting our help when tracking down your own human monsters, right?"

As always Cole considered that counterbalancing point of view. When he and Fox first met and Cole was taken into the Order's confidence, he had agreed to the equitable arrangement. Using the Bureau's resources, he would assist the Order track down and, if need be, eliminate those in the order who were or had turned to Shades. Although to date, his assistance lay in shielding and covering up the unusual murders and disappearances, making them appear to be the work of common serial killers, rather than inhuman monsters. In turn, the Order, utilizing their vast array of information resources would supply him with promising leads to human murderers. When he thought about it, eliminating killers, human or inhuman, still had a positive outcome from the point of view of a policeman. Cole shoved another piece of pie into his mouth.

Fox looked the man in the eyes and probed beneath Cole's unemotional veneer. Satisfying himself that Elijah would live up to their agreement he took a sip of coffee before continuing. "Target's name is Irma Meyers, she and her Servicio Norman Stiles live in Meyers Hall, about five or six miles from here."

"Meyers?" Cole rolled the name in his mouth. "Any connection to Otto Meyers?"

"Yup, the very same, but he's out of the picture, definitely not a person of interest, besides he's human. Lives in a swanky old folks home in Claremont City, he'll be dead within the month, even got a plot ready for him in the local cemetery." Lyle paused. "Apparently Otto emigrated from Switzerland and started building the manor in '47, Irma Meyers joined him less than a year later under the guise of Otto's niece."

"Swiss as well?" Elijah asked.

"No, German. Our fraulein and Norman Stiles came over together. According to Blas, Norman figures she started to lose it last November, got real bad only three weeks ago. That's when she started prowling closer to home. That guy whose autopsy you attended, Eddie Swan, she did him and the other dude that was with him that night."

"Ike Tate..." Cole wiped his mouth with a napkin. "Never found him."

Lyle set down his fork on the empty place mat before him. "Not likely to. Norman tells Blas that there's a veritable blast furnace in the Hall's basement. Norman had it put in ten years ago or so, after Irma began taking the odd meal among the locals. He's the janitor and cleans up after her."

"Why didn't Stiles tell the Order what she was up to from the start?" Cole asked.

"That's no concern of theirs. So long as she maintains a reasonable degree of discretion they simply don't care. That's part and parcel of being a member within the order. You don't interfere in the business of other members and they don't butt into yours. Norman followed the rules as laid down by his caste, the Servicio, and with her blessing. Notifying the Order of her predations, allowed them to track and deflect the possibility of any suspicion arising from the local authorities. Worked too didn't it? Neither the Sheriff's department, State Police or even the FBI had a clue, flew right under the radar, at least until she turned and became careless. Now we're here to take care of business and tie up any loose ends, right?"

"Yeah... you'll have to excuse me." Cole rose from his chair and looked about for the bathroom. "Sorry, this pie isn't sitting well with me." Nor had their conversation.

29

Blas Velez was late for today's session. Teun had entertained himself playing solitary with a deck of cards he had found in his room, he hadn't won a single game. A member of a superior race indeed he mused.

"Teun, my apologies. I asked a girl go to inform you of my delay, but she couldn't locate you." Blas walked up to the table that had doubled as a bar during their sessions.

"I think we ended the last session considering how a Sempitor may die or be killed. For starts, you are quite unlikely to be felled by disease or illness, a Sempitor's constitution seems to know no bounds. Poisons are certainly disabling, but are a generally ineffective means of death for any Sempitor aged over a century or more. Seems slow exposure to most natural compounds seems to build resistance over sufficient time in your bodies.

For example, you might have heard tell of a Russian by the name Grigori Yefimovich Rasputin, ah Rasputin is name enough isn't it. He was one of the Order, and was purported to have been born January 21, 1869; this of course was a total fabrication on his part... yes, he was most certainly born on January 21; but three hundred years before in 1569. He had no problem keeping up his secret, Russia in those days was quite backward; it was a huge country and Rasputin simply moved from place to place over the interim.

Anyway, he came to the attention of the Order near the turn of the twentieth century when he began hobnobbing with Russian Royalty, the Romanovs. Several Sempiterno who were lesser members of the royal families in Europe at the time, soon began running into him. Later they brought him into the fold. Rasputin was a member of the White Order and had significant powers of empathy and influence and perhaps even what some refer to as "second sight." My Mistress actually met him during a visit to St. Petersburg. Personally she didn't care for the man at all and I believe her description of the man was, and I quote, "a very complex individual." I digress, excuse me.

Rasputin managed to worm his way into the Romanov family and enjoyed a reputation as a spiritualist, healer, clairvoyant and what not. Some in your Order warned him through his Servicio to keep his distance from the Crown, but he didn't heed the advice. Involving himself in politics and gaining considerable fame he became a political target. In fact, in November of 1916, a prominent Russian politician, Vladimir Purishkevich stated, "the tsar's ministers have been turned into marionettes; marionettes whose threads have been taken firmly in hand by Rasputin and the Empress Alexandra Fyodorovna - the evil genius of Russia and the Tsarina…" Vladimir had no idea how close he was to the truth.

On July 14, 1914, a supposedly mentally deranged woman stabbed our Sempitor in the stomach, for a human the wound would have been considered severe, but for Rasputin it was a mere scratch, even so he had to feign a long and difficult recovery. Then on December 30, 1916, Rasputin was lured to a noble's home, their intentions were to assassinate the Sempitor. From an account given by one of the assassins; it seems Rasputin dined on cakes and tea laced with cyanide - with no ill effect. Feeling parched, Rasputin then asked for some Madeira wine, also poisoned, and drank down three full glasses, once again without detrimental effect. Becoming irritated, one of the attending nobles shot Rasputin in the chest with a revolver leaving his supposed corpse in the basement for an undisclosed period of time. When the noble returned to deal with the body, Rasputin jumped up and attacked the man. The noble managed to free himself running upstairs with Rasputin in hot pursuit. It was only when others repeatedly shot Rasputin that he collapsed and his body thrown into the Little Nevka River where it was purportedly discovered under the ice several days later. Unknown to the authorities and those who conducted the autopsy, the body they found did not belong to the Sempitor but was instead that of his Servicio. This is a true story. If you doubt me you can ask Rasputin yourself, he's a middle aged Sempitor living on an island off the coast of Africa on a vineyard, cultivating grapes and bottling the Madeira wine he is still so fond of."

"Seriously?" Asked Teun while wearing an expression suggesting "this is bullshit" on his face.

"Yes, seriously. May I continue? I have other duties to complete." Blas scolded. The youth nodded and wiped the look from his face.

"Other methods of reliable death include severe bludgeoning of the head, or beheading, a somewhat rare occurrence unless you are unlucky enough to have crossed ISIS. Explosions that cause irreparable damage from which there is no return as is consumption by fire, particularly effective. My standard example is Jeanne d' Arc or Joan of Arc. You might remember her as that young woman who led the French armies against the English? At any rate, she was thought invincible; at least for the most part - she is particularly known for plucking an arrow from her right shoulder and returning to battle in less than an hour and winning the day. Some say she possessed a magic helmet that protected her in battle; others cite it was God's will. Her bishop, one of the first of our Order states that she was actually a young Sempitor of unusual power. Jeanne died, burned at the stake by the English; this is yet another shining reason as to why Sempitors should not meddle in the political affairs of humans.

Let's carry on. Death by hanging is usually ineffective since the spinal cord is extremely durable and regenerative; once removed from the gallows or circumstance, the sempitor's physical processes will begin anew; it will regain consciousness within a day or so and complete mobility within a week. The old Dracula myth of driving a stake through the heart is actually effective, but only if the stake remains in place ensuring the Sempitor is unable to properly renew itself and is denied of sustenance. In this case, and past an uncertain point, the body will eventually die and rot.

This brings us to bullets, knives, spears, arrows and the like. Partial incapacitation is usually assured and if enough damage takes place, the Sempitor may appear to have died, but true death from these causes, are in fact quite rare. One of our more prominent members, a medieval pope no less, postulated that Christ himself was one of the Sempiterno. Consider that the man displayed incredible and frankly inexplicable powers of influence among his followers and even gained admiration among those of his enemies. As for miraculous healing, my Mistress, who is herself the present head of our Order, is capable of transferring limited amounts of life energy to others, although she finds the effort terribly draining. The Christ suffered terribly on a cross and died and was then placed in a tomb. Three days later we have his resurrection and subsequent appearance among others for several months afterward. There are also wide spread, although highly doubtful and unfounded rumors of Jesus Christ appearing in Western Europe some centuries after his crucifixion. I should tell you now that Sempitors, especially those of the White Order should not necessarily be viewed as evil. If Christ was indeed a Sempitor, then history records that he was surely motivated by a desire to do good in the world.

Sempitors may also be found within any race. Li Ching-Yuen a Chinese national is documented as having lived at least 200 years before dying in 1933. Moreover, the Imperial Chinese Government is on record as having congratulated Li upon reaching both his 150th and 200th birthdays. It is said that his memory was perfect and he would recall events that took place 150 years before. Interestingly Li originally stated he was born in 1736, but a professor from Minkuo University discovered evidence showing Li was actually born in 1677. Li's followers claim the man had followed the secrets of longevity; learning these from a man who was over five hundred years old. Of course the Order knows this to be false, at least that last bit, he was in fact, that same five hundred year old man. When he actually passed in

1933 he had reached the ripe age of seven hundred and fifty six, he is the only Sempitor to have had even a portion of their unusually long lives properly documented.

Rumors of other possible Sempitors include Noah – who purportedly reached an age of nine hundred and fifty years; yes the shipbuilder in the bible. Also Moses who was said to have died in his prime at only 120 years old, yet no one ever found his body or a grave, those in the Order presume he simply grew bored in his role of deliverer and taking up a different name continued to live elsewhere until his death. And of course, let's not forget Methuselah, the Grandfather of Noah who is claimed to have lived to be nine hundred and sixty nine years old.

Now let me focus on you; personally. Your unusual birthright, has entitled you tentative - I say again tentative, admission into the most prestigious of clubs. It could truly be said that you are one in millions. As you entered puberty, you became aware of having certain talents that remain unshared by others of your peers. You are possessed of an extraordinary long natural life span, and for want of better words, exceptional durability.

I think it quite likely that you will live at least three to four centuries; accurate records suggest the oldest of our kind have lived over seven hundred years. You will quickly rebound from all but the gravest injury and will be extremely difficult to kill. This said you would do well to remember, you are not immortal.

Before getting Elijah Cole's request to join him in Hansel's Creek, Lyle Fox had been waiting patiently in line behind an angry old man standing at a counter. The young woman facing him worked for the government registry office in the sleepy town of Milk River, Alberta. Having failed to present the required medical documentation, the old fellow had become incensed when told the clerk could not renew his driver's license without it. Despite the girls every attempt to politely calm her customer, he quickly became more agitated and argumentative, his cane striking the floor as he accentuated each demand. Several more tense minutes crawled passed until the short bespectacled man, realizing he wasn't getting anywhere with the clerk, muttered something nasty under his breath and spun about on his heel. As he turned from the counter his right shoulder collided with Lyle's chest and the older man staggered back against the counter.

Noting the imposing demeanor and athletic stature of the man he just bumped into, the old fellow became startled and with a rather diminutive and timid voice managed to squeak out "Sorry Sir." The fellow continued toward the exit at a brisk pace, his cane click-clacking and marking time beside him as he crossed the tile floor.

"No problem." Fox called after him as he stepped up to the counter. "Hi Gayle. I'd ask how you day is going but I already have a pretty good idea." He watched the clerk shake her head, her long blonde pony tail swayed behind her neck.

"The joys of working with the public." She quipped. "So Lyle, what can I do for you today?"

"Need a copy of a land title for one of my places." Lyle stated.

"You selling?" She smiled as she brought up the search screen in front of her. Her fingers stabbed the keyboard, her right index finger punched enter.

"No nothing like that. My accountant tells me I can receive a tax benefit by subdividing a section of property I own out near the river. Don't ask me how that works." He shifted his weight to his other foot, the new boots he bought the day before were killing him. It'd take another day or two before he'd broken them in.

"Nothing coming up." The girl wore a puzzled expression.

"What name are you using?" Lyle asked.

"Yours of course... Lyle Fox." She looked at him.

"No, sorry. That won't work, try Ipapo Otáátoyi," he leaned into the counter and produced his status card that declared him a member of the Blackfoot Nation.

She looked down at the card. "Ok, um, how did you say it again?" she asked.

Lyle slowly pronounced the name in his native tongue.

"I had no idea..." she repeated the name slowly back to the man before her.

"Literally taken, it means "lightning flash Fox." He grinned. "I think it loses something in translation." He laughed, "That's why I stick with Lyle, seems to work for everyone."

"I sorta like... Flash Fox..." she grinned and laughed, "Ok, here it is." She studied the screen in front of her. "Hmm, here they are." There were no fewer than seven separate property titles registered to that name. "Now... which one is it?"

Lyle leaned forward and peeked around the monitor so he could glimpse the screen and the property description listing. He ran a finger quickly down the list then stopped. "This one... right... here."

"Ok thanks." Gayle hit the print button and a second later handed Lyle a piece of paper from the printer. Do you need it notarized?"

"Yes, thanks." He stepped back.

"I'll see if the notary is in this morning." She paused turned away slightly then laughed, "Well I guess I am." Gayle ran the entire operation herself.

The clerk studied the document. "This date can't be right." She paused. "1885?"

"Yes it can." Lyle stated straight faced. "Actually, my family has lived on that particular parcel well before even that. You can look it up in the archives if you drive up to Edmonton."

"Ok, yeah, but the name on the title was never changed since it was first registered." She replied.

"I actually have two legal names, Lyle Fox, the one I use for most things and this one that I share with my dad, my grandfather and even my great grandfather." He explained. "My grandfather and great grandfather didn't write, for them and the government at the time, it was just easier for everyone if they just kept the same name."

Lyle finished up his business in the registry, met with the real estate agent before going to his bank and paying the monthly bills. An expert with computers and modern technology, Lyle could have easily done most of, if not all of his transactions on line, but truth was old timers like him didn't put a lot of faith in internet security. And Lyle was very old indeed.

One of Lyle's first recollections as a child was playing on a buffalo robe within the family's tipi and listening to his mother's voice as she sang a Lakota lullaby to his baby sister. He saw his father; Lone Bear lift the flap of the tipi and enter the tent. Stepping inside he was accompanied by a tiny blizzard of snowflakes at his back driven by a strong but abnormally warm January wind. His father called the wind the "snow eater," a phenomena commonly known as a Chinook in later years. Lone Bear sat between Lyle's mother, his first wife and his own sister who he had taken as a second wife. It was not uncommon that those of his nation to have multiple wives, nor uncommon for fathers to trade their daughters for horses or other sundries.

Lyle's father, a lesser chief of the Lakota nation, was the headman of their Óspaye; the small group made up of Lyle's family and close friends. Back in those days, his people were nomadic hunter gatherers living on the prairies and foothills lying along the eastern slopes of the Rocky Mountains. Numerous aboriginal nations called the northern region of the Great American Plains home. Some were allies of the Lakota who made up one of the three tribes of the Great Sioux Nation, while others like the Shoshone were fierce enemies. All lived in lands that would eventually evolve into the US states of North and South Dakota to the east, Wyoming and Montana to the south and in the Canadian north, Rupert's Land. That huge Canadian Northwest Territory would divide to become the provinces of Alberta, Saskatchewan and Manitoba some hundred or so years in the future.

A quick learner and eager to please, Lyle enjoyed a happy childhood. From his mother the boy learned survival skills - how to make fire, what foods to eat and others to avoid. As he grew older, he learned to hunt at the side of his father and uncles. A good life was to be had within his small village. Every couple of years his Óspaye would meet with others of their nation in a large pow-wow or gathering of the tribes. Banding together, these large groups would hunt the buffalo, often stampeding entire herds over steep cliffs or buffalo jumps, and then butchering the dead or dying animals lying below. This was the most efficient and least hazardous method of hunting these magnificent, bad tempered and dangerous beasts. These were also important times for the elders, who would discuss news and events occurring throughout their loosely defined nation. But perhaps, more importantly still, the gatherings were also a time for courtship and marriage. Intermarriage between members of different Óspaye was not only encouraged but an important necessity to ensure a large and varied gene pool.

As Lyle grew toward manhood his abilities were already recognized among his people. He was expected to become a great hunter and provider to his Óspaye. Some thought he might one day take his place about the fire as one of the great chiefs of the Sioux Nation but this was not to be. Instead, Ipapo Otáátoyi - lighting flash Fox - would be obliged to take another path, one far less travelled among his people or any others in the world. It was at one such gathering, as Lyle entered his sixteenth summer that he chanced upon a meeting that would guide him toward his true destiny.

Over the previous winter and spring, Lyle had begun to notice subtle changes within him. Gradually his sense of sight and hearing was becoming incredibly keen and focused; his body unusually strong and swift, beyond that indicated by his average size and most certainly when compared to other boys of his age and stature. As his hearing grew acute, Lyle discovered he could hear the faint movements of small animals rustling in the bush or listen in on quiet conversations taking place in tipi's on the far side of camp. His eyesight was also in flux, these changes no less impressive. Lyle could identify objects, animals, and sometimes even people's faces at considerable distance, but it was at night, especially at night, when the nature of these changes became most apparent. He could walk along a dark forest trail seeing and avoiding rocks, roots, fallen branches and other obstacles on even the darkest moonless nights. As these abilities continued to manifest, Lyle became increasingly worried about what these changes meant; yet he couldn't bring himself to speak of it to anyone. What would his people say? Would they fear and banish him from his home and family?

The Sioux, like other aboriginal nations living on the plains, were a spiritualistic people. Their belief system encompassed multiple deities, the greatest of whom was Inyan who created the sun, moon, and the earth. Many lesser gods were also known and respected among his people and believed responsible for good works, but there were other forces distinctly evil in nature. Lyle had heard tell of all these legends while sitting upon his father's knee or crowded about large communal fires where the Shaman or wise man would instruct and remind the tribal members of their spiritual legacy.

Beginning to develop these abnormal abilities, Lyle feared he might be under a curse. Such things often happened, he had seen a young cousin a year or two older than he, suddenly fall ill and waste away in the space of several months. There had been no identifiable sickness, the Shaman told the boy's parents and relatives that this could only be the will of a god, maybe one that his cousin offended in some manner. It wasn't much of a stretch for Lyle to hold the belief that he might be turning into some sort of monster; one in particular, the Waheela, had sprung to mind. According to legend this demon could shape shift becoming a man or a giant wolf at a time of his choosing, though mostly at night. The creature was said to be able to hear clouds as they floated across the face of the moon, or see clearly in even the darkest cave; it also had the unfortunate habit of ripping the heads off anyone it found walking alone at night.

It was this fear that led him to consult a Wicasa Wakan or Shaman attending the great gathering. Seeking just any shaman would be a relatively simple task as he'd already seen several, but Lyle felt that only the most esteemed holy man could explain what he was going through and perhaps lift the curse before it went any further. Finding such a man would be more difficult. As it happened Lyle saw a small group of the Nation's elders walking toward a particularly large and specially adorned tent used during the pow-wows. At their side was an old man, his clothing and the articles he wore on his person suggested he was a Shaman. More importantly to Lyle, the fact that he was entering the Pow-Wow tipi together with the Nation's most important chiefs spoke volumes as to the man's standing.

A short distance from where the elders were meeting, Lyle sat down at a small fire, tended by three old women whose job it was to cook and see to the needs of those cloistered within the Pow-Wow tipi. The three women gave him odd looks as he settled at the fire. After some time, one woman came up to him and told him directly he couldn't expect any scraps and advised him to leave. When the boy respectfully explained he was there to have a word with the Great Shaman, their attitude immediately changed. As Lyle patiently waited throughout the hot sunny afternoon and later into the cool of the late evening, from time to time one of the old women would offer him a drink or something to eat.

Much later as the stars blazed in the night sky, a light mist swept over the entire camp, the cooking fires that were still tended and others that would be left to smolder until morning became small islands with the mist. As for the women, two of them had already left for bed, there remained only one to tend the fire or see to the needs of the elders. Lyle had fallen into a sound sleep; his head wrapped in his arms and propped up atop his knees before the small fire. Sometime later, the men emerged from the Pow-Wow tent going their separate ways, but one man noticing the sleeping boy became curious. The woman standing near the boy beckoned the Shaman to approach. As he neared the fire, the woman told the old man the boy had been waiting since noon to speak with him. Without another word she turned and walked away. The Shaman smiled then observed the boy closely, as he did so his expression became unreadable. The old man closed his eyes holding one arm outstretched toward the stars while his other hand grasped the medicine bag hanging from his hip. He stood that way for some minutes before sitting down beside the boy and facing the fire. The Wicasa Wakan were reputed to be wise and holy men, having the ability to communicate with spirits, divine the intentions of the gods, interpret visions, and on occasion even predict the future with considerable accuracy. The last talent had ensured the old man's entry into the Pow-Wow tipi.

Sometime later, Lyle awoke to find the Shaman sitting cross legged beside him, poking the fire with a stick and gazing into its ruby embers. Without acknowledging the boy, the Shaman began to speak softly telling Lyle that he knew the boy's father and uncles; as such Lyle was a worthy person, descended from a worthy family. Upon hearing the Shaman's words Lyle felt the dread and apprehension begin to lift from his heart, but what the holy man would say next bewildered him.

A bright meteor streaked across the sky drawing their attentions upward. While the old man had been speaking, the northern lights; the Aurora Borealis had appeared. Alternating curtains of green, blue and deep reds shone above them. The old man spoke, "dance of the dead men," he paused before continuing, "The spirits have come to visit us tonight. I can hear their voices as they speak in my head."

"Ipapo Otáátoyi, you must leave your people for a time, you must undertake a vision quest." The Shaman looked into Lyle's face and studied his eyes to see if the boy understood.

Lyle was fully aware of what a vision quest entailed. This was the rite of passage he was expected to undertake allowing him to become a man and a recognized member of his people. Up until now, Lyle had never understood it required the participant to leave his family; it was a spiritual passage - not a physical journey. Without questioning, Lyle listened to the old man's words, the inflection and qualities of the voice held him in rapt attention. Behind the wise man's left shoulder, the sharp horns of a crescent moon had broken the eastern horizon, a "buffalo moon"; the upright horns in every way resembling those of the great beast. Lyle considered it truly an omen of some import.

"I see a long life ahead, extending beyond years of count. This is puzzling." The Shaman paused a moment then continued. "You are unlike the many men who walk the world; I sense a spirit emerging within you. Whether for good or evil I cannot say, it is not ready to tell me; perhaps it doesn't know what it will choose to be." The old man stirred the ashes with a stick managing to coax a small flame to life above the hot coals. "Until it has made its choice it is dangerous for you to stay, especially to those who care most for you."

"When will I know, how long must I be away?" Lyles voice quavered and his eyes teared.

"Soon, within a passing of four seasons, then you will know your destiny and what lies ahead." The Shaman reached into his medicine bag and removing a pinch of Gray powder sprinkled it above Lyles' head. "I will ask the Great Spirit to watch over and guide you on your journey."

Hearing this, Lyle stretched his trembling hands toward the fire, seeking to warm them before the yellow flames. "I'm frightened. Am I to become a Waheela?"

The old man chuckled. "Have you a hunger for human blood and meat?"

"No!" Lyle looked back at the Shaman with genuine distress.

"Then do not fear." The Shaman's voice was soothing and Lyle relaxed somewhat.

"You must begin tonight; take only what you need and say nothing to anyone. I will tell your people of your journey." Lyle's eyes followed the old man's face as he raised it up towards the heavens. The greens and blues curtain had fled the sky, now replaced by a blood red glow that extended from horizon to horizon. "Another powerful sign... here, take this with you and keep it around your neck at all times." The Shaman removed a stone amulet suspended from about his neck with a piece of rawhide and handed it to boy. Lyle examined the gift; the flat stone had a hole near the top allowing the rawhide to pass through. Approximately two inches by one inch in size, intricate inscriptions had been cut within the stone's surface, but as to what they might represent, Lyle knew naught, never the less he thanked the Shaman.

"Go north to Milk River, enter the land of the Blackfoot but do not fear. I foresee they will let you pass without harm should you meet them." Slowly the old man rose up from the fire, arching his back and stretching his tired muscles. "Wander among the holy rocks you will find along the cliffs near the river; there you will see the sacred signs set in the rock, they will appear much like those on the amulet. Your spirit guide may come to you in many possible guises, but you will recognize it. Camp near the hallowed ground, allow yourself time to understand its message. Go now and be safe."

Lyle left the old man; he could feel the Shaman's eyes upon him as he walked away. Making his way to the family's tipi, he quietly opened the flap and stepped inside. No one stirred among those who slept peacefully within the tent, Lyle wondered when or if he would ever see them again. He packed his few belongings and several essential items he would need on his journey. Stepping out of the tipi, he noticed the Aurora had ended as quickly as it had begun; early twilight was growing in the northeast.

Lyle often recalled those first lonely weeks he spent travelling along the quarter mile wide buffalo trails. These paths were permanently carved into the prairie by the hooves of migrating animals whose numbers counted in the millions. The odds were distant that Lyle would meet anyone whether friend or foe, for in those years the western lands were relatively empty of humans and instead full of wildlife. It has been estimated that the entire Lakota nation numbered fewer than ten thousand souls in 1800. Europeans had yet to make an appearance in any number in the south. To the north, there were a few more but most often these were the mixed blood Métis who worked trap lines for the Hudson Bay Company that held the fur monopoly throughout the vast expanse of Rupert's Land.

The long sunny days of July were hot and dusty on the plains. Sometimes to escape the heat of the day Lyle would follow game trails leading down from the surrounding prairie into steep ravines where the air was fresh and cool. The same trails often brought him to small creeks running along the length of the gully. There he could obtain water and hunt small game and birds. If possible he would camp atop the edge of the deep ravines, where the air still held some of the day's heat and the tree line provided some shelter from the season's frequent thunder storms.

One such night while camped a considerable distance away from one such ravine, something disturbed his rest. Rest... Lyle came to the conclusion that he never really slept anymore; some part of him was always awake and alert. Nor did he dream, at least not in the usual sense of the word. As he lay in the long hours of darkness, he would revisit his memories which were as rich and vivid as the day they were made. They were also of great benefit along the trail. Lyle found he could clearly recall the more important landmarks his tribe would use to navigate their way across the often featureless plains.

As the sun rose above the horizon, something roused him to full wakefulness. Some half mile distant he saw a small group of horses and their riders working their way westward following the edge of the ravine's tree line toward his position. Lyle attempted to discern who the riders might be, but dawn was to their backs, the sun in his eyes nearly blinded him. His ears rather than his eyes, told him he was facing danger. The language the riders spoke was unknown to him.

Lyle scolded himself, while he had been trying to decide who the men might be. They were much closer than he had first thought. Lyle quickly stood, placing the small sack containing his few belongings, his bow and its small quiver of arrows about his shoulders. Then holding his spear in one hand, and his tomahawk in the other, he moved quickly and quietly, putting as much distance between him and the riders as possible. His footsteps fell upon the hard sun baked ground in rapid succession then stopped after several minutes to listen and look behind him. What he saw wasn't good. The men had wheeled about and were moving in his direction; fast. He picked up his speed though he knew that there was no way he could hope to outrun mounted braves. He had no choice but to pick a spot and make his stand. Up ahead was a small group of aspen, too few and thin to provide shelter yet it was better than being completely exposed in the open. Lyle readied himself, crouching low, his back braced against several of the larger trees. His spear and tomahawk lay on either side, while he held his bow at the ready, an arrow notched on the bow string. He closed his eyes and took a deep breath saying a prayer to the gods to spare him harm and then waited for his inevitable discovery.

There was little doubt of the danger approaching him; it was a small raiding party. Lyle recognized the men as belonging to the Shoshone tribe, sworn enemies of the Lakota. Lyle chose the brave who appeared to be in charge as his target and drew his bow tight preparing to let loose an arrow as soon as the man rode within range. The group of riders swept toward the stand of aspens then suddenly stopped. They turned and twisted about on the backs of their ponies as if confused. Lyle held his bow in check while he watched the leader signal to the other men to spread out in different directions while he urged his own pony into the aspen grove. The small horse stepped slowly among the small trees while its rider carefully scanned the ground. At one point when the man's gaze fell directly upon Lyle's position, the boy felt his fingers relaxing; allowing the bow string to gently slip. The man had approached within a dozen feet or so, any second now Lyle's bow would release and propel the flint tipped arrow toward the rider's chest.

The something very odd happened. The rider's gaze didn't pause on his position. In fact it didn't hesitate for a second, but moved on continuing to search the grove for the man the riders had seen minutes earlier. Lyle tightened his grip on the bow string and waited.

Nearly a dozen Shoshone braves surrounded him on every side, and yet it was as if he were invisible to their probing eyes. Lyle could tell that the men were becoming frustrated, it would have been impossible for someone to elude the group after they were spotted; there was nowhere to hide. Several of the men began to talk excitedly. If Lyle could understand their language he would have understood they believed a demon had been teasing them. When their leader spoke out in an angry voice; the other men immediately fell quiet, although the leaders eyes betrayed his concern. With a quick shout, he turned his pony in the direction from where they came, the rest of the party galloped after him.

Motionless, Lyle watched them ride out of sight. Although assured the Shoshone had left, he never the less spent what remained of the morning concealed in the aspens, unwilling to chance another encounter. Throughout that morning his mind continued to wrestle with the situation, trying make any sense as to what had happened.

Three days later Lyle came upon the grassy banks of the Milk River, a relatively insignificant tributary of the magnificent seven hundred and twenty nine mile long Missouri River. The Milk River's slow summer waters meander through the dry dusty prairies, the silt and soil it carries lending color to the river and earning the waters their name. He followed the ancient river as it weaved westward, towards its headwaters hidden

213

somewhere in the still distant foothills to the west. The boy passed along alternating series of steep cliffs on either side of the river, a result of uncountable spring runoffs. Opposite and downstream of the cliffs, pebbled shallows glittered in the sunlight. Infrequently, Lyle discovered a sandy beach along the river where its banks widened, allowing the current to slow and deposit the alluvium to settle as the river shed its burden.

High above, Lyle watched a pair of red tailed hawks circle and soar in the updrafts. His incredibly sharp eyes taking in every detail within their opinions and the way their aerodynamic frames cut through the air. The two birds were slowly moving off, gliding further west over a set of distinctly odd looking cliffs on the north bank of the river. Lyle forded the river, another half mile further he reached the strange geological formations known as the Hoodoos. A jumbled collection of asymmetrical rounded rock chimneys rose up from an ancient eroded cliff some half mile northwest of the river. He rested and ate some rabbit along with Yampa and Camas roots he had cooked the night before then began to explore the area.

The sandstone cliffs in this bad land drainage basin had been eroded by flowing water and the fracturing action of freezing and thawing over millennia. The weather beaten sandstone cliffs were easily climbed in many places and in a few spots Lyle simply stepped up wide flats of rock resembling steps. The hoodoos themselves were spires of a soft rock, mostly mudstone along with some poorly cemented crumbling sandstone. Some structures were of considerable height and atop of many sat a flat capstone of hard rock, mostly limestone or well cemented sandstone. The caps protected the soft column of rock below from the effects of erosion.

It was on the lower sections of cliff in the area that Lyle first saw the petroglyphs carved into the vertical sections of soft sandstone. He began to compare these to the light carvings on the face of the amulet given to him by the Shaman. It became clear to Lyle that the cliff carvings in this area were much older, the weathered appearance of the carvings edges were worn nearly smooth. Near mid afternoon, Lyle discovered a small cave, perhaps ten feet deep and six wide. It would make an excellent base from which to explore the area. Inside the cave within a small circle of rounded river rocks, he found several pieces of aged charcoal and scattered animal bones that he recognized as belonging to deer and rabbit. Evidently someone else had used the cave as a domicile before him... the sun bleached charcoal bits lying near the entrance suggested it was a very long time ago indeed.

A month later, the sun was rising later and setting earlier each day. Autumn was on its way and the leaves would soon be turning color. Lyle had prepared to spend the winter in the area, but not within the cave, it was too exposed and the rocky floor would steal away the heat despite insulating the floor with the many robes and hides he obtained while hunting. If anyone could call what he did hunting?

His ability to remain hidden from human eyes also extended to that of the animals. He would quietly work his way close to the edge of the herd and remain motionless, the animals never seemed to detect him, not even his scent. When they drew very close, he would use a well placed arrow to slay buffalo or his spear to kill deer or elk. He felt badly that he had to waste most of the meat from the animals he took, but without the skins and hides he would never survive the winter.

Lyle chose a location for his winter camp at the base of a south facing, leeward line of cliffs. The river had narrowed significantly at that point into a series of small rapids that ran into a round deep pool. The flow and action of the water would limit freezing and guarantee Lyle access to water except during the very coldest days of winter. The open water would also attract water fowl and other game animals in the area. His shelter was small; of a lean-to design rather than a tipi, but built to be highly water resistant and very spacious for him and his gear. Its opening faced south and he constructed the simple structure within the tree well of a huge spruce, its branches forming an umbrella over top the lean to and living walls on either side.

Lyle also constructed a very small fire pit within, digging into the earth and laying a series of interlocking flat sandstone rocks that would ensure the fire wouldn't spread into the roots of brush and trees growing nearby. A small flap at the top of the shelter would allow the smoke to escape while a series of small holes beneath its walls provided a fresh flow of air - it was important that the hides forming its walls were able to dry occasionally. He felt confident that when the days grew short and frost reclaimed the land he would be as ready as anyone could be to withstand the rigors of the winter ahead.

That particular year Lyle found the winter extraordinarily mild, the warm snow eating winds visited often and the snowpack remained light. He had spent the evenings and inclement days working on a pair of snow shoes but come the spring he hadn't yet needed to use them. He spent most days visiting his snare line and hunting what game he needed. Most of his nights were spent in meditation and listening to the creaking of the spruce branches as they waved back and forth in the strong winds. Sleep still eluded him, at first he was worried but in time he realized he simply no longer required it. Instead he took solace within his memories, reliving and organizing them into a filing system that a modern executive's assistant would be proud of. This would prove an invaluable asset as the years and decades of life passed.

The days of winter stretched thin and the hours of sunlight slowly grew longer while the winter constellations disappeared and those of spring took center stage. Lyle took heed of the changing positions of the Great Fisher (Big Dipper) and his son, the Little Fisher (Little Dipper) immediately after the sun had set and the stars had appeared. His father had often said, "When the Great Fisher arises in the east and the Great Buffalo (Orion) descends in the west, spring will soon arrive."

It was a warm sunny afternoon in early spring and Lyle was sunning himself on a flat limestone escarpment jutting out seventy feet above the Milk River. Across the river lay a gravel delta and beyond that the Gray brown prairie swept out as far as the eye could see. With the first rains, the grass would begin to turn various hues of green. At present, myriads of purple crocuses already dotted the landscape, even peeking through melting patches of light snow. Lyle hadn't seen another human being since his close brush with the Shoshone raiding party the previous summer. His gaze wandered nearly a half mile down river, on the opposing river bank a sizable herd of elk or mule deer were fording the river. Within seconds he became aware of his mistake. The shapes were people; some on horseback, others on foot, while still others guided pack horses carrying heavy burdens or towed canoes along the edge of the river.

Lyle sat up continuing to watch their progress, his eyes straining to identify to what nation they might belong. There was something very strange about these travelers, their dress and even in the manner they moved; this begged closer inspection. Lyle jumped to his feet and ran along the now familiar paths leading down toward the river bottom. Although highly confident that no one could see him or even guess his presence even at point blank range; he decided not to take any chances with these new comers. Lyle chose a good hiding place close enough to the river to allow him to observe their approach, yet affording him an unseen escape route within the hoodoos at his back.

The party of fifty or so were passing within twenty yards of Lyle's position and he had no trouble identifying several Shoshone who travelled near the front of the troop of strangers, one of them was a young woman with a papoose. From the amazing stories he had heard at the Pow-Wows fires, he knew in his heart that these new people belonged to the numerous white tribes who lived a great distance east from here. Some described the whites as devils who possessed sticks that killed as they spoke and spewed fire. He would have to be extra careful. He noticed some of the men had looked in his direction but gave no indication of seeing him; this gave him the confidence to abandon his hiding place and follow the group upstream, remaining unseen as he moved among the rocks and cliffs.

Once the group had moved past the crags and cliffs lining the river's narrows, they came to a large flat delta where they stopped and made camp. Lyle observed every detail of their movements. It soon became clear that two of the white men, well dressed in waist long buckskin coats and leggings were in command; the three Shoshone braves who Lyle assumed were guides, communicated with them by way of signing or speaking in halting words that Lyle took to be the language of the strangers.

One of the leaders, a brawny man Lyle assessed to be well over six feet tall approached his position near the river's edge. The man looked up and down the riverbank and then relieved himself on the sandy bank before lighting a short pipe filled with an aromatic tobacco. For a moment the smoke clung lazily about the man's face and shoulders before wafting toward Lyle who nearly sneezed and coughed as it filled his lungs and stung his eyes. The white man turned his back on the water and walked from the river bank removing the wide brimmed hat he wore and mopping the sweat from his brow with a sleeve. Lyle gasped; the white's hair was as red as fire! Perhaps he was a devil? The boy continued to watch as this man approached the other equally tall man Lyle decided was also a chief. The second man possessed piercing eyes, medium brown hair and wore a strange triangular hat atop his head. This one seemed in charge of setting up the camp, casually giving orders to the other white men of the group as they unpacked the horses and canoes or erected their strange square canvass wall tents. Lyle noticed that several of those working with the canoes wore colorful garments that peeked through openings beneath their buckskins.

Lyle continued to watch the group; growing increasingly fascinated with the odd smells emanating from their cooking fires, the lilt and pitch of their language, and the way they interacted with one another. The sun had set and it was well into late evening when the whites and Shoshone had gone to their tents. Their attitude seemed to be unusually confident, seeing as how they failed to bother posting any one on watch. Lyle waited for a full half hour until he was sure most of the party were sleeping before cautiously making his way among the small village of tents and having a good look about. Finding there was little else to see for the moment; Lyle retreated to his own camp for the night to contemplate what he had seen and properly file the experience away in his memories.

As the stars wheeled above his small campfire, Lyle set about piecing together the fragments of language he had heard spoken that day together with articles and actions to which they referred. Within a week's worth of observations made at the camp and while following either or both the leaders as they made short forays into the surrounding lands, Lyle came to realize he was able to make sense of much of their conversation. The white men referred to the brown hair chief as Kaptn and the red hair chief as Lootehnut, it appeared to Lyle that Kaptn had the final say in most matters. Lyle found it curious that the young Shoshone squaw didn't address the chiefs as did the other men in the camp; she was on a much more familiar basis, something not uncommon between chiefs and the women of his own tribe. Instead Lyle sometimes heard her call them as Meriweder and Loowes.

Lyle had watched the group for nearly two weeks and was growing bored, they were little more than an elaborate scouting party and of little consequence to the outcome of his spiritual journey; Lyle couldn't have been more wrong. It was the squaw Lyle had come to know as Tsakaka-wea, or "Bird Woman" in Shoshone, who would soon involve Lyle into direct contact with the white travelers, but for now Lyle, would give the group a wider berth as he continued to explore the stone etchings on the cliff walls.

It was exactly one week later and Lyle had just discovered cliff side etchings nearly identical to those shown on the amulet given to him by his shaman. The cliff was only a quarter mile distant from the white's camp. Lyle studied the similar designs he found along the vertical base of the large sandstone outcropping, memorizing each in turn he would later consider them further during his nightly dream quest. He heard someone approach quietly from the direction of the white's camp. Whoever it might be was still a good distance away. His ears spoke to him. The steps weren't intentionally clandestine, but simply made by a person of small size and weight. Lyle broke from his study of the rock face and found a position nearby that would permit him to identify who was approaching. It was the young squaw, Bird Woman, she was picking her way along a nearby rocky trail. A papoose rode on her back, a small brace of rabbits dangled limply at her side. Evidently she had been out checking her snares earlier that morning. Lyle was about to turn away when he heard another pair of footsteps following behind those of the woman. These were made by a man of some size, a man who did not wish discovery; the footfalls of the man were attempting to match those of the woman. They would stop or continue, carefully timed with her pace - Tsakaka-wea was being stalked.

A minute later the man belonging to those steps came into view. It was one of the white men Lyle remembered unloading one of the canoes. The man sported a heavy black beard, wore a white and blue striped shirt and buckskin leggings, a long knife sat in the leather sheath upon his belt. The man walked within several feet of Lyle, who remained completely invisible, and then carried on following the woman. Sensing the man's ill intentions, Lyle followed.

Ahead in a small clearing, Lyle watched Tsakaka-wea prop her papoose carefully against a small tree before bending to reset a snare along a well worn rabbit trail carved out in the brush. That was when the black bearded man rushed forward toward the woman. Hearing his lumbering approach, Tsakaka-wea began to stand and turn toward the noise. The man was on her in an instant grabbing her by the shoulders, his powerful arms holding her fast before him. Tsakak-wea's face betrayed her fear as she recognized her attacker. She was about to scream when black beard struck her across the face with his open hand sending her spinning into the dirt. The man followed the woman to the ground pouncing atop her small frame. There was no mistaking the man's intentions, Tsakaka-wea cried and struggled under his superior weight.

While Lyle sympathized with the woman's plight; it was still very much her plight. Getting involved with such things usually gave rise to unfortunate consequences, the man would have his way and the woman would leave little worse for wear in the long scheme of things. Lyle prepared to leave, but stopped in his tracks when he saw the man take the long knife from its sheath. The woman tried to scream but the man's left hand was clenched tightly on her throat, all she could manage was a high pitched squeak. Black beard brought the knife upward... it was clear to Lyle the man would stab the helpless woman beneath him.

Moving with incredible grace and speed, Lyle grasped a fist sized rock in his right hand as he ran toward the struggling pair. Black beard never heard him coming and even if he had, the outcome would have remained the same. Lyle swung the rock in a tight arc bringing it crashing into the man's right temple. The knife fell from black beard's grip as the big man swooned and collapsed to cover Tsakaka-wea in an unconscious muddle. Lyle dropped the rock and grabbing the man's shirt collar with both hands yanked black beard off Tsakaka-wea and literally tossed his bulk several yards distant.

Sensing her good fortune the woman immediately rolled to the side, leapt to her feet and ran to check on her child. Lyle smiled as the woman reached the small bundle slinging it gently onto one shoulder. She turned to leave, but paused and looked back towards the Lakota boy who had saved her. She didn't smile or say a word, not that Lyle expected anything otherwise, after all their tribes were sworn enemies. Instead she simply gave a slow nod while looking him in the eye.

Something incredibly loud roared behind him and simultaneously Lyle felt a tremendous force knock him off his feet and sending him tumbling to the ground. His mind spun with the pain that burned in his left shoulder. His final image was that of Tsakaka-wea, who now ran to where he laid, her hands waving at someone who stood beyond his view, her voice screaming shrilly in his ears just as he lost his senses.

It was early afternoon when Lyle became aware of his surroundings. Light headed and exceedingly weak, he realized he lay on a low cot in one of the white man's square canvas tents. The air within the tent was close. The smell of hot canvas nearly suffocated the boy, even though the flaps and sides of the tent had been rolled up for ventilation. Tsakaka-wea sat nearby with a wet rag that she occasionally dipped into a bowl of water on her lap and applied to his forehead.

Behind the squaw was a white man that Lyle had seen over the time he observed the group. Unlike some others in the party, Lyle had determined that this particular man was no stranger to wilderness life. Lyle had had an opportunity to watch him stalk and hunt a small herd of skittish white-tailed deer with a bow. The man's movements were confident and practiced, as was the aim of his bow hand. Falling in and out of consciousness, Lyle recognized the man was preparing an herb poultice of a type commonly used among the First Nation tribes. The man stepped to his bedside with the poultice in hand. For the first time, Lyle realized he lay naked from the waist up; turning his head slightly, he stared in silence gaping at the horrendous wound to his left shoulder. Gently the man smiled at him and nodded before applying the wrap atop the wound, while he and Tsakaka-wea conversed in a tongue Lyle had never heard before. It soon became evident that the two were family; the child in the papoose was obviously that of Tsakaka-wea and that of the white man administrating to his care.

Lyle heard the crunch of a man's footsteps outside the tent, a large shadow swept over the cot and a familiar face swam into view before him. It was Lootehnut, the number two chief. The man studied the boy before him for several minutes then spoke in English. "Well Toussaint, will he live?" His caregiver approached the bed.

"Oui, he is young and fit." The man grinned at the chief, "It's also a good thing you are a poor shot with the rifle, non?" Understanding the general gist of what was being said; Lyle couldn't believe the man had the audacity to insult his superior in such a manner.

Lyle was amazed when the chief laughed, "Quite fortunate indeed Pompy, especially for our young friend here." The man towering over Lyle paused then looked down at him and smiled. "I very much regret shooting you lad, it was a terrible mistake, but we'll get you up and on your feet as soon as we can, I assure you."

Tsakaka-wea spoke to her husband in French. "Le garcon restera-t-il dans notre tente?"

Toussaint explained, "Yes. Lieutenant, my wife wants me to ask if the boy can stay in our tent for the night... She would like to tend him."

"Very kind of her, but I'm sorry, no." The lieutenant sent a warm smile towards Tsakaka-wea. "I know nothing of the young man - our Shoshone guides tell me the Lakota can't be trusted. No I'll have him bunk in one of the tents with the other men." The lieutenant noticed the frown on Tsakaka-wea's face. "Don't worry; I'll see nothing happens to him."

"What about Newman?" asked the Frenchman.

"Hmm, John Newman... right now he's sitting in the sun chained to a log." The man mused. "Doesn't look very happy. The boy here gave him a hell of a goose egg with that rock. Even so, I would bet that the flogging he'll receive following his court martial will take his mind off his head and onto his backside. When Captain Lewis returns tomorrow we'll have a discussion." The chief looked to Tsakaka-wea, mispronouncing her name as he continued to speak. "And Sacagawea, how are you dear." The girl looked at him, smiled but said nothing.

A third man approached and standing at the tent's entrance interrupted, "Sorry Lieutenant Clark Sir. Thought you'd want to know Captain Lewis has returned to camp."

"Thank you Jones. Carry on." Lieutenant William Clark, second in command to Captain Meriwether Lewis, of the 1804 – 1806 Lewis and Clark Expedition continued. "Well, I suppose we'll have that particular discussion sooner rather than later." The man strode from the tent. "Meriwether! What brings you back so early..."

Later in the early evening, two of the permanent members of the Expedition moved Lyle out of Tsakaka-wea's and Toussaint's tent. Tsakaka-wea followed and watched while the two men propped the young man up onto a cot that they somehow managed to squeeze between four

221

others within the cramped quarters of the wall tent. Lyle now lay alone in the tent, but before leaving him, Tsakaka-wea had provided a canteen of water, a plate of beans and a small portion of venison. He wolfed these down greedily, took a long drink from the canteen then lay back on the cot and almost immediately fell into a deep sleep.

Sometime in the quiet hours of darkness, Lyle awoke to the sounds of snoring. The chorus of drones originated among those asleep in the other cots about him. On the cot and covered by a thin blanket, he lay on his back with his face turned upward remaining motionless. Keeping his eyes closed, he allowed his keen sense of hearing to explore the tent and the camp outside. Everything was quiet; aside from an occasional movement of horses or small animals moving in the bush, nothing else disturbed the night. He placed a hand to his shoulder and allowed his fingers to probe cautiously beneath the poultice, gently exploring the outer edge of the wound. Lyle was pleased and greatly surprised to find there was no pain. This surprise only grew as his fingers reached the center of the exit wound. At the point where the bullet had exited the front of his shoulder, tearing through skin and bringing with it bone fragments and shredded flesh, all that now remained was a low depression in his skin; the wound had completely healed over!

Faced with this amazing revelation, his allowed his eyes to open and quickly surveyed the tent's interior. A portion of the roof and the front flaps of the wall tent were bathed in a flickering glow of a Kerosene lantern, the camp light was positioned several yards outside the tent. Lyle thought it strange that the whites seemed to find comfort in such a small flame burning throughout the night. He propped himself onto his good side and lifted his head to look about him. He was astounded by what his eyes told him.

From each of the four sleeping men, faint tendrils of ethereal light wound about and stretched toward him, each making contact with his chest. Slowly he passed a hand through one such wispy strand. Doing so the feeble light pulsed gently then disappeared while an almost soundless whimper came from the direction of the sleeper to which his eyes had traced the origin of the light. He remained quiet and assessed his condition before slowly sitting up in the cot and swinging his feet to the earthen floor. In doing so, he broke contact with each of those surrounding him, their snores first slowing, and then becoming silent. Cautiously he moved his arms, hands, and fingers. Beginning each small motion, he expected pain or at least some discomfort while performing the activity, but there were none. How very different from earlier in the evening while he was being moved; every step, every twist or even the slightest movement brought with it waves of searing pain.

His mind played over the last several minutes, studying each nuance of what had taken place. As each of the faint vines of light had been broken, Lyle had felt a subtle drop in energy, as if he were somewhat weakened but only temporarily. In fact, he felt much better than he had for some time, more alive, more vital. His mind had also sharpened as he reviewed all of his detailed memories made during the previous winter and spring within only a matter of seconds. Returning to the present he reviewed his situation and considered his options; there were none, he must leave. Aside from the obvious difficulty in explaining his amazing recovery there was no reason to remain. He would return to his camp and keep an eye on the expedition in the morning. Would they search for him? Not likely, and even if they did they wouldn't discover him. Even their most experienced and skilled in wood lore couldn't follow his trail; he moved like a ghost across the plains and within the forests.

Silently, Lyle slipped away from the tent, as he did so he heard the snoring start up once more among those inside. Within five minutes he had left the camp far behind, the stars of early summer blazing forth in all their glory above him.

Very early, the next morning found Lyle watching the camp from his favorite vantage point along a nearby ridge situated to the east of the expedition's campsite. Some one hundred yards distant, his keen eyes and ears watched and heard whatever was taking place among those below. The morning's usual activities began well before the sun breached the summit of the ridge where Lyle hid.

He watched the camp's cook and assistants, gather firewood, draw water from the river, light the cooking fires and prepare for breakfast. As the minutes went by, the rest of the camp began to stir and men slowly began to emerge from their tents. Lyle saw Tsakaka-wea emerge from her tent, her papoose slung across her back. She immediately approached her family's fire pit and within a matter of minutes had started a small fire. Her husband Toussaint appeared shortly afterward. The couple were speaking French, a language Lyle could not comprehend, but from their expressions and actions, it appeared that the Shoshone squaw was concerned about Lyle's welfare. She gestured toward the tent that Lyle had left late the night before indicating that she wanted to check on his condition, but her husband held her by her upper arm and shook his head, "non le garçon ira bien. Vous pouvez voir comment il va après le réveil de l'homme." Tsakaka-wea would obey her husband's wishes, but wore a frustrated expression watching her husband walk away and approach a fire where Captain Lewis and Lieutenant Clark stood engaged in conversation. For the next hour, Lyle could see her look over toward the tent anxiously.

The sun climbed above Lyle's shoulders. He had watched Toussaint and another man Lyle took to be a fellow hunter leave the camp several hours earlier, followed by several Shoshone scouts who rode off from the camp in different directions. Lyle watched with interest as the prisoner John Newman, the man he named Black Beard was led in chains from a tent and secured to a heavy log near the tent where Lyle had been billeted. In the rest of the camp the day was well underway and men went about their daily chores and duties, yet from his tent there was still no activity.

It was mid morning when the Captain and Lieutenant made their way over to where an unhappy John Newman sat cross legged yet still defiant on the ground before them. They spoke for several minutes; Lyle watched the prisoner's face fall as the two expedition leaders pronounced their decision regarding his fate. There would be no formal trial.

The leaders began to turn away when Tsakaka-wea approached them speaking rapidly, "Wait, I need to check on the boy, but no one has left the tent this morning!"

The two men looked at each other, Clark checked his pocket watch. "Damn odd Meriwether, nearly 10:30. Those lay bouts get into the rum last night?" They chuckled and walked to the nearby tent, the flap were closed and there wasn't a sound from inside. It was clear to the woman that the men figured she was mistaken and the men had simply gone about their business without her being aware of their leaving.

Clark lifted the tent flap. Peering within, he and Meriwether's faces wore expressions of first surprise and then anger. Lyle heard the officer shout and curse the sleeping men within. At the sound of Clark's voice he heard the men stir and begin to move about with some haste. Moments later four men stumbled out from the tent blinking and shielding their eyes from the bright sunlight. Abject apologies were quickly extended toward the officers, but an explanation as to why the group had overslept was still lacking.

As the officers continued to question the men it quickly became apparent the officers were now concerned for the health of their men. As a group, the men looked awful. Their eyes were red and sunken, their faces a definitely unhealthy pale Gray Shade, several of the men had a light cough while yet another ran behind the tent and retched violently before collapsing in a heap. Meanwhile Tsakaka-wea propped her infant several yards distant then quickly entered the tent. Finding no sign of Lyle she re-emerged with a panic.

Afterward there followed an animated discussion among all within the group. Captain Lewis called out to one of the Shoshone guides who noticing the hullabaloo had made his way to see what the fuss was about. While Tsakaka-wea looked on accusingly, Lyle heard the officer ask if the Shoshone braves had removed their enemy sometime in the night and done away with him. The Shoshone looked completely baffled and denied the accusation. After several minutes and in speaking with a number of other men who had gathered inquisitively about the tent, it was agreed that Lyle had probably slipped away on his own volition. After all, the boy could only have considered himself a prisoner held by a group of enemies or at best strangers, unsure of his future did he really have a choice? Since it was highly unlikely that the boy had the strength to go very far from the camp, the officers instructed everyone to leave the camp in various directions and try to locate the boy who they presumed lay somewhere nearby, quite possibly dead.

An hour or so later, the search was abandoned and the incident of Lyles disappearance pretty much forgotten, the attentions were returned to Lyle's tent mates, who had now appeared to have recovered considerably following a light breakfast and coffee. They would remain free of duties to rest and recuperate until the officers were assured there wasn't a serious disease stalking the members of the expedition.

Lyle continued to watch throughout the remainder of the morning and into the early afternoon. He was about to leave the camp for the last time when he saw the officers and a group of men approach the prisoner John Newman. Black Beard was stripped to his waist then lashed atop the large log where he had previously been chained. As Tsakaka-wea and the rest of the camp looked on, one of the men produced a rawhide whip and proceeded to expertly apply one hundred lashes to the man's back leaving it a mass of angry red welts and shallow bleeding wounds. Once the punishment had been meted out, the camp cook washed Black Beard's injured back with water then applied a light layer of tallow atop the open wounds that might stave off infection. Black Beard chains were restored and the rest of the camp left the man to contemplate his transgressions.

That night, and over several more nights following, Lyle sat by his fire thinking through all that had happened since setting out on his spiritual journey. He had done as the Shaman had instructed and in doing so had discovered abilities he hadn't known within himself. He had found the sacred etchings on the rocks matching those on his amulet. He had

225

discovered the white men and learned their language. He had been shot with one of their fire sticks and survived; somehow miraculously healing only hours later by what Lyle concluded was his ability to "steal" life from his captors. It was time to leave for home.

The following morning Lyle packed up those possessions he could comfortably carry and left for home. After crossing the silt laden river, the trail took him to the top of a large hill. Looking back in the direction of the expedition's camp he could no longer see the smoke of the camp fires. Lyle paused and allowed his vision to pan across the distant horizon. After a few moments he had picked up a dark column snaking its way westward across the prairies toward the distant peaks of the Rocky Mountain.

It would only be many decades later when he learned of the historical moments he had shared among the Lewis and Clark expedition as it made its way toward the west coast on their mission of discovery. He had known Captain Lewis and Lieutenant Clark; he had saved and cared for their famous Shoshone guide, Sacagawea, the woman he knew as Tsakaka-wea. Lyle picked up his small pack and slinging it across his back began the long walk back to his home and family.

30

The Shade that previously called herself Irma Meyers stood motionless above the ruined body of her long time Servicio and friend, Norman Stiles. In those final seconds, their previously broken mental connection had flashed to life one final time before it vanished forever as Norman died. Responding to the intense stimulation, the consciousness of the fading Sempitor rose to the surface. Irma surveyed the damage and calculated the terrible loss wrought through her affliction. Still her recognition of the act and its consequences were wholly inadequate; for perhaps the first time in her life as a Sempitor, she found herself at odds with her own existence.

How long had it been since her consciousness had last surfaced? Irma felt the desperate urge to feel something, anything other than the terrible nagging hunger she had recently experienced without pause or recourse. She walked toward the open kitchen window and stood facing it. Closing her eyes, she felt small puffs of air brush against her face and tousle her hair, she took a deep breath, the delicate perfumes of the night forest wafted and danced within the light breeze.

How long had she stood there, she couldn't say, but eventually she became aware of movement through her closed eyelids, upon their opening Irma watched the rhythmic motions of the fluorescent light swinging above her. Like Norman had done before her, she peered into the shadow strewn yard watching the tree limbs wander to and fro caught within small gusts of wind. Aside from the vegetation, nothing stirred in the garden. She allowed her eyes to shift their focus from the distant trees at the edge of the yard, moving closer to the weed strewn garden and closer yet upon the shrubs still tapping out their indecipherable message in Morse code against the side of the house. Her eyes finally came to rest on the window pane itself.

As the light above her head moved and swayed, she caught glimpses of her own reflection in the glass. Horrified, she reached up and stilled the light with her hand, or what used to be a hand. Irma surveyed the unimaginable visage that somehow returned her stare. How odd she thought, that this monstrosity could still manage to show some small but present measure of sadness within its eyes. When she could no longer bear looking at what she had become, she turned her back and was once again reminded of her terrible crime. How did it come to this? Why hadn't she listened to the warnings in her heart, and those of her loyal Servicio?

After some thought, she decided she would seek a proper resting place for Norman; a resting place among those of his own kind, among the humans, among people like himself. Tenderly, she wrapped the body in a wool blanket. Placing the bundle atop a shoulder Irma walked through the front door and into the gloaming. Once Norman was properly interred, she would do what must be done, what should have been done months before. Now in the first lucid state of mind she experienced in some days, she walked clear headed into the darkness - making her way down the long graveled laneway toward Big Bend Road, Hansel's Creek and God's Angel Cemetery.

31

It was seven miles from Meyers Hall to God's Angel Cemetery if you stuck to the roads, half that if you ventured cross country. The average person would cover that distance in just an hour; Irma Meyers managed to do so even while carrying Norman Stiles body over her shoulder, all in less than half an hour. Her eyesight, like that of cats and other night hunting creatures, caught and augmented the dim light, turning night into something approaching that of day. She sped through the forest as easily as would a deer picking a foot sure path along the rocks and roots of the dense undergrowth.

Following the train tracks that bisected Big Bend Road, Irma skirted the north edge of town entering the newest area of the cemetery and walked among the grave markers and monuments dotting the grounds. Some two hundred yards distant a large marble mausoleum with a barred gate stood sheltered beneath the boughs of a towering pine tree. A light rain fell as she approached the damp entranceway. Looking within she saw it contained four tombs, judging from the inscriptions on the brass plates, all were apparently occupied. Irma tested the gate, it was latched but unsecured. Opening the gate she stepped inside and carefully laid Norman's body in a far corner then approached what she thought was most likely the oldest tomb. Pushing the heavy lid of the tomb aside with an easy swipe of her arm revealed a desiccated partially denuded skeleton within.

Approaching a second tomb, she performed the same exercise, but the body within this tomb had been interred quite recently. As with most modern burials of this sort, a thin sheet of metal had been stretched across the opening sealing the contents within. Irma ran a sharp taloned finger down the center of the seal tearing it asunder. A gassy hiss escaped the tomb and the odor of corruption filled the air. Without pause, Irma returned to the first tomb and scooped up the bones of its occupant dumping these unceremoniously together with the second partially decomposed body before sliding the massive lid closed.

Bending low, she took Norman into her arms and gently laid him in the empty tomb. She stood above her friend and soon found herself lost in thought and memory for many long minutes. An unusual sound snapped Irma back to reality. Listening closely she caught the hum of an electric motor and the subdued patter of rubber treads rolling quietly a nearby asphalt pathway. She chided herself for her lack of caution; Irma turned toward the entrance and began to approach the openings iron gate but stopped before she was halfway there and instead crouched out of sight behind a tomb. The vehicle approached in the rainy gloom coming to a stop on the side opposite the mausoleum.

Four hours earlier, Larry O'Reilly had cursed his boss under his breath for the umpteenth time. Jimmy Jones, the manager of God's Angel Cemetery was nothing if not forgetful. Once again Jimmy had forgotten to mention to Larry that a new grave had to be dug and ready for tomorrow morning's funeral. Normally Larry wouldn't care, not a big deal, but Larry's holidays were scheduled to start tomorrow. He'd arranged a week long fishing trip with two of his oldest buddies and they planned to leave Hansel's Creek not later than 5:00 a.m.

Digging a grave wasn't a time consuming ordeal, the backhoe made quick work of a three by ten foot hole, even one dug to a depth of six feet. From beginning to end it shouldn't have taken more than an hour. He'd make his final rounds and be home sipping a beer and ogling that big titted babe on the six o'clock news before he knew it. At least that was his plan until the backhoe refused to start; dead battery - again! Jones, that cheap bastard had put off springing for a new battery until the last possible moment. Well, this afternoon was that moment. Larry marched from the equipment garage into the adjoining offices, a cigar protruding from his mouth like the barrel of a gun. "Jimmy, that GD battery's as dead as a doornail, get me a voucher, I'll drive into Claremont City and pick one up!"

Two hours later Larry returned to the garage and replaced the battery. He looked at the clock, nearly six in the afternoon and he still had to dig that GD hole. The machine's engine sprang to life the second the key was turned in the ignition. Larry steered the backhoe down a paved pathway leading to the location of the new grave; it would be dug out among other plots recently occupied. Within forty minutes, Larry stepped down from the unit and walked about the grave's perimeter. Satisfied with his work he stepped back up into the unit and reached behind the seat to grab the green ten by twelve foot tarp he'd spread over the mound of fresh dirt lying near the yawning hole that sat silently awaiting its guest. Grave side etiquette demanded he leave as little evidence as possible that might remind the mourners that Aunt Lucy or Dear Old Dad was about to be planted in the worm farm. His hand returned empty; the damn tarp wasn't there. In his mind's eye he could picture it lying across the counter beside the old battery he had replaced.

Well maybe he'd leave it for Jody, the part timer who'd act as his replacement while he was off snagging a couple of fat trout. That's when he felt the first drops of rain on his face and hands. "Shit!" By morning the

230

rain would turn the grave site into a sea of mud. He'd have to fetch the tarp, return to the grave and cover the dirt pile before he left for the night. He gunned the engine and drove the backhoe toward the shop. Christ it was already getting dark, he flicked on the vehicles lights. The rain was falling heavier now, in the powerful beams of the tractors overhead lights, thousands of rain drops streaked downward, like miniature shooting stars before splatting upon the asphalt pathway.

He checked his watch, it was nearly seven forty, and he could count on a minimum of another twenty minutes before he could lock up the shop. He parked the tractor in the equipment garage, jumped down and stormed off grabbing the tarp and a powerful flashlight, then leapt into the electric golf cart they used to travel about the grounds and raced down the pathway heading back to the grave site.

Several minutes later Larry arrived at the site. Springing from the small vehicle he walked through the wet grass carrying the flashlight in one hand and the folded tarp in the other. The rain had stopped and the air was deathly still as he went about covering the small hill of dirt and weighing it down with some cement blocks he had the foresight to stow behind the golf cart's seat. Finished at last, home time!

He steered the cart about pointing the golf cart toward the garage when his nostrils picked up a disgusting odor wafting toward him. Shining the powerful flashlight in the direction of the stench, its diffuse yellow beam fell upon the bars of the mausoleum's open gate. He fought the urge to simply drive off before his sense of duty got the better part of him. Shaking his head from side to side, he climbed from the cart and walked over to the structure. A light smattering of rain resumed while a small breeze sprang up, thankfully dissipating the nasty odor he caught earlier. Larry laid a hand on the bars and was swinging them closed when his light chanced to illuminate the interior of the structure revealing the partially open tomb near the back wall.

"God Damn" he muttered. Swinging the flashlight in every direction, he looked about him. The cemetery had experienced episodes of vandalism in the past; only last Halloween a bunch of high scholars had gotten all pissed up, walking around the grounds tipping headstones and monuments. They would have gotten away with it if that Jackie Baker kid hadn't passed out.

That night a neighbor living close by on Church Street, called the cops when she saw flashlights bobbing about in the cemetery. The cops came cruising and it didn't take long to figure out what the little bastards had been up to. Making a quick sweep of the grounds, the cops found Jackie barfing his guts out near the main gate. It was close to 3:00 a.m. when Jackie's mom and dad got the call, 3:30 when they arrived, and 3:45 when the Baker kid gave everyone up. The cops weren't stupid, they just left Jackie alone with his old man, Dan Baker; the meanest S.O.B. in the creek. About mid morning the next day, Larry and the town cops watched the parents drop their kiddies at the shop. All of them looked much pretty hung over, but none of them were quite as sorry looking as Jackie who sported not one but two blackened eyes.

Larry waited for nearly a minute before he figured who ever had been in the crypt had left, probably well before he arrived in the golf cart. It was quiet and he hadn't heard anyone while he worked only yards away. The squeal of the rusty gate or the grinding of stone on stone while opening the lid surely would have alerted him to the trespasser. Even so, Larry had a bad feeling about the whole business. It was one thing to kick over a monument and quite another to open the GD lid off a tomb. That stink was still hanging about the mausoleum. He reached into his breast pocket, removed a stogie and lit up. That was better... or maybe worse. Larry mused that the tainted smoke tasted like a turd, something his wife was always fond of saying about his cigar habit before she left him.

Something about this whole situation unnerved the man. Larry had half a mind to drive back to the garage and call up the Sheriff's office, then he checked his watch; nearly eight. If he called the cops he'd have to hang around for only God knows how long while they finished bullshitting over coffee and doughnuts down at the Fast Gas cafe. Piss on it! He went over his plan, dash in - quickly slide closed the lid - dash out - shut the gate and fuck off. No big deal right? He had to work to quell his fears for half a minute before he managed to work up the nerve to put his plan into action.

Irma watched the caretaker begin covering the pile of loose soil. He'd soon leave and she'd be free to take proper care of her Norman. The one thing Irma hadn't counted on was the hunger returning so quickly and with such urgency. To her credit she fought the instinct that welled up inside of her. She felt it subside briefly as Larry climbed into his cart and began to leave, but when he stopped in front of the mausoleum and walked to the front gate, Irma felt her control beginning to slip. Even now, if Larry left the tombs and walked back to his cart, she wouldn't have followed but now he stepped inside. Walking past her, Larry stood before the tomb where her Norman lay. Irma's eyes hungrily studied the nervous man from where she crouched in her dark corner; her nostrils flared detecting that wonderful aroma of fear combined with salty sweat. Her ears listened to the elevated rhythm of his heart beating within his chest. She felt herself slip and then fall, all that had been Irma Meyers disappeared forever, swamped beneath dark waves of hunger and blood lust - the Shade reasserted control over her body and pounced.

Larry stood beside the tomb, lifted his light shining it down into the depths of the crypt. He'd been in the business long enough to know that a fresh body lay wrapped in the soiled, bloody sheet. "Fuck this shit!" he purposely allowed his voice to rise in volume trying his best to insert some measure of defiance and anger within the profanity laced expletive. Larry was rather dismayed to hear his voice return sounding so weak and frightened. He spun on his heel and took a step toward the door, but something was blocking his path, something terrible. The flashlight dropped from his hands and upon striking the cement floor flickered and went out.

Although Larry weighed a full two hundred and fifty pounds, Irma tossed him about as easily as a rabbit in the jaws of a ravenous wolf. Now drawing the broken man close to its breast, it rejoiced in his screams of pain and terror; dark notes strummed upon her icy heart. Larry fell silent, had anyone been standing upon the pathway and looked toward the mausoleum they might imagine a couple sharing an intimate embrace within the darkness of the tomb, then only puzzle as a mysterious glow slowly formed, suddenly flared, then brilliantly flashed between them.

32

It was almost time to go. The couple stood on a long wood planked landing outside the main entrance to the administrative headquarters in Oświęcim, Poland. They had worked together for more than a year and although they frequently discussed the prospect beginning new lives in Brazil following the war; Irma wondered if she, Josef or anyone else in Germany could truly survive the awesome scope of the coming destruction. A large black sedan waited at the curb; inside the back seat were two young civilians, a man and a woman.

Only a week earlier, Generalfeldmarschall Albert Kesselring's entourage had landed at a local air strip stopping over briefly to visit the administrative headquarters in Oświęcim before continuing to Berlin. The visit required secrecy to protect the high ranking officer, and so the stopover came as a surprise to the camp's commandant SS-Obersturmbannführer Rudolph Höss when the Luftwaffe Field Marshal arrived at the administration office. At that moment, Höss was meeting with his SS Supervisor Irma Grese and Doctor Josef Mengele. Höss had introduced his two subordinates to the officer with some pride, as though they were persons of some importance. Kesselring simply nodded dismissively in their direction and told the commandant that he was expected in Berlin at his earliest convenience.

Obviously embarrassed, the commandant dismissed Grese and Mengele saying their meeting would continue at a later time. Throughout this short introduction, Irma had allowed her mind to softly probe that of the Field Marshal and in doing so quickly gained insight into the reason for the visit and how the war was progressing. She left the office regretting her curiosity.

Apparently, Rudolph Höss, the camp's commandant was also a cousin of Kesselring's wife. The Field Marshal had promised his wife that he would warn Höss of the Third Reich's looming defeat. From a personal point of view, Kesselring would have enjoyed lining Höss and the entire officers' compliment up before a firing squad. These butchers weren't soldiers; they were sadists, murderers and gangsters who donned the uniform of the Reich for their own purposes. Kesselring had no problem killing civilians who obstructed the objectives of the Reich, he had recently done so in Italy, for reasons both logical and rational whereas this - this was simply madness.

Just twenty minutes after his arrival, Irma and Mengele had stood in the lobby of the Oswiecim's administrative headquarters watching Kesselring leave the camp for the airstrip, gravel and ice spit up behind the officer's car as the tires struggled to grip the frozen ground. Irma spoke of what she learned with Joseph. They held few secrets from each other and Josef was well aware of her psychic abilities which for some reason far outstripped his own. Mengele quickly decided it was probably time to put their escape plan into action.

The Nazi's had been working on a German version of America's famous "Underground Railway" that would see prominent party members secreted away from Europe to various locations around the globe. There they would adopt new identities and patiently wait for circumstances to swing more favorably toward their cause. Unknown to all of them, they'd wait out the rest of their lives in futility; the world would not soon forgive or forget their wartime atrocities.

Mengele would travel along this escape route, he and his two protégé, both of whom shared a almost unique commonality with the good doctor and his one time lover, Irma Grese. Although he tried to convince Irma to go with them, she declined often saying "why would anyone care about a young woman guard forced to work in the camps, no they would go after the big fish." Besides, given her talents and abilities, she could simply vanish into the general confusion following Germany's capitulation. She would join Josef and the others in their new community the following year.

While Mengele understood the source of Irma's motivation to stay, he hardly approved of it and she knew it. Upon their first meeting in the camp three years earlier, they immediately recognized the other as to who and what they were; like to like, kith to kin, or as Mengele had recently confirmed, a subspecies of homosapien sapien. Not to put too fine a point on it, theirs was a generally parasitic, though in some cases, predatory subspecies, whose existence rested upon feeding from the larger group, in this case, humans.

For several months Josef and Irma reveled in the discovery of another being like themselves. Their minds intertwined and their thoughts bonded to a degree that would be wholly unimaginable to humans. Humans, those pathetic souls who's every relationship was dependent upon the frailties of spoken language and its often misconstrued meanings, descriptions and intentions of mere words. In comparison their liaison was metaphysical, an equal amalgamation of mind and body, they shared a tangle of vivid images, emotions and powerful memory; not dissimilar to the slow peeling of an onion, each offering the other full access to their personal history. In Irma's case this history was comparatively brief, little more than one hundred and fifty years whereas Mengele being by far the elder of the two, had recollections spanning more than three centuries and might span over five more before extreme age would finally overwhelm his incredible vitality and bring his life to a close.

This enhanced camaraderie of shared natures, however strong, proved insufficient to overcome the emotional barriers that her loathsome behavior elicited within him. Mengele's approach to humanity, while cold and too often pitiless and cruel, still fell within the normal parameters of his kind; after all, how much room for emotional empathy exists between a person and his or her piece of steak or bit of potato? An appallingly inhuman fiend as Dr. Josef Mengele no doubt was, this was not the case with Irma, a true monster in her own right.

When it came to feeding, the woman was possessed of a seemingly insatiable appetite accompanied with a twisted fixation toward the extreme and bizarre. As Josef came to know her, he recognized her sadosexual addiction and believed whatever gave rise to these perversions lay deeply buried in her distant past. Josef had often seen similar behavior among humans, but never within others like himself. Whatever lay at the root of the problem was deliberately kept as a mystery, even perhaps to Irma herself. Mengele also considered that she may be unaware this behavior deviated from the norm, since Josef was the first of her kind she had ever met.

Mengele believed it was this compulsion that underlay her reasons for wanting to stay behind and remain at the camp. The strength of that addiction must be extraordinarily strong for Irma to place her safety at risk. Even considering their kind proved highly resilient and difficult to kill, there were still inherent and significant risks associated with remaining so close to the approaching front lines, stray bombs, falling buildings, fires and the like that could prove impossible to avoid.

Yes, Mengele thought, the reason for her delay lay in the close proximity of so many vulnerable people, especially women, who Grese could safely exploit and victimize with an impunity virtually guaranteed by the Reich's policies regarding the Jews, Poles, Romani (Gypsies) and other supposed subhuman groups marked for extermination within the camps.

With the commencement of war in September of 1939 and the opening of Ravensbrück that same year, Irma recognized the opportunities each provided her and had eagerly signed up as a guard in the relatively small concentration camp; an unusual facility in that its prisoners were solely women. At that time, the grounds of this particular camp were unlike any others in operation. The manicured lawns, the exquisite flowerbeds that lined the Great Square and its peacock-filled birdhouses created awe within the women and children who entered the camp given the squalid ghettos of their previous incarceration. This description was to quickly change. The small work camp had been built to house five thousand prisoners, not the fifty thousand plus pressed into the cramped quarters. Food and clean water was limited while the toilet and sanitary facilities were nearly non-existent.

The newly formed Aufseherinnen or Overseers units, one to which Irma was assigned, like the prisoners they guarded were also exclusively female. Ravensbrück would train thousands of female guards who would eventually be sent to camps throughout the Reich and its far flung territories. Grese flourished within the despotic atmosphere of camp life, impressing her superiors and most especially her commandant, all with whom she had frequent sexual liaisons. Her attitude, hard work and efficiency allowed her to quickly rise within the unit ranks. Irma thrived and flourished among conditions that tested the physical and mental resilience of her fellow guards; a comparison not lost on her commandant who often quipped that Grese was not unlike a delicate flower arising from a stinking mound of dung.

It was while at Ravensbrück that she first developed her unbridled taste for sadism as well as a seemingly unlimited hunger and craving for food. For Irma, each naturally went hand in hand with the other. During her night shifts, she often found herself the lone guard in the medical ward that held the "rabbits." These unfortunate women occupying the ward had been selected for medical experimentation. The medical teams tested the efficacy of antibacterial drugs to be used to treat soldiers on the battlefield and to that end would purposely cut into and infect their subject's bodies with foreign objects and disease. The medical teams also experimented with bone transplants and nerve regeneration, conducting amputations and transplants among the rabbits. As expected, the ward had an exceptionally high rate of mortality among its occupants. That rate quickly rose as Irma learned she could feed at will, engorging herself with the life energies of the women she consumed whilst her fingers, hands and occasional tooth worried her victims' swollen festering wounds. The "rabbit's" prolonged and tortured cries gave rise and crest to her libido, and after several horrific hours finally satiated the demonic hunger raging within her. Following her latest gruesome feast, the unholy beast would lie quiet for a short time; at most several weeks before she judged it was safe to feed again and the opportunity presented itself.

33

A late model black Caddie slowly pulled up to the main gates of God's Angel Cemetery then stopped completely. Jimmy Jones leaned forward over the steering wheel staring out through the windshield toward an open wrought iron gate. Scarcely believing what he saw, he checked his watch before taking his foot off the brake and cruising into the cemetery. O'Reilly had apparently forgotten to close the gate before he left for the night!

"Son of a bitch!" The fat man cussed out his employee. "Just couldn't wait to get the hell outta Dodge to go fishing for some God Damn trout." Jimmy shook his head and struck the steering wheel with the heel of his hand. The car rolled along the asphalt laneway, the office and equipment garage came into sight. The overhead door was wide open and O'Reilly's dilapidated half ton sat in his parking stall.

"Oh..." Jimmy sighed, his anger dissipating instantly. Something must have come up for Larry to be at work this morning. Jimmy pulled the Caddie into the manager's stall, stepped out and walked into the office and to the coffee pot finding it cold and empty. Joanne normally made the coffee but she wouldn't be in for another half hour. Jimmy had come in earlier than normal to open up; after all they had that funeral at 10:00 this morning and you don't leave things to the last minute. Jimmy made the coffee and went into his office spending ten minutes on the Fox News website catching up on the antics of his president. He, like so many of his Republican friends had voted for the guy after running out of patience with the Democrats but now an orange haired clown was turning the White House into a three ring circus.

The smell of fresh coffee wafted through the air. Jimmy grabbed his mug. Having taken care of the immediate business of the morning, it was time to ask what brought Larry back into work. Jimmy walked out into the morning; last night's rain had stopped earlier and now the sky was clearing from the west. He took a deep breath filling his lungs with the pine scented air. At least the weather would be nice for the mourners. Jimmy lit a smoke then walked into the open garage. The backhoe was parked in its usual spot. He walked up and examined its shovel; the earth caked on the blade was dry and crusty, Larry must have dug the grave the night before, but where was he.

"Larry? Larry." Jimmy called out. The words echoed in the shop. He checked the washroom, it was empty. He was on his way out when he noticed the golf cart was missing. Larry must be checking things out.

"Good man..." he muttered, now sorry for having bad mouthed his employee earlier upon his arrival. Still, he was interested in knowing why Larry was here this morning, but right now he had things to do. The Simpson's monument hadn't been delivered yet and the family was starting to get annoyed, not that it was the fault of the cemetery, but folks don't look at things that way when a loved one's grave was concerned, and certainly not when coughing up ten grand or more to plant someone.

Joanne arrived in the office promptly at nine, and no... She hadn't heard anything from Larry about canceling or postponing his vacation plans. Quarter after nine, Jody, the part time grounds keeper arrived, late as usual. If disheveled was a uniform, then Jody was the leader of the band. His hair was a mess, sticking up here and there in every direction; his face wore two days stubble, the long sleeved shirt beneath his jumpers were nearly as filthy as his mud covered boots. Jimmy shook his head - Christ he couldn't let Jody anywhere near the burial looking like that.

Jimmy glanced hopefully out into the parking lot; there still wasn't a sign of the golf cart. Joanne still hadn't seen Larry yet this morning.

Jimmy walked out into the main office. Jody was making his way to the coffee pot, he didn't look so hot. "Another rough night Jody?" Jimmy asked. The young man just nodded and grunted while he reached for a mug. "Forget that for now Jody, I need you to find Larry, he's not in the shop."

Jody looked disappointed but seeing anger upon his employer's face quickly answered and straightened up. "Sure boss, I'll grab the cart and have a look for him." Jody replied while heading for the door.

"Don't bother with the cart, Larry's got it. Just hoof it." Jimmy glanced at his watch, it was nearly nine thirty. The funeral home's lead man would be here shortly making sure everything was ready to go. Jimmy hoped it would be, and half ways considered driving down to the grave site himself just to make sure. He'd give Jody ten minutes tops to have Larry back at the office or he'd go himself.

Five minutes later, Jody drove up to the office in the golf cart, minus Larry O'Reilly. Right on his heels was Jake Daniel's from Worthington's Funeral Home. Jimmy walked out to greet the two men and was grateful to see Jake remaining in his car talking on his cell phone. Jody plodded up to the front steps reporting to his boss that while Larry wasn't any where to be found, he'd found the cart parked on the laneway next to the gravesite. Everything looked ready for the funeral.

"Thank Christ for small mercies!" said Jimmy. Jake had finished his call and was opening the car door. "Jody, now get your ass into the shop bathroom and clean yourself up. Larry keeps a couple of pairs of clean coveralls in the closet." Jimmy waved and smiled at the funeral home's assistant director who was walking toward him. "And for Christ sake son, run a comb through that mop of yours..." Jimmy broke off and took several steps forward showing off his best smile. "Morning Jake, looks like we can rule out the umbrellas this morning..."

Jimmy sat in the golf cart parked several hundred yards distant from the grave side ceremony. Jody sat at a similar position, but directly opposite to that of Jimmy. The funeral was a big one, there had to be over two hundred people down at the gravesite. Jimmy had counted over eighty cars in the procession; he figured they were mostly from the Creek and Knot's Ridge, with more than a few from Claremont City. It seemed that John Pederson was a popular guy or maybe he just had a big family, or maybe both. Jimmy glanced down at the funeral program; Pederson had been a realtor and once held office as a ward counsel man in Claremont City, which explained the good turnout and the number of vehicles. Jimmy wondered why he chose to be buried in the Creek. Most of the mourners had parked in the cemetery's parking lot and walked in, but there were a lot of old timers tagging about and they'd parked on the laneways along with the family's limos.

Larry's attention was drawn to the entrance to the large mausoleum across from the Pederson ceremony. A small flock of crows were perched on the roof, several were squawking ever so often causing some of the guests to glance over at the building from time to time. Jimmy could see Jake Daniels standing at the edge of the crowd wearing a noticeable frown. "Tough shit" thought Jimmy, welcome to nature Jake."

The morning cloud broke up earlier than expected. The late spring sun had risen high in the sky quickly burning off the gentle mist that formed above the asphalt laneway. Anyone standing in the sun would become overheated if not downright hot. Many of the guests at the graveside had already removed their jackets and coats and stood with their garments slung over their arms. Jimmy checked his watch for the umpteenth time. Hell this was a long one, even for that windbag of a preacher the good reverend Jackson. Folks were getting antsy, the men shifting from side to side while a few ladies in pumps were standing on one foot then the other.

A raucous cackling and squawking drew Jimmy's attention back to the mausoleum across from the graveside service. Now a large number of crows, magpies and even a few large ravens were jostling about on the roof fighting for position. Several had even landed at the tombs entrance, walking about and crossing in and out of the gates iron framework. Jimmy made a mental note to have Larry or Jody come by later with the pellet gun.

Meanwhile, Jackson's droning seemed to have let up and a number of the mourners were starting to leave the gravesite, some walking back to cars parked along the lane but most toward the pathway which would take them back up to the main parking lot. Jimmy started the golf cart and began slowly driving toward the mausoleum where he planned to park the cart and stand hat in hand as the family members made their way to the limos. Jimmy always thought it was a nice touch.

Jimmy was about ten yards out from the mausoleum when he noticed several of the women who were walking along the pathway had covered their mouths and noses with handkerchiefs. Some of the men accompanying the women wore disgusted looks and waved their hands before their faces. In the meantime, the birds remained undaunted by the approach of the humans and were flocking down toward the tomb's entrance. Jimmy's golf cart came to a stop a couple of yards away from the tomb. Immediately his nostrils were assailed with a mixture of rot, old death, and the coppery odor of fresh blood and gore. It reminded him of his first job at the Randall Slaughterhouse in Claremont City where he had worked as one of the cleaners who manned the hoses, spraying down the killing floors and channeling the blood, feces and sanguine fluids down into the sewers.

He stepped out of the cart. Slightly upwind of the tomb, Jake Daniels, Reverend Jackson and a small knot of mourners approached the tomb's entrance to see what the birds were fussing about. Seconds later a cacophony of the women's shrill screams, and the men's shouts and expletives filled the air. A number of the birds took wing and flapped about the disgruntled mourners managing in the process to cause even more panic and chaos if that were possible. As the people retreated along the pathway, they ran smack into the sordid stench that wafted downwind from the mausoleum. Jimmy saw several women dry heaving while Jake blew his cookies across the blacktop.

"What the fuck!" Jimmy said aloud and ran to see what had caused the panic. Just as he arrived at the tomb's iron gate, a large raven flew out from the structure, a small length of bluish brown intestine held tightly in its beak. Bile leapt in Jimmy's throat as he fought the impulse to vomit yet he stood his ground staring into the deeply Shaded tomb. He was promptly greeted by a bloody hand which poked out from behind one of the crypts, the marble crypts on either side of the mausoleum were spattered with dark blood and remnants of God knew what or who.

Jimmy ran upwind from the tomb and leaned against the trunk of a large oak. As he took out the cell phone from his breast pocket, he saw Jody running toward him.

34

Marty Denton sat at a small desk, in a spare office within the Hansel Creek Sheriff's Office listening to a telephone ring at the other end of his line. After five rings no one picked up and the call went to message. "This is Deputy Director of the FBI, Elijah Cole; please leave your name, phone number and the reason for your call. Thank you."

"Elijah, its Marty Denton, you can catch me on my cell or call the Sheriff's Office. Listen it's important I speak to you as soon as possible, I'd like to apply for a warrant to search Meyers Hall. I'll tell you everything when I see you. Thanks."

Marty placed his phone down beside the computer keyboard and read what he'd typed so far in the Search Warrant Application. In cases like stolen property, assault or even robbery, most judges simply skimmed the document to get the gist of the investigation before cutting to the chase asking you to outline your grounds for the warrant. Like everyone else, Judges talk shop over drinks or after dinner. They discuss the nitty gritty of interesting cases, the performance of District Attorneys, defense lawyers and cops; especially cops. If the judge knew the officer to be a straight shooter, he or she would sign the warrant, wish you happy hunting and you'd be on your way in ten minutes. If not, they'd sit there for an hour reading every word twice and then send you back to correct any grammar mistakes; in other words you weren't getting shit.

Getting a search warrant to assist in a murder investigation was a different kettle of fish. It was a big deal; you had to cross all the T's and dot all the I's. A judge who signed poorly constructed warrants concerning serious cases risked his or her reputation. So far Marty had written a total of three pages, all of the information as factual and to the point as much as possible. It wasn't a creative writing assignment. When writing a warrant, Marty always imagined hearing the voice of Detective Joe Friday from that 1950's cop show; Dragnet - "just the facts Ma'am, just the facts". Doing so hadn't steered him wrong yet.

In this instance Marty heavily relied on the fact that one of the murder victims found at the cemetery was Norman Stiles. Stiles had resided at Meyers' Hall but all attempts to reach the Hall's other resident Irma Meyers had proved futile. Marty had driven out to Claremont City to meet personally with Otto Meyers. The old man stated that while he worried for Irma's safety, he no longer lived at the Hall. He went on to correctly point out that as such he couldn't give police permission to enter a home that was no longer his own.

Marty had to be careful how he approached the warrant. If he made out that it was only a case of checking on Irma Meyers' welfare but omitted anything suggesting he suspected the woman might have something to do with the murders, he could probably kiss any evidence found in the house goodbye during any subsequent trial. On the other hand if he started going on about a supernatural entities prowling Hansel Creek he'd be shown the door in quick order. He reviewed his application thoroughly; satisfying himself that he had covered all the bases. Marty would ask Elijah Cole to read over the document and approve the application before taking it before a judge; having your superior, a Deputy Director of the FBI, place his signature below that of the applicant would go a long way to grease the wheels of justice.

"Gets harder each year doesn't it?" Sheriff Billing's voice took Marty a bit by surprise. Given the facts of this particular case he figured he had good reason to be a little jumpy.

Marty glanced back toward the door. Norm Billings leaned on the door frame. "Sorry Norm, what was that?" Marty asked.

"Getting a warrant or expecting any other God damned help from the courts." He scratched his chin. "Used to be we were all on the same side, hell even the defense wouldn't put up too much of a fuss if they knew their guy was guilty as sin."

"Yeah, I guess." Marty said. What he didn't add was that if the cops had done their jobs properly in the first place they wouldn't have to endure the scathing public and judicial oversight of recent years. "I think I've done as much damage as I can here. I just need Cole to approve it before I bring it to a judge. Any suggestions as to who should sign it?"

"Hmm. That's a tough one. Dickson's probably your best shot, he's fair, a bit of a stickler, but has a good rep as does Mahoney. Just stay away from Ross; he's a little too chummy with the defense."

"Ok, thanks Norm." Marty printed off three copies of the warrant application and stuck all three in a large manila envelope. He almost made it to the door before Norm reminded him to pick up his phone. He checked his watch, nearly twelve. "You want to get some lunch Sheriff?"

"No sorry, Maggie and I are meeting my daughter Julie and her newest boyfriend. I just hope this one's better than that last sorry asshole. Nice girl, sweet girl, but no common sense when it comes to men." He brushed his thigh with his Stetson and started out the door. "Good luck with that warrant Marty; if you need some manpower just let me know."

"Will do, thanks Norm." Marty's phone rang; it was Cole.

Another bright sunny day, Marty pushed open the door and walked into Misty's bar then paused to allow his eyes to adapt to the dim light. Over in the corner sat Deputy Director Cole with another fellow at the table. He saw Elijah raise his hand and wave him over.

The waitress spied her new customer, grabbed a menu, and a set of cutlery wrapped in a table napkin and beat him to the table, "Just wave when you're ready to order."

"Yeah, thanks." Marty said offhandedly. Elijah rose up from the table and the two men shook hands in greeting. The other fellow with Elijah remained seated at the table sipping a beer.

"Marty, I'd like you to meet Lyle Fox. Lyle's one of our regional crime scene investigators.

The man at the table remained silent and didn't rise. Instead he placed two fingers to his forehead and tipped a casual salute. "How you doing?"

"Good." Marty replied and took a seat at the table. Marty thought to himself, what's his story?

As Marty sat, Fox rose from his seat and stood at the table. Reaching down, the man grabbed his beer glass and drained the remnants in one gulp. He looked at Cole, "I gotta get going. I'll call you later" as he threw down a ten dollar bill on the table, turned and walked away without acknowledging Marty.

"Ok Lyle. You do that." Cole replied. He looked at Marty and just shook his head. Once Lyle had exited the bar Elijah spoke. "The guy's got the personality of a slug, but he's a crackerjack crime scene man. He's on his way to give court evidence in Claremont City." Elijah lied.

"No matter... I typed out the warrant application and brought the copies with me. Give me the ok and I'll get them signed this afternoon." Marty tapped the manila envelope he had placed on the table when he arrived.

The waitress came up and stood at Marty's side. Seeing her, Cole pointed to Marty then asked, "You want anything?" Marty looked up at the waitress and ordered a coke and an order of fries while Elijah removed the warrant and read it thoroughly.

"You write a tight warrant Marty. That should do the trick." Cole took out his ballpoint, signed and approved all three copies, and then quite unexpectedly Cole crossed out Marty's name on the warrant and printed his own. "Sorry Marty, this isn't a reflection on you, the warrant is top notch, but this morning I was assigned by the Director to take personal control of this one. I'll take this up to Claremont City this afternoon. I know a District Court Judge we've used on occasion and I've already discussed the investigation with him so he's familiar with the facts in this case."

"If you don't mind me saying so, I find this pretty unusual." Marty tilted his head and tried to read Cole's expression.

"Not so. You'll find the FBI operates a bit differently than a city department or even the state police. If I'd had the chance to speak with you before you drew up the papers, I would have told you not to bother. I'd have given the job to a Special Agent; you're still pretty low on the totem pole, this sort of case is a high priority and can easily become politically charged. I've got politicians from no fewer than four states breathing down my neck. They pay the bills, so they seem to think they can call the shots." Cole grinned. "Hope you understand."

Marty nodded. "Makes complete sense." And it did.

"I'll set the entry time and execution to run between 3:00 pm and 11:00 pm." Cole took a sip of beer. "If we run into anything that will take longer than that I can get an extension by telephone; another reason we like to use judges familiar with the way we work."

The waitress appeared with Marty's coke and fries. "Billings offered manpower if we need it."

"I think we'll be good. I've told Fox I'll be needing him for the warrant, he'll travel back to the Creek with me after I have the warrant signed. We'll meet at the Sheriff's office then take a single vehicle out to the Hall. Shouldn't be much later than 4:00 tops."

"Sounds good." Marty agreed and the two men finished their lunch.

Marty and Elijah Cole left the bar squinting in the bright noon time sun. "Catch you later." Marty said as the two men parted ways.

Cole got into his vehicle and drove off in the direction of Big Bend Road. Yes, he was going to Claremont City but he had no intention of applying for a warrant; it would disclose too much information and leave a paper trail, and he didn't want any loose ends. He and Lyle Fox would finalize their plans and make whatever preparation they could before facing the creature that Irma Meyers had become.

35

A cold December wind pierced the thin fabric uniform pants of Captain Josef Mengele and swirled about the knee high stockings of Rapportführerin Irma Grese. The lone couple stood upon a long wood planked landing outside the main entrance to the administrative headquarters. Mengele had already taken his leave of Rudolph Höss, the camp's commandant furnishing the doctor his required papers and permits that would allow him to travel unimpeded anywhere in what was left of the Reich without question, those papers having been signed by no other than Heinrich Himmler Reichsführer of the Schutzstaffel himself.

The driver of the black sedan had been patiently waiting for his passenger for over ten minutes while that supposed Doctor and his black hearted bitch Grese said their goodbyes. He lowered his head slightly and leaned over toward the far window to check on their progress and was shocked to find both Mengele and Grese looking intently in his direction, their flinty eyes expressionless and unreadable. His blood ran cold and he hastily reassumed an erect military posture, gripping the steering wheel with both hands and staring straight ahead.

Irma queried, "I trust you'll admonish your driver's lack of respect for his superiors?" her face wore a thin smile.

"Of course, I believe our charges Kezia and Jakub will require additional nourishment during our trip, it will be of considerable duration." Mengele replied nonchalantly, "the last of our twins in Block 10 were hardly a solid repast." Mengele referred to the brief stop in the hospital ward where the last subjects of his required eugenic experiments; a set of young half dead twin girls, had what was left of their lives emptied and consumed by his precious protégées who were to accompany him to Brazil.

Strange companions for a Captain of the SS, Mengele thought. The girl Kezia was a Romani or gypsy, while the boy Jakub was a Polish citizen and a Jew no less. To him they were the culmination of his life's work, the work that revealed the relevance of his own past and that of Irma and all his kind; and that work would continue when they reached the new world. A thought came to him from the person who stood beside him; "time to go."

December 21st, 1945 - 18:00 hours. Irma reached forward and taking his cold chapped hands in her own, she gripped them strongly as the last rays of the sun disappeared below the bleak Gray landscape of the western horizon. A mile distant, the branches of near leafless elms and willows bent, shifting to and fro in the strong icy breeze, ready to greet the winter which would officially arrive at 22:03 hours marking the occasion of the year's winter solstice.

Face to face, hand in hand, they allowed their thoughts to merge and intertwine. Questions wordlessly asked and answered, safety and speed wished for the trip before him, hopes for safety while she remained, promises of a future meeting and much more were exchanged all within a single heartbeat. Mengele turned away and descended the wooden platform, his back turned toward Grese. Upon reaching the pavement near the sedan's front passenger door, he reached for the handle and pulled the door open a crack, and then turning ever so slightly paused throwing a thin smile in her direction. "Auf Wiedersehen... abschied". Entering the sedan he seated himself on its hard bench seat. Closing the door, Irma saw Mengele nod almost imperceptibly to the driver who immediately placed the automobile in gear and drove off.

Mengele's car left the barbed wire fenced compound and turned westward onto a narrow secondary roadway, shunning the main boulevard that ran off to the east, toward the avenging Soviet armies steadily sweeping toward the camp. The SS Guard watched the sedan's slit covered headlights occasionally flash in the deepening twilight and its tail lights trace out its progress as it negotiated the frequent hills and curves.

A few minutes later the car disappeared from sight and with it the only other of her kind she had ever known. She continued to stand on the windy platform, shrouded within the growing darkness as the icy wind bit her exposed face, hands and legs. The intentionally dimmed yard lights mounted on the guard towers suddenly flashed to life. Above each of the camp's concrete blockhouse doorways, smaller shielded lights also appeared.

Irma felt the old ache of despondency creep up into her chest and hollow out her heart - alone again. It had all been so brief, that sense of belonging, of being something more than just her. What if all their carefully laid plans didn't come to fruition? If that were to happen, how many long lonely years or decades would pass before she would meet another of her kind? An almost human sigh escaped her lips and hung in the night.

Suddenly an unexpected urge stirred in her loins and belly. Growing stronger she felt the familiar excitement and anticipation rise up and banish all gloom from her thoughts. The beast within awoke with a vengeance; yes, yes... the Hyena of Auschwitz would prowl within the walls of the gray concrete blockhouses, stalk their hallways and enter the crowded cells of the damned and forgotten. As the hunger raged and coursed through her veins, Irma walked down the office building's steps and strode quickly in the direction of her barracks some distance away.

In the barracks common room, a small group of men and women laughed and joked as they stood about a large potbellied stove, passing around a large metal beverage mug obviously filled with something other than coffee or tea. The consumption of liquor, forbidden on camp grounds with the notable exception of the officer's mess, was a rule that had been lately overlooked and completely unenforced, the senior officers obviously believing that drunken soldiers and staff were highly preferable to deserters and empty posts. None the less, there was a collective intake of breath as Irma threw open the door and walked to the middle of the room. The SS Supervisor's very presence immediately extinguished all camaraderie; an essence of fear pervaded the entire room. For a long moment, Irma stood glaring at the guards and soldiers, then without a word walked out of the room, down the hall unlocking the door to her private quarters.

Irma tossed her coat onto the bed and opened her locker where she stood quietly for several minutes, taking time to admire her favored accoutrements; her steel toed boots, the whip, the dagger, the club and of course her pistol. She removed the 9mm Luger from its highly polished cross draw holster. Irma lay the automatic across a palm and read the Latin inscription etched across its blued gun barrel; "si vis pacem, para bellum" - "if you seek peace, prepare for war." The exquisite parabellum pistol had been presented to her by Höss upon her most recent promotion. Tonight she would properly blood the weapon.

Soon her half starved dogs would feast on a prisoners yielding flesh, soon a special squad would attend her on her evening rounds; the "Sonderkommandos." Normally these unhappy units were composed of pitiful death camp prisoners forced to perform whatever unwholesome task their Nazi masters set before them - on pain of death or worse. But there were none of those in this particular unit. No, the members of this group needed no such coercing; these handpicked devils were volunteers all, only too ready and willing to do the bidding of their mistress.

A half hour later, beneath the dim glow of the overhead lamp an unholy group assembled in the entranceway of blockhouse #4, a woman's dormitory. In full uniform, SS Supervisor Irma Grese, the pride of Auschwitz would follow behind the attack dogs and their handlers. As the group started down the main corridor, Irma Grese's blue eyes sparkled and danced while the sick twisted expression on her face mimicked the "deaths head" insignia pinned upon her forge cap. The tips of her steel toed jackboots would occasionally flash, reflecting the harsh glaring light of the bare bulbs that hung down from the ceiling while the staccato of her boot heels rang upon the concrete floor like a snare drum.

The men's howls of anticipated delight mixed with the excited barks and snarls of the German Shepherds, echoing throughout the block's half open doors and unshuttered windows. The unfortunate women and children cowered in filthy, overcrowded bunk beds or sat upon the cold dormitory floors. Listening to the rapid approach of their tormentors and knowing what lay in store, they despaired.

36

The Boeing 747-8 wide bodied transport touched down in a steady rain at Seattle's Sea-Tac commercial terminal just a little after six in the morning. The massive aircraft had flown directly from Brasilia, Brazil covering over six thousand miles in just over twelve hours. The cockpit crew and three other airline employees who were deadheading along with the cargo disembarked and made their way to customs. The flights passengers were cleared to go on their way, while the Captain and his co-pilot signed the papers transferring the plane's cargo into bond until it could be properly cleared by US customs personnel.

Passing by a small bar in the terminal, the Captain's ever wandering eye caught sight of several beautiful young women in a nearby lounge. "Aleixo, feel like getting a drink before you head out?" The Captain grinned.

Aleixo Silva had followed his friends eyes towards the pair of long legged blondes who started to twitter among themselves when they noticed they had caught the handsome pilots attention. "Abilo, you dog. What would that pretty bride of yours say if she could see you now?"

"Silva, did anyone ever tell you you're a kill joy?" Abilo laughed and slapped his friend on the back.

"Constantly." His smile faded. "I'd like to, but I'm expected at my sister's place for lunch. She's meeting her fiancés mom and dad and feels the need for support. If I'm late I might as well not bother showing up at all."

"Fine, be that way." Abilo smiled and gave a small wave toward the girls, who if possible somehow broadened their perfect smiles and returned the gesture. "All the more for me... drive safe my friend; I'll see you in four days." The man chuckled and entered the lounge.

Aleixo Silva walked straight to Hertz, picked up his rental and drove from the airport heading eastward on the I-90. He checked his watch; at this rate he'd arrive in Claremont City before noon, visit his aging Servicio before heading off to Meyers Hall. Aleixo was already dreading what he might find waiting for him there.

37

It was nearly 3:00 and afternoon shift had just begun for the Hansel's Creek deputies. The secretaries would be leaving the building in another half hour. Near the equipment room a half dozen officers were milling about, checking their gear and swapping out portable radio and cell phone batteries.

Marty was chatting with Deputy Henry Templar who was about to go off duty. "I wish I could help you out with the warrant. Ever since I was a kid I've been itching to see the inside of that place."

"I'd love to oblige, but I don't think the Sheriff would spring for the OT." Marty smiled.

"Not too likely. Ah, besides I promised my girl a movie tonight... take care Marty." Henry replied. The deputy looked over toward the other officers and called out. "Hey Ed, hold up a minute I have to talk with you a moment." The office double timed it to the equipment office.

Marty's cell phone rang and he answered. "Denton here."

"Hi Marty, thought I'd give you a heads up. We're on the road. Lyle and I will be at the Sheriff's office in about forty minutes." Elijah's deep voice nearly blended in with the road noise.

"How did it go with the judge?" Marty asked.

Elijah Cole, who was seated in the SUV's passenger seat, smiled, looked at its driver, Lyle Fox and winked. "Oh it went very well, just as I thought it would."

Marty asked, "Do you think we'll need some extra guys on the warrant? If so I have to let them know before they go out on shift."

"No, I think we can handle it. Just let them know we'll be out there in case the resident gets nervous and calls the Sheriff's office." Elijah flipped the front windshield visor down to block out the glare of the afternoon sun.

"Good point, you know a uniform or two might not hurt, once we're in, it'd be business as usual." Marty suggested.

"No Marty." Coles voice grew stern. "The FBI will handle this alone. I know you and Norm Billings have a good rapport, but I don't need this thing to turn into amateur hour. Are we clear?"

"Crystal Sir." Marty affirmed. "I'll give them our location and our radio channel. It'll be just us."

Cole's voice grew more affable. "Ok Marty, sorry about the attitude, it's just been one of those days."

"No problem, I've had a few of those myself. I'll see you when you get here." Marty replied.

"Ok, we're just leaving Claremont City; should see you at the Sheriff's office in about half an hour." The men said their goodbyes ending the call. As Marty put the cell phone in its holder on his belt, he waved at Henry Templar as the Deputy left the office for the night.

A few minutes later Marty cornered Sheriff Billings coming out from his office. "I gave your offer to Deputy Director Cole; he says thanks, but not to worry. Here's our radio channel if you'd like to monitor, or if we need the cavalry." Marty smiled.

Billings made a mildly sarcastic face, "I figured as much. Ok. If you need us we'll be there. By the way, what time you guys figure to be outta there?"

"Unless we come up with something unexpected I wouldn't think much past six. Why." Marty queried.

"I'm going up to the cemetery to pick up some of the lighting equipment we set up in the tomb." Billings stated.

Marty broke in, "Lighting equipment?"

"Yeah, never heard the expression dark as a tomb? Even in the daytime you can't see shit in there. Now our guys already been through the scene, taken some photos, dusted, you know that type of thing, but I sure would appreciate your crime scene man give it the once over before we turn it over to cemetery management tomorrow morning. Apparently, the family of the recently disinterred are making a fuss, can't say I blame 'em."

"I think we'd be able to oblige. I'll let you know as soon as I can." Marty assured the Sheriff.

"Thanks Marty. Good luck, talk at you later." The Sheriff slapped his back and walked off to the parade room where the afternoon shift officers were already seated listening to the office sergeant provide the day's crime reports and departmental information."

Marty was outside on the sidewalk when a dark blue SUV pulled up to the curb. Elijah gave a wave with his hand as the window rolled down. "Jump in, daylights burning." He chuckled. Marty climbed into the back seat and looked toward the driver who simply looked at the road ahead giving no acknowledgment of his new passenger.

It was a twenty minute drive from Hansel's Creek to Meyers Hall. Running off the pavement after crossing the South Bridge the SUV sped due west along the long gravel lane leading to the Meyer's place. Disturbed pebbles and bits of gravel pinged and clinked as they struck the vehicle's undercarriage. Marty hadn't been out this way for as long as he could remember. On either side three foot high dry pack rock walls lined the road. Looking to the south, heavy brush and forest past by nearly unbroken while to the north the landscape consisted of shallow marsh and fen stretching for nearly a mile until the ground rose toward Devil's Head Hill.

The SUV slowed then came to a halt, its forward progress obstructed by a set of heavy wrought iron gates that led into a circular courtyard and the main entrance to the Hall. From a distance of twenty feet or so, Marty could see the gates were locked shut with a heavy steel chain and padlock of a size that would be tough to cut through with even a large bolt cutter. Without a word being said, Lyle Fox exited the vehicle, walked to the gate and took the padlock in his hands inspecting it closely. Beyond Fox, Meyers Hall squatted on the north side of the compound, the smooth Gray rock of its walls baking in the hot afternoon sun.

Elijah and Marty remained in the car. Marty saw Fox remove something from his breast pocket. "Watch this Marty. This is why I bring this guy along on jobs like this." Marty continued to watch as Fox opened a small leather case and chose some implements within and set to work picking the lock. Denton knew modern locks weren't easily defeated; it would take an experienced locksmith with a bucket of tools a minimum of ten minutes to... Marty's chain of thought was broken as he watched Lyle remove the padlock and begin decoupling the steel chain from the gates bars. Lyle pushed the gates open and walked back to the vehicle.

"Good job Lyle." Elijah grinned.

"How about that white man?" Lyle looked back at Marty through the rear view mirror and gave him a sly smile.

"Not bad... not too bad at all." Marty replied as Lyle put the SUV in gear and pulled into the compound. The Hall was an ugly building and a little bigger than Marty thought it would be. The rock walls, relatively few small windows and single narrow doorway reminded Marty of something he'd see in 17th century Scotland, not present day Washington State.

Lyle Fox seemed to have read the detectives mind, "Otto Meyers had it brought over from somewhere in Europe - stone by stone - then reassembled here. Crazy huh?"

They stood at the side of the vehicle for several moments, the place looked empty. Marty walked across the compound over to the garage and tried the side door. It was unlocked. He poked his head inside and flicked on a light switch. A series of overhead fluorescent lights flickered then brightened revealing a large well organized shop and a three vehicle carport. Two recently washed and obviously well cared for vehicles were parked side by side. A windowless Gray panel van and a gleaming midnight blue Mercedes-Benz S550, Marty walked around the vehicles and looked in each... empty. Killing the lights, Marty closed the door and rejoined the men who had obviously just returned from surveying the building's perimeter.

Elijah looked toward Marty. "Find anything?"

"Two vehicles inside, nothing else." Marty replied.

The three men approached and stood in front of the doorway. The weed choked lawn ran along the front foundations of the Hall then continued, only ending when it reached the black wrought iron fencing that lay some sixty feet or so distant. Elijah looked at the men and nodded to Lyle who pulled a large caliber automatic from his shoulder holster and let his arm fall to his side. Seeing this, Denton followed suit. Elijah grunted, "You just never know eh boys?"

Elijah Cole patted the right side of his suit. He could feel the hard chunk of steel resting against his ribcage. Satisfied, he reached forward and pulled on a thick metal handle suspended by a heavy braided cord next to the door, somewhere inside the Hall, a set of bell chimes rang harmonically for five seconds or so. The men waited. Nothing moved within. Elijah gave another tug; once again the chimes sounded yet no one answered.

"They have a land line. Let me give it a ring." Denton took out his cell phone. A moment later they heard a quiet ringing in the house, after a minute or so, it remained unanswered. "Guess there's no one home."

Cole said nonchalantly, "Ok Lyle, do your magic."

"No magic to do, I can't get through this lock; this is unbeatable." Lyle stated.

"We'll have to find another way in." Cole mused.

"No actually we won't." Lyle continued. "I figured we might hit something like this, when Stiles had the door installed, he inquired if the Order could recommend a security firm. They did and he had the front and back doors installed at the same time the security came on line. I had one of our associates make some inquiries." Lyle punched a series of numbers into the keypad and the door locks began sliding back. "Bingo."

"Ok gentlemen, until we clear the house I want everyone to keep within sight of each other. We still don't have a clue what we might be up against." Cole was the first one to walk through the door; he'd taken out his gun leveling it in front of him. As soon as he cleared the entrance way he shifted to the left and stood waiting and watching while Lyle entered and immediately stepped off to the right taking up a similar stance. Standard entry tactics Marty thought; but only standard because they worked. Everyone watched their lines of fire while relying on their partners to watch theirs, and everyone watched the backs of everyone else present. Marty finally managed to locate the lights and the afternoon gloom was instantly dispelled.

The trio carefully made their way across the great room's travertine floors, into the dining room and toward the kitchen. A faint odor of blood, urine and feces greeted them and grew stronger the closer they approached the room. Marty fully expected to see a body, but nothing but blood and the stain of partially dried bodily fluids remained. Lyle walked along the edge of the mess pointing down to a trail of dried blood leading away from the kitchen and toward the back door.

Lyle walked to the back door and propped it open saying "might help getting rid of some of the stink..." He walked out on the back porch, then down two stairs that brought him to the overgrown lawn. His keen eyes surveyed the area as he continued into the yard. When he reached what had once been the garden, he bent down and inspected the ground then returned to the Hall.

"Someone was killed out in the garden. Lots of blood, trampling of vegetation." Lyle paused. "From the blood spatters on the porch, I can say that someone brought a body into the house, not out."

"Ok, but whoever died in here was taken elsewhere." Cole stated. "The question is who this mess in the kitchen belongs to."

The group carefully made their way from the gore spattered kitchen and back into the great room. Lyle pointed up toward the corners of the room. "Cameras. They're everywhere, in every trap zone on the main floor, you can't avoid them."

"Yes, the place is also well secured and of course alarmed. I'm surprised we haven't received a call from the Sheriff's department concerning an alarm." Cole located a small digital alarm panel on the wall near the front foyer. "Looks like the alarms been deactivated and never set before whoever it was last left the premises. I wonder if the alarm system is even monitored externally."

The group made their way to the stairway and climbed to the second floor. Narrow rays of sunlight poked through the small, uneven glass panes of the western wall's few windows. The bedrooms were lost in shadows, their windows all faced north. Lyle flicked on the room lights before the men cleared each of the upstairs rooms.

Marty discovered the Hall's security monitoring room tucked away in a bedroom closet. Lyle took a quick look and whistled. "Man, this stuff cost a bundle, all cutting edge equipment." He poked around for several minutes while the other two men looked on. Lyle activated the computer and its monitor. "You guessed right boss, this setup isn't externally monitored. Strictly in house, but linked to multiple cell phones, I wonder whose?"

Cole spoke up. "You'll have time to look at that later. Let's clear the basement, then we can poke around. I don't want any surprises." Cole led the men down the stairs and onto the main floor. The basement leading to the door was slightly ajar.

Marty opened the door and the men were greeted with the unmistakable stench of death and decay. "Good Christ Almighty!" The detective pulled out a handkerchief and covered his nose while he stepped onto the top floor and turned on one of two sets of lights. The cellar was large and open; the switch nearest to the door activated a series of dangling light bulbs positioned just outside the bars of three cramped iron barred cells. "It's a prison." Marty took a few shallow breaths and flicked on the second switch; several long banks of florescent light fixtures flickered and then steadied flooding the basement in light.

The men began walking down the long steps. About half way down Marty pointed to what looked to be a pizza oven; its substantial doors covered its opening. "A crematorium..." Marty stated. The men reached the bottom of the steps. Marty pointed to several crumpled heaps that lay in front of the oven. "Bodies." A quick check identified the corpses of a young man and woman.

Lyle took Marty by his upper arm. "Wait, don't go any further. I don't want any contamination of the scene. Let's just check the rest of the basement to make sure there's no one else here, or anyone requiring attention."

Cole added. "Good idea. Then let's see what the computer security cameras can tell us."

A few minutes later, the men stood about Lyle who was opening various video files stored on the computer's hard drive. The videos bearing today's date showed the three men entering the Hall and their progress as they walked room to room. "Geez Elijah I had no idea you were so photogenic." Lyle smirked.

"Ok funny man. Let's see what happened yesterday." Cole quipped.

A few moments later Lyle had all the camera footage up and running on a grid of sixteen small image squares on the large fifty two inch monitor. "I'll just take us back a few days. From the condition of the bodies in the cellar and the blood in the kitchen, I'd guess about three days back. That would be in line with Stile's body and that caretaker found two mornings ago." Cole nodded his agreement.

A few moments later, one of the screens showed the motion activated rear porch light suddenly illuminating. Moments later the back door opened and someone entered the Hall. Lyle enlarged the image to fill the monitor's entire screen. A hooded figure, dressed in black from head to toe entered the doorway; it had what appeared to be a bundle slung over its shoulder. "Well, what do we have here?" Lyle added. An arm and hand dangled down across the figures back. Lyle paused the video and enlarged the victim's arm and hand; a man's wristwatch came into view as did the partial sleeve of a blue and red quilted shirt. "I'd guess that's one of our friends downstairs." Lyle said matter of factly.

As the figure left the rear doorway, the outside light went dark, but having low light infrared ability, the video cameras continued to follow the as yet unidentified person from room to room while it carried the victim over its shoulder not unlike a sack of potatoes. Every once in a while and arm or leg moved indicating the man was still alive. One thing was very clear; the figure bore the man's weight with alarming ease. The basement door opened and the person and its victim descended into the blackness of the cellar.

"Are the lights on in the basement?" Marty asked.

Lyle replied. "Not at all, what you're seeing is what you might call a false image. False only in the sense that the camera is picking up slightly longer wavelengths of light our eyes can't detect and then decoding the images into wavelengths of the visible spectrum that we can see." Lyle paused. "In the meantime, this guy is moving in near complete darkness without breaking a sweat." Fox didn't mention that he had performed the same feat many times over the last several hundred years.

"Any sound on the video?" Marty looked over Lyle's shoulder drawing close to the monitor.

"Not activated." Lyle replied.

The men watched the figure carry his victim to the center of the basement and then stop. Slowly it raised the semiconscious man so that they were positioned face to face, then slowly the distance between the figures dwindled until they appeared to be one on the camera. Marty heard himself gasp in surprise as a light glow filled the screen and washed out the image until the camera adjusted its dynamic range and compensated for the flood of visual light now entering its lens. The image steadied and the men witnessed the intensity of the glow rapidly increase between the two bodies until a brilliant flash erupted. The victim slumped in the other's arms. Seconds later the glow all but subsided and the room once again fell into the realm of the infrared.

The figure released the unmoving man who fell in a heap on the floor. The shape suddenly spun towards the stairs facing the position where the camera was mounted and revealing a face taken right out of a nightmare. Marty and the others stared at the screen. The face was angular, the features were jagged and accentuated, its teeth long and sharp, the flesh of its cheeks absent, but it was the eyes that held Marty and Cole mesmerized. They were oversized and glowed with a light of their own; their pupils appeared distinctly oval, if not catlike.

Marty was about to speak to the men regarding Rachel Kaplan's paintings and her diary, and of course the medium's reading but suddenly the large image suddenly shrunk to a small square on the monitor.

It was Lyle who called their attention to the small section of screen showing the back door. It was Norman Stiles; he was dragging a young woman's lifeless body into the Hall. The porch light revealed the corpse had been horribly mangled. The arms and legs had been bent and twisted at impossible angles while the head lolled loosely dangling on an obviously broken neck. "Look at the thing in the basement... it hears something, its waiting."

Norman was seen to lay the woman's body on the floor then leave the doorway momentarily before returning with what looked to be a linen sheet. Stiles dragged the body onto the sheet then wrapped the corpse binding it tightly with some twine he found in one of the kitchen drawers nearby. At various points on the sheet, the linen gleamed wetly as bloody crimson blossoms continued to grow as blood slowly leaked from the terrible wounds inflicted upon the corpse. After turning on the Hall's main floor lights, Stiles dragged the body to the top of the basement stairs then dumped the bundled corpse down the stairs. It tumbled end over end until it thudded against the cellar floor.

Norman hit the basement lights and Lyle immediately switched over to the basement camera, the images of Stiles and the hooded creature filled the screen. As soon as the lights came on, the creature used its arms to shield itself from the bright light. As Stiles walked down the stairs, the camera position showed his lips clearly moving, raising then lowering his arms as he did so. He was obviously speaking to the thing. Marty thought he may have been trying to calm it.

Reaching the bottom of the stairs, Stiles grabbed an end of the sheet and dragged the corpse, leaving it beside the other body. The creature fled the light and ran to a far corner where the shadows still gathered. Continuing his gesturing, Stiles slowly walked to where the figure now crouched, its hideous face pressed close to the rocky corner. Norman grabbed a small stool, brought it over near the corner and sat near the unmoving figure. When neither figure moved for some time, Lyle hit the fast forward until movement was detected. The time at the top of the screen indicated Norman had been sitting with the creature for nearly four hours. They watched Norman climb the stairs, turn off the lights. Stiles walked into the kitchen where he sat at the table, placed his head in his arms and fell asleep. The infrared camera in the basement showed the creature who remaining motionless in its corner.

Lyle adjusted the security program to sound an alarm if any captured motion from either the basement or kitchen cameras were detected, then he joined the other two looking about the upper rooms. It was Cole who located the floor safe in what they decided was the master bedroom. It took Lyle only minutes to open the safe and drag out its contents handing them to Cole and Marty who spread the items out on the bed. So far there was about twenty thousand dollars in cash, a good number of American and Swiss passports in the names of Otto Meyers, Irma Meyers and Norman Stiles. Nothing out of the ordinary, until Lyle brought out a small wooden chest, a silver and black outlined swastika emblazoned the lid. He handed it to Cole.

Elijah opened the lid and began to remove old personal papers, photographs, news clippings and some unusual pieces of memorabilia, handing each man a stack of papers to assess. Unfortunately, none of them spoke or read German, the language in which nearly all of the papers and documentation were written. Even so, it soon became apparent that Irma Meyers was in fact Irma Grese, the head female warden in the Nazi's Ravensbrück and Auschwitz concentration camps. There were also photographs of Grese and an SS Captain who Marty immediately recognized from his and Ann's internet research as Josef Mengele, Auschwitz's Angel of Death.

Denton read one of the few English news clippings aloud. "The headlines read: Belsen Beast Irma Grese hanged with nine other horror camp aides - It says here the woman was hung on December 13, 1945 10:00 am in

Hamelin Prison and buried in the prison yard. Yet we have a 1946 passport of Irma Meyers showing a photograph that looks strikingly similar to that of Irma Grese." Marty spread out a small stack of documents on the bed then picked up two American passports, one dated 1953, the other 1966. He opened the pages of each to the photograph of the passport holder, Irma Meyers and compared them to the German passport issued in 1946. "This doesn't make any fucking sense! The face of the person shown in each of these photos hasn't aged a day although the hair color in the last photo appears to show some Gray."

"Elijah, hand me that photo at the edge of the bed please." Marty pointed, "Yeah that one, with Irma and a guy on the beach." Marty took the photo and looked carefully. "Good Christ, this guy is Mengele. Look at the banner they're posing under - The Orange Cup Regatta Florida 1966 - Either these two have the best plastic surgeon in the world, the images are photo shopped, or they just don't age. Hell, this bitch should be a bag of bones by now!" Marty took the cell phone from his belt; "We need to get more help up here and toss this place top to bottom."

"No... I don't think so." Marty looked up and saw Cole and Fox first look at one another and then back to himself. Cole said resignedly, "Marty, I think it's high time we had a talk."

38

He always enjoyed the drive along I-90; certain sections of the interstate reminded him of the Bundesautobahn or simply the Autobahn, a term most non-Germans preferred. He always smiled when he heard Americans speak of their interstate highway system as if they had somehow come up with the idea on their own. Fact was their American president, Dwight D. Eisenhower, the Supreme Allied Commander in Europe during the Second World War; had become so enamored with the Nazi's federal highway system, that he pushed the US to adopt a similar plan in 1956.

Aleixo made good time arriving in Claremont City nearly half an hour earlier than he had planned. He bypassed city center, instead taking a ring road that would avoid noon hour traffic and bring him directly to the Shawnessy Home for Seniors. He turned into the parking lot, pulled into an empty visitor stall and exited the vehicle. While walking to the entrance, Aleixo noticed a familiar face, as did the receptionist who immediately picked up the phone. By the time Silva arrived at the glass entrance doors, a tall thin man in a well tailored business suit was already bustling from his office to greet him. Aleixo entered the elegant foyer and was immediately escorted into the manager's office where the receptionist inquired if he would like his usual, a double espresso.

"Please, that would be lovely. Sharon is it?" Aleixo asked pleasantly. Since moving to Brazil, Aleixo had grown fond of the strong caffeine laced beverage.

"Yes, Mr. Silva, I'll be right back." The receptionist disappeared out the door softly closing it behind her.

"Wonderful to have you with us again." The manager, Walter Tiggs voiced the greeting in flat even tones while his face continued to display the same benevolent yet tightly controlled expression since Aleixo had arrived. Silva considered the man and not for the first time thought with his disposition, Tiggs could easily double as a funeral director.

"Thank you Mr. Tiggs. I've come to see my uncle, but also to inquire as to his health." Silva continued. "When I last spoke with him on the telephone, his voice sounded, well... rather weak."

"Of course, of course. One moment please." Tiggs picked up the phone, punched a button and began to speak. "Sharon?"

The door opened suddenly and Sharon stepped into the office along with Silva's espresso. "Ah Sharon..." Tiggs replaced the phone on the receiver.

"Sharon, Mr. Silva would like to speak to someone regarding Mr. Meyers health. Could you please ask Dr. Lee and his nurse to come to the office please?"

Sharon placed a small cup in front of Silva and left the office.

Nearly five minutes had passed and Tiggs noticed Aleixo had nearly finished his cup. Looking somewhat apprehensive, "I'm sure they'll be here directly, probably just stopped to pull Mr. Meyers file."

There was a light knock then the door opened. An Asian gentleman in a white lab coat accompanied by a rather stern looking matron holding a manila file both entered the room.

"Dr. Lee, I'd like you to meet Mr. Aleixo Silva, Mr. Meyers is his uncle and has travelled all the way from Brazil just to visit Otto." The two men shook hands, Tiggs gestured to an empty chair at the side of his desk and Lee sat down.

Lee smiled, "My nurse, Judy Hood." The nurse obviously aware of her status stood behind the doctor and gave a silent nod in Silva's direction.

The doctor began his assessment. Silva watched Tiggs visibly blanch as the doctor spoke; he was obviously not expecting such a guarded prognosis concerning one of their most esteemed residents. The doctor certainly wasn't pulling any punches. Otto wasn't expected to live past the end of next week and could go at any time. Aleixo listened carefully, asked a number of knowledgeable questions before fully agreeing with the doctors assessment. The level of Aleixo's medical familiarity prompted the physician to inquire if Aleixo was a medical practitioner; Aleixo simply replied he was a pilot and asked to see Otto Meyers without further delay.

Silva dismissed Tiggs and the others preferring instead to enter Otto's room alone. With the appearance of his old and so very close friend, tears rolled down Otto's wrinkled cheeks and he outstretched an enfeebled hand toward his visitor. Aleixo instinctively drew back within himself, girding his emotions and fighting to retain an optimistic expression on his face with great difficulty. He wasn't prepared to see his Servicio in this advanced state of decline. The man's health had precipitously faded since his last visit which was only two months earlier.

Aleixo pulled up a chair and sitting at Otto's bedside grasped the old man's hand within his own. Nothing verbal transpired between the two, there was no need for words; the cerebral connection between the two was as strong as it ever was. Aleixo's Servicio brushed aside his master's concern for his wellbeing, concentrating instead in relating everything that had happened since their last meeting. As the seconds ticked by, a constant flow of information and vivid memory passed between the two. Finally, Otto allowed his mind to relax; he had performed his duties admirably. In return, Aleixo shared their most distant shared memories, their travels, adventures and most importantly his deep emotional attachment to the old man.

Locked in their mental embrace, the Sempitor and Servicio were as one. Slowly Aleixo removed the old man's hand from his own and reaching across Otto's body placed his palm gently against the man's chest and closed his eyes. The old man smiled at his friend as his heart beat slowed and finally stopped. A single tear rolled down the Sempitor's face as he rose from the bedside. Leaving the room, Dr. Lee and his nurse hustled into the room, immediately realizing there was nothing more to be done.

Aleixo filled out the required paperwork in Tiggs office then left the building for the final time. He drove quickly, leaving Claremont City and heading towards Hansel's Creek, where Otto assured Aleixo he had urgent business.

39

It was almost 7:00 pm when Sheriff Billing's Suburban rolled through the gates of God's Angels Cemetery driving down the driveway toward the main office and equipment shop. Seeing Jimmy Jones' black caddie parked in the managers parking stall, Norm pulled up beside it. He had no sooner killed the engine when Jimmy's secretary Joanne, walked out the front door. He stepped from the big vehicle and began walking toward the main door.

"Hi Joanne, I take it the big guy is still here?"

"Afternoon Sheriff. Yes he's been on the phone all afternoon with the lawyers."

"Whose lawyers?"

"Every ones." Joanne chuckled. "I shouldn't laugh, poor guy." She threw Billings a wave and walked toward a small car.

"Good night." The Sheriff waved back and continued up to the office door. Stepping inside, he took off his Stetson, enjoying the air conditioning. This had to be the hottest day yet this spring. Norm walked over to the small fridge where he knew Jimmy kept spring water, sodas and hidden in the very back - a few beers.

The Sheriff looked over through the open door to Jimmy's office. The man was on the phone, looked in his direction and nodded his head toward Norm, put up two fingers then continued talking and writing notes. Norm grabbed a couple of beers and headed into Jimmy's office seating himself across the man's desk.

"Yes, I understand completely Mr. Anders. I can assure you that we'll have the situation remedied by tomorrow afternoon... latest." Jimmy's right hand formed an impression of a pistol, placed his index finger to his temples and dropped his thumb pretending to shoot himself. "Ok Mr. Anders. Yes sir, thank you for your patience. Yes it's been a pleasure speaking with you as well. Good bye now."

Billings grinned at the short balding man who now pointed a finger toward the beers then back to himself. Norm handed the cold can over to the manager who immediately held it up to his forehead. "Christ, what a fucking day." Jimmy seemed to sense something the Sheriff wasn't saying. "Norm, please, please don't tell me I can't begin cleaning things up down at the tomb! I just promised that family's lawyer..."

Billings interrupted, "No, no... It's nothing like that. I've got the FBI coming down tonight to take a last look, then you'll be free to do what you need to. I just came to ask you not to lock the main gate, or if you give me a spare key, I can lock up after we're done then have one of my guys drop the key off tomorrow."

The manager's face showed genuine relief. "Oh yeah, sure." Jimmy opened the top drawer, reached in then tossed a key onto the desk before taking a long pull from the can. The two men talked sports for a while over their beers until Jimmy noticed the time. "Hell, sorry to rush you Norm, but I gotta get on my horse."

Both men were about to enter their car when Jimmy piped up, "Hey, your photographer, Al ... ah Christ what's his name, he's still down there at the tomb."

"Al Jenkins." The Sheriff nodded his thanks, started the Suburban and slowly cruised toward the mausoleum.

Arriving at the tomb, Billings made sure he parked the vehicle in the Shade and well upwind from its entrance before parking. Despite the bodies having been removed from the mausoleum the day before, the place still stank to high heaven, today's unusual heat hadn't helped matters. He stepped from the vehicle, grateful for the evening's cool gentle breeze that stirred the leaves on the trees and brushed atop the cemetery's sprawling lawns.

The Sheriff looked about. The tomb lay sixty feet or so from the vehicle wrapped in ribbons of yellow police tape, their ends flapped and danced in the light wind. The sun had just dropped below the tree line and Norm figured it would set in the next ten minutes or so. Looking off to his right, he saw a camera and tripod set up some hundred feet distance. Al must be taking some general photos of the scene, always a good idea, provides frames of reference for the judge and jury, if it ever comes to that he mused.

Billings took a pack of smokes from the breast pocket of his uniform and lit one up. He looked about for his deputy, Al couldn't have gone far. He would never leave the camera equipment unattended. Jenkins was probably just out behind a tree somewhere taking a piss. Norm placed his back against the truck and enjoyed the pleasant evening.

40

"So, there you go, you got the gist of it." In Meyers Hall, Cole, Fox and Marty sat at the polished dining room table. The front and back doors had been propped open in the hopes of dispelling some of the nastier odors. A fresh breeze sprung up and swept through the room entering from the front door and exiting out the back. As the time passed, Marty's nose had already become desensitized; but Fox was different Marty mused, it seemed that nothing seemed to bother him, not in the slightest.

At first Marty was at a loss to explain why Cole and Fox insisted that the Sheriff, his men, or even the coroner wouldn't have any part in this investigation, let alone be allowed to attend the Hall. When Marty angrily protested, Cole produced his handgun from his shoulder holster and leveled it at Marty's chest while Fox removed Marty's 10mm Glock as well as his 38 cal snub nose from his ankle holster.

It was nearly 7:00 pm and they had been sitting at this table for nearly an hour. Marty felt as though he had entered another world. So far, he had been told that Irma Meyers, aka Grese and god knows how many other aliases, along with Josef Mengele, perhaps a thousand others and even Fox himself were Sempitors; members of the Orden Sempiterno - a secret society whose members consisted of a long lived race that occasionally preyed upon humanity. Cole and Fox explained there were two different orders within the Sempitor; the White and the Gray and how they differed from each other. They spoke of the "turning" and described the manner in which some Sempitors ended their lives as "Shades," vicious monsters that killed without reason or regret until they themselves were either killed or their rapidly aging bodies starved to death.

According to Fox, he himself was over two hundred years old, their target Irma Grese was about the same age, though some in the Order thought Mengele could be nearly four centuries old. They explained how the Servicio worked, how Norman Stiles had become indentured into servitude. How it had been Stiles who had notified others of his own caste that his master had begun to "turn" and how he had tried and failed to convince Irma to end her life. How the Order had assigned Cole and Fox to destroy the Shade and eliminate any evidence that might make humans aware of their presence.

Rachel Kaplan's paintings and diary, the medium's strange reading in the library, the bodies of Eddie Swan and the poor kids that were lying down in the basement, and finally the official documentation he had read with his own eyes less than an hour ago brought the facts home - in an indisputable fashion.

At this point Fox ceased to speak and looked toward Cole who in turn laid his hands upon the table and looked directly into Marty's eyes. "Marty, the Orden Sempiterno, came together about three hundred years ago. Having amassed very considerable wealth over their long lives, the need to properly invest this wealth forced them to associate with others of similar social and economic standing, even royalty and the like. While socializing within these circles, the Sempitors began recognizing others of their kind. You see many of the Order are empaths, only a few others are actually telepathic, to a limited degree. As they came together they realized the benefits of working together, but only in a very loose fashion. Being a long lived species, they saw firsthand the dangers of politics and interfering in the lives of others. This in fact is their one and only inviolable law and unless one of their kind transgresses this law, they will take no direct action. When a member of the order "turns" and becomes a Shade, they place the entire membership at risk. That's where we come in."

Cole continued. "Lyle, who is of course a member of the Order, is also an agent working on their behalf. He'll work in the capacity of an agent for a few decades and then be replaced with another volunteer. Everyone takes their turn, sort of a patriotic duty I guess."

"These agents often work with the support of the Servicio, as well as law enforcement professionals, like me; and what do I get out of it. I can see it in your face, and yes thank you, upon retirement I shall receive a golden parachute courtesy of the Order, but I'm not a simple assassin. Before you start judging me you should know that the Order has access to the global intelligence assets of the world's nations. They make these resources available to agents like Fox and in turn the agents provide people like me information of human serial murderers.

"The Order gives a damn about serial killers?" Marty smirked sarcastically.

"Not one iota. What they do give a shit about is our ability to cover up Sempitor killings and to do so in the field before it comes to the attention of the legitimate authorities. The Order employs people to "mine" the internet and intelligence data searching for trends that might indicate one of their own members has gone rogue. In doing so, they naturally uncover leads, if not the actual identity of possible serial killers. These they share with us, a trade if you like for our assistance. But that is all they share, they don't involve themselves in world politics or causes; they take the long term approach, given their longevity, I suppose they can afford to."

Marty was beginning to understand. This certainly explained Elijah Coles amazing clearance rate within the bureau. "How many Sempitor's have you assassinated?"

"I, working with Fox, have "retired", only two Shades over the past four years. In the same time, I have overseen the capture and conviction of no fewer than twelve serial murderers, eleven of these resulted from information I obtained from the Order. I believe that to be a pretty good deal… for humanity."

"And what about the people the members of the order prey upon and kill. What of them?" Marty asked indignantly.

"Ninety percent or more of the Sempiterno belong to the White Order. As a rule, they don't kill anyone, certainly they steal small amounts of the victim's life expectancy and then move on, but these thefts are never noticed. The Grays on the other hand are most certainly killers, but still for the most part only kill what they need to survive, although some employ methods of killing that would make the Marquis de Sade himself pale in comparison. There are some such as Irma Grese a sexual sadist, who become addicted to such perversions, and as all addicts yearn for ever more frequent moments of ecstasy."

Marty scowled. "Don't these killings work to bring suspicion on the members of the Order?"

"As a rule… no. These days, the Grays normally operate far from home, third world countries are a favorite as are theaters of war and areas where genocides are actively taking place. They must also notify the Order of their destination and how long they expect to be active. This way, the Order's contacts within the local authorities, people like me, can cover up their activities if by chance the killings surface. This is an extremely rare occurrence."

"Genocides." Marty mused, "Is this why Grese became a warden in the camps?"

"Yes. She could operate for years without drawing suspicion to herself." Cole answered.

"Ok, but how did she come back from death?" Marty asked.

"She didn't come back from death, since she never died." Fox spoke up. "Hanging is unlikely to kill one of us. You would consider our recuperative powers to be utterly amazing. The hangman did a proper job; his noose ensured that her neck snapped when she dropped from the scaffold. She also most certainly appeared dead, even to the British Army doctor who check her vitals and confirmed her death."

Cole spoke up. "She was interred in the prison graveyard, as the newspaper reported. While lying in the grave, her body repaired itself. The Order's contacts at the time reported that one night, several weeks after her hanging, several workers at the prison who idolized people like Grese, dug her up and stole what they thought was her corpse. They placed another woman's body in the prison grave then spirited Grese's from the grounds. They intended to give Grese a proper burial in a place where other Nazis and their sympathizers could come and venerate at her grave. This didn't turn out quite as they expected. Irma awoke while in transit and consumed them both; leaving their desiccated corpses in a roadside ditch where they drew no attention. At the close of the war, such unburied corpses were a common sight in Germany."

"Ironically, theft of deceased Nazi celebrities was a concern within Germany and still is today. In December of 2019, Berlin police investigated the opening of the unmarked grave of former SS officer Reinhard Heydrich, a ranking Nazi assassinated by Czech partisans in 1942. Police claim nothing was taken, but the robbers would have had the foresight to replace Heydrich's bones with those of someone else who had died about the same time."

Cole continued. "In 1954, authorities moved what they thought was Irma Grese's body to a cemetery in Hameln. In the 1980's, she was moved to an unmarked grave, the original plot became a site of pilgrimage for right wing radicals."

Fox spoke. "Upon her return, Irma found she was not without friends or means, one of these being Otto Meyers. It was he who arranged passage to America along with her recently acquired Servicio, Norman Stiles. The rest I think you know or have at least already guessed."

"So what happens now?"

"Marty, you have a decision to make. Simply put are you with us, or against us? Cole asked. "Those are your only two alternatives."

Marty sat for several long minutes in thought staring at his hands as one massaged the other in turn. "If I don't go along with you..."

"If you don't, then it's quite simple, you will disappear along with the other bodies in the cellar." Cole stated flatly. "If it helps, Fox offered me the same choice. I agreed and haven't regretted doing so."

"I thought as much. Well given the choice I guess I'm in."

Cole looked at Fox who spoke up. "I see in his mind he's with the program, at least for the most part. He knows there's no way out and has already assumed the Order has more than enough clout to either discredit and ruin him if he goes back on the agreement later on."

Marty looked at the man. "You read my mind?"

"No, but I can gauge your emotions, the rest is simple logic." Fox answered. "I believe we have an appointment with Sheriff Billings, we should leave now or we'll be late. We'll clean up here tomorrow and start searching for Grese tomorrow first thing."

"Will she be hard to find?"

Lyle laughed hoarsely, "Hell no Marty, it's even money she'll find us first."

41

Sheriff Norm Billings crushed his cigarette butt beneath the sole of his boot and reached for the radio in the cab of the Suburban police vehicle. "2101 to 2105 portable..." he paused then called Al Jenkins's call sign once again. " 2101 to 2105 portable..." Nothing but dead air.

"2101 dispatch." Billings thought maybe his partner had picked him up, but that didn't explain the camera equipment sitting in the middle of the lawn.

"Dispatch. Evening Sheriff. This is Avery, what can I do for you?" a friendly female voice answered his call.

"Hi Avery, I'm trying to track down 2105 portable, Al Jenkins."

"I've got Jenkins out at that crime scene at God's Angel Cemetery. He booked out there two hours ago." Avery answered.

"Who's his partner tonight?"

"John Sweeny, in 2105. I show him out at a 10-09 (shop breaking) on Old Spar Road."

"Ok... Avery do you have Al's cell number handy?" A few moments later, Norm called Jenkins's cell.

Off in the distance, well beyond the camera and tripod, the Sheriff heard a faint ringing. No one picked up and after five rings the call went to voice message. "Al, its Sheriff Billings, I'm out at the cemetery. Give me a call back on my cell or radio."

Billings looked towards a stand of trees where he judged he heard the ringing and started walking toward them.

It was 8:15 in the evening when the three men in a dark SUV drove through the open gates of God's Angel's Cemetery and headed down to the mausoleum to meet Sheriff Billings. The ride to the cemetery had been a quiet one. Cole was worried about Marty or more correctly what action Lyle Fox would take if he became convinced Marty couldn't live up to the terms of their agreement. Elijah truly liked Marty and knew he was still only a thought or two away from winding up in the Meyers Hall's crematorium. As for Marty, he was trying to make sense of not only what he heard and experienced over the past several weeks, but how his life would change in the future; both for good and bad.

Fox was content in the knowledge that Marty would go along with their agreement. Fox lied to Marty and Cole when he said he possessed only empathic power, that was true when he was a young man of fifty or so, but

272

as he aged his mental abilities slowly grew. After two centuries of life he could pick up snippets of thoughts at close range, highly useful, but nothing approaching the uncanny abilities of some in the Order. While at the Hall, he probed Marty's thoughts as the man considered his options. Marty hadn't dwelled on the fear that he would be killed, within mere seconds he shelved those thoughts aside and moved on. The man possessed a decisive mind, both intelligent and highly intuitive. Marty was driven by a burning aspiration to excel in his career and an honest desire to protect the public; Fox remembered himself thinking "how rare a quality" in a mere human.

Instead while traveling the twenty minute journey to the cemetery, Fox was thinking only of the trio's inevitable confrontation with a very powerful Shade, this was one of the reasons he had considered Cole's request that Marty be recruited as an agent of the Order. The physical abilities of such a creature could only be referred to as "super human", but what really concerned Fox was the possibility that the beast still retained some degree of reasoning, not to mention her mental abilities, a fact of which Fox had been warned were "formidable". Their best chance now rested on the hope that Irma Meyers had reached the final stage of her existence. A good indication she had reached this point was the murder of her Servicio and the gruesome manner in which she had dispatched the cemetery worker, leaving both corpses where they could easily be found.

Norm Billings approached the stand of trees and brush, a small narrow forest that separated the newest plots from the very oldest then stopped in his tracks. The sun had set and the shadows of twilight dominated the cemetery grounds. A vague sense of foreboding swept over him and then vanished just as quickly. Before him, a red shale path stretched out running westward meandering among unmarked depressions in the earth, faded stones and weathered monuments. Once more, Norm called his deputy's cell phone and placed it to his ear praying the man would answer, none came. Instead the ringing in the distance was now louder, more insistent, sounding well inside the old cemetery; urging Norm to continue down the blood red trail leading to the west.

Fox pulled up beside the Sheriff's Suburban. The three men got out and walked toward the mausoleum. There was no sign of Billings or his deputy. Reaching the tomb, Fox immediately activated the twin halogen work light within the structure, pulled apart the police tape and stepped inside. It wouldn't be a long examination, Fox didn't expect to find anything useful to their task, but there was the slim possibility that a piece of incriminating evidence might point to the Order.

Cole stood by the entrance way. Ever since his experience within Tallahassee's Old City Cemetery these places gave him the creeps. He reached into his breast pocket for a smoke. If his wife Tina knew he'd bought a pack the day before she'd probably kill him herself. Pulling out the pack, his hand brushed his gun holster. Lighting up and taking his first puff, he immediately felt more at ease.

In the meantime, Marty noticed the camera and tripod sitting in the distance. His eyes scanned the surroundings and he saw Norm Billings walking several hundred yards away. He was about to shout out, but something told him not to disturb the brooding silence of the place. Marty looked toward Cole who had also caught sight of the sheriff, Marty pointed in the officer's direction and started walking. Cole just nodded and waited for Fox to emerge from the tomb.

In a couple of minutes Marty arrived at the shale path, he could see Norm walking in the distance. In the enshrouding gloom, the sheriff was no more than a silhouette against the dimming light of the western sky. Off in the same direction, Marty heard a cell phone faintly ringing.

Having reached the center of the old cemetery without seeing any sign of his deputy, Norm dialed Al's phone yet again. He was almost on top of the ringing now. Norm was positive his deputy had been moving since his first call at his truck, there was no way he would have heard the ringing from this distance. The Sheriff's eyes were guided by the cell phones chimes. As far as he could tell, it originated from an odd looking gravesite beneath an ancient spruce tree that probably predated the cemetery itself. Norm looked to either side of the pathway letting his hand fall to his side. His fingers felt for, then unsnapped the leather catch on his holster. His palm and fingers closed about the wooden butt of his hand gun. He began to walk forward.

Norm neared the strange gravesite, his eyes struggling in the murk to make sense of what he was seeing. He drew his gun. Holding the weapon at his side Norm called out his deputy's name. There was no answer, but the Sheriff was certain an unmoving human figure lay ahead. Norm's feet refused to move, with his free hand he took his flashlight from his belt and shone it ahead of him. What he saw nearly made him jump out of his skin; the image of a shrouded figure breaking free of its own tombstone and emerging from the grave lay frozen within the yellow beam. His handgun rose level with the figure and his finger played lightly upon the trigger. Finally after several very long seconds, he came to realize the figure was that of polished marble and lowered his gun.

Norm muttered under his breath, "Sweet mother of Christ..." His flashlight swept the area; there was still no sign of his man. He tried to swallow but his mouth was as dry as dust. Once more he hit the redial of his phone. The ring from the deputy's phone was almost deafening in the silence and it came directly behind that hideous grave stone. Norm slowly walked toward the grave but purposely stayed off to the left of the stone, if someone... or something other than Al Jenkins was behind the monument he wanted to provide himself some distance and reaction time to deal with it.

He walked beneath the branches of the huge spruce reaching the point and angle that allowed him to view the ground to the rear of the stone. There an oddly positioned body lay prone atop the dewy lawn. Norm slowly approached. His flashlight beam slowly revealed the bloody tatters of a police uniform, the body's arms and legs were splayed out at impossibly odd angles. "Oh Al. No!" Norm's voice was little more than a strangled croak as he cried out. That's when he heard something move in the spruce branches above his head. There was a loud crack and then something fell toward him in the dark.

A minute earlier, Marty had been walking toward the Sheriff as the officer's flashlight played along the ground on either side of a large stone monument. He heard Billings mutter something unintelligible then the man suddenly looked upward, his attention drawn to something within the branches of the tree beside him. Marty was impressed with the speed of Norm's reactions to whatever it was he saw in the tree.

The Sheriff spun on his heel; his arm bent sharply bringing the handgun up to chest level and aimed upward. There were two rapid gunshots. The flash from the gun barrel illuminated the surrounding area like the brilliant flash of lightning on a night as black as sack cloth. Marty was frozen in place while he saw a deep shadow drop from the tree and land upon the Sheriff. The two figures hit the ground, rolling and grappling only some twenty yards from where he stood. A faint but unmistakable glow of light began to form between the men. Marty heard Norm groan loudly and the Sheriff's arms fell to his side.

Marty swiftly drew his gun and shouted, "Federal agent, I'm armed." The cloaked figure atop the sheriff pause for perhaps a second before its hands closed upon either side of Norm's head and twisted viciously. Marty heard the unmistakable sound of snapping bone, and the Sheriff's body bucked and kicked as the figure at once leapt to its feet and began loping toward him. From beneath its black hood, an angular misshapen face appeared, its hungry eyes glowing orbs of flashing silver.

Marty didn't waste any more time, as there was simply none left to waste. His Glock bucked lightly in his palm sending a barrage of heavy hollow point shells speeding toward the approaching figure. Now only mere yards away, Marty's sense of urgency increased exponentially and he quickly emptied the remaining shells of his clip into the horror that glided toward him. Denton hadn't heard the roaring report of his gun fire, or noticed the flashes and smoke from its barrel; all he heard was the sound of his heartbeat while seeing the frightening visage of the specter that dashed toward him. Then suddenly - quite unexpectedly - the creature fell before Marty's feet, unmoving and still as death.

Marty stood motionless; the smell of gunpowder wafting in the surrounding air. Hearing the sound of breathing nearby, Marty's fear surged once more. He looked down at the figure lying before him. Stepping back from the creature, he ejected the clip and slid another into the handle with practiced ease and prepared to fire anew before he grasped that the rapid breaths he heard came from his own lips.

"Marty..." a soft voice called behind him. He spun about, the barrel of his weapon following his eyes toward two men standing nearby. Cole spoke in a slow rich baritone. "Marty. It's Cole and Fox... now lower your weapon, everything is going to be fine."

Fox and Cole walked up beside Marty and all three looked down at the creature before them. Its eyes were still open but only a faint silvery gleam remained of the burning fury Marty had witnessed only moments ago. "Well, now what." Marty's voice sounded small and uncertain in his own ears.

It was Lyle Fox who broke the silence. Fox held something out toward Marty. The steely gleam of the machete's blade reflected what little was left of the evening's light. "Now Marty. It's time for you to join the family."

42

Aleixo Silva drove south down Big Bend Road then turned eastward toward the South Bridge and the laneway leading to Meyers Hall. Today the sun hung high and hot in the clear sky, there was barely a breeze save for that provided by the rental car's passing as it traversed the five mile distance to the Hall.

Silva slowed the vehicle as he approached the gates then stopped immediately upon seeing them open and a dark SUV parked in front of the front door. He backed the vehicle slowly out of sight of the Hall, made a u-turn and headed back the way he came taking a right as he reached Lakeside Drive. Two hundred yards further along the drive he once again turned right, this time onto the Forestry Trunk Road.

Intimately familiar with the area, Aleixo was heading for a roadside turnout leading to a scenic lookout point within walking distance of the Hall. From there he would park and leave cross country to determine who was at the Hall and what they were up to. He pulled into the small parking lot, his was the only vehicle. Aleixo would have found it interesting that two of Irma's recent victims had chosen to park and cuddle in exactly the same stall his vehicle now occupied.

Exiting the vehicle Aleixo walked to the vehicle's trunk. He quickly changed his clothing and footwear to something more appropriate, sliding a small pair of binoculars and a large sheathed knife onto his belt and shoving a forty five caliber automatic in his waistband. Leaving the car, he began running along the walking trail that led to his destination.

While he jogged, his mind mulled over the information Otto had provided concerning recent events. Aleixo knew that a policeman, Marty Denton, from Hansel's Creek had come to the lodge to speak with the old man asking him details concerning the Hall and its occupants. Otto also told him that Norman Stiles and a caretaker had been found gruesomely murdered at the cemetery. There could be no doubt as to who was responsible for the killings. Aleixo rebuked himself for having waited so long to return to the Hall, he might have provided his beloved a graceful exit from this world, but now?

Otto had been terribly remorseful that he was physically unable to contact his master and pass along Norman Stiles updates concerning Irma's rapid progression from that of a rational Sempitor to an unreasoning beast. It was only a week later when he received an encrypted message from Norman Stiles that Aleixo had become concerned and arranged travel to the States.

Norman had also warned that agents would soon arrive on behalf of the Order. Silva knew Irma's Servicio had notified the Order as to his Master's deteriorating condition. Not he blamed Norman Stiles. The man did exactly what any other loyal servant would have done in his place. Still Aleixo mused; the presence of experienced agents knowing exactly who and what they were dealing with would complicate matters.

Silva had arrived and crouched among the bushes lining the rear grounds of the Hall. Using the binoculars he surveyed the scene. Inside an upper window he saw several figures leisurely moving about. In his experience, he believed the people were busy tossing the place; it was highly unlikely they would be doing so if Irma was on the premise. In fact he surmised it would be highly unlikely that any would still live if she had.

He was about to leave his position when he saw someone looking out the window into the garden. He swung the binoculars to the window; it was Marty Denton. Otto had mentally shown Aleixo the man's image back at the lodge. Silva waited until the policeman turned from the window and then rose to his feet and began making his way to the front of the Hall. Aleixo realized that he must both observe the actions of the men as they left, but also required the time necessary to return to his car and take up a position allowing him to follow their vehicle as they left. Silva also thought the absence of marked police vehicles made it likely that Marty and the other figure or figures he had seen were agents.

Aleixo Silva knew his beloved must die, but he was resolute that he could reach her mind and draw her back into a state of reason. She would pass at his hands instead of those belonging to the uncaring calloused hands of an agent. He also avowed that if someone prevented him from doing so, that someone would pay dearly. Silva hadn't survived the last five hundred years without accumulating some degree of knowledge and experience in such matters.

He reached the front gate of the compound but did not enter right away preferring instead to reconnoiter the scene instead. Aleixo found a spot where he could observe the interior of the Hall through several of the larger windows along the first floor. Given the poorly defined views through the uneven antique glass panes, he was still able to establish that three men were involved in a discussion at the dining room table. The time had come to act.

Silva ran to the edge of the building and slunk toward the front entrance where the SUV sat in the hot sunlight. Reaching one of the Hall's windows providing a view of the dining room, he carefully raised his head and peered into the room. The men continued to sit at the table, obviously preoccupied with their conversation. Still crouching, he ran to the left rear corner of the vehicle, took his knife from its sheath and forced the sharp blade between the tire treads stopping when he heard the quiet constant hiss of escaping air. Mission accomplished he ran back to the building, had a final peek inside before running a short ways beyond the gate and taking up a well concealed observation point. He would wait for the men to return to the vehicle and use the binoculars to identify the intruders and anything or anyone they might remove from the Hall.

Silva didn't have long to wait. Only fifteen minutes had passed since he disabled their vehicle and now three men stepped out the front door. He knew Marty Denton but couldn't place the other two, one a large black man, the other a North American aboriginal. His incredibly accurate memory would have remembered everything about them if he had. The binoculars showed the men carried nothing in their hands. Aleixo watched the black man take a spot in the front passenger seat while Denton sat in the back. Experience suggested that it was likely the black man was the Sempitor of the group, and therefore the one in charge. Denton was more likely his number two while the aboriginal who walked to the driver's door was likely subservient to both, a Servicio perhaps.

Aleixo lay low, the grass and brush covering his form completely, he was satisfied he was quite invisible, just one thing more to do. He concentrated his mind and drew himself inward, silencing those parts of his mind that constantly probed the world around him. Failure to do so would alert the Sempitor to his presence. Forcing his mind to remain static and inactive still left him able to discern a similar probe without the risk of detection.

The driver was about to enter the vehicle when he noticed the flat tire. Without a moment's hesitation his eyes scanned the entire compound. The other two men exited the SUV and stepped around to its left side. Marty crouched and examined the sidewalls for any punctures, there were none, but his ears detected a soft hiss near the center of the tread. Denton concluded the flat was a result of a simple puncture and not the act of a person. Cole was obviously of the same opinion and gave a satisfied grunt as he too continued to look about the compound and beyond.

It was Lyle who was unsatisfied with Marty's rather hasty deduction. His mind stretched forth in unison with his sharp eyes and sensitive ears for nearly a full minute. Unable to sense anything out of the ordinary, he shook his head and prepared to help Marty change the tire. With the men's attention so occupied, Aleixo quietly retreated further into the brush before making his way as quickly as possible to his vehicle.

Silva drove from the lookout and stopped his vehicle in a location along the road allowing him to see any vehicle turning from the laneway onto Lakeview Drive while restricting anything but a quick glimpse of his own car from the same intersection. It was nearly twenty minutes later when the SUV containing the three men, turned onto the Drive and headed toward the Creek. Knowing the traffic along the roads was bound to be very light, he gave his target a good lead, waiting nearly thirty seconds before following.

At the drive's intersection with Big Bend Road, Silva waited patiently to turn, then slid in behind a pickup truck keeping the truck between him and the SUV. The SUV crossed the railway tracks several miles further and then turned right into the cemetery parking lot. Now aware of their destination, Silva continued past the entrance and took the next right onto Church Street. He parked the rental half way down the block, next to a secondary entrance to the cemetery.

The sun had already set in the west when he entered the grounds. Passing by a grave he bent low snatching a small bouquet of flowers from a ceramic vase and continued walking deeper within the cemetery grounds. He checked his watch, nearly eight thirty. He rounded a small hill and caught sight of the Sheriff's Suburban parked near a mausoleum sporting a web of yellow police tape. Shifting his eyes about surreptitiously, he saw the Sheriff walking up the path toward him, only some fifty feet away. Pretending not to take any notice of the officer, Silva stepped from the path and walked to a nearby grave where he stopped, made the sign of the cross and bowed his head. For a second, Aleixo thought the officer had wanted to ask him something but thought better of it not wanting to disturb the grave's visitor. A soft probe of the Sheriff's mind suggested the man was looking for someone, maybe one of his men. Out of the corner of his eye, Silva watched the man turn onto a red shale pathway and walk away to the west.

Meanwhile ahead of him, some three hundred yards or so distant, the dark blue SUV with the three men had just arrived and parked beside the police vehicle. He watched their actions closely; once again he couldn't pick up anything of interest. He saw the aboriginal enter the tomb and the black man light up a smoke. That's when Denton started to walk up the path toward him, obviously on the trail of the Sheriff who had passed by only a minute before. It was time to go. Silva waited until Denton was closer before he moved to the head of the grave and laid the bouquet at the gravestone. As expected, the detective didn't take notice of him. Even though the cemetery was empty, to Denton, Silva was just another visitor checking in with the dearly departed.

Aleixo walked back the way he had come until he reached the street before following the street westward, his eyes tracking along the cemetery grounds as he did so. Every so often he'd catch glimpses of the Sheriff or Denton moving among the bushes and trees. When he could no longer see either of them through the thickening brush at the cemetery's edge, he jumped the fence and re-entered the grounds. He paused, closed his eyes while allowing his mind to probe the area, his eyes popped open with the realization that - she was here – his beloved was only a short ways distant.

He moved quietly through the brush bordering the lawn and its host of stones and crosses. Silva saw the Sheriff approaching what he knew to be Otto's unusual choice of a monument. Far too ostentatious for anything he would have chosen for himself... but then again it was Otto who would have to rest beneath that monstrosity for all eternity. He removed the binoculars from his belt and took stock of the situation. Silva's interest peaked as he saw the officer draw his gun and sweep the area ahead with a flashlight. He sensed Irma was very near, yet even closer to the officer, but where? Walking behind the Sheriff and rapidly closing the gap was Denton, lagging further behind him were the other two. He closed his mind off from the rest of the world - there was nothing he could do for Irma at present, he'd have to be patient.

A moment later, he heard the officer cry out while at the same time a dark shadow leapt down at the man from a large tree. Several shots rang out before the figures grappled in the shadows, he knew in his heart that the dark shadow could be no other than his beloved, although the horrific image in his binoculars contrasted his memory of the woman. He watched Irma break the Sheriff's neck then began to lope on all fours toward the detective who held a flashlight on his swiftly approaching attacker.

For one of the few times in his extraordinarily long life Aleixo found himself paralyzed, the binoculars dropped to his side, his eyes fixed on the scene before him. Time had slowed to a crawl. The men behind Denton were running in slow motion - Denton's gun was spouting rivets of flame and lead toward his Irma – and for every step his woman took, a bullet tore at her body sending small bits of flesh, fabric and a fine spray of blood out the exit wounds in her back.

As Irma fell to the ground so too did Aleixo. He sat staring at the three men who surrounded his lover. Something was said that he couldn't quite make out then the aboriginal pulled a long flat blade from his waist and handed it to Denton. The detective stood above his woman and raised the machete bringing it down upon her neck. Aleixo nearly screamed in rage and indignation, but the sound died in his throat.

Remaining silent and unmoving, Silva waited in the brush watching the aboriginal walk away leaving the other two men alone with Irma. Minutes later a pair of head lights appeared, bobbing and flashing in the dark as the SUV traversed the uneven ground stopping near the body. Silva watched the aboriginal man remove a body bag from the back and lay it on the ground. The men placed her body inside, zipped the bag's opening closed then loaded it into the cargo compartment.

His growing rage finally overcame his inaction. He would have his revenge, on all of them. He left the cemetery and walked to his vehicle. Time for more surveillance, more planning, he reminded himself he could take his time... after all, didn't he have all the time in the world?

Reaching his car, Silva could hear the wail of police vehicles and ambulances on their way to the cemetery.

43

The SUV idled in the parking lot of Motel 6. Inside the vehicle Cole, Fox and Denton discussed their options for tomorrow.

It had been a long and difficult night. Several hours ago, they had thankfully managed to kill Irma Meyers at considerable risk to their own lives. Marty felt he owed his life to Norm Billings who drew the Shade's initial attack allowing him a chance to kill the beast at distance. After providing their prepared and carefully tailored statements to the Sheriff department's investigators, Marty caught a case of the "guilts." He'd never deliberately lied in a police investigation before. He replayed the summary of his falsified statement over his mind.

There was no need to lie about why the FBI was there, it was common knowledge they attended to assist with the crime scene at the mausoleum. There was no need to lie about following the Sheriff as he walked into the old cemetery. But... there was the absolute requirement to say after he heard the Sheriff discharge his weapon, he saw the Sheriff and the other man; a very large man struggling on the ground. Marty announced his presence and gave due warning, so as the culprit ran from the scene he fired his own weapon multiple times, perhaps wounding, but failing to bring down his man. He and the other members of his team tried to resuscitate the Sheriff but to no avail. They immediately called for assistance.

Cole and Fox gave eyewitness statements supporting that of Marty's, neighborhood inquiries produced other witnesses saying they saw flashlights and heard multiple shots coming from that direction, and of course Marty's pile of empty shell casings and the two from the Sheriff's own weapon lay where the man fell. The fact that it was dark enough to require flashlights certainly helped account for Marty's rather disappointing marksmanship. As luck would have it, the Sheriff department's dog man was in Seattle for the weekend, while the canine unit called in from Claremont City couldn't arrive for several hours. Given the amount of activity taking place about the two bodies, it came as no small surprise that the dog man failed to establish a viable track upon his delayed arrival.

The three men exited the vehicle and stood about finalizing tomorrow's plans.

"Ok, listen up. I'm done here. I'm heading home to Canada tomorrow morning. You two guys should be able to take care of things back at the Hall, right?" Lyle Fox directed his comments to Elijah Cole.

"Yeah, Marty and I will take care of it." Cole looked to Denton. "Marty, tomorrow about nine or so, I'll pick you up and we'll drive out to the Hall. We burn the documentation we found and all the bodies in the crematorium clean out the ashes and take the teeth or anything else that might provide identification. We wipe the computer memory clear with this thumb drive program Lyle's provided, "thanks Lyle", then torch the place and burn it to the ground. By the time the police and the basement savers arrive, we'll be sipping a couple of ice cold beers back in town. "

"Ok. I guess that's the plan then." Marty acknowledged then turned to Lyle. "Thanks for your help." The men shook hands.

"What help, you did most of it, I just changed a tire." Fox laughed. "You know you're not too bad for a white boy, if you ever want to go fishing up north, I know all the best spots."

Cole extended a hand toward Lyle, "Thanks brother. I take it you'll handle our report to the Order?"

"Of course, just as soon as I get home to a secure computer... well, take care you two." Fox walked toward the motel entrance.

The SUV pulled out of the parking lot. A few minutes later Cole pulled the vehicle up to the curb in front of Reggie's house. Marty stepped out, gave Cole a small wave and walked to the front door where the porch light had just flicked on. Cole saw a pretty young woman rush out onto the porch and fall into Marty's arms. Watching the tender scene reminded Cole of his own wife; man, he could sure use some of her loving right about now. He grinned to himself and set out for Claremont City, he'd give Tina a call tonight.

Aleixo had expertly tailed the three since they drove from the cemetery. Why was it cops never imagined that someone could or would surveil them? These clowns were too easy Silva thought. He watched Cole's SUV leave Denton's place. He had planned to take his revenge killing Marty as he slept that night, but now seeing the young woman, he rearranged his plans to take advantage of something a little more apropos. All he had to do was sit back and wait for the house to go quiet.

44

The morning dawned bright and sunny. As was his habit, Lyle Fox was "up and at 'em" checking out of the hotel and strolling over to the Ihop just before six bells. Grabbing a paper from the vending box sitting at the entrance, he walked into the restaurant and sat at a vacant table. Lyle looked about the restaurant. Not too busy, a couple of truckers whose rigs idled out on the lot, a young couple that looked as if they'd been partying all night, and a family of tourists hoping to get an early start before the highway traffic became congested.

Fox sipped his coffee and read the paper as he waited for his order. The Claremont City Press had run a special edition to cover the murder of the Creek's Sheriff and Deputy. The paper had run a number of photos supplied by a local freelancer. In several, he could make out Marty and Cole's faces among the other officers and ambulance personnel in attendance. Thankfully his was nowhere to be seen. After giving his statement to the investigators, Fox had wandered along the length of the cemetery's wooded south border. Earlier than evening, when Marty had delivered the coup de grace bringing the machete down on Irma's neck, Fox was almost positive he had heard a faint gasp somewhere a hundred yards or so to the south.

His eyes didn't require a flashlight, but saw the dark ground he moved above quite clearly. In the brush, he detected something – footprints, here and there the dewy grass was crushed and beaten down at regular intervals. He followed the track that paused when they drew due south of the police units with their overhead and alley lights illuminating the crime scene. Bending low Lyle could make out a larger section of trampled vegetation. It almost appeared as if someone sat down or suddenly fallen, Lyle followed the trail of prints as it lead to and then over the south fence. The track ended there, whoever it had been had walked away using the sidewalk.

Lyle looked up as the waitress brought his breakfast to his table and refilled his coffee.

Using his binoculars, Aleixo Silva watched Lyle's movements from a vehicle parked on a vacant lot situated a good distance from the restaurant. Past the idling trucks and a family's station wagon, out across the roadway leading out of town. Silva heard a faint thumping coming from the trunk of his rental and got out to investigate. He reached the trunk and looked around, not a soul about. He unlocked the truck and lifted the lid. Ann

Oaks lay inside, moaning quietly, every so often a leg or arm would twitch slightly. She would soon become conscious.

Silva reached into a small black bag he'd brought with him from the front seat. Removing a hypodermic needle and a small glass bottle containing a strong sedative, he filled the syringe to a particular measure and then injected the drug into the woman's arm. He waited momentarily until he was sure the drug had taken effect, then closed the trunk lid and resumed his observation of the distant restaurant from the driver's seat of the car.

Lyle paid his bill and left the Ihop with the newspaper beneath his arm. Earlier he'd packed his case in his Ford 150 truck, now he walked back to the Motel's parking lot and jumped into the driver's seat. He'd taken special care of the Ford and the truck responded by providing excellent performance. Having put well over three hundred thousand miles on the vehicle, Lyle still wasn't ready to part with "his baby" just yet. He rolled from the parking lot and drove out toward Big Bend Road. Looking down at the fuel gauge he decided to stop in at the Fast Gas and fill up before hitting the highway.

Silva watched the cherry red half-ton leave the restaurant then followed at a reasonable distance so as not to be noticed. He had devised several options for this morning. All of them ended with the killing of the man who now drove ahead of him. When the red truck turned into the gas station to fuel up, Aleixo finalized his plan. Without slowing, he drove past the station and took the left turn at Devil's Fork then continued onward for several miles before parking his car on the shoulder of the road. He watched in his rear view mirror and waited patiently. This time in the morning the roadway was quiet, only one or two vehicles would likely pass by. It wasn't long before he saw his quarry, the red truck was about a mile or so away and coming up fast.

Silva put on his left signal light and crept into the travel lane alternately gunning the engine then coasting making it appear he was having car trouble. When the truck was a quarter mile or so distant, he killed the engine completely, activated his hazard lights and now sat unmoving in the middle of the roadway. The truck slowed as it approached his rental. Silva got out and flagged the approaching vehicle down.

Lyle saw the maroon Toyota pull out from the shoulder, and noticed it accelerate then fade before stopping completely. Even before the Toyota's driver flagged Lyle down, his keen eyes had seen the vehicle's license plates indicating it was a rental. Had the vehicle been local, he'd simply have slowed, asked the driver if he had a phone to call someone, and then left the guy to his own means. A rental was different, he'd found himself in unfamiliar territory and in a tight spot before. He'd stop and help, maybe drive the guy back to the Fast Gas then carry on his way.

Fox put on his own flashers and stopped the vehicle behind Silva's. The guy was already trying his best to steer and push the vehicle onto the shoulder but was having a hard time of it.

Lyle jumped out. "Let me give you a hand there."

"Thanks friend" Aleixo replied, seeing Fox at the rear of the vehicle and pushing it forward. The car quickly rolled onto the shoulder. Aleixo turned toward his Good Samaritan who was approaching with a smile on his face.

"If you need a lift..." Lyle's eyes widened as the man suddenly pulled a gun as though out of thin air. He heard four rapid "thups" from the barrel of the gun, the impact of the bullets spun him one hundred and eighty degrees as he fell to the asphalt roadway. "Wow that was fast..."Just as Lyle lost consciousness he was almost sure he felt the light fleeting touch of a mind upon his own.

Aleixo was pleased with his shooting; three out of four shots from the hip had landed near the heart and lungs. He walked up beside the man and gave him a swift kick in the ribs. No reaction, not that he expected any, this guy was past the point of ever feeling anything again. Aleixo turned the man over then quickly removed his wallet and cell phone. In the distance Silva heard the approach of a large diesel truck, a more in-depth search would have to wait, he quickly manhandled the body into the back seat closing the door just as the truck blared its horn and blew past both vehicles while its driver flipped him the bird.

"Fuck you too asshole." Silva muttered under his breath. He ran over to the half-ton, killed the hazard lights driving it onto the shoulder and parking it ahead of his rental. Returning to his car he quickly looked into the back of the Toyota. "Shit!" The guy'll bleed out all over the back seat. Either Aleixo would have to give the car a good cleaning before he returned it or maybe he'd just dump it and claim it was stolen.

Aleixo checked his watch, nearly seven. He'd have no trouble getting over to the Hall and preparing a fitting reception for Denton and the Sempitor agent who he was confident would visit later today.

It was almost eight in the morning when the phone rang. Reggie Denton picked up. Elijah Cole was on the other end.

"Good morning Mr. Denton, its Elijah Cole, is Marty up yet?" Elijah said pleasantly.

"Couple of hours ago. He's out in the garage right now. Do you want me to call him in?" Reggie asked.

"No, that's ok, I would've called his cell but I didn't want to disturb the young couple this early in the morning."

"Disturb the young couple?" Reggie's voice grew cool. "What are you implying sir? You should know I don't tolerate those types of shenanigans beneath my roof until folks are properly married."

"Mr. Denton, I'm sorry, I didn't mean to offend..." Elijah backpedaled.

Reggie's voice warmed. "Ah... not your fault, not with the way the children behave these days. It's the internet don't you know." On the phone, Elijah heard a door open and close in the background.

Reggie addressed someone else in the room with him. "Marty, its Mr. Cole, he's needing to talk to you."

"Thanks Dad, by the way is Ann up yet?" Marty made his way to the phone.

"Nope, hasn't stirred from her room, want me to knock?"

"God no, just let her sleep Dad; we were up talking a little late last night." Marty explained.

"Ok son." Reggie left the room.

"Hi Elijah. Just got back from the gas station, filled up a couple of jerry cans we had in the garage, thought they might come in useful this morning. What time you stopping by?"

"Just pulling up out front as we speak. See you shortly." Cole hung up the phone.

Aleixo had completed his preparations for his visitor's arrival. He parked the rental in the vacant stall in the garage, used a tarp to cover up the body in the back seat then carried Ann inside the house and up to a bedroom where he strapped her arms and legs to the bed frame and taped her mouth. Given her condition, Silva figured it he had at least several more hours before she'd start to come around. He'd given her a couple of heavy doses of sedative. Not that he cared for her welfare; she wouldn't live past the end of the day at any rate.

He checked the Hall out from top to bottom, disappointed to discover the contents of the safe spilled out in another bedroom. When Aleixo saw the twenty thousand or so dollars lying on the bed with the documents he confirmed his previous belief that all the men were in fact agents. Only agents and their associates wouldn't bother taking such a sum, they had all the resources in the world at their disposal. He spent nearly ten minutes looking at the papers and photos of Irma and himself, the person one time known as Josef Mengele. He quickly gathered them up and placed them in a satchel he had brought with him.

Walking to the closet, Silva sat down before the computer running the security program. He studied each of the individual camera frames and went over things in his mind... he was ready.

Cole and Marty drove through the still open gates and into the Hall's compound. Nothing appeared to have changed since the evening before. The SUV stopped at the front door and the two men got out and walked to the cargo area in the back. Marty removed two five gallon metal gas cans and lugged them onto the porch then returned to help Cole with the body.

There was no need; Elijah already had the body bag draped over a shoulder. "Weighs next to nothing, naught left but skin and bones." Elijah shook his head in wonder. "How could anything like her be so God damn strong and do what she did?"

From the security closet, Silva watched the two walk through the front door. The way Aleixo had it figured, the manner of their relationship suggested the detective was an inferior to the other, likely the Servicio of the black man, who was undoubtedly the Sempitor. The detective left the gas containers at the side of the door then accompanied the Sempitor to the cellar door and switched on the lights below. The two men walked down the steep stairs into the basement with the body of Silva's beloved Irma.

Silva watched the men reach the basement placing Irma's body down next to the other two. After placing one of the bodies in the oven, Denton pissed about for a couple of minutes trying to figure out how to get the crematorium started before Cole walked over and turned a valve on the gas line. The furnace came alive. Silva walked out the bedroom, down the hall, and descended the long stairway to the main floor. Standing for several moments at the top of the cellar stairs he took the handgun from his waist. It was time for introductions.

Upon reaching the basement floor, Marty and Cole had been obliged to place handkerchiefs about their mouths and noses, the reek was abominable. The men set Irma's body bag down, opened the furnace door and quickly placed the body of the young woman inside. After some initial difficulty lighting the oven, the furnace roared to life. A minute or so passed and the odor in the room began to clear slightly, the black oily smoke from the crematorium's fires mixing and rising together with the rancid cellar air as it climbed up and out of the exhaust pipes.

Cole stood quietly and bowed his head while Marty crossed himself and spoke a quiet prayer for the souls of the young couple. It had been difficult over the last weeks, in another hour it would be over. At least until the next time the Order beckoned.

"Sorry to disturb you gentlemen..." Aleixo nearly spat out the last word.

Cole and Denton spun about and faced the man belonging to the voice. Given the din of the blast furnace, they hadn't heard his approach. Silva stood at the bottom of the stairs, his gun leveled squarely in their direction. "Your weapons please, on the floor, one at a time. You first Denton." The two men complied and lay their guns on the floor.

"Both of you get into the cells... separately." Marty and Elijah looked to each other and paused, "Now!" Silva growled.

Marty and Elijah did as they were told, Silva locking the cell doors behind them.

"It's a shame you couldn't have waited just a few more days. My Irma could have been dealt with in the proper manner. Aleixo's voice virtually dripped with hate. "Not falling under the bullets and knives of... assassins."

Marty studied the man's face, he mentally removed the thick moustache and glasses, comparing it to the photos he saw the previous day, to the photos he and Ann had seen on those websites. "Josef Mengele."

"Well, I'm flattered. Yes, I've gone by that name, and many others in the course of my life." Their jailer's face grew thoughtful. "Yes, so many others."

Silva addressed his next statement to Cole. "You of all people should have understood Irma's dilemma. Couldn't you have helped her along?" Cole just looked at him blankly, clearly not understanding the man's meaning. Silva's face betrayed his puzzlement when Cole did not answer then turned back to Marty.

"And you Detective Martin Denton. When you brought your knife down on my beloved's neck did you truly not think she would be avenged?" Marty wasn't proud of what he had to do, but spoke up in rebuttal.

"The woman became a maddened beast; it killed as it wished, without mercy or regard. If we had not taken the actions we did, others would have died as well." Marty raised his open hands to his waist.

"Well, you young man will come to know what it is to see your woman butchered before your eyes." Silva's eyes became cold and steely while a sneer ran across his face. He watched the growing understanding in Marty's eyes then continued. "You didn't think I knew about Miss Oaks?" Silva paused, "Oh, did I mention she's here with us today? Just upstairs partaking of a little beauty rest. I'll bring her down in due course."

Marty ran to the cell door and strained on the iron bars. "Let her go you bastard, she has had nothing to do with this."

"Good, good. Such emotion, you must love her very much..." Aleixo smiled broadly.

Silva looked to Cole's cell. "Oh yes Sempitor, I dealt with your little Indian friend earlier this morning. He died like a dog in the street. Would you like to see his death?" Silva stretched out his consciousness and enveloped Cole's mind in his own, then as quickly as he did so, he pulled back. He had knocked on the door, but no one answered. Silva moved on to Marty, savagely probing his mind causing Marty to hold his hands to his temples and cringe in pain. Aleixo immediately realized neither man was Sempitor or even Servicio.

"So the Order has run out of qualified agents... what a shame." Silva saw Cole glance behind him and went cold.

"Not hardly..." Fox's voice boomed out and echoed loudly in the cellar, as it did, a strong mental probe ripped at the very fabric of Silva's conscious mind. The Sempitor spun on his heel, his face a grimace of hate and malice. Fox leaned against the stairway's handrail; his gun already bucking twice from the recoil even as Silva began his turn. The first bullet struck Silva in the forehead, the second in his chest; he hit the floor with a thud a moment later. "Hard to beat a double tap, eh Cole?"

Fox slowly made his way to Cole's cell and unlocked the door. "Fox you look like shit." Cole helped Lyle to a nearby stool.

"Took four in the chest just this morning, how good do you think you'd look about now?" Fox chuckled and coughed weakly. "Good thing he didn't suspect I was a Sempitor. He just nailed me and thinking I were dead threw me in the back seat of the car. Would have been a problem if he'd thought to use the trunk." He coughed again. "Gents forgive me, but we gotta get going. Eventually the authorities are going to figure the Hall is at the center of this mess and they'll be all over this place like "ugly on an ape."

Cole opened Marty's cell then gestured toward the stairs with his thumb. "You take care of Ann; I'd do what needs doing here." Marty didn't wait to be asked twice, he took the stairs two at a time.

After cremating the boy, Cole cleaned out the ashes; nothing survived the tremendous heat of the oven.

291

Cole placed Irma inside and was about to close the door. "Wait... put Mengele in with her." Cole looked at him questioningly. "I know what you're thinking... no matter who they turned out to be, they were still like me. Elijah you can't imagine the loneliness of living so long without the companionship you short lived humans seen to take for granted."

Cole nodded somberly, gently placed Mengele into the oven beside his love. Moments later the flames roared anew. Cole went to help Fox off his stool and leave but instead Fox placed a hand on Elijah's arm, "Wait for it."

From the direction of the oven, Cole heard a series of thumps. These were followed by several frantic heavy thuds; the heavy steel door of the oven shuddered but failed to give way. Slowly, the banging sounds within the oven ceased and only the sound of the gas fed flames was heard.

"Fox, you're some sort of an asshole!" Cole stated frankly.

"They were Grays, damn sorry ones at that. Besides, they tried to kill us." Fox smiled slyly.

"I meant to ask, but I thought the Order only killed members who were turning or disobeyed the rules?"

"Yes, that holds true in all circumstances." Cole cocked his head questioningly. Fox continued, "Yes, we never kill members unless they turn, but Silva wasn't a member of the Order in good standing. Josef Mengele on the other hand was, but he died in 1979, this was established by DNA analysis when it later became available. You see, Mengele took the identity of Wolfgang Gerhard, later Gerhard was reported drowned, having suffered a massive stroke while swimming off the coast of Brazil. From that day on, we of the Order heard nothing of Mengele. His Servicio, Otto Meyers also confirmed his death. He would have either committed suicide or have been dispatched by agents, but Irma insisted on his remaining alive and living with her and Norman Stiles. This is sometimes allowed."

"Ok." Cole asked a final question. "But why didn't you kill Mengele before we put him in the oven?"

"Oh that... perhaps I failed to mention that Valeria Diaz, who is as you know the Director of the Orden Sempiterno had a granddaughter who married a Polish Jew. They were murdered in Auschwitz." Fox paused then continued. "Never forget my dear friend, the Sempiterno possess exceedingly long memories."

Cole supported Lyle Fox as they slowly climbed the stairs.

Lyle Fox slumbered in the passenger seat as Elijah Cole drove the SUV past the gates of Meyers Hall. In the rear seat Marty cradled Ann's head on his shoulder. Behind them, Meyers Hall became fully engulfed in the flames of purification.

45

It was the final day of Teun's instruction, today he would choose to either join the Order, or live outside it. Choosing to live outside the Order brought with it certain risks. He would enjoy no protection from other Sempitors he might meet by chance; members of the Order could deal with him any way they wished without repercussion arising from the fellowship. Teun would not be given access to the Order's vast array of intelligence gathering abilities. Finally, the Order could at any time declare Teun a liability and send their agents to dispose of him. There were no advantages of living outside the Order, only grave risks.

Blas Velez opened the door leading to the sitting room where they had met so many times before, but today he paused before entering, holding the door for an exquisitely dressed woman.

Teun De Torres knew exactly who the woman was and knowing his place, bowed low in deference. Valeria Diaz, the Chair woman of the Orden Sempiterno entered and sat at a chair. Blas looked to his pupil and nodded his approval, then followed the woman and stood at her side.

The woman placed a hand palm up, gesturing toward a chair near the spot where Teun stood. Taking her direction, Teun seated himself across from the woman. She began to speak.

"I have it on good authority that without exception, all forms of higher life on this planet are directly or indirectly sustained by the death of another creature. When man first roamed the African savannah, he was fully aware and accepting of his limited position within the hierarchy of predator and prey; above some and below others. Someone becoming a meal for a predator was an everyday occurrence, but within this hierarchy, his position advanced hand in hand with his advancing technology. Now long accustomed to his rightful place of supreme ascendance, he becomes fearful should he discover his position is perhaps more tenuous than he first imagined."

Valeria Diaz stopped speaking, yet her thoughts continued to flow into the boy's mind, and were at once understood and comprehended.

Man's fear of being destroyed by something out of his control fuels the entertainment industry. World engulfing cataclysms whether natural or as result of man's own warlike folly, while terrifying and unfortunate are both expected and accepted. This acceptance runs contrary to acts of unsolicited violence perpetrated by one person upon another; such acts are regarded as universally evil and wicked - sins against the laws of God and nature. This same judgment is also mistakenly extended to mere animals, parasites or predators whose actions simply follow God's intentions; they themselves exist without knowledge of sin.

I find it interesting to watch the world rally to ease the plight of an individual or even that of an animal while at the same time choosing to ignore death and destruction of thousands of its own species. In fact, humanity will continue to ignore any number of unimaginable horrors, until forced to see those multitudes possessing a human face, the ability to understand and accept a simple precept "there but for the grace of god go I."

A genocide taking place on the other side of the world, especially involving that of another race is certainly unfortunate, but to be expected as a matter of course; too bad – so sad. But... should this happen to one of your race; your family, your friends, your neighbors, anyone resembling yourself or holding a view of the world similar to your own; this immediately becomes a tragedy, a great evil to be fought and overcome by any means whatsoever.

This brings us to our own rather precarious situation. Within each of us is the embodiment of humanity's most primal fear. At best we are parasites with humanity as our host - at worst we are rapacious predators of sentient prey. The Sempiterno are a force of nature, created by God or nature as you prefer. As such, we are no different than any of the world's creatures except in the way that our existence might be viewed by those upon whom we prey - IF they were aware of our existence. Now add an impossibly long life expectancy into the mix? We would see mankind marching on our bastions with torch and pitchfork in hand. Any who survived would be driven into exile, a haunted, isolated existence.

Before you elect to join our number, you must first understand who we are, how we live, and the risks you might pose to our entire race... if you fail to accept our few but important rules. Now choose.

The question thundered in his mind. Teun felt the layers within his mind being peeled back to reveal his honesty and commitment should he decide to agree to the membership being offered. Teun's hands flew to his temples, his brain felt as though it would explode. Suddenly, the pressure subsided then ceased.

Valeria Diaz, the Chair woman of the Orden Sempiterno rose from her chair. Walking to Teun, she bid him rise. Now standing face to face, she offered her hand and then spoke. "I have seldom encountered as powerful a mind as yours at such a tender age. It is possible that one day you may stand where I now stand. In the meantime, welcome to the Order."

Ann Oaks pushed open the back door with her hip and brought a tray of cheese, crackers and cold cuts out to the picnic table. Laying the tray on the table, she called over to Marty and his father Reggie, who were having a game of catch on the lawn. "Come and get it boys."

About to sit, Ann suddenly stopped short then walked back into the house. "Forgot something."

Reggie glanced toward Marty, over to the table of food, then back to his son. "Marty, we've been at it a while, I think my lumbago is starting to act up again."

Marty laughed, "Sure dad, no problem. Besides our beers are getting warm."

The men walked over and sat down digging into the snacks. Stuffing another cracker in his mouth Reggie garbled, "Got a good woman there son."

Marty smiled and took a bite of dill pickle. "I do don't I."

Ann suddenly returned with a small white book that Marty immediately recognized. She lay the book down on the table in front of Marty who recognized work when he saw it. "Ann, I promise we can choose the photos together, maybe after dinner."

She frowned and poked the top of the book with her right index finger. "That's what you said yesterday, and a week earlier. The photographer has given me two phone calls about this already. Don't you want to choose what goes into our wedding album together, you and me? Like most couples?"

Marty looked apologetic. "Why sure honey, this is important to me too!" Silently Marty thought, yeah, like most couples, the guy usually disappears when faced with the task. "Ok let's do this right now!" He saw his wife's face light up.

Inside the kitchen, the phone rang. "Oh bother, I'll get it." Ann walked through the door into the kitchen and picked up the phone. "Hello? Oh, hello Cole, how are you and Tina." Pause "Good. Yes he's here... no... no interruption, I haven't even started dinner yet. I'll get him. Bye now."

Ann walked to the door and propped it open a crack. "Marty it's for you. Elijah Cole."

"Be right there." Marty grabbed his beer and rose from the table. "Be right back." He walked into the house.

Nearly half an hour went by before Marty returned beer in hand and as promised set it before Reggie. "Sorry for the wait." Marty sat at the table. "That was Cole."

"Yes, Marty I know?" Ann smiled sweetly, while Reggie grinned.

"You remember that fellow that helped us out, the Canadian from Alberta?" Marty asked.

"Of course, he was with you and Cole when I was saved from that maniac!" Ann exclaimed. Marty hadn't told her the full story, nor would he ever.

The three men simply explained the man was an active serial killer operating in the region. Fox was injured in Ann's rescue. The men surrounded the place and were waiting for Sheriff's deputies to assist when the house burst into flames. Lyle Fox urgently required a hospital so they couldn't stay. When they left, the hall was fully engulfed in flame, its roof caving in; no one could have escaped. Several days later when the scene had cooled sufficiently, the fire investigator concluded the tremendous heat had left nothing to be found of the body.

"Of course." Marty continued. "Lyle called Elijah. Apparently there have been several rather strange deaths on both sides of the borders of Montana and Alberta. The authorities are blaming animals, bears or maybe wolves, but Lyle thinks the deaths are suspicious. His argument is that a single man eater, no matter the species, doesn't kill one fellow here, then another several hundred miles away, all within the space of twenty four hours." Marty took a sip of beer and looked toward his wife who was wearing that all too familiar look that said she knew what was coming.

"Cole says since the killings occur on both sides of an international border the FBI has an obligation to look into the matter. I guess the Canadians have the same concerns, the RCMP suggested a small task force be cobbled together." Cole hadn't offered any connection between the killings and the Order and when asked said such a correlation was highly unlikely.

"How long will you be gone?" Ann asked.

"A couple of weeks? Maybe only a couple of days... who knows?" Marty shrugged and pulled the preview folder over in front of him. "Meanwhile, let's get started on our wedding album shall we?"

About the Author

As a writer, I have always been drawn toward fiction rather than real life. Real life has the ring of finality; I hate the idea of our lives being bound within the confines of time, locale and circumstance. Many of my writing ideas initially present themselves within the realm of dreams, and like all dreams, some are pleasant and peaceful; others harsh nightmarish landscapes. The combinations of these two extremes lend contrast to the stories I strive to tell.

Perhaps the greatest benefit of beginning a writing career in your sixties is being able to transfer a lifetime of experience onto the written pages of a short story or novel. Adding emotional and motivational dimension, and perspective, to the characters bring them to life while helping to shade the narrative.

We learn that true Villains and Saints are never born, but only forged within life's crucible. We find our world is never black and white; nor does it exist in the dullest shades of gray. Instead, we all bear witness to life's vivid bursts of color as unforeseen events explode upon the ever-changing backdrop of time itself. Time, that unrelenting colossus who presides over the full measure of our lives, driving all else before it.

I hope you enjoy my books as much as I enjoy writing them for you.

In another life, Steve was a police officer before beginning his writing career. A Detective Sergeant and seasoned criminal investigator working in robbery, vice, and general investigations, he took point on several complex and lengthy wiretap investigations within the Calgary Police Drug Unit. A recognized expert in the field of Traffic Collision Investigation and Reconstruction Steve received his training at Northwestern University, Illinois, and under the tutelage of the Royal Canadian Mounted Police.

Stephen lives in Calgary, Alberta, Canada with his lovely wife Wanda. His favorite hobby is his family, sons and grandchildren. Other past times include amateur astronomy, playing guitar, singer/song writing, military history and following political news and trends.

Discover Other Titles by Stephen G. Kirk

Velogenic: The Dragon's Crown
And Midnight Came to Call

CPSIA information can be obtained
at www.ICGtesting.com
Printed in the USA
BVHW071240161120
593415BV00003B/70